GRACE AND
FAVOR

Also by Thomas Caplan

Line of Chance
Parallelogram

GRACE AND
FAVOR

A novel by

THOMAS CAPLAN

ST. MARTIN'S PRESS

NEW YORK

A THOMAS DUNNE BOOK.
An imprint of St. Martin's Press.

St. Martin's Press gratefully acknowledges the permission of A. P. Watt on behalf of The National Trust to excerpt from Rudyard Kipling's poem "The Return."

Production Editor: David Stanford Burr

Library of Congress Cataloging-in-Publication Data

Caplan, Thomas.
     Grace and favor : a novel / by Thomas Caplan.—1st ed.
        p. cm.
     "A Thomas Dunne book."
     ISBN 0-312-17106-4
     I. Title.
PS3553.A584G7   1997
813'.54—dc21   97-15664
                                     CIP

First Edition: November 1997

10 9 8 7 6 5 4 3 2 1

For Isabella
and for George

God please bless

One foot in Eden still, I stand
And look across the other land.

Edwin Muir
(1887–1959)

If England was what England seems,
An' not the England of our dreams,
But only putty, brass, an' paint,
'Ow quick we'd drop 'er! But she ain't.

Rudyard Kipling
(1865–1936)
"The Return"

GRACE AND FAVOR

1

I T SEEMS THAT fate is on my side. I have given the matter some thought, over years now, and can find no other satisfactory explanation for the fact that I so often enter situations at their crucial moments. Do not mistake me. I have no wish to brag or complain about this particular aptitude—least of all to exaggerate it. It is, rather, a trait—perhaps a talent—I have come to take for granted, as a traveller on an exhaustive journey far from the expected signposts of home might take for granted certain tickets, visas, even the entertainments of his itinerary. As long ago as school, I recognized and relied upon it. In fact, as the Sixties became one thing and then another outside the high windows of our classrooms and the Japanese cherry blossoms and the white dogwood and the weeping peach all would shiver and dance, I could nod off, my mind caught by dream or memory, then, by instinct, return my attention to the master just before he would impart the answer to a question later to be found on the term exam. My eye could wander from a football game only to come back for the crucial touchdown, the yearbook snapshot—and so on, whether the matter under consideration were the World Series or the more emotional, intricate contests of teenage sex and love.

Everyone has luck, of course, and lacks it at the same time. And I would not make so much of my own, except that I am suddenly afraid. I am afraid because it is three o'clock in the morning and my wife is not in bed beside me. Her breathing is absent, her smell diminished; her long periods of stillness and her sudden body shifts, the basic rhythm of our night together, like her weight upon our mattress, have vanished. And responding to this untimely lack of her, I have snapped awake from a vivid and disturbing dream with the immediate feeling that we are at the beginning of some new phase in our lives. There is no light, no sound of water or coughing from the bathroom. The door to our bedroom, however, appears to be ajar, as though pulled with too much care for whatever noise the latch might make. And Julia's dressing gown, which had, as usual, been draped over a bedpost, is missing, along with the oversize T-shirt (this one faded, from a Dire Straits concert years before) she habitually removes once she is safely under sheet, blanket and duvet. Married a few years now and still foreign to each other in innumerable ways, we continue to sleep naked, Julia and I. The physical was the promise of our attraction and we continue to make love more frequently and carelessly than, I have read, experts say is average for people who are as used to each other as we.

The carpet is cold when I step onto it. The air, damp and tomblike, plays on my skin as I walk toward the wall socket, bend over and press the switch beside it that will send current directly into the electric heater. The coils of the heater redden quickly. But I hesitate. Perhaps my wife will return in a minute, I think. Perhaps, if there is a problem, it is one for the immediate family rather than those, like me, who have married into it. Perhaps Julia heard a noise in the kennel, wheezing from her brother's room at the end of the long hall or a telephone. Or, perhaps, after our large meal, including two champagnes and two Cointreaus that I remember, she required some medicine from a cabinet in a distant room. Any number of explanations for her departure are possible, and yet I know that time will prove them wrong. We are on the verge of things too mysterious for comfort. I'm positive. I can feel it.

Our room is not the one Julia occupied as a child. That is smaller, brighter, nearer to the narrow stairs that lead up to the morning nursery. Ours is a great cube from which, from evening until breakfast, enormous solid oak interior shutters exclude all daylight. Until our marriage, it had actually belonged to what were then called the State Apartments. But no sovereign having come to stay at Castlemorland since an expensive re-decoration was undertaken in the Thirties, Lord Cheviot decided to allot this suite's principal bedroom to us, his most frequent visitors, and to set aside a few less august, if still superbly cheerful rooms against the possibility of a visit from Her Majesty. I like to think—and have occasionally convinced myself—that the gesture was meant, in some way, to signify his approval of me as his daughter's husband; to settle once and for all (in the English way: without declaration) any lingering question about the desirability of an American marriage for a girl of Julia's background. Of course, as was many times hospitably pointed out to me, Julia's grandmother had been American—Midwestern, in fact, from Chicago. But I understood that this was a different thing entirely. Her grandmother had brought a substantial fortune with her—the bulk of the famous mining fortune which had permitted the Midleton-Lyghams to keep and improve Castlemorland when other ancient families had already begun to vacate their piles. And even had she been less rich, she had come into the family at a time when there was no question that a woman would assume her husband's name, would dissolve her identity into his, bear and bring up his children and live wherever he chose. I, on the other hand, might, by the very nature of a merchant banker's life, simply pick up one day and announce that Mr. John and Lady Julia Brook would henceforth be found at Park Avenue and Seventy-third Street in New York City, or in a cottage off some quaintly named lane in Greenwich, Connecticut, or even, God forbid, for an indefinite spell in central Tokyo. Indeed, I could imagine circumstances under which I would have no choice without compromising my hopes for our future. But added to this, which would have been as true for any ambitious Englishman, was her family's natural, unspoken fear of the difference between us, their apprehension that, at some pivotal moment in the future, I might become homesick. I discounted the idea. I knew myself, I thought. And I was not wistful. I loved my wife, loved her house and our children. Still, I could see that others had not yet been able to dismiss the notion so blithely. Thus, I had been tempted to read into the assignment of a bedroom, as into many unremarkable events, more than was there. The fact is that I know as well as anyone why our room was given to us: to lure our return.

I can hear nothing as I wait, trying to decide whether—and, if so, when—to go in search of her. Is she ill? Unhappy? Deceiving me? I put the last thought out of my mind. It is impossible. I would know. I would have felt the tension in her hours before. We would not have made love.

I step into my slippers and put on my crimson dressing gown—my glasses rather than bother with the soft contact lenses soaking in their vials. Then I hear a door, voices, a door again; and it is once more quiet.

I go into the hall, dimly lit by sconces, the strip of red carpet lush beneath faint puddles of lamplight, the stone walls, the vaulted plaster ceiling formal and cold. The noise has come from downstairs and I move carefully, alert but trying not to appear overly concerned should Julia come upon me. On the grey-and-yellow marble stairs, I pass the muralled portraits of Adrian and Julia as children, then that of Charlotte, the sister who arrived between them only to die of leukemia at the age of six. Charlotte's expression is impish. She is less pretty, but her smile once again strikes me as even more theatrical than my wife's.

The overhead light in the vestibule is on. Beneath it, draped from a peg in the right wall, I can see a tan covert coat. Even through glass panes, it is clear from the limpness with which it hangs that the coat is wet. It must have rained, I think, since we brought the dogs inside before resting. In the hallway a green canvas-and-cowhide overnight case sits on the floor, beside a console table. Wet keys lay on the table's marble top, next to several loose coins and a clutch of hand-addressed blue envelopes waiting to be posted. I recognize the keys, the top coat and the case.

All four doors leading to the reception rooms are closed at this hour. I look up to the infrared projector at the cornice, then check the signal box mounted just inside the adjacent boot room to be sure that the alarm has been turned off before I place my hand on the door to a sitting room. The door, it develops, has already been unlocked. It gives way slowly, but the room is dark. Outside the french doors in the far wall, clouds obscure a late harvest moonlight. The far courtyard is indiscernible. The double door which joins the sitting room to the library, however, is open—about a quarter of its way. The damasked panels of the first door face me squarely, but I can tell that the one behind it, which opens into the library, remains tight. I make my way around chairs and sofa, being careful of lamp and television cords, and, for an instant, press my face against the glass of the courtyard doors. Beyond them a thin rain continues, steadily, without energy. Then I place my palm against the ivory hand panel of the final library door and nudge it. Cautiously. Julia's voice grows from a whisper, apparently unaware of my presence. I am about to announce myself with a second, more forceful, more flourished push when I hear her say, angrily: "He claims to have *proof*, but what could he have?"

I let my arm go limp at once, curiosity—actually, the beginning of fear—overcoming any shame I feel at eavesdropping.

Her cousin Rupert says, "I can't imagine."

"There isn't any," Julia assures him.

"No," he agrees, then pauses long enough to swallow some liquid. I can hear ice shift in a glass. "I know. None at all. What does he want?"

"Power over me."

"Power—of what sort exactly?" This is the analytical Rupert I hear speaking: Rupert the deal maker, the City-wide success, cool, direct, keen, impolitic. There is none of the more familiar nightclubbing style in his tone.

"No *sort*," Julia answers. "Just power. For me to know he has power over me."

"Bastard," Rupert utters dismissively.

Very quickly their voices fade. I make out the phrase "deal with them" in Rupert's tired voice, then the word "yes" in Julia's; but the context of their words—any specific intention—is unclear. Then I hear Rupert leaving by the library's other doors, those that lead directly back into the hall where he has left his case and keys. And he is quickly on the stairs. His next words, when they come, fall from the first landing. Whispers thrown from a height, they seem to gather strength before reaching their target—and me. "Not to worry," he says. "We'll make short work of him when the time comes. Now, night, darling. Got an early start in the morning."

Julia remains behind, presumably to lock up and re-trigger the alarm.

I am careful not to disturb anything as I retrace my steps. I have caught the atmosphere of stealth I suspected on waking and do not wish to be found out. I do want to be found, though, because I do want answers. When Julia subsequently comes upon me in the Great Hall, it can look to her only as though I am on my way to the kitchen with a hunger attack. I hear her voice over my shoulder and immediately there is something distressing in it: a lack of surprise, which catches me off guard. I have not had a midnight hunger attack in ages—if I think about it, probably since my senior year at The University. It is, therefore, unnatural that Julia, while she must reach this unavoidable conclusion, should show so little amazement.

"Are you looking for me?" she asks.

I hesitate, wince, then turn. "No," I hear myself tell her.

She looks horrified—well, mock-horrified, biting her lower lip, dejecting her brow in a way that lets me know that whatever is to come will be unpredictable.

"Actually, I was going to the kitchen," I explain, aware at once how this lie has trapped me and will require others to support it. It is a mistake, I realize, just as it has been a mistake to listen in on her conversation with Rupert without disclosing my presence. Unhappily, though my wife and I are in love and share many of our most intimate secrets, including those of our pasts and of our friends, I recognize it in the nature of our marriage that some privacies can be violated only with dangerous risk. We are modern people who have committed ourselves to one another out of desire and with considerable hope, but also a measured amount of realism.

"Oh, I see. Let me get this straight. You wake in the middle of the night and, finding your lover gone, head off not to find her, but in pursuit of what?"

"A chicken leg?"

"Didn't you notice I wasn't there?"

"Yes," I smile. "I noticed."

My wife, at thirty-two and after bearing twins, still has the lithe figure of certain northern European women: long, perfect legs rising to a shape only just beyond the androgynous hiplessness of adolescence. Her breasts are still as exquisitely modelled and as erect as they must have been a decade earlier; when the occasion is right they insist upon no brassiere, no bikini top, to put forth the illusion of youth. Her hair is dark, burnt almond even after long exposure to the sun, a gift from her paternal line; her eyes, magically green and large—cool and damp in their ovals. With her mood, they can be reticent, enigmatic, or utterly suggestive; and their limpid intelligence saves her face, with its fine English complexion and bone structure, from the parochial dimensions of any nationality. I kiss her cautiously. For a moment our tongues entwine and we hold our breathing, then she breaks away, abruptly studies me, and decides to kiss me once more with even greater fierceness, her hands clasped momentarily behind my neck. It is as though I am about to lift her when she breaks away and leads me, through narrow pantries, to the kitchen.

"I couldn't sleep," she explains, as we forage for a snack. "Not very well at any rate, after the first hour or so of the deepest sleep had worn off. I don't know why. Too much on my mind more than likely. Lying awake—you were out cold, your head sandwiched between pillows, as usual—lying awake, I heard a noise. A normal enough noise for a house like this, *however.* There wasn't really any reason to investigate, but it provided an excuse to get out of bed—away from nagging thoughts, I mean—and I guess I hoped that doing so might be a way of putting me over the brink of exhaustion."

"And?"

"It turned out to be Rupert—just Rupert. He drove up from London after dinner with a client. He nearly got done on the M-4, he said and would have, he bets, if it hadn't been for another car that undertook him, weaving back and forth across lanes. The police went for that one instead." As she relates this information, Julia fusses with a blue enamel kettle, tilting it to better judge the amount of water it contains. "Would you like coffee?" she asks, lifting back the cover of the AGA's left ring. "Or a cup of tea? Do I bother?"

"I don't think so," I say.

"No," she agrees. "You're right."

"Did Rupert have any other news?" I ask, striving for a definite matter-of-factness of tone.

"Nothing." She speaks the word nervously. I cannot tell if she has guessed at my suspicions.

We take an apple, a wedge of Camembert, a plate, knife and paper towels into the library and sit beside one another on the worn velvet sofa with the double-depth seat. Near it, facing us from its mahogany stand in a small alcove, is a century-old globe on which Britain and its empire have been painted in pink. The hemisphere of Europe, Africa and Central Asia is visible to us. From England at the upper left to the mass of India at mid- to bottom right, the globe is splotched with the brilliant hue of vanished power, remembered glory. I imagine long summer twilights a hundred years ago when those who beheld this globe—the men who used this library for an office from which to oversee their estate or who merely gathered in it after dinner—were, more or less, in control of what they surveyed; when each day brought to them new reasons for confidence in the future. My wife is, in many ways, heiress to the anxiety which followed the demise of their pre-eminence. And though she and her friends have been bequeathed an attractive sureness of manner, they wear it more often as armor or decoration than as an outward manifestation of abiding faith in themselves or their situations. If truth be told, I believe they are frightened—not so much by change as by the rate of change lately, the speed with which ways of life are ravaged.

Again, I prompt Julia. "You were telling me," I say, "about Rupert."

"No. That was all. We chatted to each other for a few minutes. Entirely banally. Then he went upstairs, completely knackered—must've all but passed you on the steps."

She has avoided my eyes. I stare at her until she turns toward me and we both cannot help laughing. "Darling," I say, "I could swear you're up to something."

"Up to something?" she exclaims, irately pinning me down. "Of course I'm up to something. It's my brother's birthday tomorrow and I hope I'm up to a lot—which I have no intention of letting you in on because, no doubt the moment he began to fish for it, you would tell him everything and spoil the surprise."

"Bugger that!"

"Don't say 'bugger that'. You're not English. You weren't at school here. You shouldn't work so hard to—I mean, you shouldn't use *so many expressions* that. . . . Never mind."

"They slip in."

"I suppose."

"*And* I don't see how they're a bit different from hundreds of American expressions that are always being appropriated by English slang. In fact, if you want to get down to it, the American language is the one that's seductive. The entire American popular culture. The world is full of people whose fantasies come from America, who want to be American and modern—not English anachronisms."

"I'm sure you're right," Julia says. "And I'm sorry." The tension of talking around the point of her discussion with Rupert has affected both of us. We are slightly disoriented. "But don't forget that my grandmother was American."

"No."

"And that I married an American. By choice. If I had wanted a Guards officer I'm fairly sure I could have snared someone. So don't tag me as some sort of snob. I like America. How could any woman in my situation not like it! I don't mean that I mind a bit about Adrian inheriting all this and my not. I don't. I was brought up to the idea. Any other policy and Castlemorland would have ceased to exist before I ever had the chance to know it. You can't divide by three and four every twenty-five years and hold on for too long. So it's not primogeniture—not any loss of material things—that bothers me. But look about you—at the pictures. The eighth Earl, the second Marquess . . . Two, four, six . . . eight family portraits in this room alone and they're *all* of men. Granted there are plenty of ladies scattered about the other rooms, but they do not form a line, except by the fact that, at some point or other, all of them married into the Midleton-Lyghams. No pictures of a Countess's mother, few enough of their daughters, none of anyone after that. It's so peculiar. I suppose it isn't very different—only less visible—in families without titles. Women, after all, take their husbands' names, or did until recently—and still tend to do, I think, even in the States, once they have children. But what a title provides is a kind of right—very nearly an obligation—to trace a single line; the line of the grandest, most formidable not to mention forbidding people back through history and bugger, as you would say, whatever strumpets find their way in, or ne'r-do-well second sons eventually fall out. Daughters, as I've said, being beneath consideration to begin with."

"Interesting," I reply, wide awake now, expecting more talk but clearly no sleep before morning.

"What *is* interesting is to imagine the female lines that have gone into a family like this one. My mother, her mother, who died in childbirth, her's and so on. Or starting with my American grandmother, on that side of the Atlantic, and going back. She was far less dispensable to the survival of this house, after all, than many of the whiskered gentlemen you see on the walls." Julia sits forward, places the plate with the core of our apple and the Camembert-encrusted knife on the coffee table. I lean forward, too, and deposit our paper towels on top of this plate; and for a moment it is as if we are about to depart a restaurant. Then, without studying each other, we both sit back and my right leg is draped over my wife's left and my arm is around her and she has relaxed her head onto my shoulder. I smell perfume, the residue of herbal shampoo, the beckoning scent of our earlier lovemaking.

"Are you trying to excite me again to prove that you are still a boy?" she inquires.

"Oh, I am," I tease, though I have suddenly come to feel unsure, even suspicious, of her. I must test the extent, the depth of our faith in one another by making her let go of herself. I must shake her famous control. "Do you want to go upstairs?" I ask.

"Not yet."

I slip my arm around her waist. My palm and fingertips rest there, then slide along the quilted surface of her dressing gown until they settle against the shape of her breast. She is leaning into me still, each breath more quiet, as though the burst of energy which brought her awake has abruptly exhausted itself and she is again on the edge of sleep. I begin to stroke the square puffs of wool.

She is briefly passive, then her own hands begin to untie the belt of my robe and, with that accomplished, to draw its panels open. It is a ludicrous posture, in this setting especially; but if I feel exposed, I am also curious, excited by the unending expressions of our physical attraction to one another, amused by the lengths to which Julia will sometimes go. I bend my head back, arch it along the top of the sofa, stare at a section of dimly lit, indecipherable frieze. I take a deep breath. I swallow.

All of a sudden she lets go. Just as quickly her fingers press into my belly, giving no massage now but a rapid tickle. She immediately shifts position, straddles me. I abandon my thoughts, my doubts, even the idea of imminent sex. I am—have always been—very ticklish and the laughter her hands draw out is involuntary, utterly consuming. It is also the gift of the child in her, of those not quite tamed, never predictable aspects of her otherwise disciplined personality. By reflex, I reach for her shoulders to push her away; but she is bent toward me and, convulsed, I lack the strength to raise her. The collar of her dressing gown slides lower at my touch, however, festooning just below the wings of her back. The gathered wool has the effect of reigning in the freedom of her sleeves. She looks directly at me, laughs, sticks out her tongue in a silly, girlish, yet provocative way. And while I concentrate on her eyes she steals the instant to bring her arms to her side so that the sleeves fall from them. Now, her dressing gown, like a blanket, descends from my knees to the floor, bundling about my slippers. Quickly casting off her T-shirt, Julia is naked, eager, but in an impish frame of mind. She tickles me once again. When she stops, she stands. Unselfconsciousy, she strides from the grouping of chairs and sofa toward the center of the huge barrel-vaulted Adam room, where she waits for me, exactly as she might wait for a glass of sherry before lunch in twelve hours time. "Not in your bloody dressing gown," she admonishes even as I have begun to remove it. "That's better."

"What's got into you?" I ask.

"Desire to please my husband," she explains unconvincingly. "That's all. Of course, if you'd rather, we could go up now. Everything as usual, with no surprises. There wouldn't be any danger of our being discovered. No chance of anyone coming in to see you as—well, not so respectable as they'd thought. Never mind me. We could go back to our bedroom, back to the safety of our past routine and, since we are a married couple, make love like bureaucrats. Everything you want as you want it. No uncertainty. You have my word. *No* tension."

"Boring," I say.

The library is a long room, with apsidal ends set off behind columnar screens. In the day it is bright with the light of four great windows and a central set of doors which give onto an interior court carpeted with grass and slate and in season, tended crescents of fuchsia foxgloves. At the center of this cloister, firm upon its pediment, a triumphant cast-iron figure of Mercury presides, while in the perfectly round pool below it water ripples in a wind of seldom determinable origin. At this hour, of course, the courtyard is dark. The moon is obscured behind rain clouds. And heavy scarlet curtains have been drawn. The room is lit by the butterscotch glow of a few shaded lamps reflected in the pier glasses that are set between the windows, and when Julia extinguishes the last of these lamps it is impossible to see. At once a sense of smell takes over: centuries of Cuban tobacco, burnt oak and beeswax perfume the air. Hearing becomes more acute: the dead of night gives off an even, compelling, monotonous quiet.

Taking my hand, leading me to the Baumbauer writing table which faces the mantle and whose back is to the set of outside doors, Julia asks, "Because a hero has to take a risk, succeed in an adventure before he can win the princess? Is that why you say 'Boring'?" This is a favorite theme of hers and I recognize it, of course, at once. It is an idea she picked up in a book she read, or a lecture she once heard. I can't remember. But she has written monographs on the subject of heroes—and especially heroines—and the adventures they pursue; their stories filled her dissertation. My wife knows the rituals, the paths exceptional people have travelled in tribes whose members she has never encountered, whose terrain she has never visited, or whose spans had ended millennia before her birth.

I laugh. "You're not a princess," I tell her. "Is that really how you think I see you?"

"Partially." She has found the armchair. She pulls it back silently, taking a seat as my pupils expand.

"How many times do I have to tell you it was love at first sight?" I demand. "Before I knew your name. Before I knew that there were such things as marquesses, much less families so eccentric they pronounce 'Lygham' as 'lime.' Before I knew about any of this: great houses and pictures and land, furniture that, because you are a woman, you'll never see a stick of."

I stand in back of her chair, my hands on her shoulders, massaging, almost kneading them; my palms slide to the sides of her breasts, applying the lightest friction before I bring them higher again. There is no draught, but the room is chilly. And I wonder how long Julia will be content to sit here—if this is an old fantasy of hers or one she has just conceived. It is from this writing table that Castlemorland has been run for centuries. From it the affairs of the house and estate are now directed by her brother, since her father's recent death. Thus, it is, in many ways, the soul of the house and its link to the land. The stacks of papers upon it detail the plans and histories of farming and forestry operations, the sale and renovation of village houses, the schedules and expenses of gamekeeping, the dates and guest lists of shooting days. It is a magnificent writing table—one Julia still calls a *bureau plat*—its ebony veneers and bronze mounts and red velvet surface somewhat taken for granted in its utilitarian role at the center of this masculine room in which Churchill and Melbourne and Pitt the younger all held forth.

Indeed, the signatures in the volumes of guest books stored in lower shelves of the north bookcases include many of the most eminent names of England since Victorian times. And one imagines, upon encountering them, a house more glorious than at present: the same treasure trove, but staffed, as it was meant to be, by no fewer than thirty servants inside; its cellar and larder and coffers overflowing. Our escapade would have been impossible then—or would it? I wonder. From some moment earlier in the century, an unbroken party seems to roll back through time, undarkened by conditions in the nation at large, with Castlemorland as its focus. Barely touched by the personalities of its owners, the house seems to have enjoyed a steady, splendorous life of its own: not the comet-like blaze of Gatsby's mansion, but something durable and mellow and more beguiling, accumulated out of the long and short stays of famous men; out of exquisite lunches, dinners and balls and a village fête held once each year. Beneath my hands I can feel, in my wife's slow breathing, her absorption of this history as well as her attempt to will herself—and, very likely, me—into the company of the ghosts that surround us. Whether she seeks merely to join or to humiliate these ghosts I cannot be certain, but it is clear that she wishes to dominate at least one indelible moment in the history of the room, to be able to see this male precinct, in future, through the memory of our disrespectful use of it. Our fun.

Still, she is keeping her secret, refusing to share it, whatever it is, with me as she has with her cousin Rupert. I wait for her to rise, to give me the slightest tug, some signal. When she doesn't, I repeat "Love at first sight" in a whisper, adding, "And it was before I knew anything, anything at all, about Americans in your past."

"Rupert never mentioned them?"

"Perhaps once or twice."

Julia's mention of Rupert's name further unsettles me. With a sudden, cold cramp in my groin, I realize now that the secret between them must be more frightening than I had thought. Otherwise, she would hardly keep it through the intimate games we are playing.

"What's the matter?" Julia asks.

"Nothing at all. I just lost track of my thought for a second."

"Are you cold?"

"Oblivious to it." I take a deep breath, stifle a yawn, sense that a moment is required before we make love.

Julia looks down from the desk at her own naked thighs. Her frown is pensive, as if suddenly removed from the circumstances in which we find ourselves. She has taken my hands in hers and she squeezes them now.

Then, suddenly, she stands. We face one another. We kiss slowly, then frantically, without embracing. In a moment I am against the *bureau plat*, testing its strength. Lying upon it, staring up into my wife's faultless eyes, I realize how effortless it is to love a beautiful woman— even when you know that she does not completely trust you. Even when you can no longer trust her.

2

ON THE MORNING of the murder (for that is how I think of it),
I wake, stirred by footsteps in the hallway, voices, the seeping
music of a full great house coming to life. In the scarce light that escapes
the door and bathroom I find my watch on the bedstand. It is three
minutes before eight—as late as we dare sleep. I throw off the eider-
down, toss my legs over the high bed and, from a standing position,
touch my toes a dozen times automatically; then I cross to the windows,
open the curtains and fold back the shutters. Light so indirect as to
cause no shadows suffuses the room. Julia tosses. She turns onto her
side. Slowly, she brings her knees higher, breathes more loudly and
then is asleep again. A small crystal and bronze chandelier hangs in the
center of the room. When I turn it on it illuminates the fading plasterwork from which it is suspended: a portion of the Midleton-Lygham
coat of arms, fire rising from sea water as in the legend of the original
Lygham knight who was said to have survived drowning during a ninth-
century voyage from Ireland.

"John?" Julia asks, her voice thick with phlegm and somehow
tenuous.

"Morning," I say.

"It can't be—yet."

"Eight o'clock. Already."

"Shit. What time are we expected?"

"Nine thirty in the hall. But you'll want breakfast."

"Yes."

"Do you want me to go in ahead of you? To the loo, I mean?"

"Are you having a soak?"

"A short one, I thought."

"Wake me the minute you're through. Promise."

"Fine. I'll run your tub and wake you."

As I confront my lathered face in the shaving mirror I hear two rumbling knocks at the door. Julia, once more unconscious, does not react, so, with a solitary bath towel around my waist, I tiptoe, taking gigantic steps, through our room. At the door, I ask "Who is it?" cautiously.

"Rupert."

"Julia's still out cold," I whisper.

"I don't care about Julia," he says. "Look, let me in."

I open the door. Across its sill, spontaneously, Rupert begins to laugh. His sense of humor, ordinarily dry, now and then responds to the blatant. He stares at the mountains of white menthol cream drying on my cheeks and neck. He says, "I find I'm out of shaving soap. I came to ask if I might borrow some of yours, among other things."

"Sure. What other things?"

"Is is brushless?"

"Aerosol."

"I don't know what we're going to do with you in this family," he complains, winding me up. "Sooner or later you're going to realize that a gentleman, whatever else he does, never shaves without his brush."

"What other things?" I repeat.

"Socks for one. Long underwear for another, if you've any extra."

"You'd think you'd come straight from Hong Kong."

"I know. You would, wouldn't you? Fact is I only stopped at my flat in a blur, between the airport and the office, whence I came directly here."

"How was the flight?"

"Not too beastly. I had Li in tow."

"Philip? Is he in London?"

"Will be. Right now, he's downstairs—in the middle of breakfast, I'm sure. Through the *FT*, no doubt, and the *Times*. Doesn't need sleep. There's no competing with them, I'm afraid, so it's just as well he's on our side. We spent the flight as we might have spent a day in the office: a Saturday, for example, without the telephone. We finished the deal memo. Crossed the last t, the final i dotted, put in the last full stop."

"The deal memo? Do I take that to mean—"

"Yes. Somewhere over Pakistan."

"Somewhere over Pakistan?"

"More or less. Somewhere about there."

"And? So?"

"Somewhere about that far through our flight, we decided we were ... that we were—"

"On *terra firma?*"

"So to speak."

"Excellent."

"It's funny. It's amazing. It's—not what you'd expect, is it? No, it's not."

"Not hardly," I laugh.

"The way these pieces fit together, the way they, all by themselves, without anybody asking, the way they *came* together."

"Quite unpredictable."

"For sure," Rupert agrees. "A & O. Asian and Omnibus. If you'd sat down and you'd made a list of the possibilities they wouldn't have been on it. If you'd made two lists—ten? You'd never have come up with A & O. Would you have done? Tell me the truth."

"No."

"You wouldn't have done?"

"No. Not in a million years. And yet—"

"And yet, there they are."

"They stepped up to the plate."

"As you would say. To get to the point, A & O are in. That's the third leg. The missing element of the equation. A & O are on board."

"Good."

"They've signed off."

"Good."

"Is that all you can say? I thought I could count on you for something better than that, something *more*."

"Sorry," I explain. "I meant to sound keen."

"If everything goes as we've planned it, you'll be a lifetime ahead of yourself. You ought to be keen. Bug all, John—you *ought to be keen* in view of the stakes."

"There's no one keener," I promise.

Rupert looks away, then back at me, his mood changed. "All right," he says, dismissing the matter. "I believe you. Never mind."

"How rich will we be?" I prod, wanting, I suppose, to reassure him of my enthusiasm.

"That depends."

"Best case?"

"Wildly."

"Worst case?"

"Enviably."

"How did you do it?" I ask.

"Charm. Basic English charm."

I WATCH HIS EYES as he reacts to my words. Rupert, it is clear, has no idea that I have overheard him with my wife. Instead, he is all business, giving me his raptor look. I have to admit I like Rupert, although perhaps it would be more honest to say that I cannot help but like him. He is, after all, one of those people whose approval others automatically value and instinctively seek. Even the right sort of glance from him can at once reinforce our confidence in our own judgments, just as his presence invariably seems to assure us that, however accidentally, we are at last at the center of things. It is Rupert's gift to make those around him (those he wishes to) feel like participants rather than spectators in whatever exalted thing is going on so that one leaves a meeting or a restaurant or a weekend identifying, perhaps for the first time, with the gazed-upon rather than those gazing. Naturally enough for someone so successful, Rupert has his enemies: competitors and colleagues who find his manner unbearably confident, his accent faultless, his background and aristocratic looks too much of an advantage. They whisper that his ascendance in the City has been, by normal standards, effortless. But I know better. Rupert is driven (as driven as anyone I have ever met) and his position in our firm and in this industry is due, almost entirely, to that drive. His mind is not merely clever; it is disciplined, it is focused. Many times I have watched his intelligence close in upon an individual or a pending deal and it is always as though he has raised some mental lens to a higher power. The person, the situation, the numbers are suddenly under microscopic scrutiny. And no one is better than he at assessing rewards and the risks they imply. Of course, his famous career at Eton and Cambridge and the fact that he bears the Midleton-Lygham name cannot have damaged his prospects. Those who hired him would have remembered his grandfather, the fifth Marquess of Cheviot, as among the preeminent Tories of his day. They—the partners of Battleman Peale—would have remembered, too, that Rupert's father, Oliver, the second of twins, had missed acquiring a title and one of the most beautiful estates in England by a matter of some two minutes and twenty-four seconds. They would have sighed, then smiled probably (that was what people usually did) at the thought of such a fateful near miss. With the Marquessate of Cheviot *and* Castlemorland, Rupert would have been too-much blessed, they would have told each other. He would have had no incentive to make the most of his talents.

Rupert's family history precedes him everywhere. I first heard it from the Dutch wife of an American banker a quarter of an hour before he appeared—breathless, from a meeting—at her dinner party on Mount Kellet Road in Hong Kong. The result was that, for the first few minutes anyway, I tended to view and approach Rupert as though he had been the victim of an accident, someone to whom something— well, unlucky—had happened. I realize now that this reaction was an exaggerated, almost silly one, but I also think it may have been fortuitous. Competition, like sea scent, hung or blew in the air of South Asia. And had it not been for the story I'd been told about him I suppose I might never have become Rupert's friend. As it happened, when I might have felt jealousy I found myself sympathetic instead. Thus, the disappointment which I imagined him having experienced—no matter how tremendous the advantages with which he'd been left—seemed both to explain and excuse a manner I otherwise could easily have put down as arrogant, or even wicked. Later I would discover beneath his merchant banker's punctilious exterior—his Savile Row suits and Jermyn Street style—the soul of a boy who had once hoped to become an actor. Over and over I would benefit from his large gift for friendship—would laugh and drink and succeed in his company.

I had come to Hong Kong with the American investment bank I had joined some years out of the Business School. This was a mammoth firm, more skilled at computer-screen trading than personal relationships. Its bright, sleek low-ceilinged trading rooms were arranged, like study halls, with row after row of aggressive boy-faced men. Uniformly slim and well-tailored and of every race imaginable, my colleagues there resembled one another more than any did his countrymen in other lines of work. They spun toward or away from their cathode-ray tubes and telephones like dancers who had been choreographed in some weird post-modern ballet. And I, who worked apart from them in a small team devoted to Mergers and Acquisitions—a division often called a "boutique" and which was not among the best of its kind in Hong Kong—felt uncomfortable, an alien in their presence. So when, several months after we had met, Rupert approached me about joining him at Battleman Peale, my answer was a quick "yes." By that time we had opposed each other in a very major deal. Neither of us had won, but I had admired the way Rupert had negotiated the bidding on behalf of his client, withdrawing, when there was no hope of victory, with a huge profit in hand and all his alliances intact. Also, there had been the defection of my partner, Philip Li, to Battleman during the interim. Philip was the only member of our group, I think, whose mind was supple enough to comprehend the intricacies of our peculiar environment. I changed firms because of him, because of Battleman's supreme reputation, but, most of all, because of Rupert, who exemplified the kind of polished, at-home-in-the-world "player" I wanted to be.

The night after I packed my boxes and left my old firm, the three of us dined at the Man Wah, then drank too much Armagnac. I awoke in the pre-dawn in tears, feverish and afraid, without knowing why. It was end of summer, brutal weather. What wind there was came from the south, from Lamma, but the mid-levels felt little of it and the relentless heat blurred the air outside my windows so that all of Kowloon appeared to shiver. The intrepid Star Ferry still stitched the harbor in each direction, but its running lights, like the ordinarily brilliant sash of the Ocean Terminal, were diffused to pastel, made powdery by the warm, thick atmosphere. And even the Venetian *campanile* that was all that remained of the old Kowloon Railway Station seemed to straggle through time—now concrete, then a mirage.

I cannot drink brandy. In any case, I have known for a long time that I should not drink it. In the distillation of the fermented wine upon which it is based, legend says—and I believe—demons are released. A few hours after a brandy has put me to sleep, it will rouse me suddenly. It will inhabit my mind, enlarging my dread of whatever, at that moment, I most fear. It will enact frightening episodes with vividness and certainty seldom experienced in a fully conscious state. It will produce sweat that is warm and cold and, no matter how I toss, inescapable. The alarm which three glasses of Bas-Armagnac brought to the surface of my mind that night was the sense that, having taken one step in my search for adventure, experience and knowledge of the world, I had somehow gone too far—had accidentally stepped over an invisible boundary and finally cut myself off from what I was and what I had been. I had said goodbye to my girlfriend in the South Pacific only two months before. I had regretted invitations to the weddings of old friends and gradually had stopped receiving them. I had refused promotions to New York. Now, without much questioning, I had transferred my allegiance to a firm of a different nation. Why? Circumstances. Still, I felt guilt and disappointment at my own ingratitude to the country where I had been born and had grown up. And eventually the brandy magnified my act to the dimensions of treason. At four o'clock in the morning, eight thousand miles from Maryland, I shivered with an urge to confess to a crime which was no crime at all. Then, after sunrise and an ice cold bath, after shaving, I felt better. I began to see myself as an adventurer rather than an expatriate. Americans, I assured myself, for all our youth as a people, carried the genes of the most adventurous men and women from everywhere. And I was one—and was proud of and unconfused by that fact, and unafraid to compete on playing fields far from heart or home. "I don't know. It's a risk," I'd replied, thinking out loud a moment after Rupert had conveyed Battleman's initial offer. I had not expected it, nor considered any of its ramifications, which suddenly flooded my thoughts.

He'd stared. "Yes," he'd said. "But isn't that what life is all about?"

Rupert's furrowed brow, his stare, is identical now as I hand over the last of the items he's come for: the long, grey St. Michael's underwear, the thick woolly athletic socks, the still-wet and slippery twelve-ounce can of Erasmic. His is the probing scrutiny of someone who must assure himself of something—innocence or loyalty—before going ahead with whatever he intends. I grin. I observe him, I think, as he is and as he was, hours before, alone with Julia. I wait for him to mention their conversation, whatever secret exists between them, and when he does not, my false smile broadens, requiring no effort to maintain. I say, "We'll see you at breakfast."

But Rupert hesitates. "Yes," he answers finally. "Is Julia shooting?"

"Absolutely," I say.

"Well, then."

The lather on my face has evaporated as we've talked. My skin feels cool, but tender, rough and exposed. Before Rupert can turn away I take the can of Erasmic back from him and press its top, jetting mounds of snow white cream into my cold palms. "Congratulations," I say, handing it over to him once more.

"Be careful," he says. "You don't want to nick yourself."

"No." I pause deliberately. "What's the timing on all of this?"

"We'll have to talk before Monday."

"It may be difficult."

"I'll look for a moment—any opportunity. When I find it—"

"You'll signal me?"

"Discreetly."

"How else?"

I understand, of course, that the subject of our talk—the reason for its urgency—is business, purely business, and that we shall in no way go into the matter of Rupert's conversation with Julia. He has had ample chance to disclose that already and by not having done so has convinced me that he means to keep it secret. It is difficult for me to separate my feelings about this from my thoughts about business, but I try to do just that.

The deal Rupert has referred to is one from which Battleman Peale and its partners stand to make an enormous amount of money. I say Battleman Peale *and* its partners because, about a decade ago, the firm decided to reinvent itself. The mahogany-and-silver ink-well partnership which served it for two centuries was rather abruptly abandoned in favor of a modern limited-liability corporation with a daily quote on the Stock Exchange. And although the partnership itself survives in name and membership, it is now really not much more than another large share owner. The capital at the disposal of the firm has increased hugely, which was, after all, the original and principal argument for the change in structure. Owners have ready liquidity where once they were subject to complicated buy-back and pay-out schedules. But Battleman Peale's results, once among the financial world's most undiscussed subjects, are now reported to the public quarterly. And there is considerable pressure, as a result, to see that they are good—good enough to support the share price if not always to drive it higher. The loftier, the more visible one's position in the firm, therefore, the more accountable one becomes for the results of deals. Those who receive the largest share of the profits they generate are, naturally, the first to be blamed when those profits lag—or when a competitor wins them instead. The firm's senior management, who in many ways pose the last in the long sequence of hurdles that people my age began to face in prep school, take a dim view of any action which may cause their net worth to decline, even on paper. Similarly, they smile—and are inclined eventually to bestow their power—upon those by whose effort and conniving they are able to afford ever more perfect farms, houses, cars and wives. These are competitive men, no matter how well-veneered their ambition, and many a merchant banker of Rupert's and my generation has risen or fallen forever according to how and the degree to which he has affected the firm's prestige and that of its top partners.

So it is in no way astonishing that Rupert, whose sights are on the chairmanship at a young age and on a good bit beyond that, should be concerned—yes, obsessed—with the deal he has on his plate. It is a deal of the new age. It is the largest deal in Battleman Peale's history. Its numbers dwarf those of deals which were the making of careers just a few years ago.

The essence of it is simple. We at Battleman Peale have been attempting to arrange the financing which will enable our client, a clique of top management at Ergo, Inc., to buy back the huge America-based company from its present shareholders. Ergo, though a name unfamiliar to most consumers, owns at least a dozen of the most recognized brands in the United States and Europe: teas and coffees, cereals, chewing gums and candies, soft drinks, juices, brands of canned tuna and cooked hams. In addition, its assets include eleven shopping malls on the peripheries of U.S. and Canadian cities, vast tracks of nearby land, a toy company (considered especially "hot" for its advanced holographic images), a maker of children's apparel, sixty odd thousand acres of timberland and any number of oil leases. There is, to boot, considerable real estate attached to many of these interests as well as the forty-nine-story headquarters on Park Avenue, one of the most cost-efficient, practical office towers in New York, if not among the most graceful. Ergo, translated as "therefore" from the Latin, grew out of a series of merg-

ers that began in the Twenties, multiplied through the Sixties and finally, after a decade of stillness, proceeded unregulated and with rapa-
cious fury during the Eighties.

Since then, Ergo has prospered, which is one reason why the current
management would like to own as well as run the enterprise. There are
other reasons, too, the most salient being their opinion that Ergo's
parts are worth much more independently than together. By taking a
wrecking ball to the company, by selling this piece to one competitor
and that piece to another, they reckon they can coin money from thin
air. They have seen others do this with less promising, less fashionable
assets and the lure of such big numbers has caused them to ignore all
risks. "Wrecking ball," of course, is not a term they use, even in their
most confidential conversations with us, their financial and strategic advisors. When pressed, they will sometimes talk about a "carefully" or
"skillfully" or "knowledgeably" wielded scalpel, but they do not like to
be pressed as to their intentions, or, for that matter, to speak "on the
record."

I CLOSE THE DOOR after Rupert leaves, step as quietly as I can past
our bed. Even asleep, Julia's body is tense. Watching her breathe, I hesitate, counting the all but imperceptible heaves beneath her covers,
wondering what secret she harbors and why. Until now, the depth of
our passion has always been matched by the depth of our commitment
to one another. We have sacrificed—she, her career; I, in a way, my
country—for a marriage without which life would otherwise seem impossible. Until now. Staring at the folds of wool and cotton beneath
which she rests, I am in awe that one person can fulfill so many dis-
parate dreams, so many needs of another. I cannot bear to think that
this brilliant, beautiful woman, who forsook a career of such high
promise in academia to bring up our twins, might somehow, for as yet
unknowable reasons, be retreating from me, mysteriously bearing my
emotions, perhaps even my children with her.

Bathing, the porcelain drenched with condensation, the swivel mirror fogged, I suddenly recall a drive to Cambridge not too long after we
met. I had never been there before. We had driven out on an impulse
of academic autumn.

The sun, already remote, already hesitant, drenched the asters and the juniper where we stopped at the edge of the university—for a moment. Islands of dark cloud, vaporous charcoal, floated above the horizon on the deepening topaz sky. It was a painterly vision: across fenland to youth.

"Daddy was unusual," Julia explained, "among men of his type, in that he very much believed in educating women. When I won my place at my college, which I had not remotely expected to do, he was immediately keen that I should go. In America, you'd expect that, but here not so much. It hadn't been that long, after all, that women had been going up to most Cambridge or Oxford colleges in the first place. My mother certainly hadn't done a degree. Neither of his sisters had. Difficult to think of anyone. But that was the thing he would catch you off-guard with: his fleetfooted way of adjusting to things, adapting himself."

"How old were you when you first went away to school?" I asked.

"Eight."

Imagining this—and at a loss—I hesitated.

"In my school uniform . . . my very wide-brimmed hat. Brown it was, the color of milk chocolate. I remember standing in the gravel at home, watching for the car that was to come and collect me, then feverishly looking back. "Bye*ee* now, Darling," my parents were calling. "Be a good girl. Mind the teachers. Write. We'll see you . . . shortly." It was the way things were done; it had been done to them. Very English, like roast lamb and steamed pudding on a boiling summer's day. . . . It wasn't because they didn't love me."

3

W HEN I ARRIVED in London to live I already knew of Julia's existence. In fact, I knew much more. I knew that she was meant to be both forbiddingly beautiful and brilliant, that she was an academic of some sort, the only daughter of Rupert's uncle, the marquess. I understood that she moved in more than one circle simultaneously: university circles, literary, fashionable and even, sometimes, royal circles. At least I inferred this from gossip I had overheard and from rare snapshots I had seen of her in the glossy magazines to which Rupert subscribed to keep himself in touch with the goings-on at home. Twenty-five then and not yet married (or engaged), she was spoken of as a prize by everyone who mentioned her. And yet, on the evidence, I was not fascinated. Her photograph did not beguile me. Her set seemed daunting. And I was looking for love, not adventure, not heartache. The fact is that, like most men my age, I was adept at compromise and had learned to fantasize what was possible. No, that's not exactly the truth: it would be more accurate to say that I had learned not to fantasize what was impossible. I knew my limits and was gamely willing to stretch them in the interest of fun—but never to their breaking point. Perhaps this was a cautionary streak left over from childhood, from some adolescent self-evaluation in which I had found myself wanting, from rejection here and there. Or perhaps it was a part of my nature buried deep in genetic code, fixing me in a hierarchy of my competitor males. I don't know. I can only say that, by the time I was ready to depart Hong Kong for London, my capacity and reticence for risk were by and large instinctive.

I arrived at Heathrow just after sunrise that August day, before the heat had risen too far. There had been a delay with the luggage and so the traffic would have already begun to thicken along the commuter routes, but it was a Sunday: London was vacant except for the tourists and those deserted few who had already spent their holidays. I had taken, on an interim basis, a flat in South Kensington that was owned by the Battleman fellow who had been sent out, a fortnight before, to replace me in the Asian market: a sitting room and two bedrooms on the ground floor of a red brick Victorian mews house. The flat proved of the serviceable, bachelor sort I had expected. But once I had un-packed and napped off some of the jet lag, I felt lonely in it with no one to call as the day waned in the sprawling, unfamiliar city. I tried a few friends in America, but it was the weekend there, too, of course, and I didn't bother to leave messages on their machines. There was little of interest on television—cricket and Australian sitcoms whenever I looked—and my eye soon wandered to the wall of overpainted book-shelves lined with thick adventure novels. I took down one or two for investigation, but they seemed to demand more attention and energy than I could summon. As I was returning the last to its place I noticed behind it and the other books, half-hidden, a parallel row of video tapes—dozens in all. These bore suggestive titles, double meanings, printed in hand along their slipcases, and I pressed one into the video, feeling the first excitement of the day, the first displacement of my imagination from myself. After minutes, though, the hard-core seduc-tions became routine and vaguely disgusting and I began to worry about the real lives of the porno actresses and actors and to search their faces for whatever hurt, signs of disconnectedness or even criminality, might have brought them into such an occupation. Imagining their lives was not difficult; it was even fun. And the more vivid these constructions be-came, the more available the stars soon seemed—in real life, in future. It was fantastically arousing. But it was also hot and I was exhausted after my long trip—the careful preparations for and letdown of un-winding from it. I glanced at some papers from my briefcase—Battle-man memos mostly—then browsed a London A–Z guide. On the screen an erect young actor lay on his back, straddled by a girl of star-tlingly innocent appearance. The actor was blonde, square-jawed: the girl, the sort of preppie coed one sometimes encountered. I was curi-ous about the couple: how they had been able to cast off inhibitions so completely, what their dreams were and why they did not fear the damage to those dreams that might—at any time, even distantly ahead—be done by such an indelible record of their exploits. Their abandon was the opposite of the reputation-obsessed timidity with which I and all the other professionals I knew conducted our lives. And, in a way too secret to share with anyone, I envied them.

In a surprisingly short time, however, their gyrations began to bore and I picked up a file on a bio-tech investment, one of whose original partners was a Battleman client in Hong Kong. But it was twenty-seven pages long, tightly printed and full of chemical symbols and diagrams of molecular structures, so I put it down again and began to page through my diary. I knew its contents pretty much by heart for almost all of its pages were blank, awaiting my new English life: new colleagues, new clients and commitments—with luck, new friends.

The pretty actress reclined in front of a campfire on a wide desolate beach, a tartan blanket beneath her. The glow of the flames rouged her skin. The camera panned to white caps breaking just off shore. When it came back, the actor had raised the girl's legs and was doing his work slowly, more emotionally, less mechanically than before.

Then the doorbell rang. It was practically a horn and it jolted me. Frantically, I retrieved the remote from the batik-covered cushion on which I had left it. The second button I pushed erased the video, turning the screen dark.

At the door stood Julia—taller, thinner than she had appeared in photographs, her auburn hair, flecked with the season's gold, blowing sideways in the summer wind. She sounded a little breathless so that it was difficult to tell if she were rushed or merely winded. "I'm Rupert's cousin," she explained, holding a small object up in her hand.

"I know," I replied—on reflection, stupidly.

"Oh." She seemed surprised.

"Come in."

"Only for a minute. I brought you these." She placed the object she had been carrying on the china tray that sat on a table by the door. It was a set of car keys on a silver ring. Beside them was a silver oval engraved with a griffin. "Rupert rang and asked me to."

"How kind. He'd mentioned that. I'd forgot."

"Apparently there'll be a company car for you, but until then—"

"How kind," I repeated. "Would you like a drink, or—"

"Yes." The speed and directness of the answer rather astonished me.

"I'm not sure what there is, but—"

"Is that vodka I see on the drinks tray?" she asked. "Very little of that with some tonic would be lovely. It's been so beastly hot, don't you think?"

"Yes. Not as beastly as Hong Kong, of course. Ice and lemon?"

"Please. But in Hong Kong people are more honest with themselves. They know it's going to be hot and so they plump for air conditioners. When the heat comes here we never really believe it will come again. Worse, we convince ourselves it won't."

"You've been to Hong Kong?"

"No. Only heard stories. Will you miss it? How long will you be here?"

"Don't know."

"Matter of months? Years?"

"Oh, the latter. At least. Several."

"That's enough time. You'll miss *it* when you leave. London's my favorite place on earth. . . . Most of the year. Not in August, nor in the dead of winter. But most of the year."

"Then perhaps I won't leave," I told her. She was not at all the woman I had feared she would be. Everything about her seemed more relaxed.

"Well, my experience," she went on, "is that people are either leavers or stayers. Of course, you can't very well be expected to stay in a place until you've seen one you like. Heavy on the vodka, aren't you? Bit heavy on the ice?"

"August," I said, as though that settled the matter.

"Do you have friends here?"

"One or two. Not really friends."

"Americans?"

"Brits. From Hong Kong. Acquaintances—that's all."

"Do you come from New York?"

"No. From . . . nearer to Washington."

"I've never been to America," Julia told me, almost apologetically, as she might have explained a failure to have studied a certain subject, or read a particular book. "Which is strange, considering that I am part American."

"I'd forgot that."

"Same as Rupert. But our focus was just—at home, I suppose, and in other directions, when one had the chance to travel at all." A single electronic chime sounded out of nowhere, followed, a few seconds later, by crescendos of human panting. The huge television, its sleep alarm apparently expired, grew once again bright as the obscene video continued its progress toward the inevitable resolution of its plot.

". . . Is that Channel Four?" Julia asked in astonishment. "It can't be, can it? Not even Channel Four . . . it's certainly not the BBC."

"What?" My eyes followed hers to the screen. I was shocked—terrified, to tell the truth, of what she might think of me. ". . . Oh . . . no, I'm sorry. It's . . . a tape. Actually."

"Really? Is it yours?"

"Came with the flat," I stumbled.

"How thoughtful of the owner. Whose flat is it?"

"Battleman bloke who went out to Hong Kong in my place."

"She's very pretty, isn't she?" Julia observed of the girl in the video.

"Very," I agreed.

"And he's rather—"

"Here, let me turn it off. I'm really sorry. It's very embarrassing. I don't know what explanation to offer."

"Why offer any?"

I hesitated, then smiled. "Point taken."

"You're sure you're not a connoisseur of those things?" she asked as the screen went dark.

"It's the second one I've ever watched. Cross my heart and hope to die. The first was when they had just come out. I bought a VCR from a friend and he threw it in as a starter bonus."

"Did he?"

"He did. Did you come in Rupert's car?"

"It's not very far."

"Then after you've had another drink . . . and I'll have one . . . I'll give you a lift back—wherever it is. Have you had dinner? No, of course you haven't. It's not that late. What I meant was, do you have plans for dinner?"

Julia smiled. "I'm afraid," she said "that I have to meet some people. . . . I *am* sorry."

"Understood," I assured her.

"Do you know about parking? You can park by a single yellow line after six-thirty, but never where there's a double yellow or you'll be clamped. Rupert's car has a Kensington and Chelsea sticker so you can park around here, but not, for example, in Westminster Council."

"I'll figure it out, slowly but surely."

"Take a bit of time, that's all."

Rupert's car was a six series BMW coupe. Julia led me to where she had parked it a couple of doors down the mews, showed me how the automatic locking system worked and then, with a wave, almost jauntily, was gone toward a broader thoroughfare of whose name I was not yet certain.

I returned to the house, swallowed the remains of my gin and tonic, then poured another, squeezing the juice of a fresh quarter of lemon into the tall glass. I was suddenly desperate as I sat again on the sofa, whose cushions bore the impress of Julia's visit, and stared into the space in front of me at those bookshelves crowned with bronze busts of hopelessly commercial grade, at the stained grey carpet and bright Persian throw rug and the lifeless TV screen.

I had come to London ready to fall in love with the city and, in time, with someone in it. But this was too soon, too abrupt and improbable. I had not yet had a full night's sleep, even a meal that felt right for the time zone. I had met no one but immigration officials and taxi drivers. I was half delirious with jet lag and alcohol after a nap that had seemed at first too short and then too long. And yet it had happened— that connection that is sometimes made between people, the involuntary transference of energy or radio waves, the sudden revving of euphoria and fear when one had expected another unremarkable moment. I had fallen in love with someone I had not expected would appeal to me—well, if not fallen in love, then at least become more than aroused by, much more than intrigued by Julia.

The ice slid to the rim of my glass and bounced from my teeth. So I put down the finished drink and went out into the mews, locking the door, with care, behind me. The sun had passed behind the lowest fringe of buildings in the west and here and there shadows disturbed an even light. It felt better in the open air, as if the sight of so many others and the scale of the metropolis might dilute one's emotions. I walked east in the Fulham Road, past shuttered antique shops and estate agencies, past a few convenience stores and pubs, then turned into Sydney Street for no reason except that it seemed quiet—pretty and residential. I wondered what Julia's take on our encounter had been, whom she was meeting, whether she had a boyfriend or, for that matter, wanted one. In a way, I thought, it would be easier, simpler, to discover that she was already engaged—or nearly so—than to find that she was available. The latter was as much as I could hope for, but then the delicious prospect of winning her would be bound to require more concentration than I was sure I had left in my emotional account. Still, I walked: now, in the King's Road; now in Birdcage Walk until, by the time I'd reached the Houses of Parliament, I was exhausted and in need of a loo. I found one, then some good kebabs in a cheap Greek place that catered to tourists. After dinner I strolled back along the river in the solitary dark and found a stray cab lingering after hours in front of the Tate.

My instinct told me it was the wrong thing to do, but the next morning I rang Julia from Rupert's car phone to thank her for having brought the car round. She seemed surprised. At first, I thought I had awakened her. "I hoped we might have dinner some night," I concluded. "Not just because I don't know anyone else in London."

Julia laughed. "Tuesday?" she asked, after a moment.

"Tuesday would be nice. Where shall I—"

"I'll come to you at . . . half-eight? Then we can wander."

We dined across a chequered tablecloth from one another at the Red Dragon, where I ordered too many courses of spicy Szechuan in order to prolong the evening, our talk. Two nights later we sat side by side on a banquette in Walton Street. Then, on the weekend, she was gone—"to the country," without a word more specific than that. On Monday, we took in a play in Hammersmith, then a quick hamburger. Julia was tired—from the weekend, the long drive back, from work; a bit bored by the play. Everywhere we went at least a few people— young women who were themselves imperfect replicas of her, young men in banker's suits or jeans and banker's lace-ups—hurried to our table for a fleeting word, a kiss, or else slowed, waved and smiled. They were, to a person, pleasant, even charming, acknowledging me as they gushed at Julia. But I found their highflown confidence, their tribal intimacy with one another unnerving. When one of them, who now and then locked eyes with her and took such great liberty touching her that I was certain they had slept together, finally moved on in the group he had come with, Julia turned to me with uncanny instinct and said "Don't worry."

"Do I look worried?"

"An urbane cynicism can mask quite a profound ignorance," she insisted, "all of England is a society of cynical urbanity."

It was this sense that she, too, saw things—or, in any event, could see them—from the outside, as much as her beauty or style, that drew me to her. But we were by then no more than friends—and remained nothing more as the summer waned, London refilled and term began again in Cambridge. Julia, having been a don until the year before, still remained close to a number of the fellows of the college where she had done her post-graduate studies. She had moved to London in order to deepen her association with The Chamberlain Institute, a privately endowed academic think tank which sponsored research into just the sort of anthropological and mythological areas that had come to interest her—and also to grow up. She felt, she told me, that she had by then lived in a university town for too long. But, of course, by coming to London, she had merely forsaken a venue in which she had fewer and fewer contemporaries. The friends she had made there—the entire famous set, virtually—had moved on, in large part to London. And the adulthood she had in mind could not be cloistered within even the noblest walls of the academy.

The afternoon we stopped near Granchester to study Cambridge across the fens in the distance, Julia seemed wistful. "Such an Eden, isn't it?" she said. "God versus nature, I mean. The spiritual and the hormonal in the same place at the same time—at their peaks. Contesting. It must have been the same where you were?"

"In Charlottesville? Almost."

"A place of stillness and movement. The *axis mundi*. When you are there and that age, it's the center of the world. Or seems so. You think harder than you ever have. Then let go of consciousness. *Think. Then let go.* Never before and never again is life like that."

We drove on and eventually found a parking space for Rupert's BMW in Queen's Road. Then we crossed the Cam on foot over Trinity Bridge and strolled the avenue of American limes until we were on the opposite back, equidistant between the river itself and Wren's library. "Do you see that weeping willow?" Julia continued, recovering herself nimbly after a moment. "There is a legend that if you sit anywhere in its shadow when the moon is full and stare at the river for long enough what you are meant to do with your life will become clear to you." She looked up. "Surprisingly, there is not a queue. I suppose the legend is relatively little known and, nowadays, not too much believed in. But some people still go there and sometimes it seems to help."

"Did you?"

"Yes. But I had few doubts in those days. More now."

Judging that Julia preferred not to elaborate, I said only "You're kidding?"

Julia's eyes travelled the ripe grange in the distance. "It's not that I mind getting older," she whispered. "Just that sometimes, I miss the certainty, that's all."

We walked then and made our way, blithely assuming the prerogatives of university fellows, across college lawns and through college cloisters and quads until at last we were in King's Parade and the mist had thickened and grown chilly on our skin. Julia bought squares of bitter chocolate fudge in a shop whose return was crowded with pedestrians. And we headed down Trumpington Street in the direction of the Fitzwilliam. "This is my best thing," Julia said as we hurried, skipping over the quickened water-flow in Hobson's Conduit which ran beside the curb. "Showing a place I love so much to someone who's never been there. Seeing it all—all this—over again. Nothing's more fun, do you think?"

I hesitated. "Unless it's seeing a place someone you care about loves," I answered then and took her hand without turning, as though I had been doing it all my adult life. I could feel her expectation, the instantaneous tightening then lessening—but not too far—of the pressure in her fingers and, in that fantasized but still unexpected second, though we had never kissed, never discussed a future together, a compact seemed to have been reached between us. Later, dry in the warmth and among the crowds in the galleries, I was transfixed by Titian's portrait of *The Pasero Brothers*, the mystical interplay of emotion and thought between siblings. And for the first time—late in the scheme of things—I could realistically imagine my life completed by love and children, the end of the quest begun in adolescence, the beginning of something new. But, of course, it was still too early, too dangerous to say this aloud. Indeed, I said, "What an extraordinary painting!" then ". . . I wonder if *I* could return the favor and show *you* someplace."

"Do you have somewhere particular in mind?"

I paused, then blurted "New York?"

Julia turned warily, as though I had proposed we move there.

"I have to go later in the week," I explained. "Boring business stuff. But it won't take all day." In fact, I had been anxious about the trip, worried that my disappearance from London might somehow disturb the rhythm of our developing friendship. But now, suddenly, the subject came easily. "It may not even take very much time," I added, "if we're lucky."

"How long would we be gone?" she inquired.

"We could stay through the weekend. I don't know: four or five days."

"I really shouldn't."

" 'Footfalls echo in the memory,' " I told her, reciting, out of nowhere, lines from T. S. Eliot that had just come to mind. " 'Down the passage which we did not take.' "

"I shouldn't," Julia repeated, then added "but I will."

We travelled as though we were already a couple. Indeed, I was pleasantly aware of giving that impression to others as we lost ourselves in separate newspapers in the lounge at Heathrow Terminal Three, spoke suddenly or observed those meaningless silences which occur between people long (or else readily prepared to be) habituated to one another's presence. It felt strange, comfortable yet convulsive, to have found Julia—as if, an infinity of possibilities having been resolved at last into a single destiny, time had turned round and become unforgiving. I understood that I had begun to fall in love not with a fantasy the pursuit of which might be put off to accommodate my work and apprehension until some perfect season of the future, but with a woman in the here and now; it was urgent that I not lose her by moving too fast . . . or slowly . . . or through any mistake at all.

All day Manhattan baked in Indian Summer, but in the early, low-latitude dusk, its treetops whispered in harmony with a cool, damp, harbor wind. Autumn. We stayed in an apartment Battleman had long kept in midtown, just east of Lexington. It was a commodious place, its fifties decor still polished and unfrayed; the doorman memorized our names at once. That first evening we found ourselves lured north along Park Avenue, oddly braced by the moisture which hid in swirls of developing darkness. I had first come here on my own from Charlottesville—for the debut at the Waldorf Astoria of the rather mousey sister of one of my fraternity brothers. Now, after so much time, I stared at the rows of illuminated windows and at the facades which

framed them and realized that only the buildings were immutable—
that in all the years since I had been at college or even since I had
worked on Wall Street the occupants of most of those rooms were
bound to have changed. I felt lost in the city, a visitor with only the most
distant, fragile connection to it. And because I had once so precisely
dreamed, so resolutely assumed that I would make a life here, I shivered
with a transitory sadness that only really passed when I began to see it
through Julia's eyes, as if for the first time.

We dined lightly then slept in separate twin beds in the same room.

The next evening, after work, I took Julia to dinner at a good French
restaurant on Fifty-fifth Street and we sat for a long time over the
claret. Afterward, we walked back to the apartment, Julia looking, without luck, for the first leaves to have fallen. We were modern; we accepted the facts of each other's pasts. And if I were wholly ready for
love, she at least seemed reconciled to the compromise with her dreams
that I appeared to represent. "Most people want to marry the person
who makes their heart beat fastest," she said as we shoved our narrow
beds together, "when, of course, one should really marry the person
who makes you most calm."

"Do *I* make you calm?" I asked, unsure what answer would
satisfy me.

Julia hesitated. "I think so," she replied, biting her lip slightly
and looking down over it, half-smiling in that comical way she had—
still has.

I gave Julia her emerald and diamond ring the next Christmas Eve,
but, despite a few hiccups that autumn, my proposal and her acceptance
seemed implicit from that September night in New York—or so it
strikes me now, in retrospect. We married in the spring in a traditional
service in the village church, which was attended by many more of
Julia's friends than mine. That congregation of Englishmen in striped
trousers, morning coats and colorful ties, of young women in floral
pastels and expansively brimmed hats confronted me with both the
charm and claustrophobia of the world into which I had chosen to
marry. My ushers ignored the usual rule and seated the bride's guests on
both sides of the sanctuary, for balance. But the imbalance of nationalities, with only my parents, my aunt and a few of my closer acquaintances from the American investment banking community in London
scattered near the front on my side, reminded me that, in expanding my

horizons, I had all but lost my vantage point—that I had taken many of my oldest friends for granted, strained the immediacy of my connection to them and so eventually left them somewhere in the misty wake of my peripatetic, work-obsessed career.

4

I T IS CHARACTERISTIC of Castlemorland, as of most great
houses in England, that its hallways and passages are quiet, unlin-
gered in. The life of each room is secreted behind heavy closed doors
and cavern-thick walls. No doubt there are practical reasons for this—
the conservation of heat, for example—but, to my mind, the most important thing about it is the sense of drama it creates when the house
is full of habitual guests and infrequent visitors, such as on this shooting weekend.

When I come downstairs, ahead of Julia, there are Barbours and
wellies, jumpers and gun cases in the Great Hall. They are grouped
loosely, one or two of each off to a corner or backed against a column
or an open area of skirting board. There is an unfamiliar black Labrador
asleep between two such piles, his nose settled awkwardly upon a worn
cowhide ammunition box. He is breathing mightily, in frequent heaves,
and his uneven sounds are the only ones about. He jolts awake as I
pass, raises his head in the manner of a very old dog, then lowers it
again, snuggling an inch or so closer to the scuffed leather. All at once
his breathing turns regular—inaudible, practically imperceptible from
the height of a man's ears and eyes.

The breakfast room lies at one end of the principal north-south corridor which, at Castlemorland, is always referred to as the Long Walk.
The Short Walk, by comparison, extends directly east from the entrance, beneath the overhanging marble staircase, to the pleasant room
known as the Regent's, which has, from its beginning, served as a sitting room for the lady of the house. In any event, the breakfast room,

east-facing and so brilliant with sunlight at this hour, is very much alive with that peculiar muttering and fitful paper-ruffling which are the definitive sounds of morning in English houses. Topley, six feet four inches and nearly eighty-three, stands by the sideboard buffet. He came to work as a footman for Julia's grandfather and recently celebrated his golden anniversary as butler at Castlemorland. There was a party given for him in what used to be the servants' hall. Julia's father gave him a pocket watch whose hunting case had been inscribed, as well as airline tickets and leave for him and Mrs. Topley to visit their daughter and grandchildren in Gibraltar. It was a pleasant, if bittersweet occasion because of Topley's ubiquitousness in the memory of every living Midleton-Lygham and also because of the unspoken likelihood that, after him, there would never again be a full-time butler in the house. The family remained at his party less than an hour—for two glasses of sparkling wine and short conversations with everyone present—and I remember how difficult it was for me to measure out affection and reserve in the effortless, perfectly calibrated way that was natural to and expected of gentry.

"Morning, Topley," I say now.

"Morning, Sir?" he asks, as though there is bad news of which I—of which everyone—must certainly be aware. News unhappy enough to contradict any notion of a 'good' morning.

I put this down to his manner, which can be testy on occasion. Whatever news there is I do not wish to pull it out of him one word or one phrase at a time. Nor do I wish to become involved in the domestic problems of a house in which I am, really, a guest. I reason that if, in fact, there is news I should know someone else will tell me. "Any eggs?" I inquire.

"Of course, Sir. Scrambled and fried."

"Scrambled, please."

Topley removes the lid of a silver chafing dish and I help myself to two serving spoons of scrambled eggs with Cook's signature traces of nutmeg and curry. I take a slightly oily crescent of baked ham with its wheel of bone attached, some burnt toast and a small tumbler of room temperature orange juice.

At the table I sit down—tentatively, never fully drawing up my chair for I realize there is very little time—at the ready place next to Philip, who presently looks up from the peach-colored sheets of the Saturday *Financial Times* and smiles. "This is a surprise," I say.

"A happy one, I hope, because it appears I'm going to be camping out with you and Rupert in the City—more or less for the duration."

"Excellent. Rupert told me the news."

"Damn good job he made of it, too," Philip adds. His face may be Chinese, but his voice is English, his diction, native rather than repatriated, that of his mates at Trinity, Cambridge. I know it well; can, by now, pick it out anywhere as the regionless purr of the reflective educated classes, its timbre and rhythm confident, ready, quick and without much mercy. In many ways, it is the most persuasive of all voices, especially when disembodied, such as on a telephone or radio, capable of selling greed as good manners, or weakness as common sense. "John," Philip says then. "May I introduce Wiley Ryan. You don't know each other, do you?"

"No," I answer immediately, "though I certainly feel like I do. Hello." For the past month, this man has been the focus of my working life and, by now, my fate is tied to his. I have developed any number of spreadsheets and *pro forma* financial statements in the technical design of his bid to take Ergo, Inc. private. I have, from each midday until well toward midnight, when Wall Street is invariably still at work, kept a nearly open telephone line to America, sounding out the key players there whose backing we will require and liaison with whom is my largest responsibility at Battleman.

"Wiley Ryan," repeats the large, red-haired man across from us. He has the shoulders, the broad-gauge wrists and beefy rhipidate hands of an American fullback. He stands abruptly, reaches over the salt cellar and pepper shaker and the domed silver butter dish to shake hands with me. "We've spoken heaven knows how many times—dozens? It's a real pleasure to meet you in person, finally," he declares. "You've been doing a helluva job, John, a *helluva* one."

"Thanks."

Wiley Ryan's voice is more voluble than most and flatly mid-Western as he nods to the lady beside him. "My wife, Taggart," he says. Taggart Ryan is a handsome woman only a few years beyond forty. Hers is the face of a nineteen-fifties cheerleader—Cupid's pursed mouth, button nose, continuously evaluating eyes—leathered by time but preserved by moisturizers. The evenness of her skin tone is a dermatological marvel. Her thick frosted hair has been laboriously coiffed and flipped forward.

"Morning," I utter.

"I've been reading the weather report," she apologizes. "Excuse me for not having looked up when you came in."

"I haven't heard a weather report," Philip explains, his eyes still flickering to and from the *FT,* "since we landed, I suppose. There was talk then of a front just west of us, if I remember."

"This is England," I remind him. "There is always a front coming in from the west."

"From anyplace," Wiley Ryan says, "except when you need one to dull the glare."

Suddenly, I understand what bothers Topley—the vague ill temper clear weather can induce in serious shooters. For them an azure sky, the sparkle of sunlight, visibility for an extended distance are soul-destroying. Though I am a good enough shot, owing to a certain calmness of nerves, I am not what could be called "serious" about the sport. But for having married Julia or found my way into a career and country where it is often practically obligatory, I doubt, in fact, that I would pursue it all. Not in the British Isles, where the conditions under which men pursue birds are so contrived and expensive. The shooting I first knew was from log blinds, at dawn, on the Eastern Shore of Maryland. Geese and ducks migrated in the flyway overhead and men camouflaged themselves and their habits to defeat them on their solitary passes. The stillness of the dark tidewater, the quiet intent of lusty hunters before sunrise, the shots—one, two, three, four—erupting all of a sudden in what had seemed an empty universe: these were the elemental sensations of life in the wild. They were natural, they were sporting. No beaters. No artificial coverts. Dogs instead of picker-uppers.

Wiley Ryan shrugs at fate. He is C.E.O. of Ergo. He is fifty-seven, windburned and freckled, a former partner of a Cleveland law firm, who was once a near-miss All American at Stanford. I know all about Wiley Ryan, whose success-after-success, institution-after-institution resumé was a principal feature of the Ergo I.P.O., as it is of the pending Leveraged Buyout proposal to take Ergo private. I know that he is a man who, when he says that he understands business, actually means that he understands finance and manipulation and how deals are cut among interested parties on the inside. And now, meeting him for the first time, I am immediately aware of other things about him. He is, for instance, fastidious, almost military in his posture and in the way he arranges his clothes. His Hermès tie, carrying a carefully chosen motif of game birds in flight, is knotted in a carefully contrived half-Windsor; his collar is short, a flyaway in the style of the Prince of Wales. He keeps his coat buttoned even as he sits and that coat, a heavy hound's-tooth, single-breasted with three horn buttons on each sleeve, has been made for him—recently, from all appearances—by one or another of London's most costly tailors.

Cross-sectioning a lukewarm fried egg, his forefingers press heavily against the spines of his fork and knife until the latter slips across the bone china, producing a high frequency shriek. He half smiles but otherwise ignores this disturbance, coaxing the abstract swirl of orange and white with a triangle of light brown toast. To deflect the conversation, he says, "We had marvelous shooting in Spain last year" and again looks to his wife.

"Oh, yes," she says. "Fan-*tas*-tic, wasn't it?"

"Partridges?" asks Philip Li.

"We shot the estate of a man called Rodieros."

"The Duke de Rodieros," Taggart Ryan adds. "We shot one of his estates. He is supposed to have several."

"Then I'm sure he must," answers Ralph Marlowe from along the Ryans' side of the long mahogany table. Ralph Marlowe is a close friend of Julia's brother Adrian—a young farmer from Lincolnshire who was with Adrian at Harrow and later at Cirencester, the agricultural college. With his chair set slightly back for leg room, his shag of hair and boat-shaped face, the first impression he gives is one of extraordinary length, of a peculiarly English gawkiness. There is a quiet tone of world-weary sarcasm in his voice, but this is not so brittle as it might be.

"No question about it," Wiley Ryan replies. "The Duke's a hundred percent the genuine article. Gave us an eight hundred bird day, laid it all on."

"Eight hundred," Ralph Marlowe exclaims. "I don't want to speak for Adrian, but I'm afraid Castlemorland can't offer you that."

"Never mind," says Wiley Ryan. "Never mind. Whatever the bag is, it'll be."

I am glad that Adrian is absent from the room when Wiley Ryan says this. For Adrian is old fashioned about the Castlemorland shoot: any suggestion of competition among the guns, any mention of the size of the bag (particularly a bet about it) would strike him as unsporting. And depending upon the length of his temper and whether or not he has had a drink, he might either explode in a tirade or turn away in disgust. In any event, it is clear that, except for the presence of Ralph Marlowe, this is not the sort of shooting party Adrian enjoys. This is a party of Rupert's invention—a party with a motive. Its purpose is seduction.

Ralph Marlowe says, "Still, it's a great shame you had to come so far—and find such brilliant light when you got here, I mean."

"It wasn't very far," Mrs. Ryan explains. "We were in the Cotswolds and—"

"The Cotswolds?" I repeat. "Were you?"

"Doing some antiquing," Taggart Ryan elaborates. "I have a little decorating business of my own back home. I have one or two clients for whom I'm, well, looking."

Wiley Ryan leans forward and looks down four vacated place settings to Ralph Marlowe. "The fact is," he says, "that we were in our suite yesterday when Rupert very kindly telephoned from his flight. Philip was with him, weren't you?"

Philip Li nods. "Absolutely." He bites into a section of marmaladed toast.

"I don't know where they were, but somewhere in midair," Wiley Ryan continues, "this incongruous thought occurred to Rupert Midleton-Lygham that, maybe, just maybe I'd like a day's shooting on short notice. Actually, it was more complicated than that. They had wrapped up the business they'd—well, he'd—gone to Hong Kong to do and, I suppose figuring the time difference, called me in America to tell me about it. Only Tag and I weren't in America and one or the other of them drew out of my usually tight-lipped secretary the fact that we had slipped over here for a few days."

I enjoy the skill with which Wiley Ryan works to win both Ralph and Philip to his side, the subtle compliments he bestows upon them and the way in which these compliments reinforce his own unique authority to praise.

Just then the door from the Long Walk opens and Julia and Rupert enter together. Minus only her wellies and Barbour, Julia is otherwise ready to shoot. Rupert, however, is still without his jacket. His hair is wet, brushed and combed, but not yet entirely into place. He has the look, as he often does—even after hours at the office—of a man who has come directly from the bed of a pulse-raising woman and who has not yet had time fully to compose himself.

"Wiley, morning," Rupert calls from the buffet. "Tag." He introduces, "My cousin, Julia." He says, "You've met John. Needless to say. You've met everyone. Sorry to be so late."

"Not at all," Wiley Ryan tells him.

I force a smile, clandestinely, yet frantically watching for clues, in Julia's or Rupert's eyes or demeanor, to the late night meeting neither will acknowledge. At the table, all eyes have been lifted to the new arrivals and I wonder who, if any among those present, might have threatened my wife. Ralph, of course, seems too close; Philip, too distant. But how am I to know for sure without understanding the nature of that threat? To my knowledge, Julia has never previously met Wiley Ryan. Still, I study their exchange of glances, the exact tone of their pleasantries for the smallest hint of recognition.

"We've put the clock back anyway," Ralph Marlowe concurs, dropping his words dryly, as if intending them to evaporate. "Awaiting more *appropriate* weather."

Julia takes two slices of burnt bacon from the hot-plate and begins munching one while she pours a few oat bran flakes and a drizzle of skimmed milk into a bowl. My wife has exemplary carriage, a leftover from a childhood and adolescence passed on horseback. She still hunts occasionally—several days each season—but the principal consequence of her early training is a posture now rarely found in anyone her age. This posture legitimizes her beauty, I think, suggesting that her fine bones and high color, much like her eyes, are manifestations of internal strengths. I am proud as I watch her, as I watch the Ryans watch her. It is flattering to have been chosen by such a woman.

Without apology or disguise, Julia settles her bowl on the edge of the buffet and, still chewing, rolls back the cuff of her jumper in order to glance at her red-and-yellow tartan Swatch. "Had no idea, sorry" she exclaims, then, without sitting, woofs the molehill of cereal and hurriedly sips some of her cream-laden coffee. "Will you both be shooting?" she asks.

"No. Just Wiley," Tag Ryan says. "Though, if I may, I'll come out and stand with him."

"Good," Julia says. "Who else is shooting?"

"In addition to you and John and me?" Rupert asks.

"And Philip. Philip, you're shooting, aren't you?" Julia inquires.

"And very keen to," Philip tells her.

"And Ralph," she adds. "Naturally."

Ralph sits back on his chair, raising its two front legs, balancing himself upon it by the balls of his feet. "Naturally," he repeats.

Julia starts slightly. "I mean you had the first gun in the shoot when Adrian took it over. He came to you long before he thought of inviting me."

Ralph stares at the cross-vaulted ceiling, appearing to study the bas relief medallions in the arch, the pendentive dome, the *faux marbre* and porphyry finishes. He pauses, then says only, "That's true."

"Does that make eight?" Julia asks.

"With Adrian. And Piers," Rupert says.

"I bloody well forgot Piers was coming," Julia asserts anxiously. "I thought his next days were later on in the season. Never mind." She glances toward me, raises and lowers her eyes quickly, as if to absolve herself of any foreknowledge of Piers Haig's participation.

"He usually shoots midweek," Rupert adds.

Julia nods.

IN THE HALL, guns are removed from their cases, cartridge bags collected. Legs are raised, slipped into hunter green Wellington boots. Fern-colored huskies are buttoned against the damp and the chill. Barbours, worn but freshly thorn-proofed with vaguely fragrant wax, are zipped and snapped shut. Caps are doffed by the men—all wool and of similar pattern; primarily tan or olive with only very subtle plaids. Briefly, there is silence: an absence of voices, anyway, if not of movement or ruffling.

On the portico, Piers Haig leans one shoulder against a smooth column as he chats to Julia's brother. Piers is not tall—no taller than

Adrian; but where Adrian's frame is broad, his neck and wrists thick, his features rounded, Piers is lithe, athletic, a once pretty boy whose conventionally sculpted face has recently begun to grow a little corpulent. His hair, which has gone prematurely white, remains childishly thick, messed by the wind.

He does not acknowledge me as I approach, does not interrupt his conversation or change his expression. Rather he lowers his voice, deliberately making it more private. But I can hear him well enough now. "The truth of the matter," he says, "the truth of the matter, Adrian, is that Matthew Paxton is, *in my opinion*, about as wide as they come. He's slippery. Not a nice man, *in any way*. He's lived on the land around here all his life, I suppose, and it's perfectly obvious he doesn't give a fig for it. Or for anything, for that matter, but cash."

"Matthew is Matthew," Adrian replies. "I've known him all my life. I believe I know what he is."

"One would think so," Piers says, still apparently oblivious to my presence six feet from them.

Adrian glances toward me then back to Piers. It is as though he were holding a hand up, politely but firmly begging my indulgence.

"Matthew's father," Piers says, "was better. He was your father's agent, wasn't he? I know he was my uncle's. And my uncle liked him, too. He was what he was, if you know what I mean. Serious. Honest. Humorless. Not clever, but plenty capable. Filled the bill, with no untidy ambitions left over.

"And the younger brother, David, of course, I knew from when he was up at Cambridge. I wasn't living too far from there then. And he occasionally moved with an older group. So Julia and I ran into him now and again."

I remain silent, but find it difficult to do so. I do not like hearing Piers pair himself with my wife, even in memory, history. I do not like to think of "Piers and Julia" or of "Julia and Piers" as though such a couple ever actually existed or had legitimacy in others' eyes.

Once, before we were married, Julia and I confessed our past loves to each other. We did this spontaneously, in my bed on a rainy Sunday morning spent unusually (because of the demands of my work) in London. My list proved longer than hers, as I felt it ought to have done. But later, driving alone in the Strand, it occurred to me that hers had not, so to speak, begun at the beginning. We had betrayed names, but out of all chronology. And, anyway, it was not until months afterward that I learned she and Piers Haig had once been "practically engaged."

"David was a different thing," Piers continues, "though I couldn't for the life of me say why."

"Totally different—in every way," Adrian agrees.

"I never knew him," I venture.

"Didn't you?" Adrian asks.

"Of course, he didn't," Piers says in a chastening voice. "John wasn't around then. Think how long it's been since David died."

"I know," Adrian says. "It's been a bloody long time, hasn't it?"

Piers looks at me. He is including me now, finally, plainly relieved to be past the awkwardness of having to greet me and decide precisely what to say. Piers's wife, Marjorie, has been in a wheelchair for more than a year, having lost the use of her legs and arms permanently to multiple sclerosis. There are rumors that she is given to long and severe depressions, rumors that Piers depends too heavily upon her inherited income to subsidize the small stabling operation he bought and runs near Newmarket, rumors that he has lately allowed his medical practice to slide and that his fidelity, once surprising to those who had known him in his youth, has at last begun to waver.

"His looks, I guess, were the basis of it," Piers says. "I mean David was so young, so new to everything, what else could it have been? He didn't look like he carried one gene from his own family, did he?"

"No. Come to think of it, he didn't."

"He didn't *sound* like any of them either. Or move the way they did. He was more . . . not athletic really, but—"

"Graceful," Adrian says.

"Yes. Graceful. That's right. There was nothing working class about David. Hell, nothing middle class either. I've never thought about it before, you know, not in this way."

" 'Those whom the gods love die young,' " Adrian says, "or something like that."

"Bugger it, if you ask me."

"They used to say that about the war dead. At school, remember?"

"Yes. They always had some justification handy for anything they couldn't explain. Do you think David was a poofter?"

"No. Absolutely not."

"I know some people who do."

"Pure jealousy."

"Hugh Basildon claims to have—"

"Rubbish."

"I don't know. There might be truth in it. He had plenty to get from Basildon—and got it, I might add. Or was in the process, at least. Hugh, if you recall, was really his entrée."

"For God's sake, David Paxton didn't need entrée, certainly not of any kind Hugh Basildon could have provided." Adrian's words grow louder until, suddenly, he catches himself and modulates his tone. "He had something much more important than entrée."

"Oh?" prods Piers. "And what would that be?"

"Magnetism," Adrian says. "David had magnetism, if anyone ever had it. From the time he was a little boy."

"My point is that magnetism can take one only so far without help. Without sponsorship."

"You have to remember that we were pretty nearly the same age, David and I. Actually, he was a few months older, but near enough. We used to play together as children, his father being my father's agent, as you said. They lived in Thorn Cottage, do you know it? It's that lovely double-fronted house on the edge of the village. Anyway, though it might not have seemed so to anyone else, I, even then, always thought of him as the lucky one. I was the heir to this magnificent estate, to a title. He was heir to nothing much at all. And yet I'd've had to have been a fool not to realize that peoples' attention was almost always riveted on him. Anything he wanted—whatever, whomever he fancied—he had only to make his presence known. Not even his desire, *just* his presence. And things would come round.

"Luck. Everything about him cried out 'luck'. And, you know, as long as he's been gone, I can still see him perfectly. When you come to think about it, how many people have faces you cannot—cannot ever—forget? Damn few. And David had so many. I can see his face at every stage of his life. I can see him reading in my father's library, which was a privilege no one else outside the family was ever granted: no one connected to the estate. An old leatherbound volume of Trollope in his hands. And Trollope's an author I still haven't read. No, David was astonishing, unique really.

"The year that film crew came, how old would he have been? Barely seventeen? Maybe not quite that. I came home for hols, I remember, and he was already here. His school had closed down a few days before mine had and he'd returned and found all this excitement he hadn't expected or known anything about. Lorries and caravans everywhere. The atmosphere of a fun fair, but with film stars about and, I don't know, a certain seriousness in the air. Art with a capital A. Those weird silvery lights. It's difficult to explain, but everything was backwards while that film crew was here. Julia seemed to understand it, to be amused by it. I can't say the same for myself. They were calling the house something else in their story—Mudlington Hall, or Madlington, I believe, rather than Castlemorland. The imaginary family who lived in it were the Lesleys, headed by the Earl and Countess of Lesley and starring their exquisite young daughter, Lady Victoria. Played by Susannah Finley, who, you may remember from the scene in the dairy, bared every square inch of her voluptuous knockers."

"You are banging on about this," Piers interrupts.

"Only because there's a point to it. By their second or third day here these Lesleys—who were, after all, just actors being paid to do a job, just fictional characters dreamt up in some screenwriter's imagination—these Lesleys had rather taken over the place. They were of far more interest to the people of the village, not to mention to the tourists who'd come to wander through the parts of the house that had been left open, than were we Midleton-Lyghams, who have lived at Castlemorland for seven centuries and farmed and fought and died for England for nearly ten."

"Poor Adrian, you felt dethroned."

"Not at all. That sort of thing has never bothered me, as you well know. We were talking about David Paxton and I only raised the matter in that connection. I suppose what I was trying to say is that the shooting of that film momentarily scrambled an ancient village, tossed people out of their assigned roles and let them grab for any new identity they cared to try on. Interesting as far as it goes. But in David's case, more than interesting. Absolutely fascinating really. You know that he was chosen for a role as an extra. An aristocrat. And you may know that the director was so taken with him that he was ultimately written into the script as a sort of *fin de race* swordsman."

"I knew he had lines," Piers says. "I didn't know how they'd come about. He was very photogenic, David; that much one had to say."

"I would never have been given that role," Adrian explains.

"Well, I wouldn't let that bother me."

"Neither would you have been."

"You'll pardon me if I find the idea of David Paxton as an aristocrat slightly hard to credit."

"What would you say to the idea of David Paxton in bed with Susannah Finley?"

"You're joking?"

"She was living in the house. She, her co-star and the director. He had it off with her there, very nearly nightly from the time they met until she went to America for her next film."

"And no one knew?"

"A few of us did, not many. Enough that he had a reputation before he ever got to Cambridge."

"It's very odd," Piers admits. "I've never heard anything about this. Your agent's son ends up bonking a girl you more than likely had an eye on yourself."

"Hardly. I was never that bold."

"And this girl just happens to be about the most desired female in the U.K. or anywhere else. And all of this takes place under your roof with your blessing. Tell me, were you after a certain vicarious thrill, Adrian, from having David play your role?"

"I honestly don't know," Adrian says quietly. "I didn't have as much confidence then. And I'd already got used to the idea that I had certain rights and so did everyone else. One's parents, for example. One's masters at school. The farmers on the estate. It was a very prescribed world in which my rights, I suppose, were obvious—all those things I was heir to. And so were David's because you were fooling yourself if you ever thought he didn't have the right—by which, again, I mean the magnetism—to fuck whomever he wanted, whenever and wherever without promising anything more into the bargain."

I look at Adrian and think, as I sometimes have, that he is more perceptive than he is given general credit for. He is my brother-in-law; I like him and am glad that we are able to share the kind of easy friendship we do, the friendship of men who would not, for a moment, wish to live each others' lives.

5

A PEWTER ARROWHEAD of cloud has risen above the beech wood beyond the park. For a few minutes, as the others in our party come through from the hall, it appears to float. Suddenly, then, this greying mass drifts southward, drawing an ever-enlarging delta of shade across the low, distant sky.

Julia is first to join us, attended, as usual on these outings, by her golden Labrador Cav (for Caveat) at her heel. Cav's grand obliviousness to others in the shooting party, his cocked chin and theatrically held profiles have, like the stagecraft of an old thespian, by now passed from affectation into habit.

"*Whose* is *that?*" she asks, with a kind of sheepish astonishment, stopping suddenly. On the swept gravel, no more than thirty yards to the left, sits a Ferrari 328 the color of a robin's egg. A last laser of sunlight ricochets from its chrome; against its left front fender, still mottled by rain of the night before, a solitary oak leaf dangles, almost as a pendant.

"What? . . . Oh," Adrian replies, ". . . it was a birthday present."

Julia swallows visibly. "Adrian! To you? From whom?"

"Someone very sympathetic to the plight of turning twenty-nine. Last time young, and all that. Namely myself. Fact is, my theory has always been that the only sensible way to measure age isn't from birth, by how long one's been here, but by the amount of time one has left. And since one never really knows the answer to that, once one's reached this age, it's presumably just as well to—go for it." Unarticulated in Adrian's glib philosophy is the fact that this is to be the first of his birthdays without either of his parents alive. His father, the Andrew for whom my son was named, passed away a few months ago—abruptly and not old—while Caroline, his sweetly dispositioned, superstitious mother, died years before when her plane missed its runway in a Northern Irish fog. She and her husband, who had been on their way to fish a beat of a famous river belonging to friends, as a matter of safety and principle, never travelled in the same aircraft while their children were young.

"Was it frightfully expensive?"

"Not *frightfully*. It's not new. Has a couple of years and a few thousand miles on it. Anyway, even John has plunged on a Porsche, which has been very good for his street cred, too. People, after all, never really trust anyone who goes around saying that a car is transport and that's all there is to it. And, really, why should they?"

"They don't call it 'mena-Porsche' for nothing," Ralph says.

"Though, if I were John," Adrian adds, "I might have a Cadillac instead."

"A very large Cadillac," Ralph agrees.

Wiley Ryan smiles.

Ahead of the Ferrari, to the right of the portico, the driveway has filled with two Range Rovers—the larger, dark green one freshly washed; the older, army-tan model splattered with hardened mud. Keeping his distance from the vehicles—and, for a moment, from us— is Mr. Cole, the Head Keeper. He is facing some women who are much less smartly dressed than we, indeed whose clothing is almost tattered; he is speaking to them informally, in his thick, rapid Yorkshireman's brogue. From his manner, it is clear that he is merely repeating something he has already said any number of times, summing up. I recognize the bright face of Isabel Wainwright, Adrian's fiancée, who has taken up beating as a hobby, also the figures of two of Julia's teenage cousins who now live three quarters of an hour away and are apt to turn up on the pleasanter shooting days.

We acknowledge each other, then separate. The women move off to join the other beaters at the first covert, supervised by the Under Keeper, Donald, while the 'guns' gather round Adrian, who now has a final word with Mr. Cole.

Mr. Cole motions toward the sky. The arc of his hand, with its many dips and rises, traces the contour of the estate, the anticipated progress of our campaign in the day ahead.

Adrian stops him. "We won't shoot that wood until—"

"Wednesday after next," Mr. Cole can be heard to interrupt, "when His Grace comes to shoot and the gentlemen who remember what shooting was."

"Wednesday after next," Adrian assures him, then pauses.

"Always some woodcock in that low ground. Never known there not to be. Also, your last drive before lunch."

"Let us hope," Adrian says. "Shall we?" He removes a small leather case from the outside pocket of his Barbour, opens it quickly and offers the exposed ivory tabs to each of us. Rupert takes a step back. Wiley Ryan withdraws the first tab, but does not look at the number engraved in blue on its bottom. Philip is next, then Piers, Ralph and Julia. I follow my wife and am succeeded by Rupert and Adrian, in that order.

We mount the Range Rovers and follow, by perhaps ten minutes, the car bearing Donald and those beaters who are relations or intimates of the family.

I have drawn the number three, which is unlucky, for it means that I shall travel between drives and shoot beside Adrian, Philip and Ralph. On an ordinary day, of course, I would enjoy the company of this lot, would relax in their conversation and playful, unedged competitiveness. But an ordinary day would not have begun with a start, Julia's departure and secret in the middle of the night; on an ordinary day Piers would not be shooting in our party, much less separated with my wife from me by the ominous luck of a draw. His presence disturbs and unnerves me, the more so as I think about it. I even begin to wonder if her old boyfriend might be the person she told Rupert she feared, the one who had or sought a hold over her. There was no sign of such tension when we gathered a few minutes ago, but Julia is facile at masking emotions when circumstances demand. The intussusception I feel so acutely may be groundless, I realize, but, on the other hand, what if it is not?

On the way to the first drive, Philip sits beside me in the back of the unwashed Range Rover. "Julia seems on good form," he says.

"Did you speak to her?"

" 'Good Morning', you know. 'You must be awfully fagged from your flight.' That's all. Why?"

"No reason. Just wondered."

Philip searches me. "I'm glad she's shooting with Ryan," he says at last. "She'll charm him."

"She'll need to," Ralph calls over his shoulder from the front seat, "if he's expecting an eight hundred bird day."

"What?" asks Adrian, who is driving.

"That's what they were banging on about at breakfast," Ralph explains. "Some Spanish grandee gave them an eight hundred bird day."

"Bollocks," Adrian says.

I test my footing beside the wooden peg which displays my number. It is dark here, even when the sun flirts with the new cloud scudding overhead and the peculiarly liquid light of late autumn can be seen upon a nearby field. Where the fir thins to my left, the distant, slanting sun throws shadows at oblique angles. A latticework imposed by tree trunks and branches appears on the ground then, at intervals, dissolves.

I have brought no dog, no loader, a single gun. The gun is the best of a pair I purchased at auction at Christie's during my engagement to Julia. It was made by W. Brenneke for a German of about my size and shape during the late Fifties and though its fit is not so exquisitely tailored to my shoulder and cheek bone as is Wiley Ryan's Purdey to his, and its walnut stock not so well matched to its mate, I am comfortable—even happy—with it. There is something about an American who takes too keenly to shooting as the English do it that strikes me— and also most Englishmen I know—as false. Equipment of a certain calibre, in any sport, should be earned by the years of experience needed to gain the advantage it offers, or it should be inherited. I would feel conspicuous shooting Adrian's or Rupert's Purdeys, both pairs of which were passed on from their fathers, for I am neither sufficiently skilled nor intent and, like so many things in my daily existence these days, they are not my birthright.

Now, standing, waiting among the loose brush, the nettles, the lusterless dead leaves, I relish this countryside, both its closeness to and distance from our lives. The joy I take in its remarkable beauty is matched by my relief that Adrian, not Julia, bears the burden of protecting it. For having helped in a small way, with advice as to its finances, I have begun to understand how large and unremitting that burden is.

Ever since last night, I have wondered whether I would remain in England if my wife betrayed me. And now, as the other guns have grown silent and no doubt ready and a trio of practicing Sabre jets breaks flight formation overhead, I still do not know the answer.

Silence.

Then a whistle, soft at first but rising. A wail—discordant notes—the percussion of tin, cast iron, heavy wood. A violent cacophony as squads of men and women proceed witchlike through the covert, beating pheasants into the undefending sky.

"Over!" comes a call.

"On the left . . ."

I shoot—and clearly well enough. At the end of the drive, there are four birds in front of me and one, somewhat shamefully, behind. I step away from my peg to make room for the picker-uppers. Though I immediately pretend to ignore the fact, I notice that only Philip has dropped a smaller carpet of pheasants.

Peg number five, to which I advance on the next drive, is in the middle of a broad clearing, near the top of a slow rise. I settle by it, preparing to load my gun. Finally, when they are over me, I take each in a difficult line of three pheasants, swinging through a short careful arc. For the next, I pivot on my back foot and when I see that there are not only birds in front of me but two more dead descending, I notice that Adrian has missed one and decide to "wipe his eyes" by killing it too.

"You were shooting like a man possessed," Adrian says afterward, "but very admirably."

"Did they teach you that on your Holland and Holland course?" Ralph asks.

"No, in Dodge City," I tell him.

"If you don't mind taking some advice," he goes on, half-smiling "as impressive as your shooting was, it would, I think, be better if you didn't appear to put so much of yourself into it. If you were able to do what you did—exactly—without such apparent effort."

"Why?"

"Why? I don't know why. Because this is England."

"It might be 'better'," I say. "I suppose that's debatable. But it would be dishonest."

"Would it?" Ralph asks. "Or would it be merely a difference of style? Why, I wonder, do Americans insist upon making every choice a moral one?"

"Because they all go on to university?" Adrian asks.

I decline to respond.

After the next drive we move off to where the other guns have gathered for elevenses of sloe gin. The area in which we collect ourselves is shadowy but well-drained and full of that vile beauty which shooting people are so expert at discerning. At first, the quiet—the absence of conversation—seems to unsettle Taggart Ryan's sunny, eager California disposition, then she begins to tell us a story. "When we were shooting here last year," she says, "that is, when Wiley was shooting—not here, I mean, but in Scotland—we found a body on the last drive." Her perfume is sweet and there is an unmistakable lushness and lustiness about her. Her hair, were it not gathered beneath a designer trilby, would fall nearly to her shoulder.

"A body?" asks Adrian. "Do you mean that someone was shot?"

"Not then and there. No. As a matter of fact, I don't think we know the cause of death: whether a gunshot or something else. The body we found had decomposed . . . and, apparently, that made it buoyant so that it rose through the wetlands and Darcy Jones—she's a very close friend and she and her husband, Darryl, were with us—Darcy's boot kicked it accidentally."

"Who did it turn out to be?" Adrian inquires.

"No idea," Tag Ryan continues. "The eerie thing is that it groaned when the keeper touched it. Exactly as though it were alive. A doctor we talked with later said that was because the air was forced up from its chest."

"I see," says Ralph. "Well, as long as it wasn't one of your party."

"We had never seen him before. It was very shocking, I can tell you."

"As anonymous corpses are apt to be," Ralph replies.

"Now, now," she says. Her laugh, her entire personality are open, but forceful, like a wide, white river. Yet, as I watch her, I realize, suddenly, how age must have mellowed her and made her vulnerable, how coveted she must have been before life had worked her over and she had settled for being Wiley Ryan's third wife, a role in a series. She has children by a former marriage. They are now in colleges I have never heard of, their lives momentarily stranded in some expanse or enclave of the Pacific Northwest, their faces, perpetually adolescent, smiling ironically from wallet size snapshots she must carry with her everywhere. I watched her show these to Rupert as we got up from the breakfast table. Look, she seemed to be saying of a pretty daughter with vacant eyes, she would be *perfect* for *you*. For your sort of life.

"Tell me," Wiley Ryan asks then. "Have you had many Americans here to shoot, Adrian?"

"Not many."

"But surely you've let shooting to them?"

"Even that not too frequently," Adrian insists.

"You're the first I can remember who've been here as guests," appends Rupert.

"Many women?"

"One or two. Hardly legions," Rupert says.

"Legions?" Julia laughs out loud. "Hardly *any* is more like it. Why do you ask?"

"Curiosity," Wiley Ryan admits. "And because I've enjoyed watching you shoot and I was thinking that by the next time we do this maybe Tag will be ready to join you." Wiley's use of the phrase "next time" brings a ripple to Adrian's expression. He seizes his cup jerkily and looks at once at Ralph—somewhat sternly condemning his school friend to silence.

Rupert, of course, understands that by inviting himself to Castlemorland again in the future, Wiley Ryan thinks that it is he who is bestowing a favor upon the Midleton-Lyghams. For Ryan is the Chief Executive Officer of a Fortune 500 company, an exceptionally canny individual; no matter how bewitched he may be by the manners and paraphernalia of aristocrats, he is aware that he comes before them on any contemporary table of precedence. It is he, not us—not Adrian or Rupert, not Julia or me, not Philip or even Battleman Peale—who enjoys and holds the confidence of those institutions that control the affairs of the world: the banks, the governments and international agencies and, most of all, the omnipotent, faceless markets themselves. We are staff, merely adjuncts; he is the principal. If our deal together succeeds, he will probably take out more than one hundred million dollars for his personal account, but that is not the most important thing. If pressed, right now, he would, I'm sure (they all do) define himself not as corporate executive—a finance man—but as a "player": someone, that is, who through a mixture of luck and ability is entitled to play the game of life while others remain as spectators, no matter how enthusiastic or capable. His is a world of players. And just as generals evaluate the skills of generals—rather than, say, those of lieutenants or corporals—in opposing armies, he measures himself all but exclusively against his equals. The buyout he is attempting and the sell-off which will follow it have the potential to raise him above even this rarified company, to make him a kind of athlete-star on the playing field of business: one of a dozen or so men in the world to whom the best deals will flow before others can see them.

No, Wiley Ryan is a realist. He knows that he brings more to the party then we do, even if that party is momentarily ours.

"I'M CURIOUS," RALPH confesses as we separate again, "whether this corporate empire you and your colleagues are hoping to take over is eventually to be headquartered here at Castlemorland."

"Whatever you might have inferred from what you overheard at breakfast," I tell him, "I'd caution you not to jump to conclusions."

"Oh?"

"For one thing there are certain laws. You cannot just act upon inside information even though you may have come upon it innocently. For another, not everything works out as one might wish it to. Markets have a way of changing directions unexpectedly."

"Here I am, speculating about an estate I dearly love—and that only—and you reply with a crash course in Stock Exchange ethics. Well, set your mind at ease, John, all of my available funds at the moment are in the form of something known as an overdraft. So I won't be taking any flyers that might embarrass you."

"I'm very glad to hear it," I placate him.

"Never mind. Adrian still hasn't answered my question."

"Nothing's going to be headquartered at Castlemorland," Adrian declares "*except* my *family*. You're talking rubbish, Ralph."

"Does your family include Rupert and all his partners and clients? You don't mind my saying that he already seems to have the shoot rather well in hand."

"No such thing," Adrian protests.

"Perhaps you're right. Perhaps Rupert will never settle down in one place long enough for us to have to worry about him around here. Perhaps he's not the kind to find someone and marry her—breed. I mean I'm not in any hurry myself; there's no reason one has to be. But he's a lot older than you and I are, Adrian; one does get on. No offense to anyone here, but you have to wonder why he would choose to as a bachelor."

"Could be he's spoilt for choice," offers Philip, who, until now, has kept a graceful distance from Ralph's xenophobic onslaught.

"Could be. Have it any way you like. Nonetheless, I'm sure there must be any number of people around who would be only too happy to come across with the ready for a gun in the Castlemorland shoot. Matthew Paxton, for instance. I understand he's flush these days."

"Whether he would or wouldn't isn't the question," Adrian replies patiently, "as there is no gun available and there'd be a long list ahead of him if ever there were."

"All I meant to suggest is that Matthew likes money; he enjoys power. And, word is, he's developed a taste for the accoutrements of both."

"Why not?" Adrian allows. "He's done quite well by himself."

"He's made a lot of money."

"How much do you think?" Adrian asks.

"No idea," I tell him, presuming he has addressed his question to me.

"Net?" asks Ralph.

"Yes. When all's said and done," Adrian says, "free and clear?"

"More than a million. Maybe closer to two."

"That's a lot, it's a huge amount, isn't it, considering—"

"—that he had no capital of his own to begin with."

"Um huh."

"You have to admire him," Adrian says, "in a way."

"No you don't," Ralph says. "You don't have to admire someone who sets about spoiling the countryside for his own account. Matthew may be shrewd, but he's a charmless shit whose ambitions have nothing to do with grace or style—or even what his baby brother might have seen as 'self-improvement'."

"Well, 'respect' then if not 'admire'. You have to 'respect' him. He's seen opportunities where nobody else has. And he's turned several of them to his advantage."

"No doubt. But not on the Castlemorland estate, I notice."

"There aren't any opportunities for him here."

"Because it's completely agricultural?"

"Yes."

"And you wouldn't like to see that changed?"

"I wouldn't allow it to be."

"But on someone else's land you don't mind the odd housing estate or shopping arcade sprouting up."

"Of course I do. It's just that that's not my responsibility."

"The odd leisure park . . ."

"You've made your point, Ralph."

"My point is that I am a small farmer and you are a genuinely landed member of the English nobility. And what I want to know is why people like you, who have by far the most to lose, are always so impressed with the ability of certain spivs to turn a cash profit."

"I don't have time of day for Matthew Paxton, you know that," Adrian says. "But I do think one should try to be fair, to give him his due."

"I suppose. Anyway, he's small time in comparison to present company."

"Is that what's put you in such a mood?"

"Adrian, we're old friends. You don't mind if I tell you that I don't like to see shooting dates used up for business."

"I understand. You believe shooting should remain the last preserve of gentlemen?"

"I'm sorry," Ralph says, "if that sounds obnoxious. Don't mean it to. It's not that I mind at all about letting dates. I don't. That's a matter of economics, pure and simple. But this business of mixing it up. One is as apt to spend all day helping Americans as having any sport. Really. What's the point of taking a gun in a shoot when you don't know anyone else in it."

"Has it got to that point, do you think?" asks Adrian sharply.

"I'm afraid it's heading there. I'm surprised this Ryan bloke didn't arrive with an over and under and one loader at least. I'm surprised he didn't hire a spike from some kennel for the day."

"This Ryan bloke, as you call him, is someone most sensible people would be very glad of the chance to get to know," I suggest.

"John's right," Adrian says.

"So it's not just as a favor to Rupert that they're here? I see. You're hoping to profit as well. I didn't know that. I take back every word I said. I do. Because I realize now—just now—that it's hopeless."

"An estate like Castlemorland can only survive if it is surrounded by a sea of cash," Adrian explains.

"Not an entirely original phrase, if memory serves," says Ralph. "It sounds rather like one of your father's."

"The phrase may not be original, but it hits the nail on the head. I'm not upset with Rupert or John for juggling the schedule somewhat. I'm grateful to them for helping to keep this place afloat. They don't have to, after all. It isn't theirs. They have other things to think about. It's just that they happen to love it as much as I do."

This argument, enhanced by the earnestness of Adrian's voice, seems suddenly to calm Ralph and, all at once in its aftermath, it is as though the score of our conversation has been shifted into a new key, arranged according to a slower tempo.

Two drives remain before lunch, the first on the wide plateau of hills near Castlemorland's western borders, the next in lower country, where a funnelled wind has frozen the banks of a picturesque stream to shards of crystal, glittering and opaque. I move through these matter-of-factly, apprehensive, when I am alone, that Julia is shooting with Piers, even though she long ago admitted that her attraction had been to "shits" in those days; that what she had responded to in him had been the false illusion cast by a slightly older medical student standing on his own—the unfamiliar challenge of someone who was neither deferential nor automatically available.

Afterward, we gather briefly in the library, which lacks the theatricality of evening at this hour: the glow of peach-shaded lamps, the crescents of shadow, the music of tongues loosened by exhaustion and whiskey and port. Nor does the dusty, diurnal atmosphere tempt the sort of naughtiness with which Julia and I filled it less than half a day ago. Topley has laid out a dozen precisely measured two ounce glasses of Tio Pepe, but there is neither a decanter nor a bottle of the sherry visible. Anyone wishing to have more than his allotted portion of midday alcohol will have to reach—and, no doubt, be seen to reach—for it.

Rupert takes me aside so gracefully that our sudden separateness from the others appears to have evolved from his previous conversation and even to have left that undisturbed. "This is going very well," he gushes. "Our man seems very keen."

"He's shooting well?"

"Quite," Rupert concludes, somewhat dismissively. "But my point is that I think he *likes* the whole thing. I think he appreciates it. I don't think he's ever shot a bird he hadn't paid for."

Adrian approaches, surveys the assembled guns and, ostensibly setting an example of hospitality, quickly swipes a second sherry from the tray.

"Isn't there wine with lunch?" Julia asks him at once.

"I don't know," he protests.

"Of course, there is."

"Is there? I honestly can't remember."

"In actual fact," Julia whispers, unaware, I believe, that she is being overheard, "you chose it. You went to the cellar and chose it yourself, as you always do. I'm not trying to suggest anything to hurt you, Ads. I'm for you. No one more than I."

"Just because you took to the straight and narrow after the twins were born."

"Straight and narrow, hell. I didn't *touch alcohol* during my pregnancy. Who in her right mind would have done? But I do drink now. Maybe no so much, but I do. You know that."

"No," Adrian says, "you've lost the knack."

The meal which follows takes place around the old butcher-block table in the center of the kitchen, now aromatic with warmed burgundy wine and fresh tarragon, for Cook has a jugged hare stew in a large enamelled cauldron.

The afternoon has deteriorated by the time we resume the shoot, a white woolen sky having lowered itself upon the landscape, painted out the temple and the distant hill upon which it stands and absorbed the earlier sunlight. Birds soar and gather against the clouds then fall like cinders upon snow and, for a moment, hearing the otherworldly clatter, the shrill invocations of the line of beaters, my mind drifts and I dream—not of pheasants high and fast on the winds of the British Isles, but of the thrilling, fearful Halloweens of my childhood.

Then, after the final drive, a heavy, wintry dark envelops the park and we are momentarily an accidental foursome: Adrian, Ralph, Piers and I; Rupert and Philip having gone on ahead with Julia and the Ryans. The boot of Piers's Jag is still open, laid with the brace of pheasants Adrian and Mr. Cole have placed there and, in the creamy light that rises just above the low campfire-like red of the tail lamps, we scrutinize one another.

"I've always said that this is my favorite shoot," Piers professes. "I've always said that having a gun in it is the last thing in the world I'd ever give up."

Adrian smiles to receive this compliment. "That's kind," he says assuringly.

"N'tall," Piers says. "Statement of fact."

When Piers has finally started his engine, muffled by its noise Ralph asks, "What kind of doctor is Piers, exactly?"

"An endocrinologist, I think," Adrian replies.

"Which means what?"

"Fat people who want to be thin. Thin people who want to be buff? You must have heard him on the subject. I'd be surprised if you hadn't. Men who want to be women, and vice versa. Diet pills, mostly, are his sort of thing."

"Oh, that's right. I remember. Speed. . . . Christ, I'd go to you— or John—for medical advice before I'd ever consult him," Ralph continues.

"No comment," Adrian says. "Any comment, John?"

"I know what Ralph means," I admit.

"Still, I think it's only fair to remember that he's made quite a reputation for himself," Adrian says. "He invented some sort of treatment—for the pituitary gland, I think; one of those—for which he won a big prize in Germany."

"Remember," Ralph says after a moment, "at Cirencester, when you had just been given shooting dates of your own, Adrian, and we used to sit up over a glass of whiskey and discuss whom you would ask?"

"Endlessly revising, I remember. Putting people into categories. The first to be invited were—"

" 'People one likes who have shooting of their own to offer.' "

"And right after them came 'people one doesn't like who have shooting.' "

"That was brilliant."

"Far at the bottom were 'people one likes who don't have shooting,' " Adrian recalls.

"It was different then," Ralph goes on. "*You* were different."

"I didn't have any responsibilities," Adrian explains. "That's all."

6

"Who's there?" Julia asks intently.

"Daddy!" Andrew calls out.

"Hello Daddy," cries Louisa.

"Hello there," I say and scoop them—first Andrew then Louisa—as their short sprints finish at my knees. I can no longer raise them as high as I was once able to do; they are five and a half ("still five" my daughter protests), too heavy to be seated for long at the crooks of my elbows, too bulky for me to clasp my arms about securely. But I give them as much of a lift as seems safe and is possible and, in doing so, I suddenly think of and begin to count all the stages they have passed through forever. For a few seconds, I am wistful as I remember their first steps, first words, sentences, toys.

As usual, they speak at the same time. "We heard guns," Andrew says. "Guns," says Louisa "in the park."

"Were they loud guns?" I ask.

"Not very," Louisa explains.

"Not very," Andrew repeats. "They were far away."

"Whose were they?" I ask.

"Don't be silly," Louisa laughs.

To which Andrew adds, "Don't be silly, Daddy."

"I'm not being silly."

"They were your guns," Andrew replies.

"Yours and Mummy's."

"Oh!" I exclaim.

"You're being silly," Louisa insists. "Uncle Adrian had a shooting party."

"I know. That's right," I say, kissing each child on the forehead before letting go. "And when you're old enough—"

"You always say that," Louisa tells me. "You always say 'when you're old enough' but we never are."

"Oh, you will be."

"When?" asks Andrew.

"Before you know it," I explain. "Before you know it, you'll be shooting in parties like the one Uncle Adrian had today."

"Will *I?*" asks Louisa.

"Why not?" I promise her. "You'll be shooting a beautiful part of this estate or some other estate—"

"Perhaps in Scotland," Andrew ventures.

"Perhaps. And you'll think back to right now and wish more than anything that you could be children again. I know you don't believe that, but it's true."

"I'd like to be nine," Andrew says more concretely.

"I'd like to be . . . sixteen," says Louisa.

"I'd like to be . . . a hundred . . . and . . . sixty-seven," Andrew says. His giggling has overcome him. Still, he studies our reactions: his sister's, his mother's, mine. "No. Three hundred. I'd like to be three hundred and . . . thirty-nine."

"Which is very old," Julia tells him.

"It's older than anyone," Andrew says.

"That's right," I agree.

"It's older than any place," he goes on, "it's older than anything."

"Well—"

"It's not older than Castlemorland," Louisa interrupts.

"It is."

"No, it's not."

"Mummy?"

"Castlemorland is older, I'm afraid, Andrew," Julia says.

"How old is Castlemorland?"

"Not this house, but the ruins on which it's built: almost a thousand years."

"See," cries Louisa. "A thousand years is older than three hundred and thirty-nine."

"Adrian said the house is two hundred years old. That's all. I heard him," Andrew insists.

"*This* house," Julia explains.

"Anyway, it's only a game," Andrew says. "We were only supposed to wish."

"Castlemorland is not just *this* house," Louisa protests. "Castlemorland is everything. When you go for a walk, into the village or to your plantation you don't say you are leaving Castlemorland. So it's older, it just is."

"In a way," I tell them, "you're both right." But this attempt at compromise finds a pitiful reception.

"You were supposed to wish," my son admonishes his implacable sister. "You—"

"A thousand years old," Louisa continues.

Andrew has gathered a stuffed figure of Babar from a corner of discarded artifacts in the nursery. The bright olive plush vinyl coat of Jean de Brunhoff's jolly elephant is torn; a black button is missing from its waistcoat. Andrew handles the animal idly, the rush of enthusiasm with which he seized it quickly diminishing. "Daddy," he inquires plaintively, after a few seconds of thought, "girls aren't really children, are they?"

Can he mean what he has said? I search his face, then Julia's. We laugh. "No," I tell him, amused and smiling, "and you're a wise man to have noticed that."

"Quiet," Julia says. "Don't pay any attention to your father. He's talking a lot of rot and he knows it. Of course, girls are children, Andrew."

"Just not in the same way that boys are," I taunt.

"Anyway," Louisa says, "who wants to be a child? I don't. I want—"

"You don't know what you want?" Andrew says carefully, as if repeating a phrase he has overheard. "You don't know what you want." His voice trails as he raises Babar and begins to chase his sister with him. This is normal behavior for this hour; his sister returns with a cocky scowl and agile evasive movements of her own. Louisa is a confident girl and seeks no protection from Julia or me.

Last year, when Julia's father was alive, such antics would have signalled the moment for them to burst from the evening nursery and run to his library. They would have sped into the narrow second floor hall, past open and glass-shielded bookcases, avoiding the stored Victorian chairs and sofas and cabinets that lined the walls beneath huge, dreary prints dryrotting in old plank frames, often behind blurry glass. At the end of the corridor, outside their nanny's room, they would have slowed—then taken the stairs in a race, possibly seating themselves upon and sliding down opposing mahogany handrails. At the foot of these stairs, however, they would have stopped short of the heavy door that leads onto the first floor hallway. They would have listened for sounds before unlatching it, then moved past the bedrooms quietly, as was the rule. There can be no running on the great yellow-and-grey marble staircase. It is too long, its surface too hard and slippery away from the central runner. A natural fear of height and falling slows and steadies children as they approach and descend it.

On the ground floor, Julia's father would have received them with a slice of cake and a certain diffident curiosity. He both loved and boasted of them, but emotion in him seldom found physical expression. When he died, of a Berry aneurism that followed a night and Sunday of lacerating headaches before it exploded the calm he had just begun to feel at dusk, he did so without a noticeable change of expression—without apparent terror or regret. "All in all, it's been a very agreeable life," he told his children from his bed, after which the pulse went out of the hand Adrian held. It was Julia who pressed closed his eyelids, Julia, most of all, who had understood him—or at least had been unconfounded by the paradox he contained. My father-in-law was a worldly, cultivated man, clever with his turns of phrase, whose opinions, insight and eloquence extended into every area except the deep and defining recesses of his own psyche.

In the event, Louisa and Andrew do not hesitate at the door to the first floor hallway. It is as if they have adjusted to the permanence of their grandfather's absence, to his inability ever again to scold or glare at them—as if they recognize a new, less particular order in the affairs of the house now that it belongs to their forgiving Uncle Adrian. Behind them, I catch the heavy padded leather door as they burst into the hallway, emitting shrieks of laughter and protest. Julia is behind me. I am ready to head them off and slow them down before they can reach the main stairwell but, to my surprise, they run in the opposite direction, down a once inviolate bedroom hall. They are fast and quickly disappear around the crook in the middle of the corridor. It is dark from there on, the only light escaping from the entrance to a book-lined al-cove almost at the end.

"Andrew," Louisa cries out, "go slower. I can't see."

"Andrew!" Julia calls.

But he does not hear, or else ignores them. "Hurry," he exclaims. "Hur—" His voice stops on a high note, mid-syllable; we can see him start back from the alcove, a silhouette in shock, leaning away from the incandescent yellow light which sets it off. "Oh," he mutters, bringing himself to apologetic attention. "Sorry."

In the alcove, a cube whose walls are covered floor to ceiling with painted shelves, Isabel Wainwright looks up from a small desk. Standing beside her, a large man also glances toward my son, aspects of annoyance and interruption less disguised on his face than on Adrian's fiancée's. From the shelves, the spines of orange Penguins, white Paladins and Picadors create a cheerful mosaic abstract.

"This is a surprise," I say.

"Isn't it?" replies Isabel. She is a pleasant looking, somewhat broad shouldered girl, a straight brunette with a perfect complexion and brown eyes that seem perpetually eager to please. It occurs to me that if she were only a little more delicate she might, in fact, be rather pretty. "Hello, Louisa," she continues solicitously. "Hello, Andrew. What's that you have there?"

"Babar," he replies flatly.

"So I see it is."

"He's jolly cross with Louisa," Andrew says.

"He's not!" Louisa protests.

"It doesn't seem very likely," Isabel ventures, "that he would be cross with Louisa."

"Well, he is," Andrew says with that inarguable authority by which children occasionally dismiss the logic of their elders. "Elephants, in case you didn't realize it, know everything. They never forget anything, do they, Mummy?"

The large man beside Louisa seems to assess Andrew—then, for a moment, to put aside his impatience. "No," he interrupts, "I believe they remember every detail for as long as they live."

Julia pointedly ignores Matthew Paxton, whose presence on this floor of the house must annoy and astonish her. Not that she is a snob, but Matthew Paxton is hardly a person likely to have been asked to stay at Castlemorland (or to visit any of its bedrooms) during her father's lifetime. Fifty, muscular, with rounded indefinite features, wind (or whiskey) rouged cheeks, pores that appear to stand wide open no matter what the temperature, Paxton is two decades older than his dead brother, David. And, in most ways, he is—or so I have gathered—David's opposite.

"I didn't know you were staying here, Matthew," Julia says. Her inflection demands an explanation.

"Some of us actually have work to do," Matthew Paxton answers flatly. "Weekend or no."

"I rather thought," Isabel says, "that, up here, we'd be out of everyone's way."

"Of course," Julia agrees hesitantly. "I keep forgetting that you work for Matthew now—I must have some sort of mental block." She smiles at Isabel—quickly—then turns.

But Matthew Paxton calls out "Andrew" and we pivot toward him.

"What?" asks my son.

"How old are you now?" Paxton asks. "You and your sister?"

"Five."

"Five! That's a fine age."

Andrew does not reply.

"You probably won't believe this," Matthew continues, "but I remember being five. I do, very clearly. And in all honesty—you may not believe this either—in certain ways, it doesn't seem that long ago."

Shyly, Louisa ventures to ask, "How old are you now?"

Matthew Paxton hesitates. "Ten times that," he answers finally.

Andrew appears confused.

"Lots and lots of people have been five since you were," Louisa declares as her brother's befuddlement finally dissolves.

"When you put it that way, I suppose they have." Matthew struggles to laugh. "A man my age has only to think of all the changes that have taken place—practically everywhere but right here on the estate—since then."

"What kind of changes?" Louisa asks.

"Where?" inquires Andrew.

"Oh, too many to list," pronounces Matthew, nodding slightly in Julia's direction.

"Best come along now," Julia tells the children. "Isabel and Mr. Paxton have some work to finish up if Isabel's going to be ready for dinner."

"Do you mind awfully?" Isabel asks.

"Not at all," Julia says. "It's practically your house, after all."

"But I don't think of it that way," Isabel protests. "It's Adrian's house—*your* family's."

"Well, until you have a son," Matthew Paxton says.

"When I have a son," Isabel says, "I shall have to quit my job with you and devote myself to him."

"Then the sooner the better," Julia snaps.

"Now, now," Matthew Paxton says. "I don't want to lose a perfectly good assistant a moment before I have to. Isabel won't be easy to replace."

"I shouldn't have thought so," Julia says.

"Even with so much exciting stuff on our horizon."

"What exactly *are* you doing now, Matthew?" Julia continues.

"The same old thing."

"No doubt. But what I meant was *whose* landscape are you preparing to 'improve' this time? Rebuild? Turn into a gravel pit or parking lot?"

Matthew smiles. "There's nothing definite yet, as a matter of fact. I don't have anything definite at the moment."

"So there's something we can be thankful for."

"Mummy," Andrew says suddenly. "Let's go."

"Yes, Mummy," Louisa adds. "This isn't fun. It's our time with you and it isn't fun."

"Let's go find Uncle Adrian," Andrew suggests.

"That's a good idea," Julia agrees, a half-fiendish smile breaking out across her face. "Well, goodbye Isabel. Goodbye Matthew. You must come again when you have less time."

"Adrian is going to marry Isabel and they're going to have a little boy," Louisa proclaims as we begin to move back toward the staircase.

"How do you know?" I ask.

"She told us."

"She's going to have a little boy and quit her job with Mr. Paxton."

"Maybe she will and maybe she won't," Julia says.

"Will their little boy be our brother?" Louisa asks.

"No," I explain. "If he's born, he will be your cousin."

"Whose cousin?" Andrew asks. "Louisa's or mine?"

"Both."

"Is Isabel our cousin?"

"She's going to be your aunt. Because she's marrying your uncle. Do you understand?"

The children nod unpersuasively. "What about Mr. Paxton?" Andrew asks.

"He had a very nice father," Julia says.

"Is Mr. Paxton our cousin too?"

"No," Julia tells them. "Mr. Paxton is no relation to you. Absolutely none at all."

Adrian is nowhere we look for him—not in the office he has built behind the cube gallery, not in the kitchen or pantry, the library or Great Hall, and not in the shallow crescent of the park that can be seen from the entrance, nor in the gravel court which is illuminated by spotlights beyond the kitchen door.

"I suppose he's still with Mr. Cole," I say.

"After all this time?" replies Julia. "I wouldn't have thought so. More than likely he's in the s-a-u-n-a. Collecting himself." She spells the word in order to forestall any further search by the children.

"You can't collect your*self*," Louisa says then. "That's silly."

Andrew stares abstractedly at a middle distance between his mother and sister.

"It means resting up, calming down, gathering your thoughts together," Julia says. "That sort of thing."

"Oh," Louisa sighs.

But I know that by 'collecting himself' Julia means that she thinks Adrian must be in one of his blue periods, at one of his low points and that these depressions have become more frequent lately than they once were. Whether they are a cause or result of his affection for alcohol, no professional has been able to declare to the satisfaction of those laymen who know and love him.

When we return to the evening nursery, the children's nanny has straightened the room and is shuffling about, preparing their tea in the small adjacent kitchen. The trays have been sent up by Cook and we sit with our children around the low white table painted with playful bears and bright balloons as they devour their portions of roasted chicken, mashed potatoes and shaved green beans. With exquisite timing, Adrian appears just as the plates are ready to be cleared away. He is dressed in a terry cloth bathrobe and Belgian slippers worn and scuffed on the outsides of their soles. His face is flushed with color, but there is no waver of fatigue or drunkenness in his bearing, no slur in his speech. From behind his back he removes a folded linen napkin which he presents to Andrew and Louisa, pulling open its corners to reveal two equal slices of birthday cake. The children's eyes widen at the spun sugar confection, swirls of turquoise and yellow, an interrupted scroll of navy blue. "I cut it myself. Snuck in while Cook wasn't looking. By the time it's served the others will have had so much champagne, they'll never notice. Not that they're very observant in a sober state. And anyway it's mine, isn't it? My cake, my birthday. And the first slices ought to go to whomever I say. Correct?"

"God, you're kind," Julia says and rises, rushes toward and kisses her brother. "Isn't he, Andrew? Isn't Adrian kind, Louisa?"

Louisa stands to hug her uncle. Andrew stands too, but more reticently—apparently glad to have only to shake Adrian's hand when he offers it. In no time, predictably, they return their attention to the slices (far thicker ones than are ordinarily cut for them) of cake.

"When one comes to think of it," Adrian continues to Julia, "as things stand now, if anything should happen to me and to you, the whole thing's theirs."

"What a lugubrious thought," Julia says.

"No. Just the honest to God truth, that's all. Oh, now don't take it the wrong way. I have no intention of kicking off for a good half-century, and maybe more, depending on what the medical people think up by then. You'll live longer. Women usually do."

"Who shot the most?" Andrew suddenly blurts out, the question uncontainable though his mouth—his lips and cheeks and chin—are full of and smeared with icing.

Adrian hesitates. "Your mother," he answers eventually.

"What a lot of rot," Julia says. "There were any number of better shots than me."

"Was it the Chinese man?" Louisa asks.

"How did you know there was a Chinese man?" I ask.

"We saw him from the window."

"He has a name, that Chinese man."

"What is it?"

"Mr. Li."

"Did he shoot the most?"

"I don't know," I say. In any case, it's not a question anyone should ask."

"Why?"

"Honestly, John!" Julia smiles, shakes her head vigorously, feigning exasperation. She is playing with me. "They're a bit young to be expected to grasp the finer points of shooting etiquette, don't you think?"

"Sorry," I tell her.

"What's ecticut?" Louisa asks.

"I think Daddy shot the most," Andrew declares.

"That's right," Adrian agrees at once. He stares me down, winks.

"And I think Rupert shot a lot," Louisa says.

"Yes. He did," Adrian tells them.

"Everyone loves Rupert, don't they?" Louisa asks. "He's so handsome."

"No question about it," Julia says. "Everyone in the world does."

Adrian remains with us for a quarter hour and when he goes it seems he does so almost involuntarily, as if required to by a pre-ordained schedule. But once we are in the hallway and out of the childrens' hearing, he says very quietly, "John, if you have a few minutes before things get underway tonight—"

"Of course," I promise him.

"Ads," Julia approaches him then, "I realize it's none of my business. So do shut me up, if you like. But is it absolutely—I mean absolutely, *without* question, in the nature of things—necessary that Isabel work for Matthew Paxton?"

"I don't suppose," Adrian says, "any arrangements of that kind can be said to be 'in the nature of things'."

"You know what I mean."

"I know he grates on you, but the fact is this isn't London or even commuting distance—by any stretch of the imagination. And Matthew *is* successful *and* interesting. Who else could Isabel work for anywhere around here and not go out of her mind? The local chemist? Motor Care? She's hardly spoilt for choice, you'd admit. And if she stayed at home, heaven only knows how her mother—who is really an appalling old bat—would meddle in her life or what would come of it. For either one of us. You take a Londoner's perspective which, I'm afraid, Julia, simply can't apply when one is in the country seven days a week rather than for the odd weekend."

"I cannot help it," Julia says. "I don't trust him. *Do not trust him.* It's more than that he grates on me, which, of course, he does."

"If it's any consolation, Isabel doesn't trust him either. She simply types his letters. There's a point: how could anyone who typed his letters and kept his personal accounts not know what he was? She goes home at the end of the day and deposits the pay cheques he gives her. That's all."

"This afternoon, just a while ago, do you know where I came across him? In the study room."

"Alone?"

"No. He was with Isabel."

"Well then. She's going to be my wife, Julia. Where she chooses to have him is her decision."

"That's what I told her in so many words."

"No doubt she was trying to keep out from under a house full of guests."

"No doubt. . . . Look, perhaps it's just me; I could be wrong. I mean, he had a lovely father—a lovely mother, too. His brother, it goes without saying, we *all* adored. But, Ads, I just can't help feeling he has a grudge against us. I can't. I'm sorry."

"Against us in particular or the world we represent?"

"Both."

"The problem with occupying high positions—not to mention visible houses," Adrian says, "is just that. You have your own life, but there is also another life which is called yours, though it is actually lived in other people's minds. You play a much larger role in their imaginations than they do in yours. The Midleton-Lyghams are a perfect example. There have been Midleton-Lyghams around this part of the country— well, forever by English standards. We were the fixed point in the world Matthew Paxton grew up in, so naturally we'd be bound to serve as models for him—as objects of his approval *and* ridicule."

"You sound as if you think you're telling me things I don't know," Julia replies.

"Not in the least. I understand that you are very intelligent, darling, and always have been and that you are superbly educated—far better than me. But Father and I spent many hours talking about just these sorts of things. I know what his views were, what his experience had been all through his life. And when it comes to human nature, to instincts about people, I really don't think I'm so incredibly weak."

"Neither do I," Julia assures him. "I'm sorry if I gave the impression I did."

"Forget it," Adrian says. "And forget Matthew Paxton, too. Remember Mother's expression, 'Consider the source'—and don't waste ten seconds of your time thinking about him."

Julia is such a good natured person. It pains me to see her distraught. "Sounds like excellent advice," I add, though, at the end of the day, I do not know Matthew very well and have simply observed rather than fathomed my wife's often strained reaction to him.

"Ads, Ads, Ads," Julia says, ignoring me, "your problem has nothing at all to do with intelligence or education or instincts. Your problem is that you don't have a cruel bone in your body. You are not even slightly malicious, much less cruel. So you don't know the . . . rush that certain emotions can give some people. You had such a splendidly happy childhood that you've refused to grow up and recognize just how evil human beings can be. What Matthew Paxton feels for us—all right, I admit it's only my opinion—is beyond jealousy. In actual fact, it comes closer to hate. Jealousy smolders, you know, and very seldom does much more. But hate—hate calls for some response from the one who feels it. Which is why I am, to be honest, slightly afraid of him."

"Why should he hate us so intensely?"

"You know the answer to that?"

"Because of David?"

"Exactly."

"You're saying that he holds us responsible for David's death because we favored him in certain ways and encouraged him? I'm not sure I agree. For one thing they were night and day, David and Matthew, and there was no love lost between them."

"All that was true until David died. But the dead David Matthew could love because the mere fact that David had become a corpse proved Matthew had been right all along. Don't you see? It must have done. David was raw material and we were the catalysts that transformed him into something else. Little things like Father's having allowed him to use the library or to hunt with us—they gave him confidence. They slipped into his mind and geared up his aspirations, so to speak. They made him more than—no, a better way of putting it is that they made him able to think of himself as more than—another handsome grammar school boy. His horizons changed because of us. Because of us, what seemed possible to him changed. If we thought about it at all, I suppose we assumed we were doing him a favor. Yet, we didn't think about it, did we? We just enjoyed his company. Even basked in it. Be honest! There was no attempt to seduce him, which is what Matthew judges us guilty of having done. Quite the contrary. David was the seducer—always! Anyway, what's the point? David's dead. The whole thing's history. Matthew will see what he wishes to see."

"Christ, Julia," Adrian's voice rises. "I don't know what you want me to say. I have no idea what you expect me to do."

"Just keep the facts straight, Ads. Don't let yourself be confused. That's all."

Adrian stands still for a moment, then nods faintly. He withdraws down the shadowy corridor toward the stairs, turning at intervals to look back at Julia and me. His step is measured, even mechanical, as though disengaged from the thought process which commands it. At this instant he seems merely a piece of flotsam drawn to the magnet of one or another obligation.

Not long afterward, I prop a bolster pillow behind my back and lie at the center of Andrew's bed with my children on either side of me. They have snuggled close to my ribs and I have an arm around each and a hand on the front and back covers of *Topsy and Tim Move House*. They know the book by heart and will spot any word I might miss, even though they have not yet learned to read.

"Please," Andrew says, "start."

But as soon as I reach the word "bath" and pronounce it in the American way, with a flat rather than broad 'a', he begins to giggle. Louisa follows. "Not 'bath'." Andrew admonishes me " 'ba*aa*th'."

"Silly," Louisa says.

"Silly," my son repeats. "Daddy, don't tease."

"Yes, Daddy," Louisa says, "don't tease, please!"

"Please don't read in *such* a dreadful voice," says Andrew.

"I think," I tell them, "when it is time for you to go away to school, I'm going to send you to America, where everyone says 'bath' and speaks as I do."

"Across the sea?" Louisa asks.

"You've been there," I remind her.

"I know, but it's still across the sea."

"I'd like to go to school at Disney World," Andrew says.

"You might grow up to be Mickey Mouse," Louisa says.

"You might—" Andrew's voice breaks off. "Daddy, are you serious or are you teasing?" he asks with abrupt earnestness.

"Teasing," I say.

"Daddy," Louisa asks, "are we English or American?"

"Both."

"We can't be both," Andrew declares. "Can we?"

"Of course you can," I assure him, though I wonder if it is true. "Of course you can."

ADRIAN FINDS ME on the great stairs just as I have set out to find him. "Hello," he calls, catching me up.

"Hello. That was very kind, bringing the cake to the children—and everything. Thank you."

"Not at all. I meant what I said. I feel close to them. How else to say it?"

"They love you," I tell him. I pause. "I believe you also said—"

"That I'd like a word. Yes. Look, the house is crawling. Let's grab a coat and step outside. Do you mind? I don't think it's too cold. If it is—"

When we clear the light of the house and, moving through cool, dark parkland, look back upon it, the yellow-white lamps at the windows, their glow turned to a flicker and distorted by mist, appears to call us back. The grass is damp, the eerily modern silhouette of Adrian's Ferrari all that fixes the scene in the late twentieth century. We walk only fast enough to keep up our body heat, without an itinerary.

"Do I have your word," Adrian asks finally, "that what I am about to say you will keep completely confidential?"

"Completely."

"Even from Julia?"

"Go ahead."

"Let me start by saying that I hope you'll forgive Ralph."

"For what?"

"What he said during the shoot. I don't know. You know. It was a lot of crap really. He shouldn't have said it. He's not really anti-American."

"To tell you the truth, it went in one ear and out the other."

"Just as well, though I'm not sure I actually believe you. I don't know how much you know about Ralph?"

"Not much. That he's your friend. That he likes to seem acerbic, I suppose. And he can be convincing, on and off."

"What Ralph does with attitudes," Adrian says, "is he tries them on, then, for a little while, he becomes what fits. Today, he was acting the part of the English gentleman farmer taking a last stand for the world as it was."

"I gather."

"But there's more to him than that. I always think—my father always said—that you have to understand a person's background before you pass judgment on him. Ralph's father was a beer baron's son who gambled away most of his estate then danced off the end of the world. It hasn't been easy for Ralph to live up to what he thinks is expected of him, in other words."

"No apologies necessary," I promise.

"The point is that he may not be everyone's cup of tea—who is?—but he's *my* oldest friend and one puts up with certain things in very old friends if only to have one's own foibles put up with in turn."

"I know that. You don't have to say it."

"No, I do. And the other thing I wanted to apologize for was Piers. You know I try to keep his dates separate from yours and Julia's, but this time, arranging everything on such short notice, it just wasn't possible."

"I understand."

"I suppose that's the problem with England. One finds a niche, such as Piers having taken a gun in our shoot, and it's there forever. No one questions it. The occasion to just doesn't arise."

"That's the good part of England," I tell him with conviction, "not the problem."

We have gone some way beyond the cricket pitch, off lawn and into field where the higher, thicker grass feels spongy underfoot. Now the land begins to slope ever less gradually until we are climbing a steep hill, a wide open rise bordered right and left by a serpentine of old oak forest. After a moment, Adrian stops. "Do you know where the word 'snob' comes from?" he asks.

I hesitate. "Something to do with shoes?" I venture.

"Hardly. That's advert rubbish. It comes from our public schools—what you call private schools, I think. When they used to make lists of their boys, in the old days, those who didn't have titles had it put after their names: *s. nob.* From the Latin *sine nobilite,* for without 'nobility.' "

" 'With*out* nobility?' "

"It gives an entirely new meaning to the word—to the whole concept of a snob, doesn't it?' "

I nod. He's right. It is a revolutionary thought. And yet it fits my experience that the most snobbish people are often those who possess the fewest credentials.

"Piers is a snob," Adrian tells me, "because, bugger his background, his perspective contains no nobility. But Ralph is different. Julia claims that Englishmen are always watching the tide go out, worrying that it will carry them or someone or something they love along with it. Who knows if she's right? I told her I thought that was just another generalization, likely to fall wide of the mark more often than not. But I must admit it describes Ralph."

Uncertain if Adrian is finished, I remain silent.

"We'll walk back," he continues. "it's cold when you stop and I'm nearly through. I didn't swear you to secrecy, though, merely to gossip about Piers and Ralph. The fact is—and it's a fact I expect you to protect with your life—Isabel and I are planning to elope."

This news takes me aback, yet I have no immediate reaction as to whether it is the right or wrong decision—whether it should come as disappointment or relief. I look at him carefully, move closer, attempt to disguise my scrutiny behind a smile. "Elope?" It is all I can do to repeat the verb, then add, "My parents eloped."

"Did they?" Adrian asks. "Why?"

"It's a long story."

"Ours isn't, I'm afraid. It won't come as any surprise to you that Isabel's mother has no money. I don't mean that figuratively, John. I mean it literally. *No money.* So a wedding party would be out of the question. But that's not the issue. We could manage that from our side if we had to. If you hadn't done so well with our accounts lately, we could have always flogged a picture at Brimbleby's. My grandfather used to have a saying: 'consign another snuff box.' Something could have been arranged.

"The problem is Isabel's family—her mother particularly. She's a boozer. You know that? A twenty-four hour one, I mean round the clock. I know, of course, people'd think I'm the pot calling the kettle black. But alcohol is more than a problem in her life. It *is* her life and she's let herself go completely. You ought to see her. Straight hair, thin as a post, sallow cheeks with spidery little red veins always breaking. Styles herself as something of a county witch. Anyway, the old boy upped and left her years ago, lives in Marbella now—or Gibraltar, I can never remember which—with his bimbo. Girl from Ealing or Barnes or somewhere in London. A real looker. She's quite a bit younger than Isabel. And it's doubtful he'd come because Isabel's mother would like nothing better than to get him in this country, where she could have him served with a writ. You get the picture?"

"Yes."

"The thought was that eloping would save everyone a lot of anxiety. There'd be no run-up to the big event and by the time people had absorbed the news we'd be back and settled in. Then, at some appropriate moment in the future, we can give a dance and everyone can come to Castlemorland which, for most of them, will be the point of the exercise anyway."

"When is all of this going to take place?" I ask.

"John?" Adrian exclaims, playing with my name as if to question my capacity to sit on such a secret.

"How long must I play dumb?"

"Not long. We're leaving tomorrow, before the others are awake. We're not telling anyone where we're going. I'm sure you'll appreciate why."

"Congratulations," I say.

"Thank you. In the event of an emergency, there's an itinerary in my safe; but it's sealed and that's the way I want to find it when I return. Unless, of course—"

"There won't be anything that can't wait. You're not telling Julia because you know she'd make a fuss?"

"Correct. It's one toast we don't need tonight."

"All right. But I've promised a lot and I want you to promise me something in return. I want you to promise me that Julia will never know I knew."

"Done. This is how it's going to work. I'm going to double-lock the door. Maybe even hang out that wonderful 'Do Not Disturb' sign I stole from the Paris Ritz when I was little. *'Veuillez ne pas deranger.'* Don't know. Maybe, maybe not. Anyway, you know how the maids stretch a thread across the door-sill before they leave at night, or when they first come in in the morning, so that they can later tell who's up and gone and who's still in?"

"Absolutely. Real cloak and dagger stuff I remember thinking when Julia first explained it to me."

"Well, I suppose. Your job, in case anyone asks where we are—in case they ask it too early is what I mean—is to remind them about that string, or emphasize the sign—or, I don't care really as long as you keep them from barging in to say goodbye. I don't want anyone the wiser before our plane has taken off. You have my total permission to give them any excuse you like. They'll believe it if you say I'm out cold. With their own eyes, no doubt, they'll have seen me tie one on before."

"Which raises an interesting point. What if you really don't wake up in time?"

"Isabel doesn't drink. And I have the feeling she'll see to my being punctual. In any case, I wake up at four o'clock in the morning in a cold sweat almost automatically—if there's anything on my mind, much less marriage."

7

TANNHAUSER PLAYS FROM the speakers Adrian has installed in the sauna. I do not know which CD it is—most likely one of the Berliner Philharmonic; Adrian has stacks of these by his new Aiwa player. I love music, but possess no talent for it and, except for the popular songs of my youth, do not recognize most pieces by name. I can tell Bach from Mozart, but not always from Vivaldi; Chopin from Wagner but not always from Liszt. I cannot tell G sharp from C. The reason I recognize *Tannhauser* is that my father played it so often when I was a boy. He played it on 78s and then on 33s, along with the rest of Wagner. My father loves Wagner. Once it was his dream to go to Bayreuth, but he never did—never felt he had enough time, enough money, sufficient business reason to justify a trip. That, at any rate, was how he explained it. In fact, I believe he found his affection for Wagner as embarrassing as it must have felt natural. He was, after all, the son of a doctor of German-Jewish background—an apparently cultivated man for whom science rather than Christianity had gradually supplanted the old religion. My father could remember tales of his father's and grandfather's virtual allegiance to the Kaiser up to—and some even claimed after—America's entry into the First World War. He could remember his grandmother's stiff apron and accent; her strudels, fragrant with warmed raisin and cinnamon, lying ready in low dishes on the deep pantry shelf; the calf-bound sets of Goethe and Kant and Hegel. He even, as a boy, could remember having felt almost German, though his mother had come of an old, if socially invisible American family, by which was meant a family whose roots were somewhere in England. So a taste for Wagner may have been inevitable, but it posed a problem and a paradox. For my father belonged to a nationality—well, came of an extraction—which, in his own time and just as he reached manhood, had disowned the likes of him. I don't think there is any question that, whether Hitler's regime derived its nightmares from or merely orchestrated them with Wagner, it stole from my father a part of his identity of which he had been proud and that this is why, though he is too intelligent not to hold the notes themselves blameless, he has never travelled to Bayreuth or set foot in Germany.

Nor, I suspect, will he. He is older now. He has grown into arthritis, a fear of inflation, a deficit of curiosity about what might be left to experience. Only a few times since Julia and I have been married have my mother and father come to England to visit us. Instead we travel, once each year at least, to see them in the States.

I remain in the sauna for twenty minutes, once in a while scooping water from a wooden bucket and pouring it over the hot stones. I leaf through a copy of *Hello*, glancing at snapshots of Julio Iglesias and the royal family of Monaco. I read the restaurant reviews in last month's *Tatler*. At one point, briefly, I step out of the redwood cube and swallow a tumbler of ice water before returning again to the heat. In the shower that follows, I keep the water hot, the pressure high and shave before changing it suddenly to a powerful blast of cold. The chill braces me and I walk back to our room in one of the fresh towelling cloth dressing gowns which are kept folded on a shelf of the airing cupboard nearby.

Julia is asleep. The air is luxuriant with the familiar scent of Florissa bath oil and she too is covered only in a dressing gown. I lie next to her. But she does not stir. I turn toward her, then away as her body heaves a little. What is your secret? I want to ask my beautiful, deceitful wife. But I don't. I glance at the clock. We have perhaps an hour before we must be ready to go downstairs. I turn onto my back and stare at the ceiling where the plasterwork knight still ascends from the sea on a column of fire. I'm tired and for a moment I close my eyes.

My father was baptized a Roman Catholic but never confirmed in the church, the initial decision having been his mother's and the subsequent his own. By the time he was old enough to pledge his soul through any church he had been the beneficiary—or victim—of an especially encompassing religious education as well as of a peculiar compromise. His parents had believed in the old adage that a boy should take his name from his father and his religion from his mother, hence the Catholicism. But when my father was very small, perhaps two or three, his mother seems to have suffered a crisis of faith. Faith, for her, had apparently been in a code of behavior rather than a process of judgment leading to alternative afterlives. And the more confident she became, the broader her exposure and perspective as a consequence of age and her marriage, the more often she tended to neglect confession and mass. Before my father reached school age it had been decided, with mathematical logic, that the only son of a secular Jew and skeptical Catholic ought to be raised as a Protestant. The Presbyterian Church was nearest. It had a jolly minister, a pretty neo-Georgian facade and a brief, comprehensible liturgy.

So within his first, most impressionable decade, my father had had a sampling of the three principal Western faiths. He knew the mixture of *Mittel* Europe and Middle East which was then Reform Judaism, for he had sat with his father beneath the Byzantine dome of the old synagogue on special Saturday mornings. The sunlight in which his friends steered their bicycles a few miles away fell in shafts from lofty prisms of granite and settled on the white tallises of hunched rabbis and cantors as they read from precious scrolls words he could not understand. He knew the mystery of incense and the authority of vestments and sometimes thought he could feel in the eucharist his mother stepped forth to receive, something which was not merely old but timeless. Latin, naturally, he found as incomprehensible as Hebrew, but there was more joy in the music, choruses of exaltation rather than symphonic wails of lament and this captured and appealed to the child in him. Among the Presbyterians, he liked, most of all, the fact that he could sing—uproariously, verse after verse, in the white and varnished wood church that was always flooded with unstained light. The naked or blooming tops of neighborhood maples and dogwood, the blue and cloud of the sky, even the random flights of ordinary birds could be seen at any moment through a thousand panes of glass and he had the idea that there he was celebrating life rather than stepping back from or renouncing it. At least it seemed they were celebrating life that was more like the one he experienced every day—a life of satisfaction and disappointment, but not too much mystery.

When my father told me these things it was not as part of any extended discussion on theology, but rather to explain how it was that he, a general practitioner's son, had arrived at his choice of career. His point was that after such thorough exposure to competing systems of faith, he had found himself, in religious terms, what he could only call a "believing spectator." Oh, he believed in God, but not that God required him to approach via one man-made ladder or another. God, he'd decided, was everywhere, always and immediately accessible to everyone—but not without work. God was like truth and the sieve with which you separated truth from the innumerable data of life was woven of persistence and skepticism. This was a convenient formulation as, right about the time he arrived at it, he was coming to terms with his talents, forming, as every adolescent must, a view of the world. And looking back on the excessive Twenties from the enlarging Depression, he concluded there seemed ample reason to be skeptical of men and their motives.

He failed biology in high school, but was named an editor—for features, I believe—of the school paper. His strengths were becoming clear to him. After college, he secured a job on a small-town paper in Western Pennsylvania and, two years later, moved to the Baltimore *Panagraph*. It was in his early days there, while covering the Society section for a reporter who was out with pneumonia, that he met my mother—and there that he remained all the rest of his working life, except for the three years he spent at the White House.

He still likes to say that he fell in love with my mother's picture before he met her. But I am not sure. It is an oval-bordered, stagy photograph in which Emily Minor appears rail thin with her hair severely coiffed according to the convention of the times. None of her remarkable beauty shows, no hint of her animation.

I have no idea how much my Minor grandparents knew about my father when he asked permission to marry her. I do not know, for example, if they realized that the name Brook had been reluctantly Anglicized from Bruchner at the height of the anti-German feeling during the First World War. Nor do I know what suspicions they may have harbored about Jews or Roman Catholics or, for that matter, the predestination assumably espoused by Presbyterians. The Minors were good north Baltimore Episcopalians, regular and quiet in their habits and inclined to expect the same of others. Perhaps my father was accorded the latitude which is sometimes bestowed on attractive newcomers to provincial cities; perhaps my mother's parents, liking what they found in him, simply didn't care too much about his background; or perhaps, by eloping, the young couple gave them (and everyone else) no chance to complain. These are things I have never been told—questions I have never asked.

My father, at six feet three, is an inch taller than I am. He was a swimmer; so am I—well, more of a diver actually. When I was fourteen, I was briefly a local champion and, though even now I sometimes find myself showing off when there are a pool and board nearby, I'm afraid I was not bequeathed that effortless tandem of eye and hand which so nimbly facilitates certain lives. My mother is more athletic. She once played A-team tennis on the inter-club circuit, but gave that up some time ago in favor of golf. Golf, goes the argument, is one sport that can be carried into old age; but I have noticed that nine holes of it tax her more than they did a few years ago and that, though she still keeps her clubs handy in her locker, she has given up her regular game.

I grew up a happy only child, surrounded daily by friends (and on holidays by cousins) with relatively little time to think. The Depression had left my parents unprepared and the long war struck them apart, sending my father to the Pacific for most of it. So by the time they were ready to have a child (or able? Again I've never asked) they were also eager to indulge it. I was born the year after my father's discharge, in September of 1946, inheriting not only what felt like the pent-up affection of an entire generation, but—or so it seemed—the world.

America was rich. America was hegemonic. I—and my playmates— were its heirs. And we were made to know it! It wasn't long before all people talked about was grooming us for leadership. I suppose it must occasionally seem to each person that his or her birth took place at the dawn of all history, and clearly it is never true. But there can have been few moments when change was so profound, so instantaneous, so implicit and lasting in its effects as the mid nineteen-forties. I came into the world a year after the first and last atomic bombs had been dropped in war, on Hiroshima and Nagasaki, yet my early thoughts were unshadowed by mushroom clouds. The suburb where we lived—even, then, the city of Baltimore itself—seemed a bright place, continually arrayed with wondrous new gadgets to be consumed. And childhood was borne along on a Plymouth, a DeSoto, a Cadillac with white wheel tires, through a bazaar of televisions, color televisions, pastel Princess telephones and DC-7 travel. I do not mean that we possessed all these things any earlier or in more abundance than did our neighbors. We didn't. My parents were sensible, if not outrightly frugal in their habits. Successful, upper middle-class rather than rich, they sought to strike a balance between providing advantages and spoiling me. But what one owned was less important than what one imagined and the images which filled my and my friends' minds came directly from American films, American advertising, American industry: Todd-A-O and Cinerama, Buick Dyna-Flow and Thunderbirds, Amanas and Maytags. Aspirations which were once but vaguely felt all of a sudden acquired brand names and a national identity.

During my childhood in Baltimore and even after we had moved forty miles (and a world) away to Chevy Chase when I was almost fifteen, I can remember only a few foreign things that were thought to be worth owning. The known world was then divided between the promise of America and the threat of the Soviet Union, green and grey landscapes, thriving and ruined harvests. Every place else seemed not so much to hang in the balance (about which there was continual speculation) as to be beside the point. The order of things recently arrived at looked to be immutable and so, without affectation, unconsciously I think, we developed the mental habits of empire.

I sometimes wonder if my love of England is in part a residual love of my childhood and its certainties. Every now and then, in a shop where confections have been set out in open cartons and time lavished on those who would choose among them, I'll shiver with the memory of an older, less hasty, more courteous America. There are mannerisms, styles of dress, turns of phrase one encounters every day in England—even now—which seem at once anachronistic and superior and redolent of a time in America before all hell broke loose.

My mother's first cousin, an eccentric, owned a record store on Saratoga Street, just off Howard, in Baltimore. And some of my earliest memories are of going there with my mother on Thursday nights. My father, procrastinating his deadline, would come over from the *Panagraph* several blocks to the southeast and we would dine together at the splendid Oriole cafeteria, which in retrospect appears as a kind of Art Deco masterpiece wherein the food was limitless and impeccably fresh, the gravies so hot they bubbled, the breads warm with silky crusts as they awaited buttering, the meringues just whipped. Usually we would shop—for clothing at Hutzler's, for Cub Scout regalia at Hochschild Kohn—and afterward our cousin would give me a 45 of which he had, he suspected, ordered too many to sell. But there was more to those evenings than mere consumption. There was an aspect of theater about them, for which, from the age of eleven or so, one dressed (with anticipation) in a plain color shirt and tie. The scent of Vetiver rose from the first floor of the Hutzler Brothers' department store. The original wooden escalators hummed and creaked and sometimes hesitated. Elevators, their innards here and there glimpsable through pairs of wired-glass doors, arrived and departed at the snap of a uniformed supervisor with a hand-held metal cricket. Even the salesmen and saleswomen had costumed themselves for the occasion: dark suits, dark dresses, starched white shirts and blouses, ready, helpful smiles.

All this, of course, has become costly and vanished, for one reason or another, into the modern sense of things. And though I have no doubt that shopping malls present their own informal sort of pageant and that, especially for teenagers who first discover and seek out sex there, they can be the most thrilling and mysterious of venues, they do not, in comparison, equal what they replaced.

I suppose the fact, as Julia once put it, is that my generation and American civilization seem to have gone through puberty simultaneously: languishing, experiencing, casting off illusions, accepting ambiguities at the same time.

The absolute confidence in the future which was expressed in the monumental architecture of American main streets—the quarried stone and masonry, the heroic scale and minute details—now seems a luxurious illusion of childhood, tragically akin to a toddler's faith in the capacity of his sand palace to resist the sea before which he and his father have built it. Today, my mother's cousin is dead, his record shop boarded with three-quarter-inch plywood. Pigeons light in the eaves of the vacant Howard Street department stores and for all I know share squatters' rights with rats within. The Victorian front behind which caramelized corn was offered for sale within a minute of popping when I was a child is long shuttered, its last veneer weathering and chewed by time. Scarce relics of the environs have ventured a move to the Inner Harbor where an attempt has been made to re-feudalize a principal shopping area in fiefdoms controlled by one or two large real estate concerns. Yet there the flimsy, passionless structures do not even pretend to permanence.

What I wonder is why all of this should be so: why the rotting of America's cities over a single century and the durability of England's houses over many should be accepted as equally inevitable. Whether there is, so to speak in the American character, a gene which will not see anything—anything at all—abide, and conversely, in the English, one intolerant of change.

If Castlemorland is a supreme expression of English confidence, it is not easy to come up with its American analog. And when Julia asked me, one morning a few years after we were married, if I thought there actually were one, I hesitated—considered long and hard before, the image rushing to my brain and lips together, answering, "The Pan Am Terminal at JFK."

"Of course, the airport wasn't JFK when Pan Am built the place," I added. "It was still Idlewild. And that really is the essential point, isn't it, because nothing had begun to go wrong until Kennedy was shot, had it?"

"Don't know?" Julia'd said. "Don't know, couldn't say."

"Because you're so young?"

"Well . . . yes." My wife's laugh teased.

"It hadn't, Julia," I repeated. "Nothing'd actually begun to go wrong."

The Pan American terminal at Kennedy, still visible as a remnant of itself, was originally built as a true circle. The new 707's tucked in against its side were embarked via parabolic concrete and space-age-metal breezeways, then took off along unquestioned vectors of American influence and interest. Rather than any sort of doors, a long rectangular prism of forced air, warm in winter, frigid at midsummer, divided the terminal's climate from that of surrounding Queens. And on the departure ramp itself, a wide arc of sculpture and anticipation perpetually lined with limousines and yellow Checkers, a choreography of fashionable and frequently exotic men and women—of crocodile and llama, ostrich and cowhide cases of every imaginable shape stacked weightlessly on the two-wheel toe-lifted trollies of eager skycaps—repeated itself in endless variations. The scattered, round desks at which passengers checked in for journeys to destinations as far apart as any could be, like the ubiquitous round trademark map of the world itself, lent an air of urgency to the room. In but a few hours, one thought, all these people will have scattered. Tomorrow at this time, while this room is full again with others, they shall stand on every continent. And so powerful and unavoidable was this idea, so new the idea of jet travel when the terminal was opened, that travellers could actually feel—as well as contemplate—the centrifugal force at work in the vast space.

No one doubted then that the world was at the disposal of Americans.

I remember the Pan Am terminal so well because it was from there that my parents and I usually set off to Christmas holidays on one or another Caribbean island. The post-Christmas weeks were slow ones in the newspaper business—ordinarily not much news and, with the sudden cutback of store advertising, fewer pages to fill. My father and mother were keen at spotting out-of-the-way hotels where the rates were reasonable, the swimming and golf better than average and where a young teenager was not apt to be alone or bored. But perhaps more than of these trips, the terminal reminds me of my first trip across the Atlantic, my first landing in England on a dark March morning when I was sixteen years old.

Only the prospect of rain. The butterscotch fog lamps were illuminated along the A-4 and at regular intervals down the concentric roads of one housing estate after another. But I had no map or knowledge of England in my head; I recognized nothing. My father had had to come on White House business, something to do with press office liaison that could be handled, he'd promised, in no time. So he had brought us along, for almost a week, at his expense. At someone's suggestion, we stayed at the old Berkeley in Piccadilly, dined there one night and at Simpson's and Rule's, took in a Noel Coward play in the West End and a production of King Lear somewhere else, watched the Changing of the Guard, went on a taxi tour which ended up at the Tower, with my mother claiming that neither she nor anyone she knew at home would have use for such jewels even if they owned them. One day my father hired a professional with a Rover to drive us into the country. In a single span of daylight, we saw Runnymede, Eton, Windsor, Oxford, Blenheim, Stratford and the bombed cathedral at Coventry. We also had a good, hearty lunch at a pub which was not so full of Americans as might have been expected.

Of course, I did not know then that such a place as Castlemorland still existed, that it—and houses like it—continued to enjoy lives as well as histories, to possess inhabitants as well as ghosts. That discovery would come later. It did not await me with the English dawn that had so abruptly followed twilight in New York. And yet I remember falling asleep in the old doomed Berkeley, a damp wind stirring the undercurtains where I had raised the window half an inch. Rooftops spread away in the direction of Curzon Street, a scape of dark board, brick and slate. A few lights burned in mysterious windows, but London had settled into its timeless sleep and I watched . . . and watched, somehow already aware of the drama its quiet masked. My ego then was still anchored to Pan Am's marvel in New York and to the dominion it implied. I was young, curious but ignorant. And though I felt many things, I could not then distinguish among my excited emotions what now seems the most obvious joy at having come—or found—home.

I DON'T KNOW exactly how it happened (I'm not sure even he does) but, as I said, early in 1961, President Kennedy appointed my father to a high position in the office of his press secretary. The news came out of the blue: a phone call one Saturday evening, a moment after we had sat down to dinner. My father had never met Kennedy, nor even covered him for the *Panagraph*. As an editor, he had eschewed the politics of both parties, believing a comfortable distance from their platforms and personalities would best serve his readers and his own peace of mind. But he was aware that he and the young President shared certain journalist friends in common and even, from these friends, that Kennedy had, on certain occasions, admired his editorials and columns. Still, a phone call from the President is a memorable event in most households and, when my father ended his by saying that he would have to talk the matter over with his family, my mother and I knew we would be moving to Washington.

As it happened we waited out the school year (which had not been my best), sold the house in Roland Park and bought a slightly smaller one which had a pool in Chevy Chase. I said goodbye to my classmates at Gilman at a moment when I felt ready to and, full of resolution to make a new more creditable name for myself, transferred into the sophomore class at St. Alban's. It wasn't that I had disliked Baltimore, my school or friends; but I had been among the same company longer than is probably healthy for the development of certain personalities. My strengths and weaknesses were so well known among them, as were theirs to me, that it frequently seemed difficult to separate myself from a reputation that had been made years before. I longed for the chance to be judged without respect for history—even, for an afternoon, to be thought a better athlete than others would assume I could be and to show that I could be as clever as the next in math and science.

To be bound for Washington was a bonus, for it seemed the center of the world in 1961. That my father would have a White House pass and that, in all likelihood, we would be permitted now and then to step beyond the usual boundaries into privileged proximity of our central national myth—perhaps to be recognized and spoken to by Kennedy himself—this seemed . . . well, to be absolutely honest, it seemed something altogether serendipitous which one might employ, to advantage, with girls. Had the President not somehow heard of my father and called him on that Saturday, I don't know how my life would have been different—whether I would have rebelled from or resigned myself to things as they were—but I do know that it would have been profoundly so. All the other changes—in stature and maturity, in suddenly imparted physical skill and grace—had occurred among my cohort by the time of our move and though the tables had been turned on some among us, I had left puberty pretty much as I entered it: waiting to come into my own.

To St. Alban's I brought all sorts of heady expectations, whatever aptitudes I had and even the part of myself I was used to keeping in reserve, by which I mean a habit I've always had of standing back, even as real things are happening, and trying to observe them as they might be seen by someone else, from a point in the future. This was neither paralyzing nor, apparently, very often noticeable to others: a few seconds, a minute at most were all it required. I needed (still need) only enough time to contrive or remember a phrase, some image that would seem to contain the essential emotion of a situation and by which I would later be able to evaluate and recall it. Of course, I suspected that, in some way, this tendency to reflect—this wish to apprehend and scrutinize essential moments—defined me. Distinguished me. Separated me from those around me.

But to be honest, looking back, I don't think it did. It was, after all, an internal thing and no matter how fervently we imagine or wish that others understand us, they seldom do. No, it was neither my nature nor my father's job that set me apart. The school was full of well connected scions, some bearing the middle names and profiles of former presidents, others the ambitions of ministers, still others the libidos of princes. Especially as a new boy, I did not stand out in their company. What established my identity among them was, in the end, simply an event, an accident: a skinny dip.

I had a Baltimore friend whose cousin, a girl of our age, lived in Washington. She was called Caroline Carswell, a name whose alliterative, come-hither quality at once conjured for me the image of a golden blonde comic strip heroine. But when I'd asked my friend what she looked like, he'd said only "Not bad. Terrific personality. Very outgoing." Still, I was alone in a new place and, remembering some advice my mother had given me that you don't have to fall in love with every girl you meet and that one friend leads to another, I decided, late in August, to give her a call. To my surprise, she was very welcoming. She said she liked her cousin and wished she saw him more often, but that no one in her family—no one she knew really—ever seemed to go to Baltimore. She told me she was glad to hear I'd moved to Washington. I'd like it, she said. There was a good group of kids. In fact, why didn't I come to a party on Saturday night at her house in Potomac? A lot of the group I would like so much, she explained, would be there.

My parents had gone to Cape Cod that weekend. The White House seemed to have moved there for the summer and my father hadn't actually had a choice. As for my mother, it was to be her one weekend away all year. She'd written her number at The Yachtsman Motel in Hyannis on three pieces of paper, pinned one to the bulletin board beside the ice box, given the second to her sister who was staying at our new house with me and made me pledge to keep the third on my person at all times.

The party in Potomac lived up to its billing and Caroline Carswell more than lived up to hers. She was the prettiest girl I had ever seen— blonde, as I had imagined, with pebble blue eyes and a pony tail she'd gathered in a sapphire ribbon and breasts that pressed the arousing outline of her bra against a plain white cotton blouse so that you could see where the material was lace and where it was opaque and even where the clasps were. Her breasts, I thought all of a sudden, were the things in the world I would most like to see, to explore. And the funny thing was, I had the feeling she knew this and didn't mind. In that way, she seemed older than fifteen—the first really adult girl of my generation with whom I'd come into contact—although she didn't look older or conceited or what we might have then called sophisticated.

Mr. Carswell was probably an arms dealer. Just inside from the patio on which we sipped Coca Cola and Hire's Root Beer, iced water and lemonade, was a panelled library whose locked display cases contained not books but guns: rifles and shotguns and pistols of every age and description. There were even scabbards and daggers and bayonets, ancient oriental swords mounted at eye level and illuminated. I can remember standing between matched tartan sofas and, halfway between the patio and the bathroom, asking Caroline if her father were a general—someone, in other words, of whom I should have heard. The music of Bobby Vinton and Shelley Fabares played in the airy distance. "No," she told me, "he just travels." It was the first time I had the sense, which I would have often again in Washington, that there were subjects other than sex about which people were guarded.

Because Caroline was a girl—and such a pretty and "outgoing" one at that—the crowd that night included several boys who were a year, even two years older and who, in consequence, already had their driver's licenses. There were perhaps a half dozen of these, wearing their arrogance nimbly, in a way they must have thought discernible only by their contemporaries and those who were younger, combing their hair into ducktails or the closest shape to a duck's ass (or "DA") its length and their parents would permit. They stood together and smoked, eyeing each girl as though their experience of her were so complete that by now it bored them. A few were from St. Alban's. Sometime after ten o'clock, one of them suggested that those of us who were left and did not have early curfews at home go out for a burger. There had been more posturing than dancing anyway and Caroline, who seemed to assume permission, said it would be a good idea.

I telephoned my aunt, who had deposited me at the Carswells, and explained that I would not need a ride home after all. Her emotions were still raw in the aftermath of an unanticipated divorce and her voice sounded relieved to have an excuse to take her pills and escape her saddened reality in a full night's sleep. And so we set out into the high summer night in a Bonneville convertible with an Impala and a black

Corvair in convoy behind. A wind gathered the ripe scents of what were then Potomac's rolling fields and gusted them toward us, all the poignancy of the late adolescent summer to be inhaled in each whiff of mown grass, tall corn and fir. We drove south on the River Road, without, as far as I can remember, anyone having specified a destination. And soon the country was behind and the suburbs were tighter astride us. The talk, to which I paid a rapt attention, was largely of the absent members of this group—people, for the most part, who were still away with their families for the summer, on Nantucket or Martha's Vineyard or some such place, in Maine or, perhaps, Rehoboth Beach. These were people I had never met and yet some of them, I realized, would be bound to be my classmates, my teammates, new friends—or rivals. So I was alert to the gossip about them that was being bandied so casually.

The driver of our car smoked Kent filtereds. He passed the open hard pack among his passengers. I took one, but could not manage a light until we were stopped at the intersection with Brandywine. There, I leaned over, sheltering the flame in the still air between my knees, and inhaled then puffed a few breaths of mentholated tobacco. I struggled, but could neither shape nor release the perfect zeroes of smoke with which the others filled the sky above the open Pontiac. At the Hot Shoppe on Wisconsin we hurried out of the cars and into booths where we sat awkwardly, quietly more often than not, until trays of shakes and burgers and fries arrived. The restaurant was not busy and the waitresses seemed to know—at the same time to tease and defer to— the oldest boys among us. These boys, who were self-regarding in the manner of those who anticipate luminous futures, cocked their heads a little each time another person spoke and, unless that person were Caroline Carswell herself, stared somewhere just to his or her right or left so as to offer only a studied angle of themselves as their thoughts travelled toward some fantasized excitement. I seemed neither to interest nor disturb them. They asked me few questions. They cared not a hoot for Baltimore or the White House, in which they all seemed to have family friends or neighbors working anyway—and, even if they had, the fact was that I was younger. The history I had possessed and been glad to shed in Baltimore I suddenly, desperately missed. And it was out of a desire to move myself from the periphery into the center of their consciousness—to be valued and liked—that, as the party seemed to be winding down, I suggested we go back for a swim in our pool.

My aunt was out cold in a guest room that faced the street and the seven of us who had come on moved stealthily across the front lawn, around the hedgerow and summer-baked flower beds that bordered a screened-in side porch, then down a slope to the pool, which lay like a lagoon in the hollow of our property. Behind it, a crescent of blue spruce protected it from our neighbors' view and leafy maple obstructed the views from most windows. Between the Hot Shoppe and our street—somehow—two six-packs of National Bohemian appeared and I was offered a cold can by the driver of the black Corvair who had already stripped to his Jockey shorts and now seemed to be standing around, waiting for some sort of signal or decision from the others.

Recalled from the precipice of middle age—a bed at Castlemorland, a marriage as certain (I hope) as can be expected after several years and the practical responsibility of children—the image strikes me as quaint and almost touching: the depilous torsoes of four young men in briefs, three young women in early-Sixties Playtex, their nervous reflections rippled by wind on the submarine-lit surface of a Chevy Chase swimming pool.

Caroline Carswell ignored me. She glanced instead at the skinny driver of the Bonneville, who swigged his beer. Then she muttered, "This means nothing," as if to me. The boy stripped and mounted the low board and, frantically grasping his shins, cried out in a pathetic rendition of Tarzan before springing himself, ass first, into the water. Caroline laughed and suddenly turned away toward the arc of spruce, but we could see her removing her bra and then her panties and in a few seconds we were all naked, floating a respectful distance from one another, laughing, splashing with various degrees of force, trying to see— really to fix in our memories—details the water and such rapid movements disturbed.

Caroline had large nipples, that much I remember vividly. They were firm, pointed. Her pubic hair was dark and not at all thick. She swam mostly underwater, without self-consciousness. One of the other girls rode a boy's shoulders in intoxicated hopes of starting some sort of water fight. She was not pretty and her pudginess and availability seemed indecent. But Caroline refused every bowed male neck; she continued to swim alone and unapproachably.

After fifteen minutes she planted her palm on the stone border and, in a blur, vaulted herself onto land then disappeared in the shadows of tall trees. We followed reflexively; we dressed in haste. There was no exhibitionism, only the vanishing thrill of the forbidden. The air was cold against our wet skin which there were no towels or sunlight to dry.

I left the others at the curb, thanking them for the ride and Caroline for the invitation, but never coming close enough to touch her. Soon they were gone. So I crept back to the pool which was still dappled by their presence and collected the empty and half-empty cans of beer and hid them in the grey iron garbage pail of a neighbor a few doors down the alley. Then I went to my room, stripped once more and lay staring at the ceiling until finally I could get hold of my emotions and force them to subside.

8

M Y OTHER LEAD in Washington cast a long shadow. He was not a close connection, but the nephew of a war buddy of my father's. His name was Chas Ledbetter and, once, when we were about nine, he had come with us on a fishing boat our families had chartered for a day on the Chesapeake. I could barely remember him: he had not then become the sort of boy other boys are likely to fix upon. He was quiet, his hair unusually thick and black, his profile almost too severe for a child's, as though it had grown into adolescence ahead of the rest of him. But I do recall my mother and aunt describing him as "fine look-ing" and wondering why, really. By the time of our move, however, bits and pieces about Chas had made their way into our household and my consciousness. I knew from my parents, who had heard from friends of their ever more distant army friend, that he was at St. Alban's. And I gathered from other sources that he was to be president of the class I would be entering. From a story in the Gilman *News*, I learned that he was a star of the JV wrestling team and "promising" at lacrosse. His picture was on the front page. And this information as well as more in its vein that followed added up to the conclusion that I might have just the right entrée into my new school if I were lucky and played my cards right. As soon as my transfer had been set, I'd called him at home one evening and Chas had taken up the conversation as though, of course, we were old friends. He asked if I had been fishing and, if so, what for and told me that he would be away all summer working as a junior coun-selor at a camp in Maine he'd once attended, then staying with his par-ents in the Adirondacks. We'd agreed to meet on the first day of school. I would "love" St. Alban's, he promised; we'd "do stuff" together.

The weeks between Caroline's party and the opening of school were especially torporous and, for me, full of an increasing subconscious panic. My father worked long hours. I mowed our lawn or clipped hedges and re-nourished worn out flower beds then sat by the pool, cramming the last books of the Summer Reading List while doing my best to keep tan in the white-hot haze. Once my mother and I took the train to Baltimore to shop; another time I spent a night there in the home of a former classmate. But I knew that I had left more than a place behind, that my personality was undergoing changes as fundamental and inevitable as those my body had recently experienced and that there would be no turning back. I had been eager for the latitude in which to re-invent myself a new school would give me, but also more each day now, I'd begun to feel anxious and apprehensive and, in every sense, fifteen.

Chas Ledbetter offered the prayer at our first Form Meeting. He had grown into his premature features and was as tall as I was though broader, less gangly. He spoke slowly, with the confident enunciation of someone who has spent quite a lot of time absorbing the method of Anglican clergy, which, as a former choirboy, he had. He talked about honor and friendship and giving one's utmost as a citizen of the school. The first thing I thought about him was that my mother and aunt had been perceptive: he *was* fine looking, just the sort of smiling, perfect-featured boy who can't help seeming a type rather than an individual, whose looks it often pleases others to account a burden. The second was that I was sure he wanted to be president one day. Everyone wanted to be President of the United States in 1961 and if a boy kept his hair a little full and parted it in anything resembling the style of JFK, that was the giveaway. I knew. I, too, counted on the job.

But Chas was far too well established in this environment for me to let myself be jealous yet. After the meeting, in the presence of the Latin master who served as our class advisor, he took me aside and welcomed me. He assured the older man that it would be no trouble at all for him to show me around, get me started in the right habits, introduce me. The Latin master told me I was lucky to be in Chas's care, I agreed enthusiastically and we went off together to Modern European History class. At every break, a new group formed around Chas and by study hall, which followed lunch, I had shaken hands with most members of my form and a fair number of athletic upperclassmen—so many that my memory could retain only a few of their names.

That afternoon, as if by his design, we walked to the gym alone. The sun shone brilliantly, with nothing of autumn yet in it, and the grass of the playing fields was pungent with the scent of sweet onion. When we were finally beyond the intricate and shifting map of gothic shadows and well below the cathedral that loomed forever under construction, Chas stopped abruptly, glanced about to be sure that whatever he said next would be private, then confronted me with a pitiless stare. "Go back to Gilman," he said. "It's going to be hell for you here."

"I don't think so," I replied automatically. "The way I see it we're at about the same place in most subjects: a little ahead in some, maybe a little behind in others, but there's really nothing I can't—" I stopped short as the ominousness of his tone and manner registered. "Why?" I asked. "Why is it going to be hell for me here?"

"Because I'm going to make it that way," he explained slowly, softly, just as he had addressed the form.

"I don't understand."

"Fuck all you don't."

"Is this some sort of hazing you put new boys through? All right, if it is, just tell me what to expect, but, Jesus, Chas—"

"It's got nothing to do with any kind of hazing. If you're as dumb as you seem, I'll give you three guesses what it has to do with and you can start with Caroline Carswell."

"Whom I have seen once in my life."

"Whom you have seen all right."

"So?"

"So? So!" His voice rose for the first time, then settled again. "You invited her over to your pool where you got her drunk on your parents' goddam beer, then you tricked her into taking off her clothes."

"It wasn't my parents' beer," I protested. "She wasn't alone."

"What did you expect would happen?"

"Not what did."

"Come on!"

"I don't know where the beer came from."

"Come off it!"

"I don't even know who was there."

"Who was there? Everyone who was there'll tell you it happened just like I said it did and that'll include Caroline. So don't tell me you can't remember who was there. Go back to Gilman, Brook. Go back to Baltimore, where you belong."

"She's your girlfriend or what? How was I supposed to guess that? How can you hold me responsible for something so—improbable? I know two people in this stinking city and they're going out, they're jealous of each other. Jesus! It didn't mean anything. I didn't mean anything by it."

"If you mention this to anyone," Chas said, "there'll be a lot of trouble. Lots. There're six people—straight off—who'll say it was your alcohol. Your idea. They'll say worse—about you."

"Chas—for godsakes."

"They will. So'll I."

In fact, I did not go back to Baltimore. Nor did I tell anyone of Chas Ledbetter's threats. Nor see Caroline Carswell again, clothed or otherwise. Instead, I carried on as though nothing had happened, as though time, as it usually did, would sort things out. I knew that I would not be believed against a hero of the school: a boy of such achievement and earnest profile. And I suspected that a tightly knit group of cynical adolescents might be more likely than not to lie on one of their own's behalf, particularly against an outsider. There was no point taking the matter up with my parents. There was nothing they could do. And it would worry them—for me and also because any charges Chas's friends might make could be embarrassing to someone serving on the White House staff. On the night Caroline Carswell had come to swim, after all, my parents had been on Cape Cod, in the President's travelling party. And I could imagine circumstances in which that kind of scandal might cost my father his job—even the reputation for probity he prized.

Because we were too young to drive, the ostracism Chas enforced did not reach so far as it might have done a year later. Like most boys in my class, I spent the weekends with my family rather than on a round of parties. But once or twice each month silence would still a conversation as I approached and I would know that there had been a sock hop or a game, a revelry of some kind from which I had been deliberately excluded. The first time this happened I had had to walk away quickly, to cry face-down on a desk in an empty basement classroom; yet I soon learned to convert the pain to strength, to draw insight from it and, most importantly, to try to put into words exactly what I felt.

In front of faculty, or parents—whenever required—Chas Ledbetter behaved exquisitely. But alone—or in the shiver he breathed along the arc of his friends and followers—he was glacial and cruel. On the morning of Halloween, for instance, we held an election for class officers. It was during our Form Meeting. When the nominations for treasurer were about to close and Chas had already been re-elected president, he raised his hand and put forth my name. Everyone looked round: at him, at me. I was astonished. In the end, though, I had three votes, to the winner's thirty-three and runner-up's sixteen. And I realized that he had savoured the speed with which his mock-flattery of me had been turned to general scorn.

The consequence of all this was to force my attention outward from school to the world at large and so gradually to re-direct my ambitions. My confidence punctured, I decided that I lacked a decent chance in politics. I would always lose to the Chas Ledbetters, whose cynicism would never give them away in public. There was something about them, a balance of intellectual and moral shallowness with emotional intensity, that the public would find more appetizing than it would me—just as Caroline Carswell and girls like her would find such boys more delicious to kiss. But they lacked poetry and the more I looked about the more I thought that poetry might be the one gift I possessed. I began to see in John Kennedy, who was a hero to almost all of us and a figure of obsession even to those who had inherited their parents' vitriol for him and his family, not a master of politics so much as a master of language. There was a program then on television—a documentary compilation of old newsreels—entitled *World at War*. Winston Churchill, of course, figured in it prominently and I remember thinking during one clip that what Kennedy was actually doing was imitating Churchill, even as others were imitating him. The times and their generations may have been different, but the pose struck was the same—the mythic pose of the hero, Julia would have called it. I couldn't be so abstract then, but I did realize that it was achieved not with a haircut, a manner, smiles or any amount of youth or handsomeness, but with ideas wrapped in words that made them able to pierce the defense of people's skepticism and stab their emotions.

Soon my papers and essays were full of alliteration and inversions, mimicking the punchy style of Kennedy's speeches. And by employing this style so often, even in mental conversation with myself, I grew to be an expert on its mechanics. That is the effect of any litany: either one comes to believe or to dissect what is being stated. In those lonely days, I did each in turn and ultimately came to feel that I was onto something more mysterious and promising than my contemporaries could imagine. It was not that I expected to rise to great power myself one day; rather that I had chanced upon and now understood the original source of all such power. In consequence, I saw the world—including those who remained aloof from me—from a suddenly superior perspective, perhaps akin to that of a physicist observing natural laws at work.

Or so I thought. In the winter, Caroline Carswell threw over Chas Ledbetter for the exotic and hipless son of a French diplomat. Her new boyfriend apparently owned an acoustic guitar, held Gauloises between his thumb and forefinger as though the cigarette paper were really a holder and sang folk songs in the languid Parisian manner. Chas, so predictably conventional, could no longer satisfy her taste for adventure. When this happened, it thrilled me. I interpreted it as vengeance delivered by fate on my behalf and was especially gratified that Caroline had told everyone who would listen that (despite his coolly silent insinuations) she had never permitted Chas to go past "second base."

Yet as spring thawed the campus, Chevy Chase, and the narrow roads and open corn fields of Potomac, the effect of their break-up was not so much to humble Chas as to humble me. For in its wake, for precisely the same act that had driven his hate, he befriended me enthusiastically. I, who had witnessed Caroline's abandon, her nipples growing erect in the swim-chilled night, the part of feint hair above the lips of her vagina, could testify to something more important than whether or not she had slept with Chas Ledbetter. Simply by my presence, I reminded people (those who knew the history) that she had been available to everyone, had teased everyone—and so come to have no value at all to a boy as prized and selected as Chas. I cast doubt upon her purity and upon her word. And huddling with the class president, the wrestling and lacrosse star and his similarly anointed friends, I, by my readiness to forgive and combine with them, sheltered Chas's ego, enforcing the illusion that St. Alban's boys were intrinsically to be preferred to those who had somehow infiltrated our group and disturbed our natural camaraderie.

I knew exactly what compromise I was making. Indeed, I think it must have been the first time I had ever been aware that a compromise was underway in my life. I had never previously thought of myself as possessing any talent nor adhering to any standard so absolute that, in the normal course of things, I might have to stand up for it against its possible corruption. But in the enforced isolation of that first semester, I had come to value my powers of observation and rhetoric, to imagine myself a kind of journalist—amateur, perhaps, but talented—who, while not relishing the distance between myself and the lives I observed others living, nonetheless appreciated that such distance was essential. I was sure (I told myself) I could not sustain my identity—my scrutiny and practiced indifference—as a full-fledged member of any "in group." Yet when the invitation came I found myself accepting it at once.

I spent all the seasons that followed—that ripe spring of cherry blossoms, the long cricket-chorused summer nights, the autumns of burning leaves, new wool and vivid football afternoons—as a member of a tiny hilltop elite, enlarging my role among my new if callous friends and in the imaginations of younger boys.

On most Friday and Saturday evenings there were parties and, as often as not, these parties dissolved from the home of one classmate or another, one girlfriend or another, to the Hot Shoppe on Wisconsin Avenue, where we were seated almost by rank (in the manner of a society restaurant) and where, to be honest, neither our prestigious school affiliation nor the fact that my father so often turned up in news photos beside the President did us anything but good.

I became a writer and later an editor of the *News*. And though I played adequate tennis and soccer on school teams, it was for my articles and profiles of teachers and students, my rare fictions themed on friendship, sportsmanship and the like that I became most celebrated. These pieces had the ring of stump speeches, for I was still finding my own voice in the imitation of others'—especially Kennedy's and that of his speechwriter, Ted Sorensen. But I knew—because I was assured often enough—that they stood out from the efforts of other boys.

During my junior year, my father arranged for my class to visit the White House, tour the West Wing and shake hands with the President. I had met the President only once before and it was clear from the abstracted way he greeted us in the oval office that he did not remember which of us was my father's son. I looked him straight in the eye and shook his hand with all the strength I felt it polite to muster, trying to assert an intimacy, to provoke a smile of recognition that would register with the others. But none came and when John Kennedy cracked his joke he looked more intensely at Chas Ledbetter than he did at me. The surprising thing was that this hardly fazed me. It was as if the man in front of us merely resembled but in no more fundamental way corresponded to the stylish image one saw nightly on television, daily in newspapers and magazines. And I think I must have realized, without then having been able to put it into words, that it was the image rather than the man himself that had entranced me—the image (words and light passing through celluloid) not the human being to which I was loyal.

When President Kennedy was shot a week after the Landon game, I felt less the heartache of personal loss, less the fear that my father's life and with it mine might be disrupted once again, than the sad paralysis of a child in a great theatre which has suddenly and inexplicably gone dark. And with the rest of my generation, I suppose, I wandered across the border to adulthood a little aimlessly from that day on, increasingly hungry for sex and experience, and curious, too—but finally suspicious of everything and anyone who made the claim of truth. For in the sudden soundless dark that followed his brilliant performance as president, disbelief crept back into the national imagination—and into mine.

I applied to Harvard, but was rather high-handedly advised by a youngish member of the admissions staff to "take a year off, travel, perhaps do a course abroad"—then apply again, with no guarantee of ultimate acceptance. Despite my B+ grades, they found me promising, he said, but also felt that I would benefit from "a little more maturity." I asked who wouldn't and went instead to the University of Virginia at Charlottesville, where, by Thanksgiving, I had lost my virginity and discovered Hemingway. His was a cleaner, edgier style than Kennedy's and I wrote sentences in it through any number of science and history and economics lectures—until I discovered Fitzgerald's more lyrical and romantic vision, which so much more closely resembled and indeed seemed to perfect my own. William Faulkner had recently taught at The University and I read him eventually, for his technique and the salutary implication that to be a writer is to be a genius, aloof from the world and above the fray. The nights I spent reading *The Sound and the Fury* and *Light in August,* with the window slanted open and Mr. Jefferson's dogwoods in bloom outside, were as close as I came, during my college years, to the separateness I'd once felt as boy. I can do this, I thought more than once, reading some virtuoso paragraph or phrase; but then, when it came to the attempt, I never could . . . I was too lazy, or there wasn't enough time. I was usually in love in those days and it was impossible to lie in bed after intercourse and imagine the pain in the heart that had made certain people artists. It still pleased me to think of myself as a writer even though I accomplished only a minimum of writing every week—even though I guessed that as a life it would demand a sterner resistance to compromise than I felt inside myself.

I graduated between infatuations, and after four years and six summer weeks of boot camp in the Army R.O.T.C. Corps, received a commission in military intelligence, then and reported for active duty and advanced training at Fort Holabird, Maryland.

I brought as much anxiety as commitment to the military and, in no time, just before and all during my tour in Viet Nam, that anxiety turned inevitably to fear. After the first patrols, the interrogations in which one was not quite sure which questions to ask nor in what order nor what to make of silences, much less answers or evasions, the fear became habit and I gradually lost any sense of a world in which it was not felt constantly.

When I returned to America, a reprieved, unwounded killer, I knew only that I wanted to do something which was not mundane and not merely remunerative. I had had enough of authorized truth and wanted nothing so much as to define my beliefs for myself—before I stood on them. I realized it was a privilege—a piece of wild luck—to have lived through all that I had and in one way I wanted to tell my story—the story of people like me—and in another I wanted to forget it. Very carefully, I re-typed some stories I had written in college or at one base camp or another—stories of first or unrequited love, of improbable friendships, or random, unnecessary deaths—and sent them off with an application to The Writer's Workshop at The University of Iowa in Iowa City. Simultaneously, on the recommendation of a captain who had been there, I applied to the Harvard Business School to do an MBA. The admissions questionnaire demanded several essays and my captain friend assured me that the answers I wrote, combined with my military references, would have more to do with whether or not I was accepted than my college grades, a few of which any good law school might have balked at. In those days, law school was the most prestigious path for young men who weren't quite sure what they hoped to do with their lives. But I was pretty certain, if of nothing else, that I had no desire to be a lawyer.

On the Wednesday of my discharge the mail brought two envelopes. The first was the same one in which I had posted my materials to Iowa, roughened, torn and patched with cellophane tape at its upper right corner and stamped in several places "Return to Sender." Through an error of the post office, it had never reached The Writer's Workshop. The second envelope contained an acceptance from Harvard.

And so, on the hinge of that event, my life swung. Over the summer I studied programmed texts on accounting and economics, then, in September, settled into Morris Hall with an old velour sofa, a wicker rocking chair and two occasional tables purchased from the tenant of the year before. I was relieved to be there, but Cambridge, like my furniture, was fraying at the edges and, although now and then I strayed into the Square, to the Coop or the Brattle Theatre or to dine with the younger brother of a St. Alban's friend who was an undergraduate in Eliot House, by and large, I kept quiet, kept to my studies and myself. I spent hours every night adding columns of figures, subtracting, multiplying and dividing—computing present values and probabilities as methodically as I avoided thoughts of the future in any personal sense.

By graduation, I'd decided that, except for one based on independent wealth I did not possess, the free-lance life was really the most appealing. Its ease and opportunities, the prospect of working hours that might be long but also fluid and unrepetitious, was part of what had charmed me about writing. So when, gesture by gesture, I'd begun to separate my fate from that of a writer, it had not been to abandon these qualities, nor out of any desire for decision-resolving structure in my life. Investment banking—as a culture, perhaps, even more than as an activity—seemed to have about it at least a bit of the swaggering, well-travelled and turned-out air of the free lance.

So I went to Manhattan with the first good firm that offered me a salary—gave them several years and most of my energy then crossed the street to another which promised to send me not just upstairs to a partner's desk, but abroad to Hong Kong. Hell, I was ready to go: my contemporaries were by then expanding into family apartments along Park and Fifth and the widest, most hospitable cross streets and I felt myself aging, for the first time, in a way that constricted rather than broadened me. The path ahead was clear—but to what? Without a wife, without children, I was an appendage to my married friends' lives, a more or less cheerfully borne inconvenience to their routines, and the unarticulated distance between us grew and grew. The fact was that I still had so many uncaptured dreams of a sort and urgency and exoticism that seemed not to burden anyone else. Having grown up and accepted the responsibilities of earning my own living, having compromised my principles, even perhaps my religion, in Southeast Asia and the purity of my ambition in the face of economic reality and the enormity of risks at home, I knew—because my instincts told me— that I would still have to travel some distance before I could ever come to rest and be happy, be content. It wasn't just wanderlust. I have never felt since so old as I did then, nearing thirty. It was as if time were running out and the geography from which dead people were forever displaced beckoned with a mystery, an immediacy, a seizure of the imagination I had only previously known in women. I went west to Hong Kong because west is the flight path most often settled upon by restless souls. But even after we had crossed the international date line and a day of my measured life had vanished—even after years—I wasn't sure I had got as far as I'd hoped to. Almost by accident, by virtue of the times and circumstances into which I'd been born or later chanced, I'd left pieces of myself in innumerable places.

"It makes no difference," Julia'd said when we first discussed such things, not as acquaintances or fast friends, but as a couple in love, deciding to marry. "People don't just inhabit cities anymore, or even countries. We exist on axes, lines connecting any number of points like the map of an airline's network or a child's drawing done by numbers."

I think that she was right and that the real enigma hides in how we end up where—travelling between the points—we do. Hong Kong beckoned me not to the China of dynasties and superstitions, but to the freest marketplace in the world, a city hectic and quintessentially modern, an undiluted chance at real money. But evolve though it had, this tenuous peninsular outpost remained also the land of *joss*, of sudden, slippery and ironic fortune. Arriving there for a year or two (imaginably five under the most lucrative circumstances) with my American employer, I had no idea how abruptly and utterly, how permanently it would change my life.

Now, AWAKE AGAIN beside my still sleeping wife, with hardly any time left before Adrian's birthday dinner, I stare once more at the plasterwork scene above us—the knight, the column of fire—and wonder: if I had never left New York, had found someone and married there, had children and raised them in my own country, given them childhoods in the image of mine, would I be as happy as I am? Or as afraid?

9

J OHN?"

"Rupert?" His voice, coming from behind, surprises me. We are the first downstairs, the first to have entered the principal drawing room, which is a high, galleried octagon set between the breakfast room and the Regent's, four of whose sides also determine the exterior facade of Castlemorland. This vast space is decorated in the trans-Atlantic liner style of the 1930s: puddles of shaded and frosted lamplight spilling over groups of empty upholstered chairs and sofas, a floral formality at once cheery and severe. There is a log fire in the fireplace and, above it, illuminated by a distant spotlight, Rubens' portrait of *Christ Between Two Thieves* disturbs the illusion that life and its luxuries might somehow endure.

"Do you have a moment?"

" 'Course."

"Quick, then." Rupert hurries us toward the enormous, floor-length gilt-framed mirror which dominates the wall opposite the fireplace, reaches behind its baroque moldings and waits as a side panel as large as a door swivels out. Ducking into the dark entry thus revealed, he beckons me, then pulls the panel closed behind us. The narrow passage into which we have come is momentarily pitch; it smells of cedar wood.

"Where are we?" I ask. "I've never—"

"No," says Rupert. "You wouldn't have done. Your father-in-law never used it. Adrian may not even know it exists; not his style. In the old days, when my grandfather was alive and there was adequate staff and things were done properly, it was a way for the family to come into the room with the guests already gathered. Not dramatically, as though a curtain had been lifted on a stage—exactly the opposite, in fact. Un-obviously. I mean, one minute they weren't there and the next they were, having materialized all at the same time, virtually like ghosts." Suddenly, he snaps on an overhead light, which refracts from a small cut glass fixture. "If you press the wall next to the cabinet, it will give slowly—there's a counterweight within the wall—but you'll find yourself back in the Long Walk, the outer door seeming just another slab of granite."

"Amazing. Speaking of that cabinet, what's in there?" The break-front's several shelves are glass and glass-enclosed, stacked tight with curious leathery pieces.

"The skulls of turtles which made soup for seventeenth-century gourmets."

"You're joking."

"I'm not. You wanted to know." Rupert is wearing a blue velvet smoking jacket with side vents, a navy silk bow tie, a studless white business shirt and—a detail I notice just now—pressed jeans over black slippers with cantaloupe piping.

"You've gone a bit Hollywood," I tease him, without thinking.

"Travelling light these days." As ever, his thin waist and broad shoulders give him a rugged skier's air, but his earlier handshake seemed oddly soft and now the light in his green eyes appears more wistful then determined. "And, as I was saying, one never knows the form around here anymore—especially now."

I regret having mentioned Hollywood, wonder if it may have upset or annoyed him.

"We don't have long," Rupert continues. "I just thought I ought to fill you in."

"Yes, please."

"Asian and Omnibus are firm."

"That's what you said. That's excellent. How firm?"

"They'll take a third of the bridge," Rupert says, referring to the short-term vehicle that will permit Wiley Ryan initially to finance his group's buyout of Ergo shares. "Maybe a bit more. They're on for the final offering, too; or at least it seems likely they will be."

"Did Philip do that?"

"He did his part certainly. The credit goes to the team."

"Naturally, but A & O—well, you know, his sponsor, what's his name?"

"Chuan Ch'u."

"Exactly. Chuan Ch'u. I'm never sure I've got it the right way round."

"You'd better practice."

"I'll be glad to."

"To my way of thinking, the real plus of dealing with that lot is that it reduces contingencies. Takes some of the sting out of the unexpected. Just by the sheer scale of their resources, the day-to-day numbers that shape their thinking."

"There's that, no question," I agree. "And it's novel. No one's involved them, to this extent, in anything over here, or in the States either. At least to my knowledge, they haven't. So, in a way, it's their chance to step on to the multi-national field. They're bound to know this, obviously; it's the kind of thing to which they're very sensitive. Therefore, they must be committed, which is nice because it will reassure others—Europeans and Americans both. Hell, it reassures me. But, what I'm getting at is that it's Philip's connection that provides the margin of comfort."

"It opened the door, I'll grant you."

"Through which we entered, minding our p's and q's, as my mother would say, but still speaking—still trapped in—our own language. We've got a lot to say that's worth listening to, but we need an interpreter and Philip's that man. As well as a common object of trust, which may mean more at the end of the day."

"Things will begin to move faster now on the other fronts," Rupert says. "You'll have to go to America, but not quite yet. I'll have to bang heads in Zurich and Geneva, then with our German friends and the Dutch. Not sure yet about when to enlighten the French . . . if you have any thoughts?"

"I think you've got the order just about right."

"*Beaucoup de prep* between now and then, however. We've got to get a mass of documentation out of the way, vet everything with Wiley, keep everyone's greedy lips buttoned. Not a small order, but the incentives are there."

"You bet."

"What I haven't told Wiley is that the Hong Kong interests are going to want a little more than he's been prepared to give. They're also skittish about the magnitude of his up-front take-out. The Cult of the Manager hasn't really caught on with them and they'd prefer to see a more efficient and ordinary correlation between pay and performance."

"When are you planning to break the news?"

"Whenever it feels right. After dinner? Smoke a cigar and talk things out in a relaxed sort of way."

"He may walk, you know, when you tell him."

"Why do you think we're discussing this in a cupboard? Seriously, though, I'm not that worried. It's just another equation we have to reconcile. He'll give a little and so will they. When all's said and done, they're still star-struck by the numbers; they're not going to desert the field. As you said, chances like this—"

"We may have to give an inch or two ourselves."

"Perhaps. If we do, we'll squeeze it back eventually, from them or someone else. That's not what worries me. What does, to be honest, is that Ryan doesn't seem focused—in the way he ought to be. He's got his eye on the reward rather than all the work we've still got ahead of us. It's surprising—as if he's bought into his own advertising. He's breathing sighs of victory prematurely. And every time he opens his mouth, I just can't wait to call out, 'Touch wood, touch wood!' "

"What can we do?" I ask, nervously conjuring, for the first time, a realistic prospect that the Ergo deal might not succeed, that it could conceivably undo rather than boost our careers.

"Not much more than keep an eye on him, I'm afraid," Rupert allows. "We have to keep him pointed in the direction we want to go."

"Because we've rather bet the farm on it, haven't we?"

"In a manner of speaking," Rupert agrees. ". . . I think the party's got going," he adds abruptly, leaning to the plaster wall, lifting a small wooden relief by its corner, as though it were a pendulum, then pressing his eye against a secret peephole. "Well, maybe not quite."

"Who's down?"

"Ralph Marlowe . . . and, hold on, the very popular Lucinda Lowe. That's all for the moment. No, I'm wrong. Here comes your future sister-in-law, the beater."

"Isabel."

"Adrian could have done worse, I suppose."

"He could have done a lot worse, couldn't he? Isabel is very solid."

Rupert savors his own smile. "Very. So is Adrian. Adrian's *very* solid."

"Don't be wicked," I say. "As far as I can see you actually got the best end of the bargain."

"How do you reach that conclusion, may I ask?"

"You ended up with everything but the house and title."

"If you say so, it must be true."

"Well, didn't you?"

"That depends upon what you mean by *everything.*"

"Everything one is left with when material things—whatever's man-made—are taken away. Inherent things. Simple as that. You're healthy. You have a wonderful brain. You've had incredible exposure—not to mention success. Women fancy you. Must I go on?"

"Strange how an idea gains currency," Rupert muses. "People assume I envy Adrian his inheritance because they believe that's what they would do, how they would feel in my situation. But I don't—honestly! Which isn't to suggest that I never did, but one eventually reconciles one's self to missing out on certain things and having others. I suppose if I thought about it for a moment and wanted to pick someone to envy I could find candidates. Adrian wouldn't be among them, though."

"Who would?"

"Couldn't say off hand. That's the point. Would love to be younger. And not in the City, I don't think. Not a financial type. You wanted to be a writer. I wanted to act. How on earth did we end up here is, I expect, the question. We tried, is the answer, but presumably not hard enough. Or weren't lucky. Maybe it's as simple as that. Maybe one craved success but feared failure more. Maybe I inherited both my mother's dreams and my father's reticence."

The matter-of-fact tone of Rupert's analysis does not so much startle me as confirm my impression that he is a keener observer than most, able to see through his own complexes.

"You never knew David Paxton—" he continues.

"Before my time," I explain, "although that's the second time today his name has come up."

"I'm not surprised," Rupert glances over my remark. "David still haunts the place—in an odd sort of way. I just thought of him because, if anyone ever could have, I suppose David might have got away with it and become a film star. It's not impossible. Not impossible, but not likely either. I will tell you something about him, though, that no one else knows. You can make up your own mind what to think. As you say, it was long before you came into the picture. David had just gone up to Cambridge, in fact, and Julia was still there. I can't remember why, but one weekend I'd come to stay here and David had also come home to visit his parents. My uncle had given him permission to use the library, quite controversially I might add, when he'd first begun to show promise at school. So it wasn't odd to find him in the house. But the thing was, I came into *this* room, which was always meant to be the deepest, darkest of secrets, the holy of holies—I mean, in a sense, *I* had no right to be here, but I'd wanted to sneak away for a few minutes to avoid someone—and whom should I find but David."

"Why? What was he doing?"

"Reading, I assume. I don't know what. Whatever it was he slipped it back before I could see."

"Did he explain himself?"

"Not really. By this time he was already famous for having fucked Susannah Finley. He had quite a layer of confidence, but beneath it I'm sure he was still afraid of me."

"So he said nothing at all?"

"Nothing."

I study Rupert. "How did you handle that?" I ask.

"I didn't betray him."

"But it sounds like you had him in your pocket from then on."

"Anyway, it turned out not to be for very long. He died fairly soon afterward, you have to remember."

"So I gather. Sadly."

"Terribly sadly. What a naughty thought, John. Still, do you know what *is* pleasant—I mean *for us*, having sold out in the ways we both have?" Rupert smiles. "Having survived and *won*— had the last laugh in our own ways. Wiley Ryan waiting in the next room for us. It's delicious, isn't it?"

"Sweet," I agree, managing the start of a laugh, somehow without his absolute faith.

GIVING NO FURTHER surveillance to the party in progress, we leave the turtle skulls and the dim, claustrophobic hideaway by its entrance into the Long Walk, opening the granite-faced door cautiously, until we are sure we are alone. When we come round, again yet as if for the first time, into the principal drawing room, the others have gathered around the large velvet companionable at its center. Topley offers saucer-shaped glasses of Krug as Wiley Ryan holds forth in his *soi-dissant* baritone.

"Man comes into a Rolls Royce dealership," he is saying. "Clever, silent fellow; looks every inch a sharpie. Approaches a royal blue Corniche, pigskin trim, top down. Stares at it—blankly—for several minutes. In due course, naturally, salesman approaches him *very* cautiously. 'Just looking, thanks.' The intense scrutiny goes on and on—and on, half an hour, maybe, and the customer is smiling more and more brightly all the time. His eyes never leave the drophead. Finally, fearing he's just another loiterer, the salesman comes up to him again. 'Well,' he asks, 'you going to buy the car or not?' Man by now's grinning ear to ear. 'Oh, I'm going to buy the car,' he says. 'I wasn't thinking about that. I was thinking about sex.' "

Laughter, quickly muted.

"Point is—"

"Car's no different from business. *To him.* Its image engages the imagination. It doesn't fill it. And shouldn't try to."

"Because one person's fantasies may not be another's?" Julia asks.

"That's a large part of it. You lay a deal on the table in this day and age and you had better have done your homework. But there's a time for crunching the numbers and working out the details and another time for sitting back, hard as that is, and letting the other fellow invest your idea with his own hopes and dreams. I hope I'm making myself clear."

"Very," Philip says. "Fantasies, to take Julia's point, not being fungible."

"What does 'fungible' mean?" asks Lucinda Lowe. Lucinda is one of Julia's oldest friends, a jolly, themeless school chum—and off and on fling of Ralph's—who cooks directors' lunches in the City and caters small dinner parties in London.

"Substitutable," Philip replies. "It's an economics term. As in one barrel of oil for another. Bushels of wheat. That sort of thing."

"No, not at all fungible," Wiley continues. "Which is why we're here instead of still hunched over a desk back at home office: to give our crop time to grow, to allow our customers to visualize its possibilities."

"It gives us a nice break, too," Tag appends. "For me, to do some antiquing, as I mentioned. And, for Wiley, to catch up on any number of details he's had to neglect lately."

Rupert smiles inquisitively.

"Tag means that I could use some new suits and shoes, not to mention a couple of dozen new shirts."

"What I tell him is that London's for men what Paris is for women. I try my best never to miss the Paris shows, *so*—"

"And invariably succeed," Wiley interrupts good-humoredly. "Where I do agree is that, now and then—and, who knows, for whatever reason, this may be one of those times—you have to be ready to step into an entirely new role. As if it were opening night, without a dress rehearsal. And, of course, your basic English tailor is not of too much help to you then. He's an altogether different bird from one in Hong Kong. He won't make you up a suit in twenty-four hours. So you have to allow a bit of time—plan ahead or else go without. Shoes are worse—a six month wait at minimum." He looks directly at me as his analysis winds down, his pause almost begging affirmation.

This feels lucky. It could also be important. Even though we are a team, I do not want Rupert and Philip to monopolize the relationship with Ryan. It is fine—and probably right—that Rupert should be the point man in Battleman Peale's work with Ergo, but I know from experience that it is wise to be visible to clients and to leave them in no doubt as to your identity and usefulness to them. For success has a way of sweeping quieter personalities from the minds of key executives—and of those who set compensation—just as failure does of singling them out for blame. Still, I cannot think quickly enough of a clever or memorable reply and this frustrates me. "I'm sure you're right," I hear myself say.

"Even you fellows have to be careful about clogging up your subconscious imaginations," Wiley Ryan says. "Technical efficiency and vision are both valuable commodities, but vision is the more valuable—by far. I keep a horse or two at stud not a million miles away from here. That's no secret. Tag and I'll stop off there when we leave here. Why—why do I do that? Because I'm a born equestrian? Because I live and breathe horseflesh and horse talk? Hell, absolutely not. It's for the same

reason I buy abstract art and teach myself about it, the same reason I'll
go off on a trek to who knows where. You see, people may think I'm not
minding the store, but I'll be at trackside or at a museum opening—or
all geared up at the edge of the polar ice cap—anywhere that's totally
removed—and I'll suddenly see, in whatever I'm looking at, a metaphor
for our business, for some situation that's right there waiting on my
plate. Nine times out of ten I'll see it in a whole new way."

Philip remains silent, which surprises me given the subject at hand.

"Would anyone else care for a cigarette?" Lucinda Lowe asks then.
Marlboro in hand, she raises her forearm until a malachite and gold
trimmed bangle has slid most of the way to her elbow. Her wrist is pale
and, like her face, freckled. With the back of her hand, almost absently,
she waves her long hair behind her shoulder, turning her face slightly
as she does. Her hair is Van Dyke red, her shoulder stylishly exaggerated beneath a designer's Chinese green and ivory brocade.

With instinctual grace, Rupert steps toward her, holding up a lit
match while sheltering its fragile yellow-blue flame in the cup of his
palm. "Thanks very much," Lucinda tells him, drawing fire into the tobacco.

"Rupert," Tag declares once he has finished. "I just noticed something. I just noticed that you have your monogram on your shirt cuff,
which fascinates me because I told Wiley, it must have been day before
yesterday, that I thought they looked so nice there when we saw that on
someone else—another Englishman."

"Do I?" asks Rupert, suddenly examining the navy blue letters embroidered on his own starched double cuff as though startled by this
forgotten detail.

"What about you, Adrian?" Tag inquires. "Are yours the same?"

"What? No, I'm afraid they're not. Just the plain old job, sadly."

Tag shrugs, her expression forced with affable sympathy. "It doesn't
matter at all," she assures. "You may not even care about such things."

Adrian slowly raises his eyes from his wide glass, then wipes his
lower lip with a single stroke of his index finger, disguising the gesture
as a yawn. "Did once," he says finally. "Used to, very much." Mock
sigh relaxed, on apparently sudden impulse, he downs another swallow
of his birthday Krug.

"Really? What changed your mind?" Tag's voice conveys a curiosity which could hardly be more intense if Adrian were the lifestyle guru of a magazine.

"It's a long story," Adrian explains. "But I'll try to make it as short as I can. I remember when I was . . . about fifteen, I suppose, and one evening Father rang me at school and said that as soon as we broke for hols I should meet him for lunch and we'd go on to his shirtmaker. I'd grown rather a lot over each of the previous summers and he'd had the idea that I'd more or less reached my size—in which, as it turned out, he proved to be correct."

"I remember that," Ralph says.

Adrian nods. "In any event, we had lunch in Mayfair at a little Italian place where everyone knew him. *Linguini Posipillo.* Funny how certain things stick in one's mind. I wasn't allowed a glass of wine, although, of course, I would have been at home. Never mind. We went round to his shirtmaker in Bury Street and I was measured and we looked through book after book of patterns for half an hour or more. He didn't appear at all preoccupied that afternoon, which was unusual when he was in London. I think I chose a dozen shirts, trying to trade even with him one colorful stripe I fancied for each solid conservative thing he thought a schoolboy my age should wear. He was never very adventurous in regard to dress. In fact, I remember he once told me that he'd been brought up with the religion that 'if you passed a man in Berkeley Square and, five minutes later, could remember what that man had been wearing, that man was badly dressed.' Anyway, I was as nervous in that shirtmaker's as I think I've ever been."

"Because you wanted brighter, bolder stripes?" Lucinda asks.

"Not at all. Because I wanted something else, which I was afraid to ask for. You must know how that is, to have something urgent on your mind which you are afraid to get round to."

"In my life, it's always been sex," Ralph says. "Would she like to do what I'd like to do—then and there and bugger whatever'd been planned? But in a shirt shop with your father—?"

"In this case," Adrian laughs, "what I'd wanted were those embroidered monograms I'd seen on some of the other boys at schools' shirts. Precisely what we've just been talking about: you know, small block letters over the left breast or on a sleeve. They were very much the *in* thing then, like a tan after Christmas or finding your snapshot in *Tatler* and having it rumored that you weren't still a virgin. You know, *very* smart. So, naturally . . . well, finally I got up my nerve. It took a lot of doing, but, I burst out with it. 'Father,' I told him, 'some of my mates at school have their initials on their shirts and I think it looks rather smart . . . and, well, I wondered if I might have them, too.' It was such a relief, I can tell you, to have it out."

"What was his response?" Wiley asks.

Adrian hesitates, his glass halfway to his lips. "He looked me in the eye, directly, but very kindly, no sternness, and said 'Adrian, if you need initials on your shirts to have other people know who you are, then, of course, you may have them.' "

"How devastating!"

"I didn't think so."

"You didn't?" asks Julia.

"I thought it was like discovering some truth. It was there to be found; one grasped it and went on."

"Have you ever ordered anything monogrammed since?" Lucinda asks.

"No."

"What are your initials, may I ask?" inquires Tag.

"A.F.H.M.L. For Adrian Frederick Henry Midleton-Lygham."

"You see, I think I agree with your father—having all those initials is what I'm saying. Wiley has only three. He's Wiley Augustus Ryan, so W.A.R., which makes a statement, doesn't it?"

"A very important statement," Ralph agrees.

Soon the clear note of a single bell chimes. As Isabel smiles, the hands of the double-sided orrery clock which stands on a table in a scalloped alcove show that it is half past eight exactly. The bronze sphere encaged above its face displays the positions of the earth, the moon, the planets of the solar system relative to Saturn.

"I'm afraid we've let your glass go empty," Rupert tells Wiley Ryan, catching this fact from the corner of his eye.

"Oh, don't worry. Not your fault. It must have a leak at the top."

"Let me—"

"Do you know what I would enjoy, if it's not too much trouble? A martini. Bad habit of mine, I'm embarrassed to say. One straight up martini before dinner, with a twist—of lemon if possible."

"More than possible. Gin or vodka?" Rupert asks.

"Oh, gin, please. The pleasing effect of the juniper berry and all that."

"My late father," Tag says, "always believed it was due to the juniper that gin was apt to perform feats of ventriloquy—too often where these were least wanted."

Wiley ignores this. But Adrian quickly picks up the thought. "Mustn't forget the coriander," he insists. "Difficult to overstate the importance of orris—also the angelica and cassia bark, for that matter. What I can't abide is the sting of gin, know what I mean?" he continues. Oblivious to the apprehensive silence he has provoked, he begins to walk toward the drinks cupboard, apparently pre-empting Rupert's bartending. The cupboard is a somewhat battered Regency affair, mahogany with hexagonal panes of glass curtained on the inside with pleated raw silk. The worn hinge squeaks as he opens the right door panel. "Solution is . . . pay attention, all of you! Solution is . . . half an inch of Noilly Prat, what have you—no more, with two parts Messrs. Gordon's gin and one part Comrade Smirnoff's vodka . . . in a shaker, which we haven't got to hand. So this pitcher will . . . simply have to do. Add ice, stir the lot thoroughly—backwards and forwards, usual trick, and . . . what do you think?" Surprisingly, Adrian does not sample the concoction he pours, but offers it immediately to Rupert, as though it is his vindication he seeks, Rupert's exquisite taste which matters.

Rupert, hesitantly, gathers a few beads of the drink on the surface of his tongue.

"What do you notice?" Adrian asks.

Rupert swallows. "The vodka takes the edge off the gin, doesn't it? Completely neutralizes it."

"Abracadabra. *So* having met the approval of his banker, here is a nice cool one for Mr. Ryan. Anyone else care to?"

"Please," says Rupert.

"The shortest imaginable one," Philip acquiesces.

"Oh, I couldn't possibly," Isabel replies apologetically "Ask John. You do make me laugh, Adrian."

"No, thank you," I tell them.

"Oh, come on," Ralph urges.

"Why me?" I ask.

"Americans are used to strong drink," he explains. "More than the rest of us. You have to admit that's true. You'll have a couple of strong ones before dinner, when we'd have something weaker in our hands."

"All evening—*and* afternoon," I add.

"Occasionally. Admittedly. But why not? With alcohol, it's a matter of time, isn't it? Not just what one drinks, but the length of time over which it is consumed."

"Anyway, I'm sticking with champagne tonight," Adrian says. "After all, I'm on the wagon—slightly." Resting the shaker and glass on the silver tray atop the drinks cupboard, he looks conspicuously at his sister and smiles.

J ULIA LEADS US into the hall and down the Long Walk to the dining room whose door she opens tentatively. Beneath three Edinburgh chandeliers, the long table that has lain all day in wait now reflects the overhead light from paired epergnes and candelabra, from a full service of Castlemorland's most brilliant implements and crystal. Antique curtains of rose velvet are drawn over most of one wall. These must be twelve feet tall; they bundle at the floor against any possibility of light invading from the park beyond.

We pass boisterously into this great room, admonished by the painted stares of Cheviots and Gravesends past. The portrait of the second Earl of Gravesend, hanging high over the enormous marble chimney piece, has been painted with that peculiar trick of perspective which makes his eyes appear to engage any viewer's, following them left then right as one passes back and forth before them, fixing the viewer uncomfortably as soon as he comes to rest in any given spot. I point this out to Wiley Ryan and explain that the second Earl, whose long chestnut hair is thickly braided but whose pale skin tones and sharp features so closely resemble my son's, has been given the nickname "Shifty" by his late twentieth-century descendants.

"It's not quite boy, girl, boy, girl," Julia announces calmly as she moves about the table "but as much so as possible. Look for your place card. Ads, you are at the head, naturally. With Tag on your right and Lucinda on the other side."

"Who cares if the numbers are even," Ralph admonishes. "This is a dinner party, after all, not an orgy."

"Thank God," Lucinda says.

We laugh as we are seated—more than enough of us to make a

party; fewer, no doubt, than would have been asked had not Julia's father died so recently. Waves of candle flame, fluttering steeples of pale yellow and burnt orange, bathe the light between us, drawing the rouge of the high damask curtains into the air itself and our complexions, transiently restoring the lineless, expectant, insubstantial faces of our youths. On the wall distantly to my left a paillette of an old master glimmers, then recedes. Beside it, in a vaster frame, Venus blindfolds Cupid. We are objects of the minatory stares of armored warriors and politicians, of dressed game and birds of prey, of a risen God and fallen angel.

"The salmon is Lucinda's doing," Julia declares, referring to the painted plates of gravlax smothered in Beluga caviar which have now been set before each of us. "The fish eggs are a present from the Ryans?"

Taggart Ryan sits to my left. I lean toward her to offer thanks just as Wiley, in a boardroom voice plainly meant to draw in the entire table, asks, "Do I gather, Julia, that you are writing a book?"

"More dreaming of writing one. Something short, just for children actually."

"But it's not your first?"

"Well, it is, I'm afraid."

"I thought Rupert said—"

"I've written a few monographs, one of which was included in a collection, but the whole book wasn't mine. That was in another life though, before Andrew and Louisa. My days are spent with dogs and children now and, really, I wouldn't have it any other way."

"What is the subject you're dreaming of?" Tag asks.

"Women who've just seemed to slip out of their history of England's families, that's all. The effects of their disappearance as much as anything else. What it might have been like if they'd remained as vivid as the men they'd married, or slept with."

"Many have, I'm sure," Wiley Ryan suggests.

"One or two queens."

"Julia started off reading Religion and Philosophy," her brother explains, "then moved over to History of Art."

"You know," she says, "slides on, eyes off."

"Seriously," Adrian says, "it's an interesting combination."

"Just a branch of the higher nonsense," Julia demurs.

"It's not really," I assure them. With drink, to which my reaction is less exuberant and involuntary than is Adrian's, I nevertheless am beginning to achieve a mild, feverish buzz.

"Of course, it's not," Adrian agrees.

"I've always had the greatest admiration," Wiley expounds, "for anyone who could write a book. If I had that talent, I would sit down and write a long one, I can tell you that. What I've seen could certainly fill a lot of pages."

"It might make an awfully good thriller," Tag ventures.

"In a way, I suppose, it might," Wiley replies. "Part thriller. Part biography. Part economics text and history lesson. The world's turning upside down and inside out, after all. What better subject?" His glance, as he clears his throat, travels upward in thought. "Most importantly, control is shifting. If you go back a few years, not long really, you'll discover that anyone with a good idea and nothing more had a helluva hard time finding capital and that if and when he did find that capital and sat down to make a deal the money men soon owned him. He'd have to give away a huge amount of whatever it was he had, because ideas and bright young men and little companies with possibilities were all thought to be a dime a dozen and the power was entirely on the side of those who controlled the cash. Borrowing, except for small amounts for operations, was out of the question; and what borrowing was possible had to be accomplished through banks or, just as bad, through finance companies that specialized in high-risk lending. The bond market, to which big companies could turn for long-term debt at manageable rates, was like a club. In order to go there you had to have been there. Admissions were, for intents and purposes, closed because it was thought that a company needed fifty years of Moody's and S & P ratings to go directly to the public for its funds. In that way, it was just like the proverbial bank which will lend you money only when it's certain you don't need it.

"Well, whatever else we may or may not have done, we've at last reassessed the risk inherent in any company—proved that a company's capacity to pay back a level of debt is what matters, much more than its history.

"And thank God. Because it would have been fatal for me and a lot of other people, if we hadn't figured this out in time. We'd have gone through our lives failing to recognize that what we wanted—no matter how stupendous or far from our clutches it seemed—was really up for grabs. *Up for grabs:* for the first time in history, the biggest operations—worldwide things, things central to our daily lives—and all up for grabs. And the only thing that could buy them was imagination."

I am startled by his candor—perplexed and frightened; so, I can tell, are Rupert and Philip.

"Are you planning to buy something in particular?" Ralph wonders.

"No, not at all. Certainly nothing specific at this point in time. On the other hand, you can never be sure what might come along when you least expect it to and it's a good idea to know, if and when something that's attractive does, that the means exist to take advantage of most situations."

Julia, concentrating, says, "Let me be sure I actually understand. You're saying that there is already enough money amassed somewhere, in the market, that's willing to take a chance, so that all of a sudden the valuable thing is the idea. If that's true, it strikes me that somehow, for all this to work, there has to have been a shift—practically a sea change—in society's perspective."

Plainly, Wiley Ryan approves. "An economy has to keep fit—just like a country or a person," he continues.

Julia nods. "Ah, but unlike an economy—or a country, for that matter—a person cannot change emphasis or outlook or the rules of nature and suddenly start over, having become young again." Her voice teases playfully.

"Are you absolutely sure? With enough available credit," Wiley Ryan smiles, "who really knows what a human being could do?"

10

W HAT DID YOU make of all that?" I ask Rupert, who has come into the loo off the Long Walk and now stands next to me in front of one of two-yard-wide marble urinals that Julia's grandfather installed in the Teens.

"What?" he asks, staring at a framed Beerbohm cartoon, just above eye level. "Oh, not much really."

This astonishes me. "For a moment," I explain, "I was afraid he was going to give it *all* away."

"Were you? I wasn't. When you think about it, in actual fact, Wiley didn't say anything at all concrete. That's an art. And he covered himself pretty well, I thought, when he announced he had no plans whatsoever to buy anything. I'm glad Ralph asked him that question. Shows he's good for something."

"I hope you're right."

"I am. Say no more."

Rupert and I collect Philip and Wiley and maneuver them to the billiards room beyond the library. The room is chilly, dark when we enter. Rupert twists a rheostat and an even, eerily purple light fluoresces, shaded by a cornice, from the ceiling. The balls are racked for snooker. "Game?" Rupert asks Wiley.

"Is there time?"

"Who's watching a clock?"

"Tag and I are off in the morning for Newmarket, as I said. But reachable whenever, wherever. Here, let me write out a number," he says and proceeds to copy onto a record card held in his cowhide note pad a cell phone number he apparently knows by heart. "What are your movements?"

"To London, in all cases," Rupert answers. "I'll be meeting with some of the Asian and Omnibus functionaries tomorrow afternoon. Clueing them in, on a need-to-know basis, of course; giving them our perspective on our talks so that we can advance to preparing documents. Philip will be along."

"Good, good. John?"

"I've also got an early start. Brunch in London with some Americans we usually syndicate to. Mum's the word, naturally; the idea right now's simply to prime them. Then there's a tremendous amount to get started on in the office. One of my colleagues will be coming in and we'll be able to get underway without the world and its sister. Be nice to have everything in order for the solicitors in the next few days. The more the better. They wouldn't like hearing me say this, but the more of their work we can do for them the better off we are. Not just because they're bloody expensive once they start their meters running, but because half the time they do more harm than good, as much to give both sides reason to break a deal as make it."

"Don't I know. Whatever you do, keep the lawyers away—from any vital information and anyone—as long as you can," Wiley implores.

"Wiley," Rupert says. "With the A & O people—"

"Chuan wants a little more than we'd expected?" Wiley Ryan interrupts.

Rupert, I can tell, tries to cover his amazement; he keeps his voice and eye contact level. "Precisely. They are not so used to the idea of management bringing quite so much value to a venture."

"Of course they aren't. No one is. We're setting the precedent. We're on the cutting edge—supposedly."

"That's been the operating premise. Which isn't to say that the value we've placed on you and your team can't be justified by the numbers. We believe emphatically that it can be."

Wiley laughs wickedly. "Agree to whatever it is they're asking—*en principe*, as diplomats say."

"I don't think we'll have to ultimately, I really don't. They'll meet us halfway, perhaps closer if we're clever about it."

"Don't be clever."

"Don't?"

"Follow me, will you? Trust me on this."

"Listening."

"Rupert," Wiley begins, "you've always said, we've always agreed we were building this deal on a tripod, am I right? From the beginning? Battleman's institutional network in the U.K. Your associates—plus some of my own and other management's—in the States. And this major commitment from elsewhere, that now turns out to be from A & O, which couldn't be better. Correct so far? So the Chinese commitment, because it comes first and with the authority of people who are pledging their own money, is our cornerstone. *Our cornerstone.* With which we fiddle at our peril. Chrissakes, they're pros. Oldest traders in the world and still some of the best. They'll understand; they'll expect it—respect us more in the end for standing up for ourselves, but until the deal is set we don't want and can't afford to jar them. So agree to their terms generally is what I'm saying, make it sound like we're willing to acquiesce for the most part. Niggle on something trivial—anything that's not a dealbreaker if you feel you have to, if it makes you happier. When we present them documents, we'll take a longer view, I promise, an altogether tougher line. But by then we'll be farther along, the last pieces of the puzzle will be in place. The whole pitch and prospect will be so eff-ing attractive, they'll never walk—never dare, never even turn their heads in that direction." Wiley Ryan smiles his country handsome smile, selects a cue from the rack, blues its tip with chalk. "Will they, Philip?"

"Pride can do funny things," Philip tells him.

"Yeah," Wiley Ryan tells him, "but I've been smoothing ruffled feathers all my life. And I expect, when the time comes to clinch things, you can do the same. I'll help you. Faith, Philip."

"There *is* another argument worth considering," Rupert suggests, pretending indifference, readying his own cue now.

"Is there?"

"That it is preferable to have things sorted out with A & O to the point where there can be *no* possible question. No imminent roadblock."

"But there is no such point in life, ever," Wiley declares, "which is the essence of my philosophy here. There will *always* be contingencies—some foreseen and provided for by lawyers; at least they'll attempt to provide for them. And others that creep up out of the damnedest places. The imperative is to be prepared and agile and charming enough to be able to navigate around them."

As the balls thunder loudly across the felt table, slamming one another, I am distraught, apprehensive—afraid: not so much that Wiley's strategy will fail in this instance as that it could lead to difficulties, a potential for disaster down the line. In my experience, a deal founded on honor, even when it has been sealed with only a handshake, can often survive disagreements of scopic magnitude, whereas one founded on a lie might as well have been made upon a hole of quicksand. Don't misunderstand me. I am not innocent. I recognize that rich men are often liars, or were in their formative years; just as I suspect that liars, as a class, possess the edge on becoming richer than most people in the world as it is. But I have also had the luxury of not having had to deal with or represent too many such people. For I am—and have intentionally fashioned myself to be—merely a professional; a high wage slave; one who serves rather than conceives or instigates deals; a name buried, if at all, deep in the text of any business story. And if there is a measure of clean-hands sanctimony, an aura of "we happy few" about those who do what I do, in such places as I do it, I don't mind too much. In a way, it is the price we are paid, the perk we are allowed for remaining in the shadows of any transaction. One of the things that attracted me to Battleman Peale, in the first place, was its almost anachronistic reputation for discretion and probity, its absolutely fussy code of honor. So I am a little angry and disheartened now at Rupert's cravenness in the face of Wiley Ryan's devious plan, at Philip's silence—and at my own. What is the point of serving as advisors to a clique of management and putative owners who value the imprimatur we provide far beyond any opinions we might render?

That is a silly question, of course. The point is money—fees on a scale that can produce not merely evanescent income, but some real wealth for each of us. *Kudos* capable of effecting a chain reaction: larger fees, leading to greater reputation, leading to larger fees still. In practical terms, the successful completion of the Ergo deal will set me on the road to being able to keep Julia and the children in the manner I would like to: Louisa's and Andrew's schooling, their holidays, the large and little extras that set childhoods apart, will be assured, no matter what happens to me. Without depending upon my job, the vicissitudes of the market or the vagaries of partnership contracts (which concern me, as many of my classmates from business school have recently lost their jobs), I will be able to pay off our mortgage and find us a weekend bolt-hole somewhere in the country. Julia, I hope, will feel a latitude she hasn't yet, perhaps even the lessening of a competitive, resentful strain that sometimes infects her relations with her brother. And, for the first time in memory, I may be able to relax. For if neither Julia nor I ever expected such wealth, and if neither of us is utterly secure in it, I suppose I am less so. It may even, I am pleased to think, be possible for me to help Adrian, in ways I cannot yet predict, to secure the future of Castlemorland itself.

Yet the converse is also true. One is given only so many real chances in life and the danger of stumbling over any one of them is that other people—younger, hungrier, stealthier and every bit as bright—will, like educated vultures, pick clean the landscape bearing your remains. Such a prospect terrifies me, but it is my turn to shoot and I try to put its horror momentarily out of my mind. I flourish the four ball into the side pocket then, after a careful set-up, the six ricochets away from the far corner, rolling evenly along the flush wall of felt. There is silence—and it lasts. Apparently, tacitly, weakly, we are all agreed. I take a long puff of my cigar, study the perfect white cylinder of ash which has accumulated around its fire.

"Will you *and* Tag join us in the library?" Rupert asks Wiley Ryan after our abbreviated game.

"Thank you, no," Wiley begs off. "I think we'd better find our way upstairs. We've got a long enough drive ahead of us in the morning and I want to be fresh when our trainer's selling us his bill of goods."

SUDDENLY MINUS THE Ryans, we settle in the library before the fire, which Adrian stirs with a brass poker and to which he adds a split log from a nearby basket. The flames roar up as he works. In the firelight, surrounded by shadows, the area between opposing sofas assumes the intimacy of a campsite. Reflexively, we gather about the enormous square tapestried ottoman that fills it. Julia quickly shifts the stacks of magazines—months of *Country Life* and *The Field*— that cover it, clears a flat surface among lavish art books and leafed-through Saturday supplements. We sit together, reclining into the old double-depth velvet sofa. On the floor, disinhibited by alcohol and the hour, Lucinda and

Ralph sit with legs kicked back, their bodies in relaxed contour. The toe of her shoe teases a ball shaped leg of the ottoman; his fingers rest on her waist. Unexpectedly, they have assumed a liberty with one another's bodies to which their well-known history together would seem still to entitle them. The vague Lucinda possesses a more languid beauty than she had seemed to at dinner. Prone, her torso cocked jauntily on the easel of a single elbow, there is a suddenly tantalizing aspect to her, her eyes uncomplicated and, in this light, very young. A slight overbite has given her lips the intimation of petulance, of all but merciless discrimination—then a single moistening stroke of her tongue, careless as a schoolgirl's, transforms this effect to one of guiltless acquiescence. Ralph feigns attention to the packs of playing cards Julia has broken from cellophane and begun to shuffle, studying Lucinda in only sideways glances. Adrian and Isabel take the sofa across from ours.

Rupert appears with a bottle of Armagnac and a Screw-pull, with which he effortlessly unwinds the cork. Philip trails, bearing short glasses, into each of which a shot is poured. A spark of jealousy seems to pass between him and Ralph when he notices Lucinda's unimagined ripeness and attachment—but it is only a spark, a regretfullness that will not last beyond the evening. Philip is a rational man, who seeks love, like any commodity, where he believes himself most likely to come upon it.

"What are we playing for?" Ralph asks.

"Not much at this hour, I hope," says Lucinda.

"Articles of clothing then?"

"We can start by taking off our jackets. The fire's damned hot," I say.

"Not articles of clothing," Lucinda says. "We don't all know each other well enough for that, do we?"

"No," Julia agrees.

"I was only kidding," Ralph explains. "Each chip is a quid?"

"Fifty 'p'."

"Fifty 'p' then."

It is agreed all around.

I am dealt the Jack of Diamonds, the two of Hearts, three of Clubs, seven and nine of Spades—and so try hard not to grimace.

Almost furtively, Rupert picks up and studies the tight fan of cards Julia has dealt him.

Lucinda is smiling.

"Haven't you ever heard of a 'poker face'?" Ralph asks her.

"What? Oh, sorry," she says. "I wasn't even thinking about my cards, actually."

Julia places the remaining deck face down on the needlepoint.

Chips are tossed into the pot. "Here's a quid," Ralph says. "More cards?"

I give up the two of Hearts and three of Clubs. Philip discards only a five of Spades.

Lucinda relinquishes nothing.

"It *is* rather toasty in here," Rupert declares.

"Don't look at me," Adrian says. "Isabel's firmly in charge of all our dealings with British Gas."

"What do you mean?" Ralph asks.

"You'll have to ask her, I'm afraid," Adrian says. Isabel sighs faint-heartedly. "Oh, darling, do tell them. It's just that it's so damned funny."

"It's mortally embarrassing, that's all," Isabel explains. "I shared a flat couple of years ago. Well, actually, I suppose I did own it, I'd bought it with everything I had plus rather a lot of my bank manager's money be-side. And then a bill came from British Gas for heat—eighty-five quid, I think—and I paid it. I didn't dare say anything. I just supposed that was what everyone was paying. Live in London, that's the price. You know."

"Sorry to interrupt, for just a second," Ralph says, "but what about more cards?"

"Sorry, Ralph. Here they are."

"Is there any more drink?" Adrian asks.

"Beside you," Rupert tells him.

"Anyone else?" Adrian implores. "Superb stuff. Where'd it come from, by the way?"

"Kai Tak Duty Free," Rupert answers.

"Better than cognac. Much. I've always said so."

"So, you paid the bill and—" Philip prompts Isabel after a few sec-onds.

"It's just so terribly boring, that's all . . . Then the next month an-other came. It was getting colder, must have been November's. And that one was for a hundred seventy-something. Which shocked me quite a bit. I took it out of my very tiny savings. I couldn't imagine how peo-ple I knew were doing this. Or, if they weren't, were they freezing?"

"I fold," Julia says.

"Same," Ralph says. "Sadly."

"Raise you a quid," Lucinda says.

"And fifty 'p' beside," Philip adds. "Sorry, Isabel."

"Don't even think about it," Isabel absolves him, putting down her own cards. "I'm out too, I'm afraid."

"The least the house could have done," Adrian tells Julia plaintively, "would have been to have rigged things slightly in favor of the birthday boy. Fold."

"Me too," I add.

"Finish your story before we show our hands," Lucinda insists.

"It's just you and Philip left," Julia says. Lucinda glows.

"It's a dreadful story, really," Isabel says. "Because December was positively frigid that year, if you remember. Brrr. Day after day. The mercury was *in*visible. And when that bill came, just under four hundred."

"Jesus. Four hundred sounds a lot. Your flat must've been massive."

"Not at all. I had a serious word with the bank manager, paid it with my overdraft then had two workmen round half the day looking for a leak."

"And—"

"None. Tight as a drum, my flat was. January, they billed me seven hundred sixty-three pounds and fifty-six pence. I remember the figure *exactly*. Seven *hundred* sixty-three pounds and fifty-*six* pence. I was on the point of tears, I promise you. Really and truly was. After I'd paid it, I was practically broke. I took the bill with me one night and showed it to Adrian. We were just beginning to have—well, you know, serious dinners. Surely, I said, everyone can't be coming up with these sorts of funds on a monthly basis. No matter how cold it's become. 'Let's have a look,' he said. And he did and it turned out that what I'd been paying in every month was the amount of a credit I'd had—after paying the start-up, I s'pose, I don't actually know where it came from—and the credit had doubled each time I'd paid it, you see, minus the running costs, which weren't much at all."

"So now you know," Adrian says. "The reason I am marrying Isabel is that we shall have free heat for the rest of our lives. Who won the bloody hand, anyway?"

"Three aces," Lucinda says.

"Two kings," announces Philip.

"I think it's time," Julia declares.

"Yes. I'm absolutely *wiped*," Adrian says.

RUPERT AND PHILIP are first up the grand staircase, their gaits betraying the honest strains of jet-lag and long hours of cunning. They are the most sober yet exhausted among us. Behind them, Ralph and Lucinda feign boredom of each other and their surroundings, advancing up the charcoal-and-yellow marble steps without a glance back from the majestic landing at one of the most splendid halls in England. She trails her hand, palm open, toward him and he follows with the blithe grace of a rich boy long accustomed to accepting presents out of the blue.

Julia and I are at the head of the stairs when the telephone rings: a pair of insistent Telecom throbs before it is answered. Julia hesitates. For who can it be at this hour? Quickly, suspending alarm, I make my way back to the library, where I find Adrian at the *bureau plat*, his father's desk, worn receiver in hand. The instant he notices me he muzzles the mouthpiece and whispers "Isabel's mother" across the hollow distance.

"Is everything all right?" I inquire.

"Inevitably."

"Good luck!"

"Thanks for *everything*, John."

In our bed, Julia stares into the dark, as raptly as though the plaster knight on the ceiling were still discernible. She breathes deliberately, collecting her thoughts. "Poor Ads," she murmurs finally. "He has such a pure soul. I just hope and pray—" Her body heaves, then falls onto its side, turns away from me as she drifts, all of a sudden, into sleep. My hand props against her. Her heel nestles at my calf.

Finally, Castlemorland is still. Any stirring now, even the lightest whisper might be discerned across an unexpected distance. Absorbing the quiet, touching and studying my wife, the memory and fear of the previous night stampede across my consciousness and nerves. *Will I wake to find you gone again?* I wonder.

Then, in my half-dream, the sound of displaced gravel arises, a powerful engine ignites, then purrrrs.

11

N OT QUITE A thousand years ago," Adrian said with astonish-
ingly natural matter-of-factness, "a knight granted his liege as
much land as would be covered by the flight of an arrow. That liegeman
good and true was my ancestor. The bow was pulled, the arrow soared
and when it came to rest it hit a goat, which was, of course, enormously
frightened and spurred on by it, but not so gravely wounded that it
couldn't run any number of miles before it and the arrow came to rest.
That's how the boundaries of this estate were set. That's why we occupy
the entire valley, but nothing beyond the hillrise; because the goat was
too knackered after running uphill to go any farther."

Julia and I had met only a few weeks before and my conversation
with her brother took place during my first trip to Castlemorland,
which had come about of a sudden. We had been to dinner with a colleague of mine and his latest leggy girlfriend. The matter of the weekend had come up in conversation; our friends were bound for Paris. In
the car, unprompted, Julia'd said, "We could go home if you like. Leave
Friday evening?" We were stopped for a light. Whether I was actually
being invited or summoned remained in some question: whether I was
simply to be rewarded for the dinners, a play at the Old Vic and concert at the Albert Hall to which I had treated Julia or, in fact, was to be
presented to her family, with all that such presentations implied, was
never made clear.

On Saturday, we'd donned wellies and walked about the estate.
Closing the gate by which we had entered a pasture before approaching another by which we would leave, Julia'd hesitated abruptly. "Best
to hurry, John," she'd said. "There's a bull in here." I'd glanced at the

herd in the opposite corner and immediately scurried, fast as I could, to the exit. When I had climbed to and gone through it, she'd laughed. "God, you're thick as two short planks," she'd teased. "There's not a bull anywhere about. Obviously."

"That's my sister's sense of humor," Adrian told me the next day. "Don't let it embarrass you. She'll only display it in the presence of someone she cares about. Believe me."

It was October, the moment of the afternoon's failure. The sun momentarily sustained itself above a line of beech, where we stood surveying a newly ditched plantation. Norway spruce. Douglas Fir. A darkening forest of *chiaroscuro*. Adrian and I had shared a pint at the village pub, then set out alone on what amounted to a working tour of Castlemorland. After inspecting the last of the harvest's grain—loose pyramids of wheat, barley and oil seed rape, drying in a storage shed, awaiting collection by a merchant—we had entered the part of the wood where plantations were named after children of the Midleton-Lygham family, planted as close in time to their births as the seasons would allow. Adjoining the one named after Julia, some ways along the plateau from his own, the felling of trees was underway across five acres. "A plantation is ditched once per crop," Adrian explained, reaching down to retrieve a branch for a walking stick.

"Ditched?"

"For draining. The felling itself takes weeks, given the constraints of manpower and farm equipment around here. After that, it's fifty years to the next clear fell." He seemed enraptured by the subject, linked to the old forest as some men are to poetry and others to the wars they fought in their youths. I watched his grip relax and tighten upon the branch. He had, I assumed, inherited the hands, the torso and musculature of his ancestors who had been farmers. For there was a solid basicness about him—a physicality as worthy of respect as, if less alluring than, his sister's beauty.

"I've never been to America," Adrian announced to me suddenly. "I know it's beautiful; it's so vast it would have to be. But this is rather special, too, isn't it? In its way? What do you think?" He pointed in the direction of a folly, half-hidden among tree trunks: a gothic tea house of fairy-tale design, silhouetted against a low mauve cloudscape. The house stood atop a distant cairn. "Built by a three-times great uncle," he muttered as quickly as he realized that I had focused upon the folly

rather than the totality of the Castlemorland Estate, which he had
meant to be his reference.

"Why?"

"To enliven a day's shooting? Wouldn't you have such a thing in
America?"

"No . . . well, maybe in the West. But it would be totally different.
It's not that it wouldn't seem so old. In a funny, primordial way, it might
even seem older. But it would seem always to have been the property of
God—you know, of nature—rather than of a particular family."

"I suppose it couldn't be anywhere else but in England. Even in Europe, where there is a long tradition of shooting, it's different. The
continuity has been broken. Ancient societies, but they've had to sustain so many blows. Practically all of them have been conquered at one
time or another; the order's kept changing."

"And in the New World people shoot where the birds fly."

"Exactly." The smell of peat floated in the cool, damp air. Beyond
the plantation, a sudden undercurtain of rain separated us from the
park. Beneath the treads of our wellies, the floor of the forest was slippery with leaves and needles, then tough where the ditching had already
got underway.

He was hardly visible in the stormy, enveloping dusk, but I stared at
Adrian for a moment. "If I were you . . ." I began.

But he cut me off. "You'd be barking in a week. *Barking*, I promise
you. Farmers with their problems coming to you. Foresters with their
complaints. Gamekeepers with their disagreements and dire prognostications. Tenants in the village: one problem after another. Woman
came in to see our agent last spring, going on about her house and
whose lease it would be if she and her husband divorced. Now, she's
four months pregnant with no thought of breaking up at all. Yours is by
far the more glamorous life, John. You wouldn't want to be me, trying
to find the money for a new roof instead of some fancy international
deal—with all life's choices made for you. You really wouldn't."

"If you hadn't been born who you are," I asked, "what would you
like to have done?"

"Farming, I'd still think. It's about the only thing I have any talent
for. It's certainly the only thing I know. If I were an entirely different
person, of course, that wouldn't be a constraint; so I couldn't say really.
It would be nice to be able to do something—well, noble and lasting.

Perhaps be a vet, if one were cleverer." He smiled suddenly. "To be honest, it wasn't until I was eighteen and finally could go to drink parties that I found something I was actually good at."

"Perpetuating all this seems noble and lasting to me," I told him, laughing off his joke and with it the subject of liquor, as I had heard he had a problem. "I can't think of many things that would be more so."

"But, of course, it's such a privilege. And one does it out of love not expectations. It doesn't seem . . . well, *fitting* to claim credit. Anyway, one is not exactly perpetuating things; it's more the job of helping into the future those aspects of the past and present which the future seems inclined to accept. That's all. Nothing stands still. Nothing's the same as it was. You have to admit that. Not England, certainly. Or America either, I imagine."

"But England is a little more like America was."

"Is it? That's probably because this is a country where one needs three planning permissions for just about anything. If my father wants to build a new farm building, he very likely can. But if, for instance, he were passionate about modern architecture of one sort or another and wanted to build me a glass house on that ridge over there, he wouldn't have a prayer of getting it through. I don't know if you knew that."

"No. I didn't."

"It's the price one pays for being able to live in a world that's free of glass houses, I suppose. Though there must be many people who would like to live in them—whose lives would be immeasurably improved by a small piece of land with one of those things on it—and they no doubt see the situation oppositely. In America, they'd prevail."

"And eventually stare into one another's windows," I said. "The valley would disappear. The silence, first. Soon enough, those who had come for the view and the quiet would find themselves in a suburb, just another suburb." As I spoke, I caught in my tone something I did not like: not a lack of patriotism—for that has never been in question—but a catty disloyalty that would hardly have sounded itself had I been standing within my country's borders. Just as it seemed imperative to defend one's country on foreign soil and to do so less critically than one might at home, so it felt unbecoming to deride the United States abroad, even justifiably. Oh, I loved England, but that love, as I have said, was also rooted in the love of a vanished America. And I had no idea then that the accidents which had brought me to live in England would continue and contrive to keep me there beyond the expiration of my current visa. At times, I realized, my Anglophilia was reaching points of silliness, cataloguing the smallest differences between English and American things: the shapes of paper clips (pointed or round), the location of flaps on brown envelopes (side or top); but, at most others, I relished the peace, the comparative lack of frenzy when judged against life in Hong Kong or New York.

"Who's to say," Adrian asked, "who's right and who's wrong?"

"The child who will come here in a hundred years and find what we found, or something else."

"That would be my answer, but then I'm fairly prejudiced in the matter. I've always felt—because it was what I was brought up to feel, I guess—that I would one day have to take care of Castlemorland, not own it outright. Would you care for a short one?"

"Excuse me?"

"Flask," he said, holding up a handsome silver one he had just withdrawn from the pocket of his Barbour. "Mercifully filled with Johnny Walker."

"A short one," I told him, somehow sensing how acutely he wished me to join him.

"Much as you want. Love Johnny Walker. Prefer the Red stuff to the Black, though. Don't know why. Not meant to, I know. . . . Anyway, a thousand years is a very long time, isn't it? Half the time since Christ is one way to think about it. Father used that comparison when he spoke in church one Sunday. I was a child. The thought passed me by—completely and utterly. Then, much later, I found it had stuck. Strange, how the mind works. A thousand years—well, almost—of ghosts bearing down on one: one can't dismiss the idea out of hand."

"No," I said. "One can't."

"I knew that my father had been 'older' when I was born. He was older than most of the other boys at school's fathers. And so I knew that in time—and in less time, very likely, than in some other cases—I would come and live here. When you think about it, I *knew* rather a lot about my future for a boy of twelve. I knew, just by looking out my bedroom window when I was home for hols where I would be buried. Even if I had no idea whom I would marry in the meantime, which I still don't. I knew my weaknesses, had some idea of my strengths. I knew that it was more important for me to be dependable than a brilliant scholar—or even athlete, for that matter. I knew that I was bound by— and at the same time a link in—a chain, which, if I broke, would be broken forever. And I could never let that happen or live with myself, if by some accident . . ."

We walked without words, until the woodland finally gave way to park and the splendid, jokey folly melted again into the high autumnal night. Across the long lawns and cricket pitch, still soft, virtually indigo before winter, the incandescent windows of Castlemorland winked and beckoned, assured and promised.

ALL THIS I recall on Sunday morning, from an iron chair beside the canal garden, which channels water from an elliptical pool on the south terrace to an ornamental lake three levels below. The canals are walled in old stone from a nearby quarry and I sit between this exquisitely conceived masonry and the boxwoods which border it in an unseasonable puddle of sunlight. It is early. I am alone with the newspapers and a tall glass of orange juice. Julia is still dressing.

On my way outside I have passed Adrian's room, noting, as sworn to, the as yet unbroken scarlet thread which the maids at Castlemorland routinely stretch across the thresholds of occupied bedrooms in order to determine which have been vacated.

Ralph is awake. I hear his footsteps on the gravel then look up to see him coming toward me, tabloid rolled beneath his arm. "Bit chilly," he calls.

"Once you get out of the shadows, it's glorious," I say. "You're up early."

"The whole thing leaves one hungry," Ralph remarks suggestively.

"Is Lucinda—"

"Out like a lamp."

"And no sign of anyone else?"

"String's still tight across Adrian's door."

"Yes. I noticed that, too."

" 'Do Not Disturb' sign hung out as well. *If* you can believe it: per-*pet*ual adolescent, that boy. As if it mattered."

"Isabel's mother called, just as we were going up. For a moment, I was afraid she might be 'hyper-ventilating' again."

"No, no. Usual . . . situation, I'm sure. She's all alone, she looks at the telephone and who is there to call?"

"I thought I heard a car as I was falling asleep. Then, the next thing I knew, the car was in my dream. Not real at all. What are you reading?" I ask.

"News of the Screws," Ralph answers, unfolding the cylinder of newsprint he has tucked away. "Interested?"

"Thank you, no."

"You off to church? Or back to London?"

"The latter, I'm afraid. Business."

"Sorry for you. Have you had breakfast, by the way? Is there any? Where?"

"Sideboard. I'm going light this morning—just orange juice."

"Thank God, they're not Catholics," Ralph says. "Wake up famished in a house full of R.C.'s—even today in lots of places—and they've got the silver locked up until Mass. You can't put knife to fork until—"

Andrew hurries, ahead of Julia, along the edge of the canal. For a second, in the windswept surface of the dark water, he seeks to steady his reflection. Louisa straggles, as if to beg attention by her aloofness from the moment.

"Daddy," Andrew says. "I want to stay."

"So do I," Louisa says.

"We've had such a nice weekend," Julia tells them, "haven't we?"

"It's only the morning," Louisa explains. "We never go home in the morning."

"We'll come back soon," I say. "You've interrupted Mr. Marlowe, though."

"Sorry," Andrew says, turning to Ralph with memorized courtesy. "Daddy?"

"Not at all," Ralph assures him, smiling at me.

But now Louisa chimes in. "Daddy," she begins.

"Your brother was talking," I tell her.

"I want to go on a horse," Louisa insists.

"So do I," Andrew agrees. "I want to go on a horse, too."

"Everyone's asleep," Louisa declares.

"We're not," Andrew says, then giggles uncontrollably.

"It's not nice to go while everyone's asleep," Louisa says. "I want to go wake Uncle Adrian."

"No, you don't," Julia says finally. "Uncle Adrian is very tired. He worked very hard yesterday on his shoot. And it was his birthday. Remember, he brought you the first slices of cake."

"Yes," they recall in chorus, almost shyly.

Louisa removes a small plastic flask from the pocket of her coat. It is green, covered in red, yellow-bordered canvas. "I'm going to fill my flask with Ribena, Daddy. And we can go for a walk, just you and me."

"Where?" I ask.

"America," she says, and laughs.

"You can't walk to America, silly," Andrew informs her. "Daddy, I want to go to your office with you."

"No," Louisa says, "that's not fair."

"You can both go to the office with me. But on a different day, not today."

"When we get to London," Julia says, "we'll have a choice. We might go . . . to the children's museum. We might go . . . to see a film . . ."

"Which film?"

"I don't know. We might . . . order a video . . ."

"A real video," Louisa insists, "not a video game."

"Or we might even go to the park," Julia tells them.

"Yes, I want to see a horse in the park," Louisa says.

"I want to ride my bicycle," Andrew says, "along the Serpentine. Like I did the other time."

"I suppose," Julia tells me, "it's just a matter of loading cases into the car."

"Will you watch them?"

"You are boring," Ralph says. "The pair of you."

"*You're* boring," Andrew says.

"Yes, *you're* boring," Louisa agrees.

"What a horrid thing to say," I admonish them. "Apologize to Mr. Marlowe, or we won't be—"

"No need to apologize," Ralph assures them before anyone else can. "I *am* boring. Not deliberately, mind you, simply by nature. I'm not ashamed of it, either. In the world, the way it's heading, it's probably the most flattering thing you can say about someone."

I leave a tenner for the maids on the night table and carry our cases into the front hall, then return to the nursery for the children's. The house is silent: not even the occasional sound of a door or shutter swinging on its hinge.

In the car, it is quiet too. The children, belted in the back, busy themselves with coloring books and crayons as we drive along the lorryless roads to the motorway.

"Did you find Topley?" Julia asks.

"Last night," I reply.

"I can't explain it," she says. "It feels so odd, tipping in one's own house. But then it isn't one's own house anymore. And I suppose leaving something is a way of acknowledging that fact as well as the staff's kindness. It's delicate, though, isn't it? I'm glad you do it."

We are in Julia's wagon, the F Registration one with childproof locks but no telephone. The radio is on Capital: Mr. Akerbilk's band is playing *Wonderland by Night*. It is music from my childhood, years before Julia's.

"I suppose we ought to have come in two cars," I say. "That way you and the kids could have stayed all day."

"I don't mind, really. Things come up." She turns and repeats, "We don't mind, do we?" to Louisa and Andrew.

"We should have brought Daddy's Porsche," Andrew declares flatly.

"Next time," Louisa says.

"You can go with Mummy," Andrew explains. "Daddy and I—"

"Or," Julia interjects, "It may be the other way round."

"We'll see," I say. "What are you coloring?"

"Superman," Andrew says, his voice at once overlayed with Louisa's so that neither's words can be further discerned.

Julia turns. "What's our motto?" she asks with a soft force. The children hesitate. "What's our motto, Andrew? Louisa?"

"Calm down," each replies.

"Take a breath and count to three and—"

"Calm down," they say again.

"Superman," I repeat the name to Julia as the children return to their books and crayons. "Do you remember—"

"I know what you're going to say."

"The night we went to Joe Allen's, after the Old Vic?"

"Yes. I wasn't looking over your shoulder, though. Wasn't staring. One couldn't help but notice them."

"I remember thinking—to myself—how intently you were looking at me, pretty sure it meant you were keener than I'd expected."

"I was interested."

"You appeared rapt."

"Well?"

"Then, when we got up to leave and I saw Superman and Luke Skywalker at that table behind me, on a line with my eyes from where you'd been sitting—"

"You were crushed."

"Totally."

"I really only *noticed* them."

"But you hadn't said anything and they'd been there the whole time."

"So?"

"So, I felt gullible when I should have been suspicious."

"Bollocks," Julia says. "One was just having a bit of fun, that's all. I married you—not Christopher Reeve or Mark Hamill, wasn't that his name?"

"I think so," I tell her.

TWO HOURS LATER. London lies in the clear aftermath of mist this morning, its pavements still darkened by early rain, its asphalt glimmering in the newly insistent, still intermittent sun. A pink reflection of the city floats above Chelsea on a bank of cloud—then floats away, borne on the determined wind. Across Pimlico Green a chalk white steeple rises against a patch of cyan sky, while, below it, a few vacated black taxis line the curb. From Bourne Street, in the opposite direction, come organ and plain-chant from St. Mary's, the celebration of the Holy Eucharist ascending from the choir and travelling like smoke on winter gusts toward Ormonde Place, where we live.

I am proud of our house, which is one of several built in the last decade in close conformity to Thomas Cubitt's original plan for the surrounding areas. Fronted with classical white stucco for its first two stories, but topped with brown brick, it stands in a corner of the low private square which has been nestled into what must once have been a lesser mews, an arch away from any thoroughfare. Hercules presides over its tiny central garden and access to cars is strictly controlled by

means of a barrier and electronic entry card system; the sole other con-
cession of the Regency to modernity being a two-car garage at ground
level.

At the time I bought it, a few months before our marriage, the house
was considered to have cost the earth. And, though I could not improve her title or bring Julia the scale of fortune which seemed on so
many minds (if still just beyond reach) in those days, it had given me the
most enormous pleasure to be able to provide her the sort of London
house most other men she knew could not, in a million years, have
done. There are advantages to having compromised one's life and when
these appear I am inclined to seize and celebrate them. Had I become
a writer rather than a merchant banker, had Iowa accepted me instead
of Harvard, it is unlikely that I would have made, much less saved as
much as I had been able to by then. In such a case, it is all but impossible to imagine that I could have found my way to England, or had the
family I have now—that I would have been able to give to my parents
not only the gadgets and holidays and first-class transatlantic tickets
that I have from time to time, but, more essentially, the comfortable
knowledge of their child's and grandchildren's prospects and security.
Had I become a writer in my twenties, and so left unsevered the imag-
inative line from my childhood, who can say what sort of life, what sort
of books might have come of it? Who can calculate the cost to the soul
of viewing human beings, day and evening in, day and evening out,
through a merchant banker's wholly practical lens, screening men and
women for their usefulness—the more immediate the better. The price
of profit is the loss of languor. Under pressure, with responsibility,
without leisure, the imagination hardens, eschews risk, grows sensible.
I have felt this in myself occasionally, without knowing how to forestall
it—if truth be told, with fear. Our house is splendid, the life it contains
a lucky one indeed. Especially in the evenings, when I return to its fire
and cheerfulness, the spontaneous laughter and pleasant disorganiza-
tion of my children, I recognize it and am utterly grateful. Yet, I also
know that the man who inhabits its rooms is no longer the boy who
might once have imagined doing so. He is wiser, but weaker, somehow
diminished even as he has become enriched.

"I don't think there's any bread," Julia says as I carry our cases and
she directs the children inside. "I know there's no milk. Cereals we
have masses of, but not so much orange juice. If they don't have the

fresh, I'll fetch it tomorrow. You wouldn't just nip round before you go off?"

"Let me just disarm the Banham," I tell her.

"Can I do it, please, Daddy?" Andrew asks.

"No. But one day. It's a grown-up secret," I answer.

"It's *not*," he says. "You just press the one, the nine, the three and the five."

"How do you know that?" I ask, astonished. "You know it's very secret, don't you, top secret? You mustn't repeat it to anyone."

"To burglars, you mean?"

"To anyone."

"It's our telephone number backwards," Andrew says.

Julia and I exchange glances: pride and apprehension.

"Is that how you remember what to press?" Louisa asks.

"Yes," Julia explains. "But even so, it's not infallible and we change it now and then, as well, just to be on the safe side."

"Blah, blah, fishcakes," Louisa says.

"Blah, blah, fishcakes to you, too," Julia retorts. "Now, I wonder if we have any interesting mail. Or any messages. Letters first!"

In the gutter by the Pakistanis' friendly shop at the corner of the Pimlico Road, the wrinkled cellophane wrapper of a loaf of Hovis bread skips in the breeze, then stops against a discarded lemon peel. There is a queue by the register and, before joining it, I check the shelves of both aisles, adding a box of Jaffa Cakes, a tube of crisps and, on impulse, a chilled can of Coca-Cola to Julia's order. The plastic litre of juice sweats cold onto the counter as I wait.

I recognize a slight increase in organ volume as I walk nearer to St. Mary's, then turn abruptly into our distant-seeming mews-square. A shaft of sunlight, liquid for having burned through cloud, glints from Hercules' torso.

The children and Julia have gone upstairs, into the library which looks out over the conservatory and small garden on the opposite side. I find them transfixed: Julia on the telephone, standing rigidly by the answering machine; the twins as if cast into mute paralysis by a stroke of the wand-like receiver to which she listens with absorbed incomprehension.

"What is it?" I ask.

Julia's hand goes up—slowly, as she continues to listen.

I wait. "Please," I say, after a minute. "What's happened?"

Her palm presses a few inches forward, forbidding us to speak or move. "Certainly. Certainly, *sure,*" she tells whomever she is talking to. "Just under two hours; we'll turn right round. No. Thank you, you're kind. . . . It is. . . . It is. . . . He's *here*, he's just come in. I will. . . . That's very . . . thoughtful, thank you. . . . Just pray, I think. That's all: just *pray.*"

At first, when Julia lowers the receiver, she misses its cradle and it thuds loudly to the floor. When she looks up, her gaze goes past us into space. It is numb, as though she is seeking to discern not an object on the horizon, but an invisible world embedded in our concrete reality. "Adrian is dead," she announces, enforcing her calm. "Isabel, too."

"What?" For an instant, my senses deflect the news she has just imparted. Then, all of a sudden, my mouth turns dry and I can feel my heart's accelerating thuds against my chest.

"They've . . . died."

"What?"

"Car accident."

"Oh, God!" Still, I cannot accept what Julia is telling me. It is too unexpected, its ramifications too many to absorb. "Just now?"

"No, last night, apparently. On the Home Farm Road. Not far."

"But—"

"He wasn't in his room, *obviously,*" Julia stops me. "They must have gone out after we went up."

"Who was that?"

"Rupert."

"Oh, Julia," I tell her, taking her hand. "I'm so sorry."

Louisa is already crying as Andrew moves to his mother. He leans against her as though suddenly fearful for her well-being.

Julia holds her breath. For the first time since our children were born her attention is distracted from them. Although they are here, in grief she seems neither to see nor hear them—neither to see nor hear me. She breathes reluctantly, as if all emotions are lost to her, suddenly spent. "They're gone," she whispers ". . . whatever happened."

T HERE ARE FEW calms as deceptive and superficial as that
which prevails on the Mergers and Acquisitions team of a merchant bank in the run-up to the sort of bid in which we are presently involved. The early frenzy of information collection and projection—the
disarray of forecasts and spread sheets supplanting one another
hourly—soon enough give way to hypotheses all the more fanciful for
the secrecy in which they are conceived, nurtured and compressed.
Plans are made, disturbed, designed again. Intriguing plans, lunatic
plans, plans elements of which are applauded or trashed. Then, finally
magically, the cartography of the deal rises from the numbers, the jumbled alphabet, as if written in alkalis on litmus paper, and it is immediately as clear and indicative as a hand-written map, from which all
tributaries, all context have vanished.

The designated journey is excitedly, hurriedly undertaken. Yet, we
in our business are also, like children, usually too eager for our destination. So, eventually, we must wait . . . wait to refine the magnitude
and probability of our dream . . . wait and reconsider our route at each
intersection.

Right now, Philip and I are in a conference room—a high cube of
glass and teak—in the very modern, much-debated annex to Battleman
Peale's ancient headquarters in the City. Stories below us, small, darkly
dressed figures scurry anonymously along the narrow pavements in the
gathering dark of a midmorning storm, while an interior wall affords a
contrasting prospect: a hundred desk-bound brokers in a gothic hall at
street level. The hall is altarless, carpeted in blue. We are its appended
loft.

I glance at Philip. "Anyone heard from Rupert?" I ask.

"Not since yesterday. He's still in Hong Kong."

"When I talked to him then, I thought he sounded rather up. Didn't you?"

"Very much so," Philip replies. "Obviously there were people about. He couldn't talk candidly. But I think he was optimistic. No reason not to be. Everyone's in place. He's just trying to keep nerves calm until the big moment. You know, it's the 'steady' stage, as in 'ready, steady, go'."

"I know it is."

"And mood is everything when you've got us Chinese—any Asians—involved," Philip laughs. "We're shrewd, we'll do the numbers backwards and forwards, but instinct still matters to us more than it does to you—the feel of the thing that can't be quantified."

I smile, long enough for it to register. "Go to hell," I tell him. "Why didn't *you* go with him, anyway?"

"Far too much to do here. And those forty-eight hour turnarounds really take it out of you. I don't know about you, but I'm not as young or resilient as I once was. And Rupert has matters well in hand. This trip. In actual fact, I think it may do him good to get away—to put some distance between himself and everything that's happened."

"Do you know what struck me as extraordinary . . . poignant and sad?" I then ask. "Adrian was buried by the vicar who'd christened him." There had been flurries, unexpected and random, blotting out the horizon as we gathered round his grave. The ice had moved on the wind and it had felt as though the living, too, were being sealed into something by the white, membranous sky.

"Sort of family you've married into, life's a very small circle," Philip says. "Thought he'd dried out, Adrian. Couple of years ago. I mean I'd no idea, really, he was still in *such* a bad way. Does anyone know what actually happened?"

"Far from it. We're still piecing the puzzle together. The sticky business has to do with Isabel's mother. Remember the telephone call he took as we were heading upstairs? He put his hand over the receiver and told us it was she. But now she says she never rang."

"She likes the bottle, too, if I recall. She might not be able to remember whom she'd rung and whom she hadn't."

"Still, it's strange that he would go driving off at that hour for anyone else. I mean, except for Isabel's mother, everyone he was that close to—would have felt that kind of obligation toward—was staying in the house."

"All I know is that when you have a brand new car, at the oddest moments, the smell just beckons. You can't help wanting to grip that wheel."

"Not a chance."

Philip nods. "I'll have to take your word for it."

Philip's parents are Shanghaiese who found a refuge with cousins in Hong Kong after the Japanese occupation of World War II and the Communist Revolution of 1949. His father is an artisan who originally specialized in the manufacture of camphor wood chests for the protection of woolen garments and in whose tiny, open-fronted shop I often saw teak treasure chests and others the size of coffins lined with camphor, the noble, ready figures of ancient warriors raised from their exteriors in formal and intricate battle scenes. Upon the dirt floor of that shop camphor shavings lay piled into neat mounds, a few stray. His father, a more diminutive man than Philip, gave me one to smell on my first visit. Its bitter aromatic scent dried my sinuses as I inhaled. Mr. Li smiled. "Nowadays, kids want to wear a suit, carry a briefcase," he explained in remarkably clear tradesman's English, as if anticipating, before I'd asked, the question of how it had happened that his son had come into my world instead of his.

Despite the enormous physical and cultural distances which separated our childhoods, Philip and I—ironically, while completing perfunctory insurance forms for our previous employer—came upon a fact which formed, in its way, a profound bond: we shared the same birth date. This simple coincidence enabled us to compare and contrast our altogether different experiences with utter precision.

In no time we began a game. One of us would summon a memory, anything to which a specific date could be attached; the other would try to recollect where he had been at that moment. We played it on the honor system and, once challenged, if either of us faltered, he bought lunch or dinner or drinks or pairs of Havana cigars. As it turned out, there were many instances when we both could recall our lives and situations. The Christmas we were three my grandfather bought my family our first television, a cherry-wood floor model Dumont, I remember.

And my father installed a set of Lionel trains—six cars from engine to caboose, the tracks upon which they ran complete with gradings, a tunnel and twin bridges—on a square of plywood painted the color of garden grass beneath our tree. Philip, then, was on a cargo ship in the *Dong Hai*, the East China Sea, having just come out of a week's dark hiding near the port and having abandoned home. It was his first voyage anywhere—turbulent weather. The seaspray stung him. His mother had to hold him back from the lifelines the one time they ventured topside. Shanghai had fallen months before. They were being smuggled, and passed almost all of the journey below, in a small compartment near the hold.

The day we were six was sunny in both Hong Kong and Baltimore. I went off to first grade proud of a new blue metal lunch pail which featured a large bright yellow decal cartoon of *Tom Corbett and His Space Cadets*. Philip carried a single notebook from his home behind his father's shop in *Chek Chue*. "We were always told," I explained, "that if we dug a hole and kept digging far enough, we'd come through to China on the other side. Were you?"

"No. We thought of America as someplace across the sea—as far away and as unreachable as paradise, I suppose."

"Was it east or west? Across the Pacific or beyond Europe?"

"That didn't matter."

The summer my father moved us to Washington, Philip apprenticed to his. He might have become a master carver, too, might have followed his father and their ancestors had it not been for an odd facility with numbers and a studious side he thought he must have inherited from his mother. Just when I was benched from the J.V. football team for the last time, Philip, having won his school's maths prize, came to the attention of a prominent local businessman and property developer. It was this serendipitous connection which opened, for him, a wider window onto the world and its possibilities. At sixteen, he pedalled his bicycle from the cricket pitch in Chater Street outside the Hong Kong Club all the way to the top of the Peak and stared at the colony from the superior vantage point which the English, more proprietary abroad than they would have been at home, reserved exclusively unto themselves. Twin desires to imitate and offend warred in him and, he said later, he thought then he might "have gone either way." But the next year, his childless sponsor, who confessed to having felt similar emotions in his own youth, encouraged Philip to sit for the

Oxbridge exam and, following the inevitable result, paid both his tuitions and once-each-year travel expenses home.

Following Philip's double-first (in history and mathematics) at Cambridge, Chuan Ch'u continued to shepherd him: through a further year at the London School of Economics, then an apprenticeship with a middle-bracket merchant bank in the City of London. It was upon Chuan Ch'u's recommendation that Philip was taken on by the same American investment bank with which I came to Hong Kong. Indeed, the fact that his sponsor was a principal client of that firm, I believe, distorted Philip's evaluation of it and he lived through seven quarters of half-hearted attempts to nourish a proper Corporate Finance and Mergers and Acquisitions side before I appeared, green and greedy, from New York.

Our trading room and offices were located across from Battleman's more sedate quarters, in a relatively modern concrete tower whose punchboard windows had already won it the nickname "Building of a Thousand Assholes." There, Philip and I worked, commiserated, sympathized and became fast friends—until, after an especially disappointing distribution of bonuses one Chinese New Year, he resigned to become the second youngest, though first Asian, partner in the long, daunting history of Battleman Peale.

I remember exactly when he broke the news to me. It was early morning—still blue November—and when I looked up from the Asian Wall Street *Journal*, Philip had come into the Luk Yu Teahouse and was approaching the booth which he had reserved and I had already settled into near the wall. The Luk Yu, in Stanley Street, was crowded with businessmen at this hour, mostly in pairs, a fair number in teams—or were they families? As far as I could see back into the room, I was the only foreigner, the solitary "gweilo." The conversation was relentless, yet muted to the level of indecipherability, choral and distant. Disappearing clouds of cigarette smoke rose from some tables. No matter the reason for any meeting, a purposeful air of concentration prevailed, an air of Oriental seriousness about tea as much as business.

A waitress in sandals, black trousers and a white jacket arrived beside us, bearing a metal tray of *dim sum*. Philip pointed to a lotus seed and rice dumpling. I chose the same.

Philip asked, "So, do you think our management will ever figure out what it's doing?"

"I'd like to believe they will," I laughed. "But I'm not sure."

"Well, I'm bailing out, I'm afraid. Time's come. No other choice, really."

I swallowed hard, drew a deep breath. I knew this meant the end of any hope for our department.

A second waitress appeared, literally chanting the names of the products she bore. I indicated a coconut milk tart and a haw bun. Philip deferred—for the moment. He seemed abstracted, glancing now at the polished brass spittoon beside our booth then at the wainscotted wall, its polished wood bright in the glow of a shell sconce.

"Battleman approached me, in confidence, a month or so ago. They've offered me a partnership," he declared simply.

We paused while a waiter familiar to us both (although I could not remember his name) brought a large lidded porcelain cup into which he placed the pungent leaves of Philip's favorite hyson, then poured boiling water over them. Almost immediately, without permitting the leaves to escape, he poured out the weak new tea into a gleaming slop bowl. Philip and I followed the ritual: bathed the cups in front of us in this same bowl, rolling, cleansing and warming them. We dipped our chopsticks into the tea as we were expected to do. Then the waiter refilled the large cup with scalding water, which brew we allowed to stand for a few minutes, until all the volatile oils, the caffeine and tannin of the green leaves had been released and the liquid cooled some, before testing it in our own cups.

"Battleman? Very heady stuff," I said, mustering what enthusiasm I could. "Congratulations."

"Thanks. John . . . I go to prepare a place for you." He smiled.

The tea had a pleasant astringency, an immediately warming and stimulative effect. Yet another bearer of *dim sum* approached. I tried a bamboo shoot and shrimp dumpling; Philip, tea in hand, a red bean pastry then a shrimp pancake. A dollop of the pastry's filling fell onto the butterscotch tablecloth, soiling it. Instinctively, Philip covered the stain with his plate.

PRESENTLY, WE MUST be about the business of examining the terms and conditions of scores of documents: checking various drafts against each other, as well as against our original notes of what was agreed—by us, by others—at various stages of multiple negotiations. The document which begat all this, of course, was the Letter of Representation, instigated by Rupert and concluded between him and Wiley Ryan, by which Ryan instructed Battleman Peale to act on his behalf. This effectively expressed the intention of Ryan and his clique to buy in the public shares of Ergo in sufficient quantity to take control of the company and, simultaneously, authorized Battleman to find them the money to do so—in two stages, over the short then the long term. Naturally, it was the most confidential of documents and, once signed, was rapidly followed by the assembly of a relevant Financial Package, which included the recent Balance Sheets, Income and Cash Flow Statements of Ergo (and its constituent parts) as well as projections derived or massaged from them. Sensitive data concerning the finances and intentions of Wiley Ryan and his crew were also included in this Financial Package, which is why a Letter of Confidentiality had to be drawn up, too, and signed by any party offered and wishing access to the F.P.

THE AGREEMENTS WE are studying and verifying—some already reached, more potential—concern the Bridge Loan, or short-term financing vehicle, which will permit Ryan, et al. to buy the Ergo shares that are tendered. This financing will be undertaken by Battleman and, for the most part, syndicated by us among institutions with whom we are accustomed to dealing, in London, New York, Frankfurt, Zurich, Hong Kong, Singapore and Tokyo; its very scale, which poses the internationally competitive challenge to which—for good or ill—we have risen, will no doubt ultimately require us to venture farther afield, to less familiar pastures. These Syndicate Authorizations guarantee that the loans can be called by a date certain, thus protecting the lenders, whose spirits are blended of greed and timidity and whose entrepreneurial instinct and latitude are bounded by tight constructions of fiduciary responsibility, if not the civil and criminal laws of their governments. The circumstances and timing under which such lenders may give up the loan (in an unlucky outcome) or maintain it in their portfolios (in the event of a happy one) are, for example, points of enormous possible consequence, to be settled upon only with diligence and a view (both practical and theoretical) to many possible contingencies, such as sales gains or losses or any change in the Return on Assets at Ergo, or even the alternative level of interest rates in the market over the interval involved, including a common definition of the "market basket" in which those interest rates are held.

Later, we will have, as carefully, to vet the kaleidoscopic combination of equities and bonds—the layers of "real junk" and "quality junk," of common, preferred and re-set preferred shares—which will take out, no later than one year from our bid, the bridge loans we are organizing. We will have to sell these in the same world markets, though, by and large, to different institutions—or at least different sides of the same institutions—before our work is done, our fee earned.

"There are ordinarily two ways—at least—to look at the same thing," Philip conjectures after a while, stretching his arms above his head then lowering them. "I suppose one could say that we are a little past our moment doing this sort of deal, slightly *too* small and British, not U.S. based, so fledglings in our way. *But*, and it's a big *but*, we are the *only* and the *best* deal around at the moment. Or likely to come along in the foreseeable future. We're hungry—well-mannered, always, it goes without saying, but with an appetite. We're not *un*sophisticated, not *in*experienced, we're wired-in globally—all that—but the real thing is the quality of the deal. Its rarity. We should be calling the terms to our advantage, most if not all of the time. Because the greedy bastards won't find anyplace like this into which to put their money. What I don't want to have happen is for some glorified portfolio manager, or some jumped-up lending officer to decide to keep us on his books at the extortionate rate we'll have to offer for the bridge any longer than it suits us to be there. Not through a technicality."

"We have to be careful not to drive such a hard bargain that—"

"Wouldn't dream of it."

"And the A & O crowd may require a bit of special handling. I mean it's actually possible they may do the bridge *and* the final offering."

"Oh, it's more than possible, I gather," says Philip.

I have begun shuffling envelopes—the morning's incomings—as we speak. But I look up at him now, then suddenly beyond him to the figure of a young woman descending a staircase behind bright glass squares across the cathedral loft at exactly our altitude. She is dressed in a pleated blue skirt and white blouse with a dark cardigan tossed around her shoulders, but any suggestion that she is a schoolgirl is contradicted by the determination of her stride. "Who's that?" I ask.

Philip turns. "Where? Oh, I see . . . American girl. Works the other side of the Chinese Wall, I'm afraid." Like every merchant bank that conducts both trading and corporate finance activities, and so fears even the appearance of conflict of interest—much less a reprimand from the Bank of England or the D.T.I.—Battleman goes to extraordinary lengths to keep its operations discrete and their respective personnel separate from each other. Our card-keys, for example, provide access only to the lifts on the east side of the building and, even then, exclusively to certain floors. The trading offices, in whose stairwell the young American woman is silhouetted, may appear to be close by, but there are no connective passages other than those sealed by alarmed emergency-only fire doors. Like the impressive trading floor itself, they are reached via another street, a different entrance, white rather than blue card-keys. Each evening a central computer prints out a list of who has gone where and when, recording each reading of every card-key. And these lists are audited, although by whom remains a strict secret. Every six weeks or so we are all recoded and there are those who relish the Le Carré-esque dimensions to that exercise: the descent to Admin in the basement, the furtive selection of a P.I.N., the backlit key pads upon which numbers scramble in the blink of an eye and seem never to end on the same positions twice, the sense of approval, access, hierarchy. Even the software and networking and topics screens of our computers are kept distinct from one side of the wall to the other. Corporate finance types—those involved with mergers and acquisitions especially—are inclined to view themselves as intellectually superior to traders, owing to the large number of MBAs and other advanced degrees held among them. Traders, conversely, are apt to see themselves as shrewder, bolder, takers of measurable and attributable risks. Within the firm at any one time, the relative regard in which the members of each group are held is determined by nothing so much as their recent contributions to profits. It is the common, continually updated knowledge of these which can create smugness or apprehension on either side of the Chinese Wall.

"How do you know she's American?" I ask.

"We met."

"Really? Where?"

"In the library, of all places. They brought her through on a tour. She's only here temporarily—on some sort of work-study program, I think. So half of it's having a look around, being won over. Who knows who her father is? Could be a client. Probably not. I don't remember her name. Didn't get it the first time and didn't ask her to repeat it the way you lot do. Figured it shouldn't be too difficult to get it off the blokes in trading."

"Are you interested?"

"She does a very passable 'fuck me right here in the stacks' look, that's all I know. When you see her close-up, you'll understand what I mean. But I'm playing it cautiously. Very damned cautiously. No need to worry."

"You're not married. I take it she's not. Why would I worry?"

"No reason. Chinese Wall, that's all. Small risk, I grant you—probably just imaginary—but why take *any* at this point? Why give *anyone* any reason to talk until this deal is done? When the public knows what we know and we've earned our bonuses, if she's still about and I'm in London, I may very well give her a ring. Bottle of Bolly, dirty weekend in the country might be just what's wanted then."

"Funny, isn't it," I say, "that there is no objection to one's sleeping on the other side of the wall, only to conversation across it. Breakfast and dinner wouldn't normally present a problem, but lunch is guaranteed to be suspicious. It's insane."

"The pretense of the thing must be observed," Philip explains, "even if we all know the substance is bullshit. And then there's the fact that losing money—in this case lots of money—can be a very anti-erotic thought."

"There's truth in that."

"For the time being is what I mean. The short while that remains. I don't know why I'm banging on like this to you. It's not something you'd understand. You've been lucky, you know that, I hope. You came to this country and, as far as I or anyone else can see, without too much effort married about the most desirable, delicious-looking woman in it. That's enough good fortune for anyone's lifetime. I mean, yours couldn't have been the first proposal she'd been offered—obviously."

"Perhaps I seemed exotic."

"No, the Midleton-Lyghams have got too much American blood already for that to be the case. You must have something else—more in your trousers or your repertoire than the rest of us expected. No offense. What interests me, though—and surprises me, if I'm being honest—is that your eye still wanders. Not your hand—well, maybe, maybe not."

"Never," I declare firmly.

"I'll take you at your word. But your eye does notice a good figure on a staircase at quite a respectable distance."

"I should hope so."

"And you are curious enough to ask whose it is."

"Because your needs are always uppermost in my mind."

"Bugger that."

"One day, Philip, you'll stop planning your future long enough to fall in love and marry someone. And when you do, you'll discover that marriage, especially when you have children, will change your life rather a lot, but your nature not at all."

"Odd you should mention that. I had a very disturbing dream the other morning and now I can only remember the end of it. Was a party, family gathering of some sort—you know, all ages and couples with children about—daytime. I was talking to one person, then the next, no one I knew from actual life, in the usual meaningless sort of way one does. For a moment, I don't know why, it seemed that I had been put in charge of some children. Then, suddenly, they were all gone—all but one. Chaos. Then quiet. I was talking to a small boy—maybe three years old, not a baby—and he was answering, very nicely, although I've tried since and can't remember the words he used. All the time—it wasn't long—he was looking away, in the same direction I was. Then he turned to look at me and I knew immediately who he was. I knew that this face which was so beautiful and so real was one I had never seen in the world, not because it didn't exist, but because it wasn't here yet. The instant he turned, John, I recognized that that boy was my son— was *going to be* my son. I did. I swear. Do you believe we sometimes glimpse the future in our dreams? I do."

I hesitate. "Yes," I say at last.

Philip examines me. "What is bothering you?" he asks at last.

"Nothing that fatal. Just that, at the end of the day, there's still a difference between creating an industry and dismantling one, isn't there?"

"Damn it, John. You know the talking points. We've been over them 'til one's blue in the face."

"I know."

"Don't let your faith lapse. Not now, John. We are hired not for our knowledge of what may or may not be God's will—not as saints, but simply as professionals. You know what they say: 'The power of the sword of Damocles is not that it falls but that it hangs.' We're not just helping Ergo to do what's necessary. We're sounding the alarm for every other company like it, before it's too late."

It is apparent to me that Philip believes what he is saying, or has come to believe it anyway. So the chasm between us is the one that always separates the faithful from the rest, but it is not so wide, I think, so dangerous or unnegotiable as it might at first appear. I am a solid member of the congregation, after all, with a long record of attendance and with too much at stake, too many people I love depending upon me, not to go the distance. I will argue the point—privately, intellectually, here, now; that's all. "I hope so," I tell him. "You don't know how much."

"Old Chinese proverb," he says as he smiles. " 'It is good to know the truth and to speak it, but better to talk of palm trees'. . . . Oh God, listen, I'm very sorry. I forgot to tell you that you had a message from Dicky Mortlake. Meant to write it down. Completely escaped my mind in all this conversation. I don't think it's too late."

"Dicky? Did he say what he wanted?"

"Wasn't Dicky himself. Someone in his office calling for him. Message was: can you meet Dicky for lunch. Said it was rather important."

"Can't imagine why," I say and check my diary. "Where?"

"Wiltons—at a quarter to one."

"Very grand, too. Seems okay. Am I supposed to ring him back?"

"Regrets only. Oh, and John, the place is bound to be full of tycoons. So try not to lose your temper."

"I just try to see things from every viewpoint," I explain. "Really, Philip. Buck up! I was bought and paid for a long time ago."

13

A ND SO, AFTER a few more hours of the gossip and speculation that often pass for analysis in the senior reaches of such firms as ours, Philip goes off to the Brasserie Rocque and I down King William Street toward the Monument Station of the District and Circle Lines. The Advent wind is crisp, heavy, almost maritime. I turn up the collar of my top coat against it. Overhead, layers of cloud—white beyond grey, grey beyond white—shuffle furiously toward Europe. Between the river and St. Paul's, they sail swiftly. Taking a shortcut through St. Swithins Lane, I pass a man I have never seen and for a moment he seems an extension of the climate: his stride temperate but not at all crisp, his expression phlegmatic. His manner stirs in me a certain low-grade, metaphoric apprehension for I wonder if we at Battleman will be up to the task we have set ourselves and able to play the American-style game we have entered. I wonder if we will actually be able to win, or what will happen if we don't.

I buy a copy of the *Spectator* from a news agent near Monument and take the uncrowded tube to St. James' Park. I page to "High Life" and read it, then "Low Life," and a review of a *nouvelle anglaise* restaurant in Battersea before my stop. In the park, there are the usual pigeon-feeders with time on their hands and a few tourists designing snapshots with the lake and Buckingham Palace in the background. The wind has quickened the dark water, even brought up white caps from its surface. Yet, despite the chill, the scene feels more autumnal than wintry. London is damp today. The air does not sting. There is no hint of the coming solstice in the grim sky, hardly any of Christmas, except in shop windows along Jermyn Street. These are decorated with the newest stripes and cheques of the most fashionable shirtmakers. I stop to admire two or three, making a mental note of a pattern which combines the palest greens, greys and blues.

I am five minutes early. At twenty to one, Wiltons is just beginning to come to life. I hand my coat, tucking my worn crimson scarf into the left sleeve, to a young man in a white waiter's jacket who stands at the near end of the bar. "Joining Mr. Mortlake," I tell him.

The young man, his black hair combed perfectly, nods. Another, fortyish and dressed as a banker, approaches. "Mr. Mortlake?" he inquires politely, then immediately continues "hasn't arrived yet."

"But he's booked?"

"Yes, indeed. You are Mr. Brook?"

"That's right."

"Would you like to come through now or—"

"I'll wait here," I say, "if that's all right." But the space on the plush banquette I have eyed is abruptly taken by a vague-seeming elderly man who has entered the restaurant behind me. "On second thought—" I add.

I am led past the Victorian oyster bar already arrayed with baby lobsters, a whole smoked turkey and dressed crab; its marble counter festive with trays of colorful North African vegetables and iced buckets holding bottles of champagne. The several places before its high stools are set and ready, but none is yet occupied. Patrick, the Head Oysterman, looks up from his preparations as we go by.

I am given a table in the front room, against the wall and opposite a row of booths. From the low olive velvet chair I can examine all arrivals. "Would you care for a drink now, Sir?" the head waiter inquires. "Glass of champagne?" he suggests.

"Why not? It's nearly Christmas, after all."

"Indeed it is, Sir. Can't think where the year's gone. Won't be a minute."

During the next quarter hour, party by party, the rooms fill. And by the time Dicky arrives, the booths across from us are occupied by, among others, a duke with unusually splendid tresses and one of Her Majesty's former Secretaries of State for Foreign Affairs, wearing a camel cardigan beneath his suit.

Richard Mortlake is a stockbroker with a reputation for being lucky, an affable—if now and then arrogant—chap whose instinct is supposed by some to give his clients an edge. He has handled several of the Midleton-Lygham accounts for years, since he himself was at Battleman Peale and met Julia's father a few days after the latter's principal broker expired of the effects of prostate cancer. Dicky is my age—or thereabout. But, in many ways, our journeys this far through life would seem to have been in opposite directions: his toward certainty, mine away. His affection for the products and conclusions of his own mind frequently confounds me. For, to Dicky, no issue is ever so deserving of the world's immediate attentions as one which has lately caught his interest; no observation so penetrating as that upon which he has just that morning stumbled. "He brings an intensely professional air to an utterly amateur talent," Philip summarized dismissively when Dicky still worked on the other side of our Chinese Wall. "Strictly second-class stuff in a third-class culture." But since Dicky left for a huge signing bonus and managing directorship in the London office of a Wall Street competitor, he has not been much on Philip's mind. He is, after all, a Sales and Trading type, not "one of ours." Yet he has managed to keep some of Julia's family's money (certain funds used to support the estate, for example) and even a bit of mine—and, in fact, to have done rather well with both.

One of the most interesting things about Dicky Mortlake—about many of the most successful people when one thinks about it—is the facility with which he straddles identities, standing out in each camp for his well-recognized strength in another. Among brokers, he is known as a technician, or "quant." Among technicians, for his skill as a broker, a man who can be trusted to handle *people*. It is this duality which separates him from either pack and gives weight to his words. Mystifying each camp with a glib knowledge of the other's arena, he leaves many people afraid to bet against him. The second son of a chartered accountant in Basingstoke, he fell in with the right crowd at Charterhouse, worked hard, then ventured west to do a degree, on partial scholarship, at the University of Texas in Austin. After graduation he joined a Battleman correspondent firm in Houston and eventually, through that connection, found his way home to London.

"John," he calls, a table away now and advancing toward me. His voice is hoarse, throaty as if in the last stages of a cold. "John," he repeats. "Sorry to have kept you. Really!" Dicky's left arm is in plaster, suspended in a sling he has fashioned from one of his wife's Hermès scarves. The scarf is white, displaying a row of golden equine profiles.

"You haven't," I tell him. "I was early."

He glances at the watch he wears eccentrically gartering the outside of his right shirt sleeve. "Oh? Were you? What's the time? Didn't realize. Felt *later* somehow."

"Long way from the City. Or were you around here to begin with?"

"Client of mine's in Park Place," Dicky explains. "So it was fortuitous when I got your message. Rang and stopped in to see him on the way—something I've been meaning to do. Goes on a bit, that one. Few minutes feel like an eternity, you know the sort. Never mind." The smile which overtakes Dicky's round, rather concave face is jovial, knowing, professionally contagious. Momentarily framed against an ochre wall and brown velvet curtains, with his receding, curly hair, he seems a corrupted, if still sagacious cherub.

"When *you* got *my* message, did you say?" I ask him. "What message was that?"

"Inviting me to lunch."

"What?"

"Here. Now."

"All right," I say. "We'll go Dutch. If that's what you'd like. Divide the bill. Not a problem."

"Hold on. You honestly thought—that I'd invited you? . . . You did, didn't you? That *I'd* asked *you*. To Wiltons, of all places?"

"Afraid I did. And conversely—"

"I thought that you had done the same. Did you think I was trying to buy you off?"

"I hadn't thought about it. If I had, I suppose I might have thought that you'd been lucky in the market. And that you wanted to talk about it."

"You're not having me on?" Dicky asks finally.

"Winding you up? No. To what end."

"Well, then, if I didn't ring you and you never rang me and yet here we both are, sitting at a table at Wiltons, who?"

"*Who* is having fun with us? Exactly."

"Cannot imagine, off hand. It would have to be one of a rather small set of people. Like the grey area in Venn diagrams. Anyway, in for a penny in for a pound as they say. Have you given any thought to the menu?"

"No."

"I'm going to have a baby lobster, I fancy. Start with half a dozen oysters. Which I can't resist. Though I'd love an Ogen melon *almost* as much."

"I think I'll stay with something hot. Bisque and grilled turbot."

Dicky nods. "Should we have a glance at the wine list then? . . . Tell me," he asks, "how did 'my' message to you come? If you can remember."

"Philip passed it on. He said someone in your office had telephoned—a while before; it had escaped his mind during our meeting. Gave me time and place, you know. Said I wasn't to ring you back unless I had a conflict."

"He didn't say *who* in my office?"

"No. I'll ask him, of course, but—"

"And that was all?"

"Yes. How did 'my' invitation reach you?"

"Same way, only I answered the phone. Woman's voice, she didn't identify herself. Wouldn't've paid particular attention if she had. Telephoning for you, she said. Very apologetically and politely. You were meant to have been unavailable. Same idea. Regrets only. And who regrets a free lunch at Wiltons? There was one other thing, come to think of it. She did imply that there was some urgency. Today better than tomorrow, that sort of thing. 'Arabesque', does that word mean anything to you?"

"Arabesque? No. Nothing."

"Maybe it's the name of another restaurant. Though I was pretty sure she said it was something you wanted to talk about. From the tone, you understand, as though it would ring a bell with me, which it doesn't, I'm afraid."

"A-r-a-b-e-s-q-u-e?"

"I suppose," Dicky replies. "Don't really know. My spelling's a bit up the snout."

"Never heard of it. Unless—wait a minute—that was the name of a film, wasn't it?"

"Anything's possible," Dicky Mortlake interrupts. "You can ask Philip if it means anything to him."

"I'll do that."

"Seriously plutocratic in these environs," Dicky says with a sigh after another moment, "if you have a look around. Seriously rich men shunning their clubs as well as *quite* a few chaps most clubs would shun, though probably not a bank in the land. Fascinating. Different scale entirely to any of ours. They're drawing buckets, these blokes. Absolute buckets they're drawing."

"Some of them. Well, I'll grant you, quite a few."

"Me, I'm just a salesman—admittedly, a glorified one, but still a salesman at the end of the day."

"Do you really believe that?"

"I believe that you make your own luck—not entirely, mind you, but to the extent that you don't, there isn't time to be fussed worrying about it. It's a very competitive world we're living in. Very. Like a game of tag, when one thinks about it. *You're* frozen. *You're* still playing. One needs to try and understand the basics of it, as best one can."

"Are you going to be more concrete?" I inquire.

"Couldn't possibly be. Not in this market. Wouldn't hazard a guess. Perverse, isn't it? I'm permitted to chat to you—well, could do if I had anything of substance to say—but for you to do the same and therefore benefit me amounts to a crime. Prison potentially. Strictly *verboten*. Bloody unfair."

"You have to put yourself in the mind of the authorities. Anyone who works on the M and A side is presumed to have knowledge the market doesn't have yet. Brokers, whatever they may or may not have overheard or figured out, are, I'm afraid, presumed to be speculating."

"Manufacturing hypotheticals," Dicky adds sarcastically. "Most days, I'd rather rely on instinct than information anyway."

"That way you can sleep at night," I agree. "I wasn't built for a life on the edge. I don't suspect you were either."

There is a famous story about Dicky Mortlake and, as I watch him cover one oyster after another with cayenne, I remember it. He was in Los Angeles, spending a year with one of Battleman's correspondent firms before returning to London. Because the markets with which he dealt were in New York and the time in New York was three hours ahead of California at any given moment, it was necessary for him to be at his desk by six-thirty—and so up at five. In Houston, he'd had a roommate with a clock radio, but in L.A. he was living alone. He rang up the phone company and attempted to organize the sort of regular alarm call his friends in London did. But to his astonishment, such service came with a forbidding charge. "What did you do, finally?" I'd asked him when he first told me of the situation. "Thought about it for a moment," he'd replied. "Then—brainstorm—rang the hall porter at my club in London. My father'd put me up blind so I was young to be a member. Five o'clock in the morning in L.A. is, after all, one in the afternoon in London. Lunch time. Perfect. After that, he rang me every weekday at that hour." "How expensive was that?" I'd asked in some amazement. "It was free," he'd explained. "Chap would ring five times then hang up. I never answered once that entire year—except on the last day, of course, to thank him."

"How are your oysters?" I ask now.

"Absolutely superb," Dicky replies, raising a half shell in his fingers, vacuuming the bivalve. Boilly's oil painting of *Les Mangeurs d'Huitres* hangs nearby and Dicky seems a latter-day replica of its intent eighteenth-century subjects. "Who the fuck is this? he asks then, suddenly replacing the shell on his plate and looking up.

Near and coming toward us, a lean young man in skin-tight black lycra bicycle jams elbows past several parties waiting to be seated.

"I'm very sorry, Sir," one waiter insists sternly.

But the young man, who seems to know where he is headed, presses on until, in a few seconds, he is beside our table. "Mr. Brook?" he asks.

"I'm Mr. Brook."

"Papers you asked for."

"I didn't ask for any papers. From whom?"

"Your office, Sir. My instructions were to give them only to you. Nobody else. No exceptions. You're *John* Brook, are you?"

"Yes. . . . Thank you."

"Signature please." The messenger places a legal size envelope beside my fork, then departs in a haste as impolitic as that in which he arrived. Two of the waiters quickly apologize to me, but I tell them it is I who should beg their indulgence.

"Everything's so urgent once you've done an MBA, isn't it?" Dicky asks. "What have they sent you that's so important you have to read it with your turbot?"

"I can't imagine," I admit, tearing at the wired cellophane tape that secures the flap. Inside the envelope are three sheets of A-4 paper, each flat, unfolded. I remove the topmost, glance at it momentarily, then study it for seconds longer. Next, I examine each of those beneath it.

They are similar in form: cash-flow statements from which all identifying headings have been removed. I do not recognize the numbers as any I have reviewed or worked on recently. "These make no sense," I tell Dicky.

"What are they?"

"Your guess is as good as mine."

"Let's have a look," he says, beginning to reach.

"No," I say, pushing the papers aside. "Best not. On general principles."

"Have it your way," Dicky says, secreting his curiosity. "As long as you're doing about the bill."

"Nothing personal."

"Understand. Better safe than sorry."

"You're not missing out on much," I explain. "If it came from *my* office and *I* can't make heads or tails of it, how could you?"

"Couldn't say," Dicky replies, "without seeing for myself. Could I?"

"How is your wife?" I ask, for distraction.

"Loving the country. Really loving it."

"Good."

"Fucking strange being married. Ever feel that?"

"Now and then."

"Myself, never thought I would be," he continues. "Oh well, happens to the best of us. . . . Most of the rest of us, too. Wife, couple of kids. Nanny, school fees—the entire route pretty well marked out. What? Not whingeing, mind you. One's lucky to be successful, after all. Not everyone is. But success does become something you have to have, after a while. Almost like food. Air. You gear yourself up for it, take on responsibilities. Overhead. Addictive stuff."

"Very."

"Period of making ends meet. Keeping up, you know. Then, before you know it, the woman's ass has spread, the kids have left home. Where are you?"

I do not answer.

"Where are you?" Dicky repeats. "Fortunate if they come round is the answer. For Sunday lunch . . . Christmas, that sort of thing. If they remember to send a card on your birthday. You're middle-aged, lusting for the sort of fuck you're unlikely ever again to find and probably aren't even capable of anymore. Memories, that's all then. The rear-view mirror. What's the point really?"

"You're letting your imagination run away with you," I tell him.

"Taking a realistic view of what's ahead, that's all. Over the long run, admittedly," Dicky says, cajoling some lobster from its shell.

"I'm not so sure."

"Tell yourself the truth, John: except for certain—and they are very, very few—lucky ones at any given point in time, there are actually, when one thinks about it, just two different sorts of people in the world, aren't there? Blokes craving sex they don't have—and aren't very likely to come by. And other blokes who have—mind you, all too often who have to have—sex they don't even want; never did, or at least don't any longer."

"What's got you so depressed?"

"I'm not depressed."

"You could have fooled me."

"Staring life in the face, pure and simple. Being honest with myself, and with you, too. Oh, I admit I can sometimes fall in love with the sound of my own prognostications. And I'll admit that now and then they're . . . a little too full of BS, perhaps, but, at the end of the day, that's my *specialité*. I flog the stuff and, often as not, it flies."

"One day, though, someone may figure out—"

"—that it's heavier than air, I know. And what then?"

"Wait and see, I suppose. Wait and see." I look at Dicky, surprised by a sense of futility I had not observed in him previously, while he continues to dismember his lobster at an imperturbable pace. He is aware, I'm sure, that he has let his guard down; having done so, he is quiet, reflective, abruptly focused upon his food.

After lunch, Dicky and I leave with still-lit cigars and share a taxi back to the City. Drizzle has begun, but by the time we reach the Square Mile it lets up. On a damp pavement near Finsbury Circus, a vagrant stands idly in front of the building which houses Dicky's present employer. As Dicky races from our taxi toward his entrance, I watch the vagrant seize a pigeon from the air just above foot level, then force it into a paper bag of more than usual strength. But the light changes and the taxi, contained in traffic, lurches south toward Battleman Peale.

14

"DON'T WORRY WHAT people are thinking about you. They're not," Julia advises.

"Of course they're not," replies Simon Basildon, the Midleton-Lyghams' fastidiously dressed solicitor.

"No. I know that," Julia goes on. "It was a sort of maxim of my mother's, that's all. I didn't mean it in any particular way. But people in this village do expect something of whomever lives in the big house— not of me, *per se*, any more than Adrian . . . any more than Daddy."

"They most assuredly do," Simon Basildon agrees.

"China tea or India?" Julia asks.

"China, please."

"John?"

"China, thank you."

"Mr. Basildon thought we ought to meet—just us," my wife explains, repeating a fact of which each of us is already aware, "in order to review certain matters." It is late afternoon, a January Thursday of midwinter spring.

"Matters of some importance to the future of the estate." A tall man with a belly beneath his tweed waistcoat, Simon Basildon must stoop as he leans forward to receive his cup and saucer. He has long silver hair, still plentiful for a man nearly seventy, and reddish cheeks. His gold half-glasses bestow an air of self-conscious self-satisfaction not unexpected in a—indeed *the*—senior partner of Pitfields.

Caveat lies in place next to Julia's chair, his eye on the gingerbread to be sliced, his restraint trained to the point of instinct.

"Julia?" I ask, between swallows.

"Darling?"

"Have you asked Rupert to join us?"

"No. I haven't."

"I'd just rather thought—"

"Well, of course, it's . . . logical . . . in a certain way . . . because he's so knowledgeable. About certain things. Where I'm not. And you . . . don't have time to be interested, really."

"Such as the shoot?"

"Well . . . for one thing. Lots of bits and pieces behind the scene. But Mr. Basildon thought it best we meet privately for now."

"Of course, I take your point," Mr. Basildon says. "Your cousin Rupert *is* both knowledgeable *and* extremely clever. I have no doubt there will be any number of times when you will want to consult him about one thing or another, when his opinion will be most valuable to you. But by the peculiar nature of things, Castlemorland is to be yours, Julia. Yours and then your children's—Andrew's, one supposes, but I am through second-guessing fate. What I *am* saying is that, in my experience of living, there are some discussions best left to those they concern, to *immediate* families. With no reflection on anyone else. I am as fond of Rupert as you are, but his life is not here. He has the title now, so be it, and prospects that would make most human beings delirious. But whenever you mix blood and money, there's apt to be an explosion, sooner or later. Best to avoid it from the outset was my way of thinking.

"I think, at this point, it might be useful to review a bit of history," he continues, angling the temples of his glasses so as to be able to read his notes. "After Waterloo, the Midleton-Lygham family acquired *even* a *more* fabulous collection of pictures than they had on the Grand Tour during the century previous. Those pictures include the most prized at Castlemorland to this day. In any event, in due course, emulating their neighbors, your family attempted to develop a new town—with a coal mine, mind you—on a non-contiguous estate. But they were defrauded by their agent. They weren't so fortunate as to have had Hillyards—or a man of the late George Paxton's quality—about in those days. The coal proved of low quality and the entire project a disastrous failure. Those losses forced the sale of some land and second-drawer pictures and, more crucially, the mortgaging of a considerable part of the Northamptonshire holding, Claydown.

"In time, as we all know, came the marriage of your grandfather, Julia, to Edna Stacey of New York. She was an extraordinarily beautiful woman, and the daughter of a mining and banking tycoon from . . . Chicago, I believe, and, later, New York."

"Nevertheless," Julia says, "it wasn't until the government wanted death duties after my great grandfather and later my grandfather died that we were forced to sell out of Northamptonshire. That's the point you're getting to, I take it: death duties."

"Your father," Simon Basildon continues, "much to his credit, invariably sought and followed the best advice. He had given over the estate to Adrian, beginning just after the government once again permitted owners of stately homes to do so, when Adrian was still at agricultural college. Andrew had no reasonable expectation of his imminent demise at that point in time and so the whole business seemed to be working out rather well. Andrew paid Adrian a market rent and otherwise continued to live in his house and conduct his life as he always had done. The two of them began living out the 'seven year curse' for which the law provides. But your father, of course, very sadly fell ill and died soon thereafter. And so what we had on our hands was a 'failed PET'—that is a Potentially Exempt Transfer. Our options then were either to pay taxes amounting to some forty percent of the value of the house and chattels or to seek what is known as Conditional Exemption, through English Heritage—which, in the end, is the course upon which we decided. Castlemorland being Castlemorland, we did not foresee, nor did we experience any problem there. Conditional Exemption was granted—conditional, actually, upon the house and its contents being accessible to the public on a regular basis. But these terms were not onerous: Wednesdays in the summer months, for instance, and, even then, only for thirty or so days each year.

"The difficulty is that Adrian did not expect to die in the foreseeable future. And so we find ourselves in a compromised position. If there were larger farms or better leases, the situation might be eased. But I fear there's nothing to be done on that front. Obtaining vacant possession of any of these anytime soon would be most unlikely."

"I have no wish to disturb anyone—in any house or on any farm on the Castlemorland Estate," Julia tells him. "What *can* you be thinking?"

"Our analysis is merely *de*scriptive—not *pre*scriptive at this point. Adrian has left the estate to you. His Letter of Wishes expresses the hope that you will make your best effort to pass it on to Andrew. And he has even gone so far as to suggest a disposition of chattels that might, come that day, be fair and equitable to your daughter. But he has imposed no legal requirement.

"The estate was entailed until, by their mutual signatures, the late Marquess—your father, I mean—and his father, Thomas, broke that entailment after the War. They wanted to look ahead, not backward. I remember them saying so—just that! It was the mood of the time."

"In a nutshell?" Julia presses.

"We will have to ask for re-exemption of both the house and chattels. One can never take such things for granted, although, being honest, it would seem a formality at this point. So, provided you are willing to meet the terms of that exemption—"

"Public access? Of the sort you describe? Oh, absolutely!"

"Then there ought to be no reason why any obligation under the inheritance tax scheme cannot be deferred. But—and it's quite a substantial *but*—you *will* owe taxes on other funds you've inherited. And, apart from those, from now on you'll be responsible for expenses on a rather different level than you may be used to. It goes without saying that Castlemorland is a rich man's house."

"That *is* a problem," I exclaim light-heartedly, trying vainly to relieve the developing tension.

Simon Basildon flicks a speck from the corner of his left eye, re-sets his reading glasses. "On the one hand, the American fortune is wearing a bit thin by now, even that part of it which found its way over here and remained undivided due to primogeniture. And there are certain anachronistic, shall we say, restrictions on the original Chicago trusts, which haven't helped their performance—such and such a percentage having to be invested in metals, steel, even railroads. On the other hand, your husband's management of the discretionary accounts in recent years has yielded a very satisfactory surplus indeed."

"I only wish," I say, "that I could take credit. But I can't. Couple of the accounts are in the hands of a broker called Richard Mortlake. Very clever, competent fellow. And even the larger ones Rupert and I merely placed in the hands of professionals we thought would do well by them. The credit's entirely theirs."

"Whatever the case may be," Simon Basildon explains, "the profits built up in the last half-decade will take much of the pressure off, even considering that, as I've said, there will be taxes due on most of those as well. Still, they should provide some breathing room. But if it is your plan to *keep* Castlemorland and to *live* here—"

"Of course, that's our plan," Julia bursts forth. "To keep Castlemorland, *certainly. Without question.* As to how much of each year, or each week, we intend to live here, that will take a little time to be worked out."

"If that is your plan, it will require much very careful thought. You may even wish, in time, to consider placing the house in a charitable trust."

"To turn it over?" Julia asks.

"Only to a trust the family would control."

"Because beautiful as many of them are, once a house becomes National Trust, even with the family staying on in some *encoignure* until the cows come home, to me it's just a glorified country house hotel. Sometimes, not even that; sorry to say. The whole idea of it gives me serious sense-of-humor failure."

"I agree," I say.

"Suppose we simply wish to go on," Julia asks, "as my family always have gone on?"

"I should imagine it can be done. Though not without some strain . . . and surely not without proper planning."

"John?" Julia asks—almost beseeches.

"We'll come through it somehow," I tell her. "Whatever it takes." Even as I assure her, though, I am concerned. Through no one's fault, an accident, the burden of Castlemorland now seems to be falling upon me and I wonder how—even if—I will be able to manage it.

"I could go back to work," she offers.

"No. Or not yet. Better you stay with the children."

"There's not a lot of money in academia, but I'll bet I could find something else. I'm sure if I looked—"

"Don't worry," I promise. "Things will come clear—pretty soon, with decent luck."

"Because I couldn't bear to be the one to break my family's connection with the land. Pretentious though that may sound, I just couldn't bear it." She stands and walks toward a window from which a rising landscape can be observed beyond a courtyard.

"Castlemorland is not a weekend getaway. Anything but," Simon

Basildon proceeds after a delicate pause. "You are right, Julia, in feeling that to live here is to accept certain obligations—to the house itself, to all the physical parts of the estate—but even more to the village and the people who live here. That can be very pleasant, much of the time, I'm sure—endlessly gratifying. Certainly, it was for your father and no doubt would have been for Adrian. But occasionally one may come to feel one is merely playing a role—doing what's expected of gentry. For an audience which no longer really cares: churchgoers who don't believe; the young whose ambitions drive them to the larger towns, or on to London at the first possible moment; professionals who've bought in the area for high prices and who sleep here two or three nights a week because they find it aesthetically soothing."

"What choice is there?" Julia asks.

"I don't know that there is one. One supposes you *could* make some arrangement with Rupert, of the sort you mentioned, if you and John decided that you definitely did not want to live here regularly."

"With Rupert? He's not nearly rich enough to buy this off me. More to the point, he's not married; he doesn't have children. And when you've had as many affairs with twenty-year-old models as he's done, how likely are you, really, ever to settle down?"

"By 'arrangement' I didn't mean to sell Rupert the estate. I meant to share its responsibilities. Granted, he'd rattle around a bit. Only in the vaguest terms did the idea even occur to me. I certainly haven't breathed a word to him."

"The truth is we're going to have to feel our way. John cannot commute to the City every day from here."

"Why not?" I ask.

"It's too far. And, anyway, we have the house in London. And a life there, which we all enjoy midweek. John's career depends on his being there and obviously we are going to need that income. We're not in a position to forego it. And he loves his work. He's fantastic at it. He has a brilliant future in his firm. Everyone says. We'll simply take life a day, and perhaps a trial, at a time—and see."

"Then we understand each other," Simon Basildon says. "I'll meet with the accountants and we'll give you a more exact estimate of liabilities as soon as possible."

"And of assets, too, please." Julia laughs.

"Why, naturally. And I'll have a word with the boys at Hillyards and maybe they can arrange a crash course in farming and forestry for both you and John."

"That would be excellent. Meanwhile, just in case, I'll ring a friend at Brimblebys. We're not in his period, really, but he has an eye, and he'd have my interest at heart in any advice he gave on flogging this or that in the event we find ourselves short. And, *most important,* John will go back to the City and set about the business of making enough money to relieve us of that and all of our other problems. What do you think?" Julia winks at me.

"With any luck," I tell my wife.

"Good, then. Better hurry up."

THERE IS A legend that a modern resident of Castlemorland saw a poltergeist and sketched him. The resident had strayed in the dark from the Long Walk; the poltergeist of his drawing resembled a medieval knight in a costume the modern man could not have seen.

Sometimes, these days especially, as the silver thin light of winter fails into an early dark, it feels as though I, too, can discern the tracery which connects us to one another and to this house—an improbable tracery of fate which bound us to this place before we knew of its existence, which sketched upon our unconscious minds, as vividly as upon that artist's, the image of its ghosts.

Time, I often think, does not warn us of its junctures: I was a tourist, on a visa from the States via Hong Kong, then, without expectation, the lover of a woman. I did not, could not appreciate the history which devolved upon her, which I assumed with our marriage vow, which manifests itself in the voices, the emerging minds and faces of our son and daughter. When I was younger, imagining the life that would unfold before me, a different wife, different children suffused my fantasies. Who was she? Where are they?

I recall sizzling platters, lamb with scallions in Hong Kong—my earliest conversations with Rupert about joining Battleman Peale. Hong Kong was on fire as he, Philip and I walked after dinner, the lofty parallelogrammatic windows of hotels and office towers incandescent with ambition. I agreed—with no deep thought of England, no real knowledge of Julia.

Now, though, I wonder if I, too, might then have rendered Castlemorland's poltergeist so faithfully. Perhaps, I think, but never mind. Never mind.

Very quickly Julia's prediction proves correct: we are going to have to feel our way. The imminence and urgency of the Wiley Ryan clique's buyout bid for Ergo—the meetings among our team and with our hoped-for syndicators, the need constantly to revise estimates of offering price and performance to reflect updated data, to consult, even console advisors and (in the case of A & O especially) advisors to advisors—require me to spend more of my time than ever in the City. And the days are short—eight-hour bursts of illumination in the otherwise pitch season. At Castlemorland, too, the demands for attention and time expand. First Monday mornings and, soon thereafter, Friday afternoons are scheduled with meetings on forestry, farming, village leases: the postmaster/confectioner wishes a new sign; the petrol station an eastward, more gradually sloping exit. The estate owns thirty houses in the adjacent village. Two are vacant, prey for squatters; one, perhaps, for sale. Thus, the week is worn away from both ends, country life gnawing at city, as well as the reverse.

I drive for hours through the early morning, the late night fog, the drizzle, the clear almost inter-stellar openness along motorway and hedge-walled lane, from or toward my dreaming children, guided only by the beam of the 911's headlamps against the fragile winter atmosphere. I listen to Górecki's No. 3; Dinu Lipatti playing Bach's *Partita No. 1* and Mozart's *Sonata No. 8 in A Major*; Chris DeBurgh and Cole Porter.

I am torn. On one hand, I am awed, dominated, excited, intrigued by Castlemorland—proud that my children share it, if afraid of the distance at which it may, inevitably, place them to my own history, my own country. The estate is, by any standard, a summit of sorts, yet the life lived there is so often occupied with trivialities—flora and fauna festivals, for example—that I occasionally feel claustrophobic, ironically trapped by a vaster, more exquisite and tangible wealth than I have ever sought. Still, they are strange and strangely powerful, this house and landscape which impart and seize one's identity in almost equal measure. Since school, I have been trained to live, work, struggle for my own prosperity and my family's. Indeed this goal has always seemed sufficient unto itself—if not all of which one might be capable, certainly enough. Yet the shadow cast by such a solipsistic perspective across the future is the prospect that, for even heroic effort, like so many others, I would neither create nor preserve any institution larger than myself— even Battleman, of which I am but a solitary partner among many. Castlemorland, though, being Julia's now by fate, mine by marriage and our children's by birthright, alters this equation; ancient past and unsure future bind us in their taut and pretty bow.

Our attempt to commute, or to handle all of Castlemorland's business over each weekend, seems doomed. On a Sunday afternoon a few weeks afterward we decide, tentatively, that at the end of the school year, between kindergarten and first grade, the kids and Julia should move into the house full time. I will come on Fridays, leave on Mondays, drive out, perhaps, on Wednesdays, in seasons of longer days and less work. The light is thin; the orange sun hesitates on the ridge beyond the temple, cool as a picture.

Later in the same week, I encounter Rupert, by surprise, coming out of the gamekeeper's office far back in the converted stable block.

"I didn't know you were here," I say.

"Didn't you? Left you a message."

"With Julia? . . . Or Topley?"

"On your voice mail."

"That explains it. I've been on the horn to Philip twice already today, going over everything: who called, whom to call. So I didn't check my own voice mail. Should've—just assumed."

"Not to worry. I've been to see Mr. Cole."

"Mr. Cole?"

"The gamekeeper."

"I know who Mr. Cole is."

"Julia asked me to."

"She did? I know she said she was going to."

"Just to make sure things were in hand. To—"

"She acts quickly, my wife."

Rupert ignores my interruption. "Unless, of course, *you'd* prefer to deal with it," he says courteously. "I don't want to tread—"

"You're not treading," I assure him. "Actually, it was my idea."

"Was it?"

"You have experience with it that I don't, after all. I mean, by now, I have a pretty good idea of what's going on and, I suppose, of what should be going on—but intellectually not instinctively."

"There *are* one or two wrinkles now that you mention it," Rupert explains, directing our slow stroll into the sunlight of the south garden. "Not that there's such a thing as a right way and a wrong way, in any absolute sense, but in the context of each time and place, I think, there is; there must be. What's got a bit muddled is what we are trying to do, really. Are we trying to hold on in the old-fashioned way, shooting the biggest bags on the best days, with friends, for pleasure? Or are we trying to turn a profit—of whichever kind? If the latter, do we hope for a direct profit or an indirect one, if you take my meaning?"

"I think I do."

"Should the paying guns and let days support the thing, in a literal sense—income and outgoing always in balance—or, given our situation, ought we to take a more sophisticated view as to the profit that can be derived from the atmosphere. Atmospheres are important. . . . I know, I know," he hesitates, holds up his hand. "The idea would appall poor Adrian, absolutely appall him. But Adrian did not live in the real world. His life was spent trying desperately—even, perhaps, courageously—to do the one thing no human being can, which is to stand still. Stop time. Now, he's not alive at all and it's up to us—to Julia and you, really—to perhaps do a re-think."

"I'm listening."

"It's just an opinion, of course, because it has always seemed to me that, when it comes to shooting, there are two elements to the equation: congeniality and sport. It's really that simple, isn't it? Taking the last first, we are not badly off. Cole's on top of that aspect. I doubt there are more than half a dozen gamekeepers in Britain who could do the job he's done—fewer who would improve upon it. So, until one of those becomes available, well . . . it's in the congeniality department where change may be wanted. Reluctantly, perhaps, but what other choice is there? What would you think of this idea? I've only just had it, so don't be afraid to be critical. Battleman, or a syndicate of us there, might take a number of dates for a good price. A *substantial* number of the most desirable ones, though, naturally, we'd keep this to ourselves. For the sake of atmospherics—as I said. To all intents and purposes, we'd be carrying on just as always. The outward and visible appearance of the shoot wouldn't change, but its finances would be, so to speak, rationalized. The traditional shoot could manage the other days. Ralph and Piers and their ilk—the others who've subscribed—would be able to go off in pristine glory. Whichever friends you and Julia ultimately come to feel you didn't want to mix in among business types, provisions could be made for—of course. But, on the whole, it might take quite a lot off your shoulders."

"Bears thought," I say.

"Doesn't it? Very little danger, if you ask me, for a not insubstantial reward. After all, why should you and my cousin bear an expense which is legitimately business? On the other hand, why on earth shouldn't you make the most of an asset you happen to have to hand? In a way, now, Castlemorland—particularly its shoot—is your calling card. *And* . . . it couldn't be more suitable to the niche we happen to occupy. No point in sending clients off elsewhere, I wouldn't have thought; is there? Better to reap the obvious advantage. The distinction between what is social and what is business is becoming nonsense anyway. Why do you think houses like Castlemorland were built in the first place? Not as a setting for quiet, unassuming times among friends, I can tell you. To impress the King; to curry favor at court—gain what there was to be had. Purely and simply business."

"Convinced me," I tell him, "but it's not really my decision."

"Nothing that can't wait," Rupert quickly defers.

"Well, it can and it can't. It's something we'll have to tackle in due course. Right now, it all does seem rather a lot to deal with."

"It would have been more complicated had they ever married and Isabel survived," Rupert suggests.

I am stunned by the brazenness of his observation. "Yes, I imagine it would have been," I say, studying his expression, which is immediately contrite. "But, frankly, it's complicated enough as it is. I have to tell you I feel strange living here when you're not."

"Because you're American. If you were English, you would have been brought up to such twists of fate. For what it's worth, and it's not worth much, *I* don't find it peculiar in the least. In no way do I find it distressing."

"Not distressing. But it's more than twists of fate I'm thinking of." At the border of the south garden to which we have come, a low and ancient fence of flatstone and remarkable durability defines the expanding park. We stop here for a moment, sashed by the light gold sun.

"I can only imagine," Rupert replies, suddenly, with a deep knee bend, reaching through tall grass that has grown up around what appears to be a paving stone. "I used to wonder why all of this had just escaped my grasp, which, I confess, was how things seemed when I was little. I used to wonder that all the time—long before Adrian was born and even more afterward. We would drive up from London. Money would be tight—never mentioned, of course, but no child could help knowing there wasn't much about. There was always tension over it between my parents, before my mother left. This pastureland was lawn, cut and rolled like a putting green in those days and I used to wander out here to this old sundial and imagine the most exotic journeys. Look at this stone—carefully: Rangoon . . . and just next to it is Kuala Lumpur. A few feet the other side of the center are stones for New York, Chicago and Honolulu, in that order. I would often stand between Chicago and Honolulu and pretend. All the cities of the New World are marked out, actually, only now, unfortunately, they've been overgrown.

"Of course, I pretty well understood that my real task in life would be to 'wife it wealthily' and otherwise do the best I could. But the temptation simply to get away from it all was strong, even if my character wasn't particularly. So I understand exactly how you feel. I do. Anyone worth anything naturally wants to strike out and stand on his own. But then fate usually intervenes, doesn't it? I'm not complaining. No point in it. Not being the marquess and having all this, I was looking for a way to trump those who were and would be and did. But, of course, that's ultimately futile and absurd and, anyway, I was young, not realistic. Even if I'd had the guts and gone into films and, against every odd, succeeded as an actor, I wouldn't have ended up where I'd thought I was going, would I?"

RALPH AND LUCINDA come to stay a few weekends later, he to advise on farming, she, purportedly, to help Julia organize the house, especially the kitchen. The weather is bitter.

"What are you doing?" Julia asks, as the afternoon vanishes hours before their arrival. Her long torso blocks light from the hallway. She stands on the door sill of the small room, tucked behind the stairs to the nursery, which I have lately converted for use as an office.

"Replying to a fax. I won't be a moment. Philip sent on the latest set of numbers. He wanted to run them by me. They're fine."

"Good. What I wondered: you wouldn't want to check the chimney flue in our guests' room, would you?"

"Not drawing?"

"Stuck."

"I'll take a look; ten minutes max. What's the story with them, anyway?"

"They both enjoyed adolescence too much. Lots of lovely bonking, no responsibilities. They're having a hard time moving on to the next stage, he more than she at this point."

"But you're sure they're—"

"Oh, they're sleeping together, but nothing more than that."

"Where are Andrew and Louisa?"

"Watching a video."

"I thought things seemed quiet."

"They have a tea party tomorrow, for one of the children in the next village. Can you drive them?"

"That might scare off Ralph."

"Be good for him. I know they'd love it if you did."

"I'm putting it in my diary just now. There it is: in ink! From next week on, it's going to be hell for a while—once our deal's announced until we've completed it. But this, as the saying goes, is the lull before the storm. We've built in so much margin for error that now we're left with everything ready and nothing to do. Holding pattern until the man says 'go'. And the man, right now, is bone fishing in the Florida Keys. Bone fishing, to steady his nerves. He goes into training—that's what he calls it—at very odd times. To clear his perspective, he says. He says that when he comes back to what he calls 'the game' he can see things fresh, what other people can't. But where I come from we call it taking your eye off the ball. I hope I'm wrong."

"I know the type," my wife says. "Don't call him on a Wednesday, or you'll ruin both his weekends. There's nothing to do but wait, is there?"

"And sweat. Hasn't been for quite some time. But everything that should be in place is. Rupert and I have cross-checked every word in every document. Philip, every number. There's not a comma, a clause in any agreement, a plus or a minus sign we haven't reviewed a hundred times—*on* paper as well as on the screen. No one here or in the States— or anywhere on God's green earth—whom we should have touched base with and haven't. *Not a soul.* All over the world right now there are people just like us: nervous and waiting, trusting only their partners and wives, in some cases not even those."

"T minus—whatever," Julia smiles, "and counting."

15

I KNOW IT couldn't sound more obvious, but the thing you have to remember about any farm or forest is that it's alive," Ralph declares. Leafless trees would seem to defy his point. We walk among them as, a ghost of Adrian years before, he attempts to explain. "You are managing life—in all its forms: new crops, but also very old trees. Land that can bear rather a lot in the way of natural violence, but is also fragile and has to be cared for. And, of course, albeit less so with the home farm, you are first and foremost managing people."

"I'll tell you what worries me," I explain, "and that is that Adrian was brought up with this. He had it in his blood. And I don't. Nor does Julia—well, she does, in a way, but not to the same extent and there's just so much else she wants to do that interests her."

"Of course there is."

"Rupert—"

"Rupert," Ralph sighs, "thinks that 'land' and 'property' are synonymous."

"That's being rather hard."

"You can't live on a working farm, or on a series of working farms, which is all an estate is, after all, as though it were London. You have to work along with nature if you want wheat or barley, whatever. You can't just call out 'Waiter.' And you have no choice but to manage an estate according to the seasons. In the winter, when the pig is fat, it's time to kill the pig, and so on and so forth. The summer is tyrannical, with all its vegetables. Tyrannical, whereas in London the blood oranges of winter are about the only thing left you can't have whenever the fancy strikes you."

"Have you ever talked about all this with Julia?"

"Not directly. Never any reason to. With Adrian, of course. Although, with all of them, there was and is always the question of how well they listen. Family trait not to—hundred percent anyway. Fact is, I've always had the feeling that if it's a frivolous matter, they take my opinion seriously, but if it's serious, they're almost bound to take it frivolously. I mean, my role's been cast—long, long time ago."

For lunch, Lucinda has thrown together long white-and-spinach-green fettucine tossed with a mildly thyme-spiced carbonara sauce. There is a rocket salad, then sweet custard for pudding.

Later, Ralph and I drive Andrew and Louisa to the party of their classmate, in a renovated stucco farmhouse a dozen miles away. En route, we stop at a novelty shop at the edge of a recently gentrified village. The children wander down aisles whose planked floors creak beneath their heavy, rapid treads. Andrew returns with a wooden tractor, umber and bright yellow; Louisa, with a boxed set of sponge paints. We decide to buy both.

On our way out of the shop, Andrew, wrapped package in hand, suddenly asks, "Daddy, why are we here?"

"To buy Justin a present," I remind him.

"Yes, silly," Lucinda reiterates. "To buy Justin a present. For his birthday. He's six. Already. You're giving him a tractor and I'm—"

"I don't mean that," Andrew interrupts. "I mean why are we *here*? Where did we come from? What happens to us when we die?"

Ralph examines my face for a reaction, but before he or I can begin to address such a mystery in any terms, much less a child's, Andrew adds, "Daddy, I think a lot of people would really like to know."

AFTER CHURCH ON Sunday, Julia and I, Lucinda and Ralph go to the pub, which is connected to the Midleton Arms, a small hotel owned by the estate but let on a long lease to a relatively imperious Austrian.

"Pint of the local?" Ralph inquires.

"Why not?" I tell him.

"A half for me," Julia says. "I love it, but it is awfully soporific."

"Half as well," Lucinda adds.

"You're not driving back to London, I take it," Ralph says.

"Tomorrow," I explain, "crack of dawn."

"We'll head off around six, I should think. Cinda can drive. Not that far to go really and all back roads—pretty nearly. You in London all week?"

"Against my better judgment."

"I would never work in the City. Never been jealous of anyone else's success there because, for me, I know it was never an option. Of course, bit of money would be a nice thing to have at times, but I'm afraid . . . All of your deals okay?"

"Static," I reply coyly. "Lots of filling up the time. Not much to write home about."

"You know that American, the tycoon who was here the weekend Adrian—" Lucinda's voice trails off.

"Yes, of course. Wiley Ryan," I reply, vaguely unnerved by her allusion to him.

"That's right. His name escaped me for a second. I'm glad you said. He was written up somewhere. In a magazine lying around one of the boardrooms where I've cooked their lunches occasionally. I hadn't actually realized he was *that* big a fish. Should have given him my card and a brochure."

"Give it to John," Ralph says. "He sees him."

"Very seldom," I insist.

"Well, whenever you happen to," Lucinda says. "He must entertain in England now and again, a man like that. I know he enjoyed dinner that night."

"Sod it all," Ralph exclaims then. "Look who's just come in."

"I swear he puts shoe polish in his hair," Lucinda whispers as Matthew Paxton, trailing his once bombshell of a wife, Rachel, makes his way to a veloured love seat.

He nods in passing. " 'Afternoon."

" 'Afternoon."

"Cold, but still lovely," Rachel offers softly, without slowing. She is fortyish, the daughter of a Northumberland publican, widening a little but recognizable, in any culture, as a former beauty languishing before the shadow of age.

At the bar, watching the froth settle on his wife's pint while the publican angles his own beneath the tap, Matthew Paxton presses his considerable weight against the blond pine rail. On a high stool beside him, creased, a section of newspaper catches his eye. "Rise in Countryside Burglaries." He glances up, ignoring the headline as soon as his order is ready; he slides the wet glasses toward him, pays. Then he delivers her beer to his wife and sits next to her in married silence.

Some years ago Matthew Paxton apprenticed at Hillyards, his father's firm of chartered surveyors. There were high hopes for him among the partners, but he proved rancorous, too aggressive as a bargainer, a poor example for family men. So I've heard, anyway.

After a few moments, he retrieves the abandoned paper, a tabloid, its Sport pages folded in. "Not yours?" he inquires of us.

"No."

"Just wanted to be sure. . . . It's owing to the motorways—primarily," he adds.

"What is?" Lucinda asks.

"The rise in burglaries. They bring traffic so much nearer. You know, Castlemorland ought to be occupied," Matthew Paxton continues. "Really, it should be. On a full-time basis, this day and age."

"Are you waiting for me to say that I agree, Matthew?" Julia asks. "Or to contradict you?"

"Do you mind if I sit?" he inquires.

"Will Rachel is the question?"

"No bother to her."

"Then, please."

"I've been thinking, since Adrian's death. About the village and its future. What with a new century, the whole next millennium coming. All that. As to what would be best. For everyone. And—I don't know, to tell the truth. I wish I did. There are many ways to live a life, so choices have to be made periodically, don't they, given the realities?"

"Which realities?" I ask.

"Time, most of all."

"Oh, *that*," Ralph laughs, then subtly begins to separate himself, with Lucinda, from what he must sense will be an imminently personal line of conversation.

"You see, my theory is that things are not just changing, they *have* changed. England's not what it was when I was a child, anymore than I am. It just looks the same—in spots. Same as me, but more so. Everyone's frame of reference is wider. Perhaps because of television, telephones, computers, travel, all the usual suspects—and even without the old empire. Villages, such as they are, don't suffice anymore; they can't, can they? There'll be a Tesco off in one direction, ten or twenty miles away; a Sainsbury's in the opposite. Well, you know as well as I do, it's the little ones who see over the horizon and nudge us. Today, a regional approach is much more in order."

"Don't you like your beer?" Julia asks.

"Yes, I do," Matthew Paxton answers, sipping some from the rim.

"Is it the local?"

"It is."

"Good. They were planning to give it up, you know. Not enough customers ordering it. It's important not to let the side down, though; I'm sure you agree."

"Wholeheartedly," Matthew says. "Which raises an interesting point when you come to think about it. Not to paper over our past differences and disagreements, but, as it happens, Julia, you and I are two people in love with the same place—with different aspects, grant you, of its past and, I guess, different possibilities for its future."

"All true—as far as it goes. But it's in my hands, not yours."

"Still, we both love it here."

"And you have in mind a proposition along the lines of the one you made to Adrian?"

"Not exactly."

"Let's get to the point, shall we?" I say.

"Of course. I approached Adrian about the rookery, specifically; that's all. A little of the surrounding land admittedly, but, as a percentage of the estate, nothing really. Everything has its own limit, after all, doesn't it—in point of fact? Anyway, circumstances have changed. Questions that were are no longer questions of the moment. You see, I have backing. Now. Which also tends to make things somewhat different."

"Backing?" Julia repeats.

"Very substantial, too . . . *and* reason to believe I could, most probably, secure planning permission."

"All comes clear," Julia says.

"A fortune—one you'd never expected—would, suddenly, fall into your lap, *laps*. Out of nowhere, so to speak."

"That's one way of putting it."

"Point is, you don't really want to be here. Not in your heart of hearts."

"*I* don't? As if that decision were entirely up to me."

"*You* don't. Either one of you."

"I beg to disagree," I interrupt.

"Disagree all you like," Matthew tells me. "What shows shows."

"No, John's right," Julia insists.

"Are you?" Matthew asks me now. "I mean, are you sure?"

"We both want to be here. Very much."

"It will bore you in time." Matthew Paxton continues. "Look, to be absolutely honest with you, I'm not certain, yet, that what I have in mind is feasible. I do believe it will prove to be, but as of today . . . As of today, well, the thought I have in mind, have just begun to formulate seems too good—for everyone, mind you—to be true. Give me just another sixty seconds?"

"Too good to be true?"

"Sketching in the broadest of outlines: I am always inclined to begin at the beginning, with first principles, as it were. The original purpose—after providing shelter, of course—a stately home, like Castlemorland or any other, was meant to serve was as a center for the area about. In some counties, that might have meant just the village—am I correct?—but in others the orbit might have stretched all the way to the next such house. Same as churches—steeple to steeple, that sort of notion—even cathedrals. Be that as it may, the vision that's been rolling around in the back of my head is that Castlemorland is ideally suited to play a role as that sort of center for the new age we're all living in. As such, it would have a prime, rather than a distress, value. You would, if all went as planned, as I believe it could and would do, realize a maximum price. The house would be fully restored where necessary and maintained in immaculate form *forever.* Any furniture or works of art you cared to keep you could. And the estate itself could go on being operated as a business with no disruption to any sitting tenant. I even suspect it would not require more than a fraction of the home farm, as it exists today, to finish off development of what would be the area's finest—"

"Center? As you said."

"Naturally, you could continue to maintain a suitable flat, if you cared to, which I'm sure you would. Utterly carefree living. But the point is, you would be able to secure the place permanently, 'against vicissitudes', as my late father used to say. I fear I may have been too direct. But sometimes that's best."

"No. I'm glad to know what you're thinking. I never have, in such detail. Only, sad to say, it's out of the question."

Matthew Paxton permits himself a small grimace, then stares at me. "Seems to me we're moving into a world," he explains, "even faster than I had expected we would, which is creating the first aristocracy built on talent since . . . the Americans headed West, perhaps, in the eighteenth century. My thought was that, as what's fresh displaces what's stale, if a way could be found to free you of certain burdens that would otherwise be bound to increase and, at the same time, establish Castlemorland securely as a fixed point in the emerging order—state of the art conference center equipped for virtual reality, sport facilities second to none, that sort of thing—well, far better to lead than follow the pack, but I've been wrong before." The beer is low in his glass.

"A theme park?" I ask.

"Leisure park. Tasteful housing, could be—always in keeping. Attractions, for all ages, of one kind or another. Haven't thought through the actual details at this stage. Open to suggestion."

"You mention America," Julia says. "Have you been?"

"Once. To Florida."

"So much about America goes back to its earliest days," Julia muses, "when people huddled together. Their cry was 'Settle the land' and 'Go west, young man'. People wanted to be protected from the unknown, from the Indians. And there was so much land, no one ever thought . . . then it was all gone.

"We've been spared that here, by and large—though I fear it may be changing—because of our history of estates that were managed for posterity as well as profit and, latterly, because of tight planning, all those good things. You are correct in assuming that this is not the future I had imagined for myself, Matthew, nor is it what John anticipated, I'm sure. But you are wrong in concluding that that fact makes me vulnerable to the temptation of a quick fix, a carefree life, as you put it, in return for abandoning my responsibilities. For selling out Andrew and Louisa."

Rising now, Matthew, with firm, formal courtesy, says, "As you wish. But I fear you'll see I'm right over the long term."

"My long term is a series of short terms," Julia calls after him. "My month a series of weeks. My week a series of days. Well, you get the picture."

DUSK. LATER AND longer than a few weeks ago. The air is damp, the distances bleak in silhouette. On the green outside the garden door, Julia bathes Caveat in floodlight, two buckets of warm water and a large white and green cylinder of Fairy Liquid nestled against the concrete step. Caveat sits remarkably still, proud head cocked, a prosperous provincial figure luxuriating in shampoo suds.

"That stuff's for dishes, isn't it?"

"I know. But we're out of dog shampoo and he's been off in the fields rolling around in horse turds, which, I suppose, must be his idea of heaven."

"He'll gleam like crystal."

"Well, it's that or else take the smell inside. I could have sent him to the Paxtons."

"Speaking of whom, Matthew was a bit brazen, I thought."

"You weren't all that firm, I must say."

"Me? I wasn't?"

"No. Who was it, I can't remember, who said that 'weakness and treachery aren't the same thing, but they produce exactly the same result'?"

"I have no idea," I answer. "Who?"

"I suppose I did."

"I don't care. That's not fair."

"No, I'm sure you don't care . . . God, I just find it *so* annoying when you take that attitude." Julia's voice, which might be expected to rise with emotion, actually trails off.

I ask, "What attitude is that?"

"Good company director. Making no waves."

"Did I say anything to Matthew Paxton that wasn't absolutely candid—or firm?"

"But what about your tone? Oh, shit, never mind, John."

"If I did, I'm sorry. But I honestly don't think I did, in any way. I tried to be absolutely direct. That's all. We both want to be here. That's the truth, isn't it?"

"If you say so."

"Do you want a drink?"

"Maybe . . . Maybe I *should* have a glass of wine. For some reason, I'm just on edge. Everything's catching up."

"Natural. See, I told you Caveat would shine," I say as she towels him. The Labrador shivers, frisks, races ahead of us inside.

"Matthew makes me nervous. I admit it. I can't help it. On one hand, I know there's nothing he can do to hurt us. On the other, I'm certain that, if I'm wrong and there is, he'll do it."

"Matthew is clearly trying to test the waters, to see what's available—if there's any weakness of will. That's all; that's the extent of it. Why don't you let me handle him from now on? Just keep your distance."

"I'll try," Julia promises.

"Do you want to come back with me in the morning? Then, after this Ergo thing is over, we can both move back here. I'll find some way to work from here. There's got to be one. I don't like the thought of you being in one place and me in another."

"No, I don't like it either. But I'm all right for the time being. Let's see—"

"We have to put the children to bed," I say.

"Then have that glass of wine. How hungry are you?"

"Not very."

"There's still some roast, I think," Julia says.

"I'm sorry if you wanted me to be tougher," I tell her. "I will remember next time."

"You behaved perfectly. I was just agitated. Sorry."

"Apology accepted. Do you know what I think?"

"Yes," she says. "I think so. That's the best idea. Let's—"

LATER, I AWAKEN, as if blinded, in the lightless room. The telephone throbs. There was a dream, now aborted. I reach across Julia, still sleeping, for the receiver. She shifts, onto her side then immediately, despondently back again, eyes closed, facing upwards. Now, I remember: we tucked in the children, read one story each, nibbled dinner, drank a bottle of *beaujoulais nouveau*. We took a shower together, lathered camomile shampoo, which stung our eyes until we rinsed it. She was passionate, at first against the tiles, like a freshman for whom it was new.

"Hello," I whisper into the mouthpiece.

"Is this John Brook? I'm very sorry to be bothering you this late. You weren't asleep, I hope."

"No," I lie. "What time *is* it?"

"Let's see. Ten thirty-eight, according to the clock on our wall, P.M., Greenwich Mean Time."

"We weren't asleep," I assure him. "Go on."

"My name is Wilson Blaine. I'm a financial reporter with Reuters, here in London."

"That must be very nice. Now, how may I help you?"

"I wondered if you cared to comment on reports we are receiving of some insider dealing?"

"Insider dealing?"

"In the shares of Ergo, Inc., Ergo, Ltd. You've heard of that company."

"I've heard of it."

"We've had news coming over the wire that there has been considerable speculation of late in Ergo shares—perhaps, some have suggested, in anticipation of a bid for that company. And that you and your family—your wife's family I'm talking about here—may have been, in some way, involved. What do you say . . . to those who say that?"

"Totally untrue."

"That's all? To the charge that you have traded shares in Ergo in violation of securities laws, or that you have been involved in the preparation of a potential bid for the company?"

"No comment."

"But you *are* employed by Battleman Peale, who are merchant bankers to Ergo?"

"Yes. That's public information. But anything involving any client— once *or* future, that *or* any other—is absolutely confidential. I'm sure you understand that. I hope you can respect it."

"Even from Richard Mortlake?" inquires the persistent Mr. Blaine.

"Sorry?"

"You do know Richard Mortlake?"

"Yes. Of course."

Julia wakes now, with the continuing drone of my voice. She sits up, raises a finger to her mouth. There is a well-fucked radiance to her, also fearfulness in her eyes.

"Very good sources tell us that Richard Mortlake has been *and is* in conversations with the Department of Trade and Industry."

"Concerning?"

"The Ergo situation."

"I know nothing about that. So again, no comment."

"You are saying that you are not involved."

"Not in any way, in anything improper. I'm afraid I do have to go. Thank you for calling."

"One more question," Wilson Blaine insists.

"I'm afraid not. I'm sorry."

"Who was that?" Julia asks groggily when I put down the phone. "And what time is it?"

"Not quite eleven."

"Where are you going?"

"Just to my office, down the hall, for a few minutes. It seems I have to make another call. You go back to sleep. I'll be back in no time."

"Good. You didn't say who it was."

"Business," I tell her. "The Week that Was appears already to have begun."

In the small office I have recently done up, I find my laptop then, in its memory, Dicky Mortlake's numbers. I stare at the ceiling, my blotter, a photograph of my parents on their twenty-fifth wedding anniversary, their flesh turning pale with exposure in a green leather and tooled gilt frame. I try to imagine Dicky's precise connection to Ergo— any other than through me; how he might have known or had reason to suspect; what he might have traded, and on whose behalf and where? My stomach turns over, fills with acids. I pick up the telephone, then think better. I have seen too many films, read too many espionage novels to take such a chance.

As quietly as I can, I find some clothes, my keys and wallet. I make my way to the garage and drive the Porsche twelve miles, to the next village but one, before I stop. This is not a village I frequent; nor is it one in which we have close friends. By contrast to Castlemorland, it is not an estate village, never was. Most of its housing was built in the Fifties, of brick and mullionless windows which seem incommensurate with the ancient landscape. By the petrol station at the far edge of town I find a traditional phone box, bright red and dank. I insert a Telecom card, press the metal keys, which stick then spring back.

Dicky Mortlake's phone is answered on the second ring, but by an unanticipated female voice. "Very sorry to ring so late," I say, parroting Wilson Blaine's disingenuous assurance. "I wonder, is Dicky there, by any chance?"

"May I ask who's calling?" Midlands accent.

"I'm a friend of his. It is important."

"Well then, I'm sorry to have to tell you this—"

"What's that?"

"That he's dead."

"Dicky. Dicky *Mortlake*, you mean?"

"This afternoon."

"Dead? How? . . . An accident?"

"By . . . his own hand, I'm afraid. Now, may I ask *your* name? The arrangements have yet to be settled."

"No, that's all right. I'll ring back."

"Really. I think you should—"

"Not now. Thank you. I was just a friend."

16

THE LAMPS BURN above the motorway median, yellow, hazy in the low atmosphere. I drive too fast, in silence: no radio, without CDs. I find that I require the absence of sound, the sense of controlled propulsion to make sense of what is happening. It is as if intensive driving, by displacing the aggressive, nervous energy of my body, frees my mind to reason.

By the time I reach the City, the tabloids are stacked by the tube stations. So far, no mention of Ergo. I breathe a sigh of relief, which collapses when I notice Dicky's picture, jowly and somber, on the cover of the *Mail*. The story of his self-negotiated hanging appears, without illustration, in every tabloid and all but one of the broadsheets.

"Philip's been swearing up and down all morning that you couldn't possibly have had anything to do with all this," Rupert says, glancing, obviously, to the pile of unruffled newspapers I have just squared at the corner of my office desk. "That you *couldn't* have known about it. Tell me that's true."

"It's true."

"Look me in the eye."

"We know each other very well, Rupert. Either you believe what I tell you or you don't. There's no need for theatrics."

"I want to believe you. Very much. But it's all over the Bloomberg—everywhere. Globalized rumor now. Ergo will be in freefall, of course, until they halt trading, but whenever they resume, it has nowhere else to go, I'm afraid. So far, yours and Ryan's have been the only names mentioned, apart from Mortlake's, naturally."

"Where's Philip?"

"With Wiley, in the back conference room. I'm meant to bring you along. One thing first, though. I suggested we bring in professional PR people who understand the City and Fleet Street, but Ryan is adamant. He insists on handling the whole cocktail himself. I think it's a mistake."

"What can I do about it?"

"Nothing. I just thought you should know."

"The only professionals he gives any credence at all to are game-keepers, loaders and fishing guides, that sort of thing."

Wiley Ryan refuses to shake my hand when I enter the conference room. Instead, he pretends to stare through its crenelated windows to-ward the morning traffic in the shadowy lane below. With him are a crew-cut lieutenant from America and his solicitor, a Queen's Counsel; neither is introduced.

Philip says, "Principally, A & O are shy."

"Doesn't that go with the territory?" I mutter.

"It's more than that. It's not simply that they are shy of bad public-ity and would prefer the good kind. More that they want none at all. Absolutely none. And, now, that would seem to be quite impossible."

"So our tripod is down?" Wiley asks, rhetorically. "I take it that's what you're telling me. Not just wobbly—down?"

"Best to assume so," Philip replies, "with respect to A & O cer-tainly. Given the level of their distress—their impending losses."

"You know them better than the rest of us," Wiley declares. "But I'm no longer surprised at the spectacle of people acting against their own interests. I've lived too long for that. How this could happen, just when . . . it defies imagination. It's fucking stupefying.

"Our shares'll head south like a Canada goose in November . . . which, I know, would seem to make the whole deal cheaper, easier, quicker—except for the fact—ironic, isn't it—that the reason they're heading that way's because everyone knows the deal has piss-all chance of going through."

"I'd like to say something," I explain, looking as intently at Wiley Ryan's counsel and lieutenant as at him, "which is that I never invested my brother-in-law's or anyone else's funds, including my wife's or my own, in *any* speculation on this deal. No matter who says what to the contrary. That's not to say Adrian had no shares in Ergo. We all did, in some cases going back years. But he—we—just rode the wave on those. There were *no* further purchases."

"I believe you," Philip says.

"Good for you," Wiley tells him.

"There's an old saying," Philip now relates, "that there are no such things as secrets, only people who find out a little later. If, inevitably, given today's on-line transparency of knowledge, everyone *knows*, and if Richard Mortlake did speculate, perhaps he did so on his own, based on his own conclusions, on information or even impressions he derived elsewhere, misreading one thing or another. We don't know; we may never know."

"How long will the inquiry into all of this take?" Wiley demands. "Start to finish?"

"Quite some time," answers his theretofore silent solicitor. "Merely for the D.T.I. to sift through the paperwork and any other evidence. Before even addressing the possibility of referrals to the Serious Fraud Office."

"Oh?" asks Wiley snidely. "That's too bad. Because if their investigation in any way bears out the rumors—"

"I don't think threats help to clarify the situation," interrupts Rupert.

"Really? Well, I'm not especially interested in maintaining a polite surface about now."

"Your plan to vest your pensions ahead of the buyout has leaked. Not half an hour ago," Rupert tells him. "As you might expect, the comment isn't good. You are being seen, by those most disposed to be charitable, as selling out your shareholders' and your lenders' interests for purely personal gain. Painted in less flattering colors by the others. I'm afraid we are all coming under the microscope."

"Christ!"

Rupert stares at Wiley, straightening himself. "The whole thing's very unsuitable," he says.

"In actual fact," Philip consoles me later, when he, Rupert and I are alone in Rupert's office, "I was never *sure* of A & O's imperturbability. You might say I believed—on the evidence, but without faith. In the back of my mind, I always suspected, I think, that something was wrong—that it might go wrong. Especially after the directors took Wiley's measure."

Rupert says, "What we know is that Dicky took a very aggressive posture at the end of the day. The accounts our family had with him were discretionary ones, unfortunately. He had done a good job for my uncle for quite some time and my uncle had come to trust him; he trusted his judgment, in fact, more than may have been justified. Dicky began buying shares, but, on whatever impetus, he quickly advanced into options—first 'in the money' then 'out of the money' calls, where the risk, but, more important to his way of thinking, the opportunity for reward were maximized. I must say his adventurousness was not matched by discretion. He bought openly and far too much, with disastrous consequences. Also, and worse still, it seems he bought extensively on margin and that is where the Midleton-Lygham accounts are horribly exposed."

"I had no idea of any of this," I assure them. "Let me say that again."

"John," Philip replies in a soothing voice, "if any of us thought you had—"

"Thanks. But I realize that it might appear—to an outsider, someone who didn't know me—that I must have done."

"If not from you," Rupert asks, "can you imagine where Dicky could have come by the idea that Ergo was going to be in play?"

"Lots of people knew. They would have to have done. At every firm in the syndicate. And solicitors—lawyers from New York to Hong Kong. You could draw up a list as well as I."

"But he was trading on your—well, your family's—behalf."

"Which is the curious thing."

"Perhaps there were others," Rupert suggests.

"It's always possible," Philip says. We have ordered in sandwiches, from Birley's in the Royal Exchange. He pauses to take a first bite. "Such things take a while to come clear," he continues once he has finished chewing.

"How long?"

"They tend to drag on, just as Wiley's man said. I don't know exactly. We can check with our Compliance people."

"Do you think the deal is crippled or dead?" I ask.

"It's dying," Rupert says. "Obviously. Which accounts for Wiley's temper. The present arrangements have pretty well been blown and it is difficult to think of any comparable players who might come in on our side. Theoretically, I'm sure they exist, but where? The thing to worry about now is other bidders, unsullied by all this, unconnected to Ergo or Ryan or us. The same logic exists for going at the target and now its price is even more affordable."

LONG BEFORE I normally would, I leave the office, drive back to Castlemorland. Once again, I need time alone. For I must separate particular from particular—must, like a lapidary, examine each, then discern, if I can, a natural pattern among them, or, at least, the one most likely to have been created by a human scheme.

Andrew and Louisa are in the last minutes of their violin lesson— Suzuki method, taught by a Russian emigrée whose daughter married an English Foreign Office man and lives nearby. Louisa is musical, conscientious; Andrew, less interested. I listen, with Julia, quietly, as though to Perelman.

"The damnedest thing," I tell her once the children are settled, "is not that Dicky did what he did, but that he was so unsubtle in the way he went about it. I can't conceive of what got into his head to cause him to turn on everything that's kept him alive, the whole code; to turn on us, for that matter. And to leave such an obvious trail."

Julia says, "I thought all brokers' calls were recorded."

"You seem to know an awful lot."

"I read. If they are and, when they play them back, there are none from you or any of us, won't that clear us, in effect?"

"Would go some way toward doing so, I suppose. Of course, the D.T.I. could allege that we instructed him in person. Or didn't instruct him at all; the accounts were in his discretion to manage."

"Yes. I see."

"It'll all depend on what view they decide to take. Whether they believe I passed along privileged information to him, or he came by it elsewhere. Why he hanged himself. It's messy."

"Not messy enough, though," Julia proclaims. "That's what bothers me. It's like having the answers to a crossword puzzle come through from the page below." She coughs—once then fiercely.

"That's an interesting analogy. . . . Are you taking anything for that? It sounds rotten."

"I've got some mist aluminum chloride from the chemist's."

"Good. You'd better watch it, though, before it turns into something."

"With our luck right now, I think so. How bad is it, John? How much have we lost?"

"Not even considering fines they might impose—"

"God forbid. I hadn't thought of that."

"I'd have to say we're out well near all the funds we've built up, all of what your father and Adrian had done. Plus, about thirty to forty percent of the estate's capital. Roughly speaking."

"How is that possible?"

"Through what is called reverse leverage. Dicky bought calls on margin—the biggest bets you can place."

"Entirely on his own?"

"I am afraid so, darling. Still, we'd given him the authority. Technically. So, when push comes to shove, we are liable."

Julia hesitates. "Shit," she exclaims. "*Shit*! . . . I'm sorry, but that's all I can think of to say. . . . I mean, I never expected to inherit Castlemorland—obviously—but I also never expected to see it lost, much less to lose it."

"You haven't lost it," I say, especially softly, trying to comfort her. "We have a problem—a big one, I grant you. But problems are made for solutions, Julia, and we'll work ours out. I promise. Don't worry."

SUCCESSIVELY, I RECOGNIZE that my career, our finances, our once-assumed trust, our marriage are each in jeopardy; even my freedom, if charges of one kind or another should be brought and sustained. So many things seem to be happening, to have lately happened. But, there being no obvious pattern among events, I wonder if fate might actually be the author of the conspiracy against me. Fate? On second thought, the idea seems preposterous. It should require more than fate to kill Dicky Mortlake, frame me, terrify Julia with some secret still beyond mentioning; at least, fate should require a helping hand.

Later, as Julia walks Caveat, I stroll in the opposite direction, across the wintry garden. I bend to unlatch and pass through the planked door, its trellises bare, that separates flower beds from gravestones. Beyond its courtyard, the church is dark; its door trembles. The light of an almost full moon slides through its windows, brightens its nave. I take a seat in our usual pew, detach the needlepoint cushion, kneel. I pray immediately—for us, for our family, that we may remain intact. Then I remember something my mother taught me: never to ask God for things, but always for strength. The strength to understand, the strength to endure, the strength to come through a particular trial. So this is what I request, pressing my eyes closed, raising them to the altar, holding my breath, waiting for some answer—in the wind, or, perhaps, tomorrow.

Driving to the office the next day, I receive, on my mobile phone, a call from a woman whose voice is unknown to me. Its accent is international, vaguely European, confluent in the style of someone schooled for a long time in Switzerland, among many nationalities, including, particularly, the English. "Mr. Brook," she asks and hesitates briefly. "I am the executive assistant to Monsieur Jason Argus, of whom, perhaps, you have heard."

"Of course," I reply.

"Monsieur Argus would like very much to talk with you."

"It would be my pleasure." At last some good—or, at least, promising—news!

"He will be most grateful. I wonder if you might do us the favor of ringing us, on a land line, at your earliest opportunity."

"Certainly. May I ask what this is regarding?"

"By all means. In due course." She gives me a number in central London, adds "Thank you so much" and is gone.

A few minutes later I pull into a Little Chef, where, against a tile wall in the corridor leading to the wash rooms, I find a telephone. The same voice answers directly. "Mr. Brook? . . . Could you be on a Swissair afternoon flight to Zurich?"

"Today?"

"Monsieur Argus wondered."

"You were about to be a little more precise."

"The matter is in regard to possible participation in arrangements you have already underway. Is that sufficient?"

"He reads the papers, I gather."

"A day ahead of everyone else."

"I don't see why I couldn't be on that flight," I tell her.

"Good. There will be a ticket waiting for you at the airport check-in. Of course, you'll keep this conversation between us, totally confidential."

Like most people in our business, I know the name Jason Argus without knowing too much that is factual about him. He is one of the leading, if most enigmatic financiers in the world, a man whose large accounts are often joined with those of others, under his management, in arbitrages of headline swiftness and magnitude. There is about his reputation the seductive whiff of scandal, not that anything has been proven—more suggested, inevitably, as a consequence of his secrecy and foreignness, his refusal to explain himself and court the media.

With little else to guide me, I must base my reaction to his sudden interest upon assumptions. The most likely sequence of these would appear to be that he has read or heard of the Ergo debacle; that despite its controversy (to which quality he must be substantively immune) he recognizes that the fundamental logic of the deal remains excellent; that he, or some party he represents, might like to supplement A & O or even some other member of our syndicate in order to reap the rewards of the buyout at an even lower price; that, before proceeding, he would prefer to meet—perhaps to judge—me, to test my knowledge, discretion, the likelihood that I am actually part of a conspiracy that could eventually unfold upon him. Of course, his thoughts may have followed an entirely different line, but, allowing for the timing, after reflection, none seems so likely. And I am willing to take the chance. The danger in any conversation seems minimal, all the more so against the possibility that I might effect a rescue of the Ergo deal, restore our fortune, isolate the damage to the corpse of Dicky Mortlake's honor.

When no one from the Stock Exchange, the D.T.I. or any other official or quasi-official body has rung by lunch, I tell Philip, "I think there may be a chance for me to sort this whole mess out."

"How?"

"I shouldn't say—can't really. You don't need me for a few hours, do you? The rest of the afternoon, say?"

"We always need you, John—which isn't to say we won't *survive* your absence."

"Cover for me?"

"Yet again." Philip smiles.

I disappear, unnoticed, into the street, and soon thereafter into a taxi.

I have read that many writers of fiction, from early childhood on, have shared the habit of thinking of themselves in the third person, as the principal characters in the narrative of their own lives. Though I have not written what I once hoped to—and may never—this is a trait I have shared with them, going back as far as I can recall. And it is just what I do now. I find myself thinking: John Brook travels west, anxiously, into the Strand, into Pall Mall . . . the Cromwell Road, stops the taxi suddenly by the Victoria and Albert Museum, enters the museum by one door, leaves by another, retraces his route into the Brompton Road and, when he is sure he is not being followed, telephones his wife, asking her to go to the hotel in the village, to wait by the desk. A quarter of an hour later, from a booth inside Harrods, he calls her there.

"I'm going to have to go away for a day or so," he tells her.

"Where?"

"Don't repeat the name when I tell you and don't say anything to anyone else. Zurich."

"What? Why—there? Seems very out of the blue. And why so much secrecy?"

"I've been *requested*," he replies, imparting a half facetious tone to the word then taking Julia's questions in order. "And it *is* out of the blue, so I'm sorry, but many good things often are. I'll fill you in just as soon as I can."

"When do you leave?"

"Immediately."

"And when will you be back?"

"Very soon."

"Can't you tell me why? At least, is the reason good or bad?"

"Oh, good. I hope!"

"The children are having their kips. Do you want me to wake them?"

"No. Let them sleep. I'll be back before they miss me."

"Love you," she says.

"Love *you*."

He takes a second taxi now, to Heathrow Terminal Three. The promised ticket, first class, is waiting; he signs for it, suddenly apprehensive at the prospect of passport control. He buys a copy of the *Evening Standard* at the W. H. Smith stall opposite the counter, turns its pages—one through five, then the financial: nothing. Nor does the immigration officer detect his anxiety, give any more than a glance to his U.S. passport, his U.K. permanent resident's visa. John Brook's name, for now, is plainly unfamiliar to the authorities.

He basks in anonymity.

17

NOW, AGAIN, THE outlaw's fear at first sight of a barrier. Zurich is dark. I mask my tremble, draping my topcoat over one wrist, then the other. But I am waved through immigration. My passport is neither examined nor stamped. It is as if some implicit understanding has been arrived at that a person such as myself, a man in a good suit, clean shaven, carrying a briefcase, presumably with money, might wish there to be no record made of his arrival in or departure from this city of depositories. A driver meets me, my name marked on a small sign—paper pinned to varnished plywood—he holds out from his waist. A young man, German-speaking with careful English, he takes my coat and case and drives me, eventually, up the Dolderbahn to the Dolder Grand Hotel.

I check into the hotel, a Swiss Edwardian palace set impeccably on the throne of a mountain just southeast of the city, amidst sport land, and am shown to my room. In the hallways, the earliest drinkers have gathered.

There is an envelope on my desk, addressed, in plain script, to me. Inside, in black ink on white matte, is a simple message: "Your driver will collect you at eight o'clock tomorrow morning." There is no signature. A lightweight overnight case rests on a luggage stand; it contains two well cut Parisian business shirts of my size, changes of underwear and socks, also a silk-covered, plastic-lined kit of toiletries. It takes no time to unpack. My room is small, mid-twentieth century in style. From a matched pair of windows, a view of gables, a residue of snow settled in their creases, frames the slope to the city, river and lake—all obscured by trees, too distant to be discerned. Beyond them, a horizontal fringe of mountain, vacant and white, reflects the steady moonlight.

After my bath I ask the advice of the concierge on a restaurant for dinner—somewhere with local flavor. He suggests the Kronenhalle in Rämistrasse, not far from the Quai Bellevue; he calls to book a table in my name. I find a taxi in the Dolder's forecourt and wind down the mountain as snow swirls in the line of its headlamps, landing, like confectioner's sugar, on wedding cake cupolas, turrets, the terraces and fairways of summer. The restaurant, as I suddenly remember having heard, is as much institution as eating place. I have a drink in the dark and crowded bar, which is full of men, as many artists as bankers. Silver blue smoke rises overhead, veiling the cornices. Finally, I am shown to a table alone, in plain view of the principal ground-floor room. I have had a whisky—a single malt, neat—mostly to quell my nervous stomach. Now, I order only a single glass of claret with *veal à la Holstein*. The dining room is full of large, happy, garrulous parties. Two others dine alone, half-reading in the uncertain light at the margin of the restaurant.

I consider venturing across the Quai into the city, wandering the Banhofstrasse, searching the windows of its shops for something to take home to Julia. Then I think better of the idea. It is essential to rest. Shopping can wait until the business at hand has been accomplished, or at least become clear.

My driver, as I have been assured, is waiting at eight the next morning. He is the same superior young German, behind the wheel of the same racing green S-Class Mercedes. The snow has let up, flakes melting now under a newly radiant winter sun. Attending to my door, the driver says, "We have enough time, plenty of time." He seems to rejoice in his own success with the English colloquial as he appraises my reaction.

"*Plenty* of time? For what?"

"Your train."

"My train? To where? Where am I going?"

"From the Banhofplatz. Twenty minutes or so away. Half an hour—worst case."

"Then what?"

"You'll take the eight forty-three to Vaduz, where you will be met."

"Vaduz?"

"Liechtenstein. Not far, only an hour's journey. Very reliable service. You have sufficient Swiss francs? You can charge your ticket, otherwise, to American Express, Visa, Access, most any credit card. Not expensive."

A queue of six people is the shortest before any window. I settle into it, and it moves quickly. The individuals ahead of me appear, on inspection, to derive from Asia and North Africa as well as Europe. People at crossroads. I hear different languages. I buy a round-trip ticket quickly, then wander about the station. Outside its main entrance there are the usual vendors, derelicts, pigeons hardened to winter. Behind it, on the Platz-promenade along the Limmat, a couple of adolescents lie in parkas and torn jeans, in one another's arms, near the steps of the Landesmuseum. The narcotized boy stares at me for a second; the girl, into space.

The carriages arrive at the platform within the minute before we are to fill them. They depart exactly on time—out of the shadows, into the sun, which is deceptively warm behind the large glass windows. I read the *Herald Tribune*. There has been a fire in Harlem, an earthquake in a remote province of the Philippines. Children have been killed, lost parents in both cases. The same unconsolability in their dark eyes.

The landscape is industrial, unpicturesque most of the way, the roadbed remarkably level through the pass. Mountains loom nearer to Liechtenstein, highest on the right, where, between lofty evergreens, parts of the spa town of Balzers can be glimpsed.

I am met by a taxi, an orange Renault driven by a man with a fringe of white mustache, and transported into Vaduz, which is cheerful, low, with russet and black tiled rooves topping modern as well as turn of the last century buildings. There is an old spired church; near it, contemporary office blocks of prefabricated steel and stucco. Beneath the medieval castle-fortress which commands it, the town has an almost Californian air, the pretty green aspect of a movie set.

I am shown into the office of a banker named Helmut Koestler. It is practical, orderly, paneled in mahogany, not large. Below it is the trading floor of a bank, but I am not sure of Herr Koestler's role; nor does he explain it in detail. He represents, he says, Jason Argus—in certain interests, unspecified areas. After coffee and some perfunctorily general questions about Battleman Peale, he offers me a tour of the principality—the "Fürstentum," he calls it—and we take his car up the lovely, snow-banked, two-lane road to the castle, from which there is a fine view. We park, but do not go inside.

Later we have lunch at Real: *foie gras aux truffes,* followed by a *suprême de turbotin* and *fraises confites au vin rouge.* We split a bottle of Chassagne Montrachet. No bill is presented. On the pavement, he leaves me alone, with a tourist map of Vaduz, asking only that I return to his office at "sixteen-thirty."

I explore randomly for an hour or so—purchase a set of the postage stamps for which Liechtenstein is famous. Then, with dusk settling, Herr Koestler presents me with a second packed overnight case, a wallet stuffed with various esoteric currencies and a false European Union passport. "You are willing to travel a bit farther?" he asks, plainly sure of my answer.

"That all depends." I am hesitant, even fearful, but what choice do I have, I ask myself.

"To Monsieur Argus, naturally."

"I was under the impression that that was why I had come *here.*"

"Well, yes. I'm certain that you were."

"Where will I be going this time?"

"You will be back in Zurich tomorrow night. Of that you have my promise."

"Why the phony passport?" This disturbs me for I realize that, by travelling with it, I will be committing a true crime, implicating myself in a plot whose dimensions are plainly beyond my comprehension. And yet, if I do not, I will forfeit my best and, perhaps last, opportunity to set things right, to exonerate myself in London. There is little time to deliberate, to balance risks. So I cross my fingers, breathe deeply, then go ahead.

"Why not?" he smiles faintly.

We leave his office among the crowd at the end of the business day. Secretaries, actuaries, tellers, keepers of secrets heading home, into the protection of the mountains. Outside Vaduz, twenty minutes in the opposite direction from Zurich, heading for Bavaria, we pull to a stop beside pasture. A few minutes later, a helicopter hovers, disturbing the loose snow. It lands, a navy blue Aerospatiale bearing narrow but equal stripes of bright yellow and powder blue. This much is clear before the headlamps of Herr Koestler's car are extinguished. He bids me goodbye, a "safe journey," his phrases and manner as cautious and formal as they have been all day.

The chopper's cockpit is upholstered in saddle leather and smells faintly of Lexol. It is dark brown, worn to a soft comfort. I sit behind two pilots. Like them, I wear a headset, although from mine issues music I do not recognize. The pilots speak to each other, apparently on a frequency I cannot intercept. We ascend, our night shadow exaggerated on the plateau as we slither toward a range of mountains. In the moonlight, on a farther savannah of the Glarner Alpen, appear three human figures on skis, it seems standing still; later, animals, in a small herd, running. We drift south across the Rhaetian Alps, above the dim twinkle of Klosters and the more brilliant one of Davos. White mountains, black water, cloud, then crystalline night. Italy: Adamello, then Lake Garda. The headphones play Andrew Lloyd Webber. We land on a day-glow tarmac at Verona, among the surreal bustle of an airport in its waning hours. I read the sign on the terminal. I have never been here and it is strange to pass through such a place in this fashion. An official, in uniform, compliant in manner, examines my passport, after which I am led across the flood-lit asphalt to a small jet, a Gulfstream IV, also navy blue and striped as was the chopper. We fly above the cloudscape, southeast into the long winter night. Except for a steward, I am alone in the cabin.

We land at Antalya in southern Turkey, at just past midnight there. Another helicopter, smaller, similar—and soon I find myself in a pleasant bedroom with a ceiling fan of which I have no need, with thick cotton blankets, a plate of fruit, a sapphire blue bottle of mineral water. The room overlooks an orchard, that orchard a ledge, balustraded in cedar, beneath which the eastern Mediterranean Sea lies virtually still. It is the room of a resort. My meeting, I am told by the local woman who has brought me and borne my case here, will take place in the morning.

There is no telephone available. This distresses me, for I am eager to call Julia. I would like to hear Louisa's giggle, Andrew's too—to be reassured that they and my wife are well. It has now been more than a day since we have communicated and the length of a working day is as long as I can go without missing them terribly, wondering about them, fearing for them.

At first light I am awakened by bells—initially one, soon a cascade. In the distance, angled around a bend in the sea and so visible from my window, is a ruin, a necropolis from the fourth century Before Christ. But nothing moves. There is no sign of life between it and me. The bells are interrupted by silence, then begin again, louder, more in chorus than before. Later, outside before breakfast, I spy the crest of the hill above the ancient tomb, a slope as green and gentle as one near Castlemorland, grazed by a herd of sheep dangling pendants of bells from their collars.

A vanilla wind, mild though pungent, arrives from the sea. After half a grapefruit and a heavy muffin studded with dates, I board a Fountain, dressed in the khakis, loose-fitting poplin shirt, cotton jumper and espadrilles I have found in the suitcase Herr Koestler provided me. The forty-eight-foot long cigarette boat is pushed away from the small dock by its mate, who coils the bow line reflexively, counter clockwise, like a snake, once he is done. The sea, at the edge of our inlet, is lime-colored, then indigo as it deepens. The transparent shallows, like the beach itself, are floored with smooth pebbles. There are mountains, capped with snow, on the Lycian peninsula in the distance.

Very soon the captain speeds the engines and we spring from cove to sea, steering around the few gullets which cruise at this season. These are plump, ketch-rigged fishing vessels whose decks and quarters have been compromised for tourists, of whom only the most determined are now about. The captain draws our wake away from their bows. In the thermos there is more strong coffee. I am offered a cigarette, unfiltered, by the mate. I take it, although ordinarily I do not smoke.

The obelisk at Xanthos, farther every moment now, watches from the coast. Weathered, bearing still its clear inscription of heroic deeds, it has so presided, over this landscape, these waters, for two and one-half millennia.

In the open Med, in just under half an hour, we slow—troll beside a schooner whose sails luff in the casual wind, its cabin still somewhat depended, its stern skirting the becalmed sea. We come alongside; our engine sputters. I climb aboard the large craft, its hull deeply glossed in enamel which repeats the colors and narrow stripe of its owner's armada.

On the bridge, alone, a squarish man in his fifties, bald and tanned by the sun, stands over a control panel, examining readouts of wind speed and sheet tension. "Thank you for coming," he says, wiping his hand in a handkerchief before extending it. On first inspection, Jason Argus resembles a bodhisattva outfitted by Ralph Lauren.

"Not at all," I tell him.

"I hope you will not consider it a complete waste of your time."

"I'm sure I won't."

"You have been to this part of the world before?"

"No, never."

"Not much is known, really, about the Lycians," he continues, "apart from the fact that they were the fiercest of fighters. In fact, we know them mostly from their tombs. They were not, shall we say, an especially literary people, having written very little down. Herodotus, I believe, claimed Creten origin for them, but sources differ. What made them—and kept them—was, of course, geography, as is so often the case. The Ak and the Bey Mountains protected them from the land. Even the Romans quit trying to conquer them and ended up recognizing Lycia as an independent state in the second century B.C. But, perhaps, you know that."

"I didn't—embarrassingly."

"Why be embarrassed, if it's not your area of expertise and you do not claim it as such? Alexander, you know, sailed these very waters—the first European *we know of* to do so. He would have seen very much what you are seeing: the celebrated Turquoise Coast. Anthony and Cleopatra, as well. And Hannibal. Pirates held the great Julius Caesar for ransom—stupidly, it turned out, for they were subsequently crucified. The Christian emperors of the Byzantine, naturally, came by river—the Koca or the Dalaman. And Saint Paul, to preach the gospel. All ventured here and left their marks. Only with you British was the objective solely one of plunder—to score antiquities for your well-known country houses."

"In actual fact," I explain, "I'm American."

"Oh, yes. I know. But a *certain kind* of American, after all. Eastern Coast. Sympathetic to England and its ways—rooted there?"

"Married there."

"Employed there."

"Yes. That's true."

"That ruin in the distance, straight ahead—you can see it?—*that* was a crusader castle. Recent history, by local measure. Coffee?"

"I'm fine. Thank you."

"Had Alexander come today," Jason Argus speculates, "no doubt he would have sailed something very much like this. You have not seen one before? I've noticed your eye taking it in."

"No, I haven't. It's magnificent."

"It's a Perini, built in Viraggio. You have been there?"

"Sorry."

"Most modern vessel possible. Most forward technology. Forty-six meters—and it can be sailed single-handedly, if necessary. By means of the toggle switches you see before you. All the winches are buried within the decks. Every rope and sheet and bit of sail has been measured exactly. The precise tensions on each sheet, in fact, are measured continuously. They are maximized by computer, but only up to the point where it is safe to do so. In other words, Perini and his yard have produced an environment whose truest beauty lies in its harmony with nature and, of course, in the means it provides to harness that nature most efficiently, elegantly and *privately*. . . . You may have wondered why you were brought here under a false identity."

"I did rather."

"For precisely such reasons of privacy. Just as some men have a passion for fame, I possess one for—*invisibility*, shall we say. Most of the time. Whom I choose to see, when, where and why are my concern. Confirming that one or another meeting has actually taken place, particularly on a certain date, might—would, inevitably—imply a reason to an educated observer. Thus, it would be bound to disturb the essential confidentiality of one's operation—*peut-être*, to disturb the markets themselves."

"I understand."

"I suppose I can be accused of carrying precautions a bit far, but better that than—well, I'm sure you take my meaning."

Over lunch of bouillabaisse, a field salad and Rhine wine, this mystagogue shows me some candlesticks and a centerpiece he has acquired from a designer in Paris. He considers the man an artist; himself, by extension, a patron. "John, my dear boy," he offers finally. "I know, of course, everything there is to know about you—things even you've probably forgot by now—and I will tell you this: you have the kind of talent money can't buy."

"Thank you." My thoughts and emotions race.

"And so I must let you in on a little secret: money's not going to buy it—in this instance."

I look at him perplexedly. "Then, I'm afraid I'm a bit confused."

"Tell me about Wiley Ryan."

"What about Wiley Ryan?"

"Just your impression."

"He's very clever, determined. Compelling, in his way. More than that, I don't think it would be proper for me to say."

"Privileged information? I respect that. He's impetuous, though, isn't he? Headstrong, too. A liver of life, as against a pursuer of fortune, really. Often a combustible combination, I'm afraid."

"If money, as you put it, is not going to buy—"

"In *this* instance, money isn't. I believe that's all I said. I am entitled—am I not?—to feel that an Ergo led by Mr. Ryan might not represent the intrinsic value which he, and even you at Battleman Peale, suggest it does. Now, tell me about Rupert Cheviot."

"He's as smart—in the American sense of that word—as any Mergers and Acquisitions guy there is. Good with the numbers; good with the people part of the equation. Actually, I'm surprised, in a way, you haven't met him."

"Really? And why is that?"

"Rupert gets out and about. He often travels in exalted circles."

"I shall accept that as flattery, although I seldom travel in any circle other than my own. No, we've never met, sadly. I met his father once—years ago. He was a lightweight. I'm glad to hear better of his son. Now, Philip Li?"

"Brilliant."

"Conceptually so?"

"When I think about it. Absolutely. I'm sure my opinions can't entirely surprise you. I am also sure you didn't summon me all this way just to hear me reiterate Battleman Peale adverts."

"It always interests me to be able to look into a man's eye. As that is the only way I know to ascertain whether he is the sort of man who knows where to place his loyalty."

"Are you going to bring each of my partners out here for the same purpose?"

"No."

"Because I haven't met your test, whatever test that is?"

"On the contrary, John, I am convinced that you are an individual capable of intense loyalty and that your ultimate loyalty, now, is to your wife and your children. You haven't mentioned them, that's true. But, despite a certain exoticism in your background, I believe you to be the most conventional of men and that is where a conventional man places his trust—his truest faith.

"You had truly hoped I might be interested in supplanting one of the shakier elements in your Ergo deal. And, I confess, I lured you with that suggestion. After some reflection, however, I fear I'm not. But the time may come—and soon—when we *can* do business together. Your firm, I freely admit, has interests which interest me, but it is also full of hungry Englishmen. Very well, you might say, but what I look for in those who represent me is what I am pleased to find in you. You are without guile, John, which is a noble, if perilous thing to be."

I study Jason Argus, more confused than ever.

"You arrived too late to dine at our little hotel, which is a pity. The first time I myself visited it, many years ago, I happened to order a lobster. They are very good locally, closer to what you might call a crayfish. Sweet. Do you know, to my astonishment, the young waiter then and there stripped off his shirt and dove from a high ledge into the sea, where he quickly wrestled a lobster for me and presented it, charmingly, before tossing it into a vat of steam. He was, obviously, the descendant of seafaring men and warriors—identical profile, identical temperament. I bought the hotel; that waiter is now managing director of the group which runs it. My point is that I so deeply respect the local attitude to life. For its durability and simplicity, its eagerness to please yet love of victory. When I die, if all goes according to plan, I shall be mummified, which may surprise you, then installed here, in a pillar tomb of great antiquity."

I hesitate. "I hope that will be a long way off in the future," I tell him, "and I hope our paths will cross many times before then."

"Only time will tell," he replies.

When I leave, via the same tender, the sun trails a path of gold from the western sea to the shadows cast by the great yacht's sails. I am frustrated, but contain my near-anger at what seems to have been a labyrinthine adventure which has yielded nothing and, in fact, provoked more curiosity than it has satisfied. By the time I am airborne, on the next leg of a return which will retrace exactly the means and route of my arrival, methane, escaping in an abstract pattern from mountainous fissures, burns a soft crimson in the enveloping dark.

18

AS I APPROACH our house, I have an eerie feeling: it's as if I can already discern in the quietude of the road, the near absence of traffic, the saunter and scarcity of pedestrians, that this is not to be a normal day.

I'd been returned to the Dolder late the evening before and rung the house from my room. This being a school day, Julia and the children were meant to be in London. But there was no answer—until the machine picked up in my own disembodied voice. I'd next rung Castlemorland, where another machine answered: Julia's tones this time. I'd assumed they were all asleep and so had caught the seven thirty-five Swissair from Zurich, setting down at Heathrow at eight-twenty local time, prepared for the worst of the in-bound rush on the M4.

Julia is not at home when I arrive. The front door to our house has been double-locked. The narrow front hallway is dark; a few letters and packages, of varying sizes, clutter the tiles. From beyond, comes a musty, unoccupied scent. A claustral hush. "Julia," I call out. To silence. "Are you there, darling? . . . Andrew? . . . Louisa? *Darlings*?"

From the immaculate kitchen counter I pick up the telephone, press Memory then One and wait. Topley answers after several rings: "Castlemorland 221." He has not added digits as British Telecom have and may be the last man in England to speak of exchanges by their once proper names.

"Morning, Topley. It's John," I say. "Is my wife there by any chance?"

He hesitates. "Lady Julia?"

"You remember our wedding?"

". . . I'm afraid has gone out."

"To London?"

"Couldn't say."

"With the children?"

"She took them, I believe. Yes."

"But she didn't say where she was going?"

"Not in so many words."

"Who else is there?"

"Only staff, I'm afraid."

"Well, then. I'll wait for her here. Is that what you would recommend?"

"You could do. I wouldn't know what to recommend."

"Why do I have the feeling something's wrong?"

"Wrong, Sir?"

"*Wrong*, Topley."

"There's nothing wrong, Sir."

"With the children? Are Andrew and Louisa all right? Why aren't they in school?"

"I couldn't say, Sir. They appeared well when—"

"When what?"

"When Lady Julia drove off. Give me a chance, please, to complete my sentences."

"Sorry."

"Not to worry, Sir."

"Look, Topley, if you should speak to my wife—"

"You'll be there? In your London house?"

"Yes. Here. Or the office. Here, probably. Try here first."

"Very good, Sir."

A new thought occurs to me and I search the house for a note, a letter, some kind of explanation. But there is none on the desk in our library, none on her bedside table, none on the mantle or on the sideboard in the dining room; none anywhere. The house is too orderly. The Portuguese daily, Maria, who has been with us on Tuesdays and Thursdays for a year, has, as usual, done her work and it has been left undisturbed, except for the small accumulation of mail. Back in the entrance hall, I sort through bills from the local newsagent, from Harrods and a furniture restorer who has recently mended a chair the children damaged; there is a mailing from their school, an advert from a nearby butcher and another, on lavender stock, for a plumber who offers twenty-four hour service via a mobile phone. There is a new copy of *London Portrait* magazine and there are several manila business envelopes bearing no return addresses. I open these to find only statements relating to the house and our bank accounts, also a short video—what looks like some sort of cutting-edge commercial promotion.

The telephone rings. It is Philip. "Morning, John. Wondered if you were there. Where in hell have you been, anyway? Never mind. You can tell me all about it later. Look, are you coming in anytime soon?"

"Of course, I'm coming in—almost immediately. I just walked in here. Philip, have you—or has anyone there—heard from Julia, by any chance?"

"*I* haven't."

"Ask Jane," I say, referring to my secretary, whom we are sharing whilst Philip is in London. "Will you?"

"Put you on to her in a sec. Congratulations, by the way."

"Congratulations? On what?"

"No need to be coy."

"I'm not. Tell me. On what?"

"The chap you went to visit in Switzerland's hired us as advisors—on one or two things. He must have been very impressed with you."

"I can't think why. I didn't know the cat was out of the bag, as a matter of fact—that anyone there even knew I'd gone to Switzerland."

"Nothing big, but it's a start. Reassuring, too, with all hell breaking loose. Have to admit that."

"Can I have a word with Jane, then? I'll be with you shortly."

"I'm sorry, Mr. Brook," Jane says when I ask her. "There have been no calls from your wife—this morning *or* yesterday. And I've been the only one answering the phones, so I am positive. Absolutely positive."

I open the fridge, snap the top off a can of Diet Coke and drink it in a few gulps. I sit on a tall varnished stool, leaning against the island in the center of the kitchen, where, as a family, we often have dinner together. While I do not yet exclude any possibility, my emotions tell me that something is wrong—that the thread of our marriage, which began to be stretched when I awoke to find Julia missing from our bed on the eve of Adrian's death, may, in my short absence, actually have snapped. The house, I know, is not merely empty. It's been abandoned.

I telephone Lucinda. Julia is not really the confiding sort, but if there is anyone left for her to confide in, after Rupert, it will be Lucinda. Lucinda will take her friend's side, naturally, but perhaps there will be something in her voice. I find her listing on a chart near the telephone, tap in the number of her flat. The call, I'm informed, is being diverted; the ring changes octaves. But soon she answers.

"Lucinda? John Brook," I begin.

"Hello, John. How nice to hear your voice."

"Yours as well. The damned thing is, Lucinda, I can't seem to track down my family. I had to be away on business for a couple of days and now, well, you wouldn't have any idea—"

"No. Gosh, I'm sorry. I don't. None at all."

"Because, in actual fact, I'm terrified. I'm at my wits' end."

"Where are you?"

"Ormonde Place."

"Did you ring Castlemorland?"

"First."

"And Topley has no idea?"

"He said Julia drove off. But where: into the sunset, into a lorry? For greener pastures, or off a cliff?"

"Perhaps for . . . perhaps the children had a party, that sort of thing."

"The children ought to have been at school."

"What makes you think they're not?"

"Topley said she left with them. If they had come to London, they'd be here. Some sign of them anyway. That seems obvious."

"I suppose."

"Think—for just a minute. Where would she go? For support?"

"Here?" Lucinda asks.

"Where are you? The call was diverted, I know."

"Ralph's."

"Not working today?"

"Semi-retirement."

"Where—if not there, though?"

"I'll call you if I hear anything. I promise I will."

"Yes. Promise. Let me give you my number at work, too. Just in case."

*   *   *

THE PHOTOGRAPHS ARRANGED on the credenza in my office reproach me: the twins' conspiratorial smiles, my wife's devoted gaze up into the lens of the professional's camera. I remember the afternoon the children's picture was snapped. Andrew's class had joined those of five other schools on a visit to the planetarium: three hundred little boys in flannel uniforms and caps, of whom he would have been acquainted with fifty or so at most. The theatre had grown quiet, then gradually dark as the replicated heavens came aglow—stars, even mists against the inky void. The instructor had made whatever points he'd sought to and now, as the children tilted back their heads to behold the expanding galaxies, two illuminated signs—one reading "No Smoking," the other displaying the outline of a camera with a prohibitive stroke angled through it—faded at the margin of the great room. Hushed silence—until, suddenly, Andrew piped up in a voice whose shrill exuberance carried it. "I suppose that means we can light up and take photographs," he dryly announced to his fellow five-year-olds.

I smile at the memory, stare into the picture.

Philip appears in my doorway. "That was quick."

"Took the tube," I explain. "Any sign of Rupert?"

"Not yet. Not sure, now, if he's even expected back. Out on business, they say. I can tell you this, though. He's plenty happy about that piece of business you brought in."

"Is he? Good," I say, deciding that there is no need to inform Philip that I have, as yet, no precise idea what business he is referring to.

"Mind you, it's all prospective. They seem to want our advice about possible acquisitions—or mergers—for one of their companies. But hope lights the way and all that and it's the first piece of good news we've had for a while."

"Funny," I muse. "Very brave of them to hitch their wagon to our horses when we—well, *I*, anyway—seem to be the target for so much right now. If I were in their position—well, what's the use speculating?"

"You must have been bloody impressive," Philip presses. "I mean, you're to be the point man. That's been clearly stipulated. It's their principal condition, as a matter of fact."

Jane enters, an awkwardly stacked sheath of papers and folders balanced in her arms. This provides Philip with an excuse to continue in the direction he had been heading when he noticed my presence in the office. "We have a meeting together in forty-five minutes," he says. "I'll see you then."

"You've had a lot of calls," Jane explains, "most from the press, but fewer each day is the good news."

"I'm pleased to hear it."

"Mr. Ryan withdrew his bid *officially*," she continues, "as you might have expected. Actually, since the bid was never *officially* public, what he did was to deny any and all rumors. PR got rather involved, at the last minute. Rupert organized the arrangements. It all went off well, very smoothly, but relations are strained—obviously."

"No subpoenas?"

"Nothing of that kind, as yet. You have the meeting Philip mentioned—Ergo wrap-up—and, before it, a couple of the managing directors would like to be filled in on your brief from the new clients."

"That will be short," I tell her. "There's nothing at all specific at this point."

"And you have an interview, your last appointment of the day, with a part-time associate who's looking to join our department full time."

"Who?"

"Young woman from Sales and Trading."

"Do I know her?"

"Name of Kristin Erikson?"

"No. Never heard of her. They're always coming up behind us, aren't they, Jane? Politely preparing to push us out of the way?" My telephone chirps. Jane waves.

Julia's voice, sharp but tremulous, issues from the receiver. "God-*damn* you, John," she shouts.

"Where are you?"

"I just had no idea," she continues. "I mean it. Damn you!"

"I've tried to reach you everywhere. I've been frightened out of my mind."

"How long have you been planning this?" Julia demands.

I begin to answer, but draw a breath instead. "Planning what?"

"Honestly, John. Please. Not now. I know. I *know*. Do you understand that? I *know*."

"For Chrissakes, Julia."

"I should have figured it out. I was stupid, I have to admit that."

"Tell me then. *What* should you have figured out?"

Julia sighs. "That afternoon when we met, when you had just come back to London from Hong Kong, Rupert's great friend and find. Had you already begun to plant the seeds then, or was it later—after you were safely married? The funny part is you seem to have ended up stealing what you already had, which is mad—positively mad. Well, I hope you enjoy it . . . Good-bye, John." The connection does not break.

"Julia, where are you? Where are the kids? Are they all right?"

"They're fine—perfectly *fine!* Missing their father, but they'll get over it."

"For God's sake, Julia. Give me a chance. I have no idea what you are talking about." My voice breaks. There are tears welling in my eyes.

"John?" Julia asks tensely, after some silence.

But, for a moment, I cannot answer. "Please," I repeat.

"There is just so much happening."

"I understand. I do. Darling—"

"*Too* much, *too* fast. I don't know what to believe, or whom or why anyone is saying or doing or pretending—"

"Take it slowly then—*very* slowly."

"I need time," Julia insists.

"Of course."

"*By myself.* . . . With just the children, no one else."

My heart speeds. I hesitate. "Okay," I promise. "That's okay. It's understandable. . . . How much time?"

"I don't know," she tells me. "I can't say yet. I just can't. Bye, John."

This conversation pins me to my chair and I stare across my office for five, ten, fifteen minutes, stunned into paralysis by my wife's words and tone, her threat. Her departure, with Louisa and Andrew, is like a piece of graffiti written across the history of our love and life together.

I cannot stay in the office. It is too confining, too exposed. I lack the composure, the capacity to concentrate on anything other than my own predicament. Without a word to anyone, to avoid explanations, I leave—and on the pavement, in the shadows of St. Paul's, on the moving stairs to the tube and waiting beside the track, all I can think is that I am dead. "*I'm dead*" is the litany I repeat, silently and over and over, to myself. "You're dead."

The tube is quiet at this time and season, the platform vacant when I first appear. I sit alone, certain, in those intervals when I can think logically, that it will be better for me to be at home than at the firm. Maybe, expecting me to be at my desk at Battleman, Julia will return to our house at midday—for something she has forgotten? As I turn the corner from the Sloane Square stop into Holbein Place, a channel of wind freezes my cheeks and ears and blows my scarf across my shoulder. Long as a schoolboy's, the color of a cardinal's robe, it was a birthday gift from my wife.

In every detail, our house is as I left it. I pour a tumbler of Malvern water, then find myself standing in the middle of the drawing room, holding the glass as though at a party; but I am alone.

I decide to take inventory—to kill time, but, more, to measure the truth and durability of Julia's departure by an accounting of what she has taken. The result is distressing. Her clothes are gone—folded and packed, I presume; removed. More terrifying, Andrew's and Louisa's . . . oh, God: there was a clock she'd loved—gone, too; pictures of her parents. A shilling piece, three rocks (captured by our children on a bucket and spade holiday in the Isle of Wight), a small jade frog (Chinese symbol of prosperity)—all spirited from the house I gave her.

Defeated by my search, fatigued, I fall into the sofa. There is an iron snake on a distant table, a cigarette lighter that had belonged to my mother's father and which, somehow, after his death, found its way to my apartment in New York years and years ago. Its wick is short, but nonetheless droops tongue-like. I stare at it, minute after minute, hypnotized.

I have stacked the mail on the table, left it there. Now, I decide to check it one more time, as I have everything else. There are no surprises. Except for the video, which is without markings, each item is self-explanatory. The video is short, obviously professionally made. I suspect the absence of a label is meant to tempt, that it will extol the virtues of a particular product or property in which I have no interest. Still, fidgeting from my stupor, I elect to play it anyway. Soon a color bar appears on the screen of the big Sony. . . . The sky is a blue field, until clouds enter from the left then blow away. The camera lowers, jerkily, and now there are treetops, green and whispering. The camera pans down and back. A perfect Palladian house, too small to be a stately home. At the far end of an oak *allée*, a reflecting pond in which the English summer sky repeats itself. Fussed-over borders of hollyhocks and gilly flowers. Fade . . .

. . . Now, the same pool, an elongated rectangle, arced at each corner, from the opposite point of view, away from the house toward a slight hillrise, before which stands a fountain. And fade once more.

It is night. The same fountain, starlit, spotlit. Cavorting with lime-stone Venus and Mars, there are people—specks, though, in the distance. Water, splashed from the wide basin, catches the ample moonlight, as well as the artificial light by which the video is being shot.

Or is it a video? For I detect a graininess, the once-removed texture of film.

A close-up, suddenly: skin the hue of marble, hair turned to honey by the sun, worn almost long. But whose skin, whose ringlets? The young man, self-regarding and alone, reclines on a single elbow against a pediment. He appears no more than twenty. A drape of folded ivory terry towel covers his waist. His head is tossed back, his arms and legs relaxed, his torso, as if painted by Botticelli, is flecked with water.

From the surface of the pool an arm rises, then another. Julia's face, her hair held close by its very wetness. My wife is younger—a girl in ripest form I never knew. She steps out of the fountain, naked and unshy; disappears to the left then quickly returns, carrying two glasses in the same hand. She presents one of them to the boy and lies beside him, her head on his shoulder. He stirs. They sip. His arm enfolds her. They kiss, entwine, shiver and pause to sip their drinks again. It is probably champagne, having a faint amber glow. Will they make love? I am riveted, disgusted, titillated. This is my wife's past, after all, part of that unspecific history she brought to our marriage. It contains no betrayal. And yet I am filled with a voyeur's adrenaline, with dread. The camera lingers—same scene, same point of view, the angle more oblique as the seconds pass. Eventually, the boy swallows the contents of his glass then lets go of it entirely. Mysteriously, Julia vanishes, then returns. There is a syringe, which she hands eagerly to the boy, who promptly injects it into his bicep. Blood sputters. He looks away, grows limp, falls asleep, one assumes. Julia stirs him, without effect. Only then does the scene go black.

I POUR A drink from an old bottle of bourbon, which is all I can find in the cupboard, oddly relieved, oddly disappointed. I twirl a few cubes of frostily opaque ice in the brown alcohol and watch the motion of the liquid. I stare into space, waiting intensely for some indefinite thing. When the phone rings, I bolt from my hallucinations and grab it at once, but it is only Jane, reminding me of the interview I am scheduled to conduct later in the day. "It cannot be postponed," she explains, in that familiar admonishing tone she holds in reserve for defending those to whom she has taken a liking, "because the recruitment committee meets to begin making its decisions first thing in the morning."

"Ask the candidate if she would mind coming round here for a drink after work," I say. "I can't face the slog back in, I'm afraid."

Jane's voice stiffens. "What are you doing there anyway," she asks, "when it's still the middle of the afternoon."

"Contemplating suicide," I tell her, cloaking the phrase in a dry, jocular English tone, so that she will not realize how close it comes to the truth.

19

A T ONCE I recognize her. She is tall, wearing a greatcoat, flannel slacks, low pumps, a jumper of royalist purple, cashmere and widely ribbed, with a turtle-neck collar; no jewelry. Gone are the pleated skirt, simple blouse and cardigan, but this is, memorably, the American girl I noticed—and Philip identified—across the Battleman atrium.

Behind a pair of horn-rim glasses, she looks on the point of smiling, yet tentative—most likely because young. "Sorry to be late," she explains, stepping unhesitantly across the threshold. "I had some trouble finding your house."

"I'm sure," I say. "Everyone does. Page seventy-six of your A-Z guide, but it's only a dot. Anyway, here you are."

"Yes. Here I am. . . . Kristin Erikson." She extends her hand in the clenching, forthright way of American women.

"Come in. It's biting out there."

"You're American, aren't you?"

"Yes. You, too?"

"You can tell?" Hers is a fetching, but lamian smile.

"Shall we talk in the library?" I inquire. "Let me take your coat. Would you like a drink?"

"Would tea be too difficult?"

"Not at all. Milk or—"

"Lemon. Please."

"Me, too."

As I walk to and from the kitchen, I am nervous, wondering, at every moment, in every silence, if the phone may ring or the door abruptly open and Julia appear. If . . .

Kristin Erikson sits winsomely in a wide, chintz-covered chair, her legs crossed at the ankles near the leather hippopotamus footstool Julia and I ordered years ago from the catalogue of a Park Avenue gift shop.

I move, tea in hand but as though someone else, toward her. The telephone refuses to ring. I say, "So you are, I gather, keen to come over to our side of things. Is that right?"

"Yes. I'd like to very much."

"Why? Why not Sales and Trading," I ask, "rather than M and A?"

"Because I'm not a quant," she laughs. "I'm more intuitive. I mean I can handle numbers as well as the next person, but I don't think they mean all that much until you factor in the people part of the equation."

"Five years out," I inquire, "what do you see yourself doing?"

"I wouldn't dare to speculate," she replies, plainly an adept. "Five years from now, all the most important deals may be being done in cyberspace. Who knows?"

"I doubt it."

"So do I." She looks down, in a charming, self-mocking way, then brings the cup to her lip. Kristin Erikson has a slight overbite, the effect of which is to give many of her expressions a playful, pouty cast.

"Are those your children?" she asks, pointing to a charcoal silhouette which rests on an easel in the corner. "You have two?"

"Twins."

"Wonderful," she says. "I was an only child."

"So was I."

"I never minded not having brothers or sisters—well, once in a while, but not as a general rule. But I did sometimes think it would be nice to have a twin. They say twins always know where the other is and how. I wonder if that's true."

"We see signs of that sort of thing all the time."

"Are they—"

"—in the country," I interrupt, before she is able to finish her question.

She hesitates. "How nice. They must love that." She is too young to have learned to mask her calculation of our situation.

"They're in the country with their mother, which is unusual," I add, "in the middle of the week. Ordinarily we go out at the weekend, but I had to be away and Julia had some business there that couldn't be done on a Saturday or Sunday and so—"

Still, the telephone has not, does not, apparently will not ring.

"That's one of the things about London I've found it hardest to get used to: how everyone has to go away on the weekends. They're almost desperate about it and the result is that you spend all of Thursday planning and most of Monday recovering. It's hard to get any work done."

"Exactly," I tell her, hearing the distraction in my own voice. "I take it you enjoy work, which is a good thing since what we do is frantic. And, as often as not, it comes to nothing."

"No one bats a thousand," she replies.

"And it can be controversial, as I am sure you are aware."

"I'm not afraid of controversy. Also, I tend not to believe what I hear until I see for myself that's it's true. Battleman Peale is a very old firm and it just doesn't seem likely that such a high-powered group, especially the same team that's been running M and A for quite some time, would suddenly put its foot so wrong. What would you have to gain compared to what you could lose? Come on, it's bullshit."

"Would you like more tea," I ask, "or a real drink?"

"What are you going to have?"

"I'm going to have a real drink. There isn't much, I'm afraid. Only bourbon."

"Bourbon's fine."

"Water?"

"No thanks. But lots of ice, if you have it."

"To your very good health," I propose. Then, after long silence, while the sweet liquor plays on my tongue and multiplies the effect of my earlier drink, I ask, "What brought you to England?"

"In the first place? I met a guy. Usual story. I was young. He was cute. I followed him. We got married, then divorced. Could have happened to anyone." She laughs, sighs, holds my stare until I, a little shyly, look away. "I got a visa out of it. Look, to be candid, I don't know much more about Corporate Finance than what I read in the *FT*, *Forbes* and *Business Week*, but I do find the subject intriguing. I don't have a business degree, but I'm a quick study and my instincts are good."

"Yes," I tell her. "I believe that." The fact is that in my present mood a part of me would like to punish Julia, as she is punishing me. I would like to stake my ground, balance things, even justify her contemptuous view of me. I would like to lose myself, to feel that, in my pocket, there is still, at least, some currency of value. So when Kristin excuses herself to the loo, my eyes follow her. Her youth reminds me of girls from my own past. The thing about women I do not understand is the ease and righteousness with which they cross from the rational to the emotional and back. I don't know any man who does. Julia has made a judgment without permitting a word from me. She would not understand nor allow the reverse and yet she feels pure and wholly right in doing so. Believing that I have betrayed her, she has betrayed me. But, no doubt, she would not see it that way. Deception and betrayal—those are the things the women in my life have said they feared. And yet, as I look back, it was I, not they, who more often than not ought to have been afraid.

"What's the matter?" Kristin asks upon returning.

"I don't know. Is something the matter? I thought I was the one conducting the interview."

Again she holds my gaze. "Ask anything you like." Her finger traces and steadies the right temple of her glasses.

"You know what?" I say. "I try to make it a point never to discuss business when there's a drink in my hand. So the only question I have is if it's really what you want. Are *you* sure? Because there's a lot in it if a person is good, but the goddam competition is something awful and, for a long time, say from the time you are your age until you're my age, it can take everything there is out of you. There's a price for everything in this world, Kristin, and, if you're not lucky, the price in our game can be your soul. That's what the deal stream demands and feeds off of: people's souls. And the other thing is that, if you do intend to have a career, I mean if you do stick with it and don't leave to have babies every couple of years, then the person you're with has to understand that you're on a beeper twenty-four hours a day, just like a doctor is or a cop. It's nuts. I know. But it's the way it is. It's expected. You aren't forgiven if you break the code. No one is. You never will be. So whomever you fall in love with, be sure he's the accommodating sort. Because that's crucial; it's the most crucial thing of all. *Accommodating*, remember that word."

"I will. *Accommodating.*" She sips her drink slowly, thinks and pauses. "Is your wife?"

"Ordinarily."

"I'm sorry. That's none of my business. I shouldn't have asked. Forgive me."

"It's all right. Ordinarily she is, as a matter of fact—always has been."

"I'll keep quiet."

"I don't mean to sound so—equivocal," I tell her. "I really don't. It's just that right now we're going through a bit of a rough patch. Nothing that can't be weathered. Anyway, never mind, a lot's happened—too much. But it'll sort itself out in due course."

"I'm glad. Because I think that anyone who's married to you should be accommodating right now."

"Thank you."

"You want to grow old with her, don't you?" she inquires almost sweetly, leaning forward toward me. Her smile seems sisterly and empathetic and without contrivance. "Come on. Be honest. I can tell."

"I don't want to grow old," I reply, then pause. "Oh, Kristin, Kristin, Kristin," I say. "What is it women want? I told you what the life you're looking at and hoping for entails; I told you honestly; I didn't hold back. Now you tell me, because I don't know anymore. I thought I did—once—but, apparently, I was way off base."

"What *did* you think—when you thought you knew?"

"Love. And loyalty. Someone to hold on to—who would take care of them. Security. A man they could share the kicks with. Children, naturally. What else?"

"Women want different things. At different times in their lives. Just like men."

"The awful thing is, when you are doing your best, it's hardly ever appreciated. When you try to earn love you usually end up losing it."

"Because the drama's gone."

"I suppose. But it's hard. Not just hard, it's impossible. Sorry for the outburst." Involuntarily, my eyes drift to the ceiling. I am just drunk enough that, suddenly, my perspective alters and I feel as though I am observing the room from a vertiginous rise. Kristin has become hazy, sinking, as she talks, toward the bottom of a canyon.

"I think I know what you need," she admits suggestively.

"What's that?" I ask, raising my legs onto an ottoman reading her. She smiles, says nothing, waits fetchingly.

"Once upon a time I could have," I tell her. "But that was a long time ago. Mind you, I can dream about going back to those days. I don't imagine anyone can ever avoid doing that. But I can't act on those dreams."

"Will you hold it against me?"

"What the hell," I tell her. "I'm flattered. . . ." I am, too, but soon afterward, Kristin and I exchange firm handshakes and she is gone.

IN THE BLACKNESS of night, just before two o'clock, the telephone trembles beside my bed and, by reflex, I reach for the receiver and bring it to my ear, doubling the nearest pillow into a bolster.

"John? John, wake up! It's Ralph Marlowe."

"Hello, Ralph Marlowe," I hear myself answer, although in a kind of half-time, like a phonograph record played at too slow a speed.

"I won't take long. I can't. I've come down into the farm office to use the other line, so that there won't be a light on anywhere else." Still, his voice verges on a whisper. "She's here, John. They're all here—Julia *and* your kids. That's what I wanted to say. Probably shouldn't have done. Promised not to. But I felt I had to use my better judgment before things go from bad to worse."

"Thank you."

"It's as if someone's cast a spell on them. Not on Lucinda so much; she's just responding to what Julia's told her."

"Which is what?"

"All about how you've looted the family fortune. A lot of fancy financial footwork that, I'm the first to admit, is well beyond me."

"And which you must not believe or you wouldn't be calling me."

"Certainly not at this hour," Ralph agrees. "Adrian, you know, was the best judge of people's characters I've ever run across. And he thought the world of you. As you know—but, also, probably *more* than you know. So I have to set some store by his opinion, dead though he is." His voice halts for a moment.

I do not interrupt.

Ralph chokes something back. "There's also the issue of common sense, isn't there, as against all this hysteria? Hell, I have absolutely no idea what's going on, but, no matter what view one takes, I can't see why anyone in your situation—married to Julia and as hopelessly in love with her as you obviously are; living in her family's house with two young children, whom, I confess, *can* be rather noisy—would risk it all just to move money from one side of the ledger to the other. No, that doesn't fit with everything else I know about you, or, at the end of the day, with Adrian's opinion, who knew much more than I. There's got to be something else. All my instincts tell me there's bound to be another explanation—that I'm the last one who's going to be able to fathom. I may be English and you American; there may be a big distance between us—"

"Three thousand four hundred forty frequent flyer miles," I struggle to joke. "There are greater divides."

"Exactly. A man's got a right to know what he's accused of, to defend himself. The way I see it, he's got a right to see his children."

"Thanks. I can't tell you how much this means."

"Simple matter of fairness, I'd've thought. Decency."

"I'm being set up," I tell him. "So is Julia, even if she can't see it."

"Inclined to agree—obviously. But why? By whom?"

"I don't know. But there'll be worse ahead if we don't figure it out and do something soon."

"Whole cast of villains in your world, it's always seemed to me. Hard to know where to begin looking for feces in a cesspool like the City."

"I could be at your place by morning."

"*Not* the best idea. They're driving back to Castlemorland tomorrow, John. For that winter *Son et Lumière* thing tomorrow night."

"I'd completely forgot about it."

"You'll find them there."

"Thank you, Ralph. God bless you." My voice is breaking. "Pray for me."

"For us both," he says. "I hope I've done the right thing."

20

S OMETIME EARLY IN the 1960s—no one alive can be sure precisely when or during what trip—Julia's parents came up with the
idea of producing a *Son et Lumière* show at Castlemorland. Apparently,
they had seen such spectaculars in the Roman Forum, at the Parthenon
and Fontainebleau and the idea had proved contagious. The conjuring
of history through sudden, graded flashes of spotlight and floodlight
and through simultaneous playlets of recorded conversation and solil-
oquy must have seemed pre-destined for a venue as populous with
ghosts as the ancient estate they had inherited. On further consideration, the form also looked to be an inspired choice to aid the Children's
Hospital in the next market town and so a benefit was decided upon.
The daughter of a friend had recently married a Londoner who was beginning to make a name for himself in the fledgling discotheque industry. This young man's advice was sought and, impressed by it, the
Cheviots eventually hired him. Thereupon, he brought in lighting people, who fitted the temple and folly, even the decrepit orangery and the
terraces and roof of the house with powerful and concealed lamps. As
well, he brought audio engineers who secreted woofers and tweeters
high in the branches of dogwoods and at the central floor of a boxwood
maze to give the effect of incantations and music welling up from the
earth itself. A control board was set up and experts brought in to run it.
The tapes which played featured professional sound effects, the scenes
having been recorded by actors, mostly students at the Royal Academy
for Dramatic Arts, according to a script over whose accuracy Julia's father labored in the months before the final take. Once the spectacle became an annual fixture of July, each new script became a lure to draw

the audience back. Every summer, a new story, within the same format, with only a slight variation in technique, was required. And, inevitably, Andrew Cheviot rose to each occasion with months of recitals and indefatigable checking of arcane facts. The story of the first Lygham knight was told in the inaugural year, that of the old abbey which had once stood on the same ground in the following. The English Civil War was re-created, with Charles I's brief sheltering at Castlemorland, protected by Cavaliers from the west and north and pursued by Roundheads, from south and east, in 1642; as was the splendid visit, to shoot and feast, of King Edward VII, on the near-eve of the Great War.

During last summer's event, it occurred to Julia (not for the first time) that the most compelling tales Castlemorland held within it were interior ones and that a second, smaller occasion, indoors in winter, might be organized to dramatize these. Her parents had long resisted opening the house itself to crowds, but she now wrote one or two thirty-minute sketches, read them aloud to Adrian and secured the permission he had never known how to withhold from her.

A story was settled upon. "Save the Date" cards were posted the day after the August Bank Holiday; actual invitations followed within a month. By mid-October, the production was fully subscribed; a fortnight later, both the tapes and lighting plan were ready. Then Adrian died.

I CANNOT SLEEP. At four A.M. exactly—just in time to witness the digits of my clock tick over—I awaken, dehydrated, the roof of my mouth, my tongue and gums dry. Immediately, I swallow a few lukewarm slugs from the plastic liter of still water on the table beside my bed, then turn over. But this is hardly enough to settle me. I feel the beginnings of a cold. I toss again. Suddenly, surprising myself, I swing my legs out from the side of the bed and go in search of an antihistamine that I know from experience will knock me unconscious. I cannot bear thought, of any kind, right now.

In the late morning, nervous, unable to work, I hike into Sloane Square, down the King's Road, back through the Royal Hospital, trying to decide what to do, how to begin a conversation that will not end abruptly, when to leave, when to appear. Julia will not, unless Ralph gives himself away, expect me—and yet, on second thought, she might.

It could, I think, occur to her that I would remember the date or somehow be reminded of it and so conclude that she will have, of necessity, to be there. I want, as desperately as I have ever craved anything, to see Louisa and Andrew, yet I recognize that it could be dangerous to present myself before the paying guests have filled the house and Julia will have no pretext upon which—and no opportunity to—escape. I kill the day in purposeless strolls, errands, idleness, deliberately remaining incommunicado until, in late afternoon, I finally set off, estimating my arrival midway in the drinks hour, when I will be able to confront my wife, assured by the presence of others that she will have to hear me out, look me directly in the eye, see then that I am telling her, as I always have, the truth.

Traffic is snarled, though, in the Great West Road for half a mile before the roundabout at Chiswick and again, because of an overturned dairy lorry, in the country. By the time I arrive, Castlemorland is dark, its first midwinter *Son et Lumière* already in progress. I pull to a stop in the public car-park and enter the house as though I were merely another late benefit-goer, in this way hoping to avoid any altercation with—any warning to Julia from—Topley or members of the household staff.

Today, miniaturization enables a simple lap-top to replace the console control board of old. Lamps are tiny, intense, subject to exquisite regulation; self-powered, commanded by radio or infrared signal, they can be sited practically anywhere.

One of these explodes, in the distance, as I enter. Having captured the attention of the audience, it quickly settles to a faint glow in a recess above the grey-and-yellow marble staircase. Children's voices can be heard from its direction; from a lower distance, in rooms beyond ours, an orchestra: Strauss, the delirious shuffle of waltzers across the parquet of the ballroom.

From upstairs, suddenly suffused again, can be heard children singing. *"Three blind mice, three blind mice . . ."*

Darkness then. And visibility, once more, in the Long Walk.

A short while later, the Great Hall brightens. An usher's voice says, "This way, please." And the audience follows him in the direction of the ballroom. I cannot find Julia. I step back against the wall, nearly out of view, to let the others pass, to watch, to wait. So far, the crowd seems approving.

"Daddy!" Louisa cries out suddenly and, dressed in a blue velvet frock, bolts across the flow of adults. "Daddy, *here* you are! Where have you been? We've missed you."

"Not so much as I've missed you," I say. "I've been in Switzerland." I raise her until her face is even with my own, kiss her cheek, feel her childish lips on my cheek, her grasp tense at the back of my collar. "Do you know where Switzerland is?"

"It's very cold, isn't it?" Andrew asks, arriving now. "And very high up in the mountains."

"Yes, it is," I answer, momentarily trading my daughter for him.

"Did you bring us a present, Daddy. Did you?"

"I did. One for each of you."

"What? Where are they?"

"In London, I'm afraid, darling."

"We're not *in* London."

"But I left them there—which was stupid, wasn't it? Do you want me to tell you what they are, or would you rather wait?"

"Tell us. I don't want to wait."

"Neither do I. I don't want to wait."

"Do you know what a yodeller is?" I ask.

"No."

"A kind of singer who works and lives in the mountains. Very high notes, like *this*—I mustn't be too loud—then perfectly normal ones, then high notes again."

The children giggle. Plainly they think me ridiculous, though in a sympathetic way.

"Yodellers wear very pretty, very colorful costumes. And I brought you a doll of a girl yodeller, Louisa, and you, Andrew, a figure of a boy yodeller."

"We're not going to London this week," Louisa says.

"I want to," Andrew tells her. "Don't you?"

Their nanny has come up behind them, yet kept her distance. She shifts her weight and glance insecurely. "I think they want us to move on," she suggests—to them and, as much, to me. "The program's meant to continue."

When the crowd has progressed, Julia approaches suddenly. It is as if she had espied me earlier and held back until there could be no witness to our conversation. "Hello, John," she says, turning a cold profile but nonetheless accepting my feeble peck for the sake of the children. "Darlings, you *must* run along now, or you'll miss the show. . . . We'll catch you up."

"In just a minute or two," I add.

My wife glares. "May I ask what prompted such extraordinary action?" she inquires, after the children and their nanny have gone.

"You took the words right out of my mouth."

"Get out!"

"Five minutes to hear me out?"

"Not five *seconds.*"

"Whatever you believe, Julia, whatever you've been told, I'm innocent. *Innocent!* I must say I find it astonishing, as well as bloody, fucking irritating that, with all we've been through and all that's at stake, most of all our children—"

"Whom you've betrayed as horribly as you have me—"

"I did no such thing. How can you say that, or *think* that? That you would rely on other people's gossip and lies and not give me a chance to clear things up; that you would *cast off everything*—"

Exhaling slowly, as if to accentuate the deliberateness and finality of her decision, Julia says, "I've relied on no one's word, much less gossip, John. I haven't had to. I've seen the evidence. And it's all there. I have evidence that can't be explained away. Can*not*; that's all there is to it. *On paper!*"

"There *can't* be any evidence," I reply, "since there was never any crime. But, speaking of evidence, I received something very interesting in the mail when I got back to London."

"I couldn't care less, actually. You may have noticed I'd moved us out of the house."

"It's a video. *You* are its star."

Julia freezes, an amazed, irritated panic welling from her eyes, her face and bearing instantly astringent.

"I don't know what it means," I press on. "I don't know when it was taken—except that it was obviously quite some time ago. I don't even know what point it's intended to prove. I thought I'd ask you before *I* leapt to judgment."

"Very thoughtful."

"Who was the boy?"

"Guess."

"No, I'm serious. You make an attractive couple."

"Am I supposed to come back with some clever reply?"

"You are not. You are supposed to look at me, to give me, if only because I am your husband and I love you, the benefit of the doubt. And if you cannot do that, for whatever reason . . . fine, but realize that very strange things are happening, very dangerous things to both of us—not only to you and not only to me—and that they are bound to be more than coincidental."

Music from the *Son et Lumière* eddies toward us.

"Christ, I don't know," Julia says. "I don't know what to do, what to think. I don't know whom to believe or even whether to believe what I can see with my own eyes. I'm afraid to guess and guess wrong."

"You're right," I say, "because that could be fatal. But ask yourself this: if you guess in my favor and you're wrong—if I really am as diabolical as you appear to have become convinced I am—what more is there that I can do to you? Kill you? Leave my children without a mother? Do you really believe that the man you've slept beside all these years is, beneath this disguise, a monster?"

"No, of course I don't. We should get out of people's way," Julia suggests, "if we are going to talk. Was there any letter, any message with the video?"

"No." I follow her into the Great Hall, where she lifts the worn velvet rope that cordons off the family quarters. This is my home, of course; at any rate it has been lately. Yet I move apprehensively, unsure if I am host or guest, unsure if I will continue to live here, or even if Julia shall. We open the door to the Regent's, her mother's former sitting room, which has been less favored by Julia. It is dark, but silent; the curtains are drawn.

"I went to the cemetery after I discovered . . . what I discovered. I'm sure that seems the behavior of a lunatic, but I don't mind what people think," my wife says. "Everyone I love, you see, except for three people, is dead. When I use that word, I mean wholly and completely. *Not* as one loves friends or mentors, even close cousins. Two of those three are innocents, they're children. So, to whom does one turn to ask if the third is a thief or a traitor? *No one* is the answer—no one who can make any reply. One asks the wind. One asks the grave. One waits for an echo. I took three small bouquets I'd gathered from the flowers the florist had shipped in prematurely for tonight—three *very* small ones.

But the graves were frozen over, those low stones covered with just enough snow and frost and ice that I could only approximate where each one lay, where my father and my mother and Adrian rest forever in the cold ground. Do you know what I did?"

"I don't. Tell me."

"I tossed the flowers. Let God carry them, I thought. Let God stray them where He will. What else could I do?"

"You believe I've stolen money, don't you?"

"I didn't at first. I didn't want to. But . . . what can I say? Nor did I imagine the records I saw."

"What records were those?"

"Me first."

"Okay."

"The video?"

"Did you—"

"No."

"Did he?"

"What?"

"Die?"

"Yes."

"Why didn't you do anything, call anyone?"

"I had no idea."

"That was David Paxton, wasn't it?"

"Yes. David. I didn't sleep with him that night. When I left, I thought he had passed out—that's all. David was . . . I don't know, *sui generis*. A thing unto itself—unto nature."

"Which you couldn't resist?"

"It's not like we had an affair. We didn't. We never did."

"How do you know what was on the video?"

"You said it yourself. *I'm* the star. All right, never mind: I've seen it."

"You've seen it?" I ask, astonished. "When?"

"A couple of months ago. Actually, it was just before Adrian died." Julia sits along the arm of a sofa. Beside her, a floor lamp she has turned on glows softly behind a shade of lemon tulle.

I remain standing—pace, then halt my pacing. I am pensive, trying to connect things which would seem to bear no connection. "How did you come to have it?" I ask.

"It came in the post, just like your copy did."

"Do you have any idea who sent it?"

"I could venture a good guess. Matthew Paxton."

"Why?"

"It would give him a hold over me. Or he would think it would."

The door to the library is closed. " 'Power over you?' " I ask. "Why would he want that?"

"So that I could manipulate Adrian, I imagine, persuade Adrian. Why else at that point? I think he hoped I might be able to talk Adrian into succumbing to one of his development schemes. Adrian had the land and Matthew had *come to have* the cash, or at least the access to it, and, more importantly, the political connections—on the various planning councils—to get things done. How much do you know about the night that video was made?"

"Not much. The basics. First, let me ask you this: how would Matthew Paxton have got hold of it?"

"No idea. There's really only one person who could have shot it."

"Who?"

"Hugh Basildon. Simon Basildon—our solicitor's son. The party took place at his house, Lion Court, which is near Newmarket. Hugh's my age. We were up at Cambridge together. He was camera crazy, very ambitious to be a photographer—always had been. I don't remember that he had a camera with him that night, but if he had, no one would have noticed particularly. I certainly wouldn't have worried about him shooting a skinny dip or anything like that. Hugh's sweet, a gentleman. He wouldn't have dreamt of it. That's what I thought anyway; it looks as if I must have been wrong."

"But from Hugh Basildon to Matthew Paxton, that seems a stretch," I say.

"It does. They didn't have time of day for each other. Not that they wasted worry over it. You'd better sit down," she tells me, her voice edged with emotion. "This is a long story. David was a kind of fallen angel, as I'm certain you've gathered. A sort of Icarus, whom fate allowed to fly too close to the sun. He fell in with a very fast set—a set which would have been enormously seductive to any person his age, but which some could handle and some couldn't. It wasn't really a fixed group, except at its core, but rather one into and out of which quite a lot of people moved. One did one's work and, occasionally, went to a party—that sort of thing. But you know how some people are: they are born without discipline. They simply can't switch themselves on when they have to, when the situation demands. Poor David! He was always at the center of whatever good time there was to be had and, given the time and place and his general weakness of nature, that inevitably meant drugs. His famous overdose took place the night of that party. He expired beside that very fountain."

"Yes. So you said."

"He was alive after I left, though. I can't prove it, but I know it's true. What you saw has been doctored somehow. I didn't give David the hypodermic. I grabbed it from him. The whole sequence is distorted—totally backwards, opposite to reality."

"I know that feeling. How can you even be sure the film was taken on that same night? Was there only one such party?"

"I'm sure there were many, but only one that I attended. Also, you can tell by the moon and by the statues of Mars and Venus, which Simon apparently had on approval that weekend and later returned to the dealer. All kinds of telltale clues."

I study my wife, finding, in her agitated eyes, a desperation I have never seen before. "Why didn't you come forward at the time?"

"And kill Daddy? Although I've never taken a drug in my life, it does show that I was in the presence of rather a lot of drugs. Draw your own conclusions. Think of what the papers would have done with the story—and if they'd had pictures, no matter how deceptive, to run with it! A thousand years of history would seem to have come a cropper, as my father would have said."

"How come you left early?" I ask.

"Thanks to Rupert. He smelled trouble—somehow. David fell asleep. The next thing I knew Rupert came over and said he thought we ought to get a move on."

"What kind of trouble?"

"Piers, essentially."

"Jealous?"

"Dealing."

"Piers was a dealer?"

"*The* dealer of choice among that set, which is the reason we broke up."

"And yet he's stayed close to you—and to your family—all these years."

"He straightened himself out. I forgave him, I didn't return to him."

"Why do you suppose the second video was sent to me?"

Julia hesitates. "Off hand," she tells me, "I have no idea."

"Who knew about the first, other than you?"

"The only person I told was Rupert."

"Because he'd been there? He knew all about it anyway?"

"Exactly. He'd saved me."

"Why didn't you tell me?"

"What would you have thought? What could you have done? Think about it. It was a secret I was keeping in order to *protect* you, not to *hurt* you. You had enough to worry about with the Ergo deal, all your work. The night you woke up and I was downstairs, that night we made love in the library—that's what I'd been up talking to Rupert about. I'd heard him come in. You were fast asleep. I was too nervous. Anyway—"

"I'd already figured that out," I confess.

"I'd just received it that morning."

"Okay, okay. So what was Rupert's advice?"

"To sit tight, do nothing until or unless Matthew asked for a *quid pro quo*. If that happened, he wanted to stall him. Rupert's view of Matthew is one of utter contempt, as you might imagine. But he wanted to stall anything—absolutely anything—until the Ergo deal was finally over with. For everyone's sake. Then he promised to deal with him himself, but, in the meantime, Adrian was killed and Matthew went to ground."

"Until now."

"It seems that way, but why would he want to frighten *you?* No, that's a stupid question. I can answer it myself: to coerce you into influencing me to give up Castlemorland—the same as he tried to do with me and Adrian. But what's not a stupid question is why he would then fax me printouts of accounts that implicate you. The two things don't go together; one undercuts the other, if you see what I mean."

"I do. Where are these printouts? Do you have them here?"

"I gave them to Rupert."

"To Rupert—why?"

"They weren't the sort of thing I could make sense of."

"And he concluded from them that I had somehow plundered your accounts? I don't believe this!"

"Not at all. He took your side. He said there had to be another explanation: Ryan or someone, which makes no sense at all. Rupert defends you, based on the fact that he knows you. He's known you for a long time and he likes you. What he can't defend or explain away is the fact that an enormous amount of money has left our family accounts and an even larger amount has ended up being credited to yours."

"What? What are you talking about?" I demand, for I have no knowledge of any such accounts. "I'm an embezzler, then? That's what you think?"

"I told you: I don't know what to think. But I *don't* think you are an embezzler. You're too clever—*much* too clever. Rupert is inclined to believe, on faith, that you are innocent. But the facts upon which even he—we all—agree, are the following: Dicky Mortlake invested a lot of the estate's funds in risky options on Ergo stock—improperly but irrevocably. The only possible way he had of knowing about the deal you had in play was from you."

"Not true. Many people knew."

"But you had lunch with him. At Wiltons."

I wipe the back of my hand across my brow. "I remember," I admit.

"Here's the thesis," Julia proceeds. "Dicky went long, with *our* money, on Ergo. You went short, everywhere you could, with yours, using all the leverage—isn't that the term?—you possibly could. When all was said and done, you were up, we were down—more accurately, you were rich, we were broke."

"But why? Why would I short my own deal?"

"Don't you see, that's exactly what I *cannot* fathom. Unless, somehow, you knew it was going to fail."

"I never took a short position. Or *any* position on Ergo. I had a few shares—very few—from before I even met you, before I ever came to England. I never said one word about them to Dicky. 'Went long' and 'went short', that's jargon, Julia."

"I just told you," she replies, "that I talked to Rupert. I had to talk to someone. Surely you'd agree."

"As long as you're so knowledgeable, just where are my accounts supposed to be?"

Julia shakes her head. "If you really don't know, I'm not at all certain you'd want to."

"You could try me."

"Liechtenstein."

"Liechtenstein? That's absurd—nuts, on the face of it. No one knows who has accounts in Liechtenstein. Of all the damned places on the earth, that's just about the most secret."

"If you don't have accounts in Liechtenstein, why did you go there? What were you doing in Vaduz, if not counting your money?"

"Trying to save us—of course, I don't expect you to believe that. Dare I ask how you knew I was in Liechtenstein?"

"A photograph came over the fax, same as the accounts, but a day or so later. Not all that brilliant—still, it's recognizable."

"I suppose you also know I went on to Turkey?"

"Turkey? Turkey! . . . Did I tell you I climbed Everest while you were away?"

"Who hates us, Julia? Enough to go to all this trouble?"

"That's part of the problem—a rather big part. I can't think of anyone."

"Wiley Ryan, maybe?"

"Whoever it is—if it *is* anyone—it's someone with a certain amount of power *and* imagination. But who fits that description? No one I can think of very readily."

"Darling, why would I steal what's yours—and will be Andrew's and Louisa's?"

"Honestly, I don't know."

"Are you going to call the government?" I ask.

Julia hesitates. "Not yet, I don't think."

"Why?" I ask, grasping. "You could—easily. You could make what you know available to the D.T.I., the Stock Exchange, to the Serious Fraud Office, all sorts of places. You could hang a noose around my neck. I wouldn't be the first innocent man to go down that way."

My wife is about to cry. "I'm afraid," Julia says.

"You're not the only one."

"More afraid than I've ever been in my life. And yet I don't really know of what. Or whom . . . *Why?* If you could just tell me why, John, I could try to believe you. My emotions tell me that I should, that I ought to, but reason says just the opposite. Don't you understand? It all begins with *why*."

"Paxton," I tell her. "I have to talk to Matthew Paxton as soon as I can. I can't think of anywhere else to begin."

"What about Arabesque?" Julia inquires.

"That's a familiar name."

"It's a holding company, run by a tycoon no one ever seems to have seen called Jason Argus. At least that's what Rupert told me. Arabesque shorted Ergo before your deal fell through. Arabesque also sent that messenger to Wiltons. Don't you remember how really strange you thought that was? It was practically all you could talk about."

"Only to you. That was a set-up."

"Life is a set-up," Julia posits.

Now, the timbre of my voice and fever of my temper rise. "There *is* such a thing as being too clever by half," I admonish my wife, "as being too ready to see every side of everything. That's what they're relying on—that we'll work it all out in our minds instead of in our guts. That way, they can stay a step ahead. I don't know what they want for themselves, darling, any more than you do. But I do know that, whoever they are, whatever it is, they won't want us around—either of us or the children. We'd only be in the way. The contest is no longer between love and hate, Julia; it's between life and death. Where do you suppose Matthew Paxton is *at this minute?*"

"Here," she answers. "He's here—in the other room."

21

A S SOON AS we venture from the sitting room to rejoin it, the
Son et Lumière approaches its climax in the long, dank statuary
hall, a gallery whose stone and stucco interior walls impart the cold of
the winter beyond. The hall houses a collection of disharmonious objects—a fractured Egyptian sarcophagus, a trio of second-rate Greek
figures, miscellaneous Roman armories, even a pair of post-War mylar
abstracts, variations on the theme of an exclamation point, cast "after
the style of" Brancusi and Moore—which have in common only the ge-
nealogy of those who procured them. It is pitch, with the edginess of a
tomb.

Magically, the darkness seems to intensify and, breathless, the audience waits . . . and waits . . . waits until, at an unexpected moment,
light of improbable softness floods a fresco on a far wall.

Modest Moussorgsky's *Night on Bald Mountain* rises to its crescendo:
the church bells of morning disturbing a witches' sabbath of the previous night.

Afterward, flute and harp continue as the lights rise. There is ap-
plause, then hot coffee in the entryway by the old ballroom entrance,
which has been opened so that the guests can move on directly to the
car-park.

I spy Matthew Paxton above my children's heads. He is at the center of a small group, including his wife and some local politicians.
Rachel Paxton is laughing heartily.

When, gradually, most of the audience has vanished, I promise to
read my children a bedtime story, then approach Matthew, who now has

his camel's hair Chesterfield topcoat in hand. "I wonder if I might have a word," I interrupt.

He beckons the others in his party to go on ahead of him. A moment later, we are alone among relics. The hall is draughty. Matthew folds his scarf once over about his neck, flips up the right heel of his brown brogue against the pediment of a high ionic column, swaying back slightly. "Very interesting theatrical," he offers at last, "though, for myself, I still prefer the outdoor scheme. Not only for the weather, but it would appear to lend itself to themes of greater consequence. No doubt, I'd find considerable agreement on that point. Armies clashing by night. Cavalries—and the magnificent thunder of their stampedes. Campfires, too, for that matter. The age-old fight for land, you know, with soldiers dying young, taking a blade or gunshot for king and country. All the stuff of Shakespeare."

I try to judge whether he means to be taken with irony, for I am keen to understand his frame of mind. "Matthew, I'll be direct. You sent Julia a video a few months back—"

"Did I?"

"And you sent a copy of the same video to me a few days ago?"

"To you?"

"Don't deny it, please," I tell him. "Julia passed her copy on to me and I gave it, in turn, to our security people at the firm, having erased its contents, of course. They, in turn, in the course of one investigation or another, occasionally trade favors with Scotland Yard and the Yard seems to have been able to connect it to you. By some sort of bio-tech test."

"Go on," Matthew says. "You're bluffing, obviously, but go on."

"I am curious why?"

Matthew hesitates. "As a courtesy?"

"Julia," I say, "believes you had hoped to intimidate her."

"Into doing what?"

"Many possibilities spring to mind."

"But all must be ruled out, surely, in light of the fact that never once did I ask for any such reciprocation."

"You wouldn't have to have done. Your interests are plain enough. But why send a second tape to me? You had no way of knowing Julia'd shared the first, so I can't see how it served your purpose to bring me into it. She might have been more likely to keep the matter secret, after all, than to have come to me herself. In that case, your hand would have been strengthened if she had had to fear my discovering it as well as anyone else's."

"I did not send you *anything ever*, John," Matthew declares flatly. His eyes so deliberately and defiantly pierce mine that I am actually inclined to believe him.

"If you didn't, who did?"

"I sent that video to Julia out of friendship, difficult as you may find that to accept. I'd had no idea of its existence until I received it a few days—no more than a week, certainly—before I passed it on. Whoever sent it my way no doubt expected me to use it to some advantage, just as you've jumped to that same conclusion. But I never did. I'm not above arguing my vision of the future and pretty strenuously, *as you know*. But I *am* above doing any further damage to my brother David, to whom far more than enough was done in his own lifetime."

" '*Whoever* sent it'? Don't you know?"

"No."

"Or care?"

"I have things of more importance to worry about. Naturally, I'd be interested in knowing, but the subject doesn't obsess me, if that's what you mean. What I thought was that Julia had a right to be warned of what she might be up against. Any day, a pictorial might appear in the tabloids—with speculation spreading everywhere, and if there was any way she could prevent that or even be prepared to respond to it, so much the better: for David's memory, for Castlemorland's reputation as well as for her. I sent it anonymously because I wanted to wash my hands of it. Sorry, but that's the way I felt. I knew I'd be assumed to have a motive that wasn't Simon-pure, like them. Look, John, I am what I am—just like we all are. About that I'm unrepentant—same as the Midleton-Lyghams—which is the proper attitude for any decent man or woman. The question here is why you want so much to be like them."

"That's not at all the question," I contradict him. "The question is why you are so bloody eager to see this family humbled."

Matthew draws a breath. "Fair point," he confesses. "So ask yourself."

"It's more than the land."

"Certainly, it's more than the land. Land can be bought. But, in the final analysis, you've got it the wrong way round. I'm not interested in

destroying this family; fact is, I've been hoping to save it. England is lit-
tered with estates sold as debris. Only the titles don't change hands so
quickly. You know that. You've seen that."

"Your point being?"

"An economic one. Moments pass. What could have been done one
day can't the next. I see an opportunity I'd hate like hell to lose. Grant
you, had Adrian lived it would have been a more difficult case to
make—even if Rupert were a married man with a family. But your lives
aren't really here. This is all a burden that's fallen on you. It *could* lib-
erate you, but it could also become heavier and heavier as time goes on.
It could drive a wedge between you, between your children, too, depending upon how things are eventually set up. You know, there was a
time not long ago when *you* would have had to change *your* name to
Midleton-Lygham to live in this house under the present arrangement,
to change young Andrew's, too. Add to that the fact that there are people who would find a leisure center, even a mega-mart—whatever—as
being no more a desecration than the idea of anyone called Brook
rather than Cheviot rattling around in here. Mr. Brook, as in Bruchner."

"Destroying Castlemorland, no matter how much you'd coin in the
process, won't bring David back," I admonish him.

"Do you think I don't understand that? David was a bloody fool. He
made the worst mistake you can make in life, which is when you come
to believe your own advertising. I think the old man meant all he did for
David kindly, don't get me wrong. But as for the others, not just in this
family, they used him. Oh, I'm not saying it wasn't mutual, but the way
things turned out, they were accustomed to sucking the life out of people and he just wasn't."

"Julia is sure he was alive when she left him at that fountain."

"Who knows?"

"One would think she would."

"Is she a doctor? I didn't know that. Anyway, I don't blame her. My
brother had a certain effect on women. If he was a casual fling to her,
I'm sure she was less than that to him. Their relationship, such as it was,
was their business. But these are hard people, John. Years of winnow-
ing out whatever made them susceptible to life have left them that way.
You'll see for yourself one day, I've no doubt. You may have married in,
but that's no assurance. When they have to, they'll close ranks without
even realizing what they are doing. You'll be the disappointing Ameri-

can, just another mistake all in all. That's how they'll talk about you behind your back and the incredible thing, which is the awful part of it, is that they won't have a moment of doubt."

I drain two cups of coffee from the percolator on the serving table nearby and hand him one, from which the steam rises in a faint cloud before his ruddy face. "Suppose," I tell him, "just suppose, for the sake of argument, that at some point in the not so distant future Julia and I were prepared to entertain your proposal. What would it be? The conference center, I know about—and our keeping a flat. But what else, if anything?"

"Endless possibilities, really. We'd have to put some plans together, factor in the council's views, maybe Whitehall's, too—you understand. But, as I've said, I have the backing as well as the required relationships. I *can* give you some figures though. In 1957, there were two thousand malls in the United States; today there are more than thirty thousand. We're far behind, but on the same road. In this country, right now, forty to fifty percent of shopping trips are undertaken by car. So clearly the object has to be to roll up leisure activities and stores which provide necessities into one venue. The present thinking is along the lines of what we call the 'hole in the doughnut', where stores and cinemas, restaurants, what have you, are grouped around a central car-park. This can be any size—from fifty thousand to half a million square feet or so. More than two hundred thousand requires approval from London, which isn't an insurmountable obstacle if a man plays his cards properly. Personally, I'm partial to the idea of themed villages, with well-designed squares—miniature centers of their own—the farther one radiates from the focal point. Because these can be developed one at a time, in response to the demand."

"Well, it's worth bearing in mind, should the day come when we have to," I say. "But that day's not here yet. And, God knows, I hope it never comes."

"Although, from what I've been reading and hearing on the telly, it might actually be the least of your problems."

"Those are lies," I say.

"Mortlake's death is a lie?"

"No. Of course not. But the story connected with it is."

"If you say so," Matthew Paxton tells me.

"How well do you know Hugh Basildon?" I ask.

"He and my brother had a mutually parasitic relationship, but I don't know him at all. I know what he is. I met him at the inquest into David's death, but I haven't seen him since. You think he took the original film, don't you? You're probably right."

"Your lack of curiosity amazes me," I say. "I just wish I found it more convincing. Most people in your position—"

"Most people? You don't know anything about most people," Matthew snaps. "Sorry, John, it's true. As for Hugh Basildon, he and I are about as far apart as two human beings can be. If I were curious about his life, I'd go into a sex shop in Soho and satisfy that urge—it would amount to the same thing and take less time. But I'm not even mildly interested, you see, not even slightly am I that way inclined. Just so you know, however, Hugh Basildon possesses neither the industry nor the intelligence nor the stomach for extortion. He'd make a pathetic blackmailer because he's obviously a pathetic man. I mean if ever there were a pawn and not a bishop!"

"I GATHER YOU'VE made a new friend," Julia utters in a mildly sarcastic tone when I arrive at Louisa's bedroom to read to the children.

"Not a friend, certainly. Truth is, I don't know what to make of him."

"Does he want you to help him?" she asks.

"Actually, I wanted his help."

"Did you believe whatever it was he told you?"

"A little of it, yes. A little of it, no. On balance, I'm not sure."

"I wouldn't. I mean I *never* would, but you know that. Does it matter?"

"I'm afraid it might, darling. It might very much."

"Can you read *Eloise*, please?" Louisa calls then.

I open the book she has taken from her shelf and settle between my son and daughter on the edge of the bed.

"Eloise is very funny," Andrew says, "isn't she?"

" 'Hello, Room Service,' " Louisa mimics.

" 'Hello, Room Service,' " Andrew repeats.

"She lives in a hotel, doesn't she?" Louisa asks. "And it's in New York, isn't it?"

"Why does she live in a hotel" Andrew quizzes, "instead of a house?"

"Because they have Room Service," Louisa says. "Silly."

Julia laughs.

"Can we go to New York?" Andrew asks.

"Yes. Can we?" Louisa pleads. "Please, can we?"

"You've been to New York," Julia reminds them.

"Do you know what?" I hear myself interject. "I think that's a good idea. I think, if all goes well and you are a perfect little lady and a perfect little gentleman between now and then, that we should probably go for Easter."

"How many nights until Easter?" Louisa asks.

"Not too many," I promise her. As soon as I finish reading, I tuck Louisa beneath her floral duvet and immediately deliver Andrew to his bed next door.

Night lights glow dimly beneath their closed doors where Julia stops me in the hallway. "Easter?" she whispers.

"It comes at the end of Lent," I explain. "You can make a list of everything you'd like. We'll call Room Service."

Julia says, "You can stay if you want to. There's no one else staying. You can have your choice of guest rooms."

"I want to stay," I tell her, "but not that way and besides there's too much I still have to do."

"At this hour?"

"Especially at this hour."

22

I T IS, OF course, a coincidence: the moon breaking away from its gauzy cover of cloud at just that moment, riding above King William Street, spearing the City with mystical light. Racing to my office, I am doused and shadowed by it, thrown into relief. Had I time, I would stop, savor the somehow delicious, ethereal atmosphere, but I have no time to dispense so cavalierly—no time to wait to be caught by fast events. A block away from Battleman, I feel as one occasionally does upon leaving the cinema: aware of myself acutely, but as another. The sight of Battleman, proud but still, lit eerily across the vacant pavement, is invested with a dream-like quality, yet the building, like the days and nights just past, is plainly solid—here in too much detail not to be real life itself.

Ever since the reporter Wilson Blaine's telephone call and the first press reports of Dicky's death and dealing, I have been waiting for the managing directors to instruct Admin to deny me access to the building. That, after all, is how things are done in our industry. One minute a person is employed, the next expelled, permitted to collect only personal files and articles under the watch of security guards. But my card-key is still properly coded and I gain entry without effort. I wave to the guard, who has nodded off, his chin against the epaulet of his uniform.

My computer screen, an animated kaleidoscope when off, stills as soon as I log on, then chimes. To thwart hackers, our most sensitive internal systems are not connected by modem to any in the outside world; it is on these that the accounts I wish to access will most likely be recorded. In my own firm account, I discover a *Provision for Undistributed Bonus* of which I have no knowledge: a small amount, just less than twenty thousand. The source would appear to be the new business of which Philip spoke—something directed by Argus or his agents. I am not surprised. In my personal account, I find a cable-credit advice, three days old, in a similar account, the funds having been wired from a bank in Vaduz.

There is absolutely no one in our offices at this hour, but I saunter for a moment just to make sure. On a laminated card in the top right drawer of Rupert's breakfront, I find his entry codes. Working with and observing my partners day-in and day-out for so long, I naturally know where to look, but this is the first time I have ever betrayed their confidence. Back at my own computer, I use the codes to invade and search Rupert's accounts. I look everywhere: *Personal; Partnership; Portfolio;* even *Miscellaneous.* All are spotlessly clean, which is to say that they disclose no extraordinary activity in the past quarter. This is not conclusive, I realize, for the design ensnaring Julia and me is an elaborately calculated one. The care with which it has cast suspicion upon me—and established a record sufficiently incriminating to support that suspicion—will inevitably be mirrored in the caution employed to protect its perpetrators.

Next, I look in Philip's temporary office, rifle his files, his desk and cabinets with a meticulousness meant to leave no trace. I am nervous, queasy as I turn over and examine his papers, looking for anything that might resemble the password to his computer. In the end, I come up with nothing.

Of all my colleagues, Philip's intellect is the most capable of conjuring the conspiracy I am beginning to glimpse, yet his character and disposition are also the least likely to have done so. I weigh this impression against the utter absence of evidence implicating Rupert, including the records of accounts that seem to absolve him and even the fact that his password has not been secreted. I sit at my desk, lean back in the tufted pigskin chair and swivel. I close my eyes, press my fingers against their lids. Things are coming into focus.

A few minutes later, I wake Philip at the small hotel in Islington at which he habitually puts up in London.

"What time is it? It's past one o'clock," he declares, coming to consciousness over the telephone. "Where are you? What's wrong?"

"In the office," I reply. "Are you alone? I need to see you right away."

"Where?"

"Here."

He arrives in just over half an hour. I notice him first from the window, a thin silhouette sprinting against a diagonal of the zebra crossing. Upstairs he settles himself against Jane's desk. "Obviously, this is major," he says in his direct tone.

"Could hardly be more so," I reply. "Look, I have to ask you something first." I try to wrap the seriousness of my question in light humor, to elicit a reaction as well as an answer, not to give offense. "I am going to trust you with something. If I'm mistaken in doing that, all I ask is that you wait until tomorrow afternoon before you take whatever step comes next. First thing in the morning I'm going to buy a very large insurance policy. That way, if anything happens to me, Julia and the kids will be protected."

Puzzlement crazes Philip's features.

I smile. "Jason Argus," I say. "What do you know?"

"Enough. Well *quite* a lot," Philip replies. "But my info may be past its sell-by date. I've met him a few times—before he became such a notorious recluse."

"Really? Where?"

"Just after I came over to Battleman, before you got here, we did a deal for a shipping company. We sold off certain assets, packaged them with others that belonged to my sponsor, Chuan Ch'u—which is how the deal came to us originally. Argus was the buyer—a bit brusque, I must admit, but his cheque was good and one rather hoped it would lead on to bigger and better things. Alas, he disappeared—certainly from our orbit."

"If so, it was temporary. Find a more comfortable chair, Philip. I'll tell you a hell of a story."

He straightens. "I'm listening," he says as he fidgets. "Just want to get this coffee-maker to work."

I nod, then recount, with absolute detail, each event, travel and discovery of my life since Wilson Blaine's unexpected call. "Who is Jason Argus?" I ask in conclusion. "Who?"

"Here's the history," Philip informs me. "He's supposed to be half Greek, half Turk and to have made his original fortune selling weapons to both sides in most wars. According to that theory, he would be about my father's age, perhaps a bit younger, but much closer to his age than mine. Never mind, though, because there's a second theory: that he is the son of a white Russian father and an English mother; and a third and fourth and so on. He's illegitimate; he's not. He's benevolent; he's evil."

"It's one of those names I've always heard and never thought anything about," I admit.

"Meaning no disrespect, I'd've thought you'd be too small a fish for him to fry."

"Entirely agree. Where's the incentive? What would his motive be? Yet, the fact is he did summon me, so he *is* in on this, which must mean he's behind it."

"No question he's a brain box—and famously sensitive to aesthetic things. But he's kept some pretty unpleasant company over the years. Perhaps he's working with someone else."

"Philip, let me ask you this: could there be a connection between Argus and Wiley Ryan?"

"Could there be? Certainly. Why not? Has there ever been any that I've known of or heard whispered? Never. It seems an odd match, too. But stranger things have happened. Also, why would Ryan have it in for you if you *didn't* trade on inside information and bring down his deal? Whoever set you up, according to what you've just told me, set you up from the beginning."

"That's what I've assumed, but maybe it's been too blithe an assumption."

Philip looks me straight in the eye. He says, "Now, you're going off the deep end, John. That makes no sense. If Ryan was in on the plot, it had to be from the beginning. But why would he bring down his own bid? He wouldn't. That's the last thing he'd ever do. You've got to get some distance from this. It's far more likely that someone used you to blow up Ryan's bid—that you are an instrument and not the object of the game."

"I need help," I tell him. "I've done my best looking through Rupert's files, but you're better with the high-tech stuff and—"

"You know his password?"

"Found it."

"And *mine?*"

I look directly at him. "That one I couldn't find."

"*Chek Chue,*" Philip tells me.

"Sorry," I say. "Matter of life and death. Otherwise, I'd never—"

"Probably, I should have learned to carve teak," Philip says, "not to want and expect so much. That was the Buddha's definition of riches, you know: not to want. *Not to want.* I might have been married by now, had children like you—" He glances away.

Over the next hour, working like a sorcerer, he summons accounts including his own and the master file on the Ergo deal, but there is nothing revelatory in any of them, no connection to Koestler, Argus or Arabesque, to Dicky Mortlake or any other unexpected source. "Our one link would seem to be the deposit in your personal account, but it's too small for your bank to have D.K.'d and we'll never know whence it came, really. Its tracks are no doubt buried in the snows of the Alps; waste of time even to look."

"I'm afraid we may be falling into their trap," I venture. "They want us to chase a fox they know can't be found when we ought to be looking in more familiar territory. The clues aren't in Switzerland or Liechtenstein or even off the Lycian Coast—that was a diversion, to give them time, to set me up for certain photographs and travel records. That deal you did when you first came to Battleman: was Rupert involved in any way?"

"Only tangentially. He knew of it. We all knew—or had some idea, at any rate—of each other's work-in-progress, but he had something else going on with the mainland Chinese. His biggest disappointment as a matter of fact. They're a nut he's always wanted to crack, as you very well know, but the lot he was dealing with then proved more or less impervious to his blandishments. No, he didn't have any connection to what we were doing."

"Philip, when are you scheduled to go back to Hong Kong?"

"By next week, for sure. Command performance."

"Are there people there—people completely out of these loops— whom you trust? There must be."

"A few."

"Then, you dig as deeply as you can from that end. And I'll start digging a hole to China here. Trust your instincts."

"And you yours, John."

BY MONDAY NOON, there is brisk traffic in Threadneedle Street and its tributaries. Outside the George and Vulture, young men in City suits, pints in hand, stare skyward at the unanticipated turquoise sky. Rupert is among them, drinkless, having been stopped for conversation by a party of acquaintances on his way in. He laughs extra-pleasantly at something one of them has said, then departs their company for mine without a word.

We are led to a stark, incommodious booth and order pints of lager of our own.

"I'm afraid I ran it out last night," he begins.

"Where were you?"

"Annabel's, dancing. Milanese model showed up on my doorstep courtesy of an old friend in the rag trade. I gave her dinner. She wanted to go for a bop afterward so we did, around midnight. Place was crawling, like a house party."

I sigh, half for effect. "It's time you found someone and got married," I tell him. "It's time you had kids, went to bed early and got up when they do. You can have them later on, sure, but if you actually want to see them grow up . . . well, you know, there's no time like the present."

"One of these days, I'm going to surprise you all," Rupert insists. "But, right now, my life feels to me as if it suits my situation. I don't expect that to be the case permanently, but for the time being . . . Do you know the problem with doing a girl like the one last night? It becomes addictive—not as much of an upper as it once was, but still necessary. I think I'd have to break that habit before I settled down with anyone I might marry. Marriage itself isn't any way to break it."

"I completely agree," I say, "that you shouldn't take a wife and start a family as therapy. Look, don't you think we should order?"

"Yes, I do. Rump steak for me. They'll bring the usual chips and veggies. Might do a stewed cheese. Or a sponge pudding."

"Julia's been in a state," I tell him. A loud din fills the room; we cannot be overheard. "But you know that."

"I do indeed."

"Where do you stand in all of this? Julia gave me some idea, I have to tell you. She gave me some reason to believe that you were on my side, or at least not entirely on the other."

"No. I'm not against you. I'm disposed to believe whatever you tell me, John. But there *are* questions that need to be answered. No one can pretend otherwise. I'm willing to listen if you're willing to talk."

"Thank you."

"You have the feeling you are being used, don't you? Framed or—"

"Precisely."

"Let's start at the beginning then. Why would Dicky have done what he did—made those trades, taken such dangerous positions without authorization?"

"I don't know. Perhaps he thought he did have authorization."

"From whom, if not you or Julia?"

"Again, I've no idea. But that's not really the beginning. The beginning, as far as I'm concerned, is the video Matthew Paxton sent to Julia."

"Yes. I'm sorry about that," Rupert assures.

"Where did Matthew get it is the question."

"No idea. You think it's connected to the Ergo business?"

"You bet your life I do."

"So do I."

"I'm glad to hear it."

"Because Matthew Paxton's last few deals have been backed by an investment consortium which is itself a subsidiary of Arabesque, Jason Argus's principal arm. That's something I hadn't known until yesterday. But I've been asking around and the answer to one of my many questions came back out of the blue. It's the first piece of the puzzle that fits with another."

"And you're sure it's true?"

"Yes, I'm sure." He raises his thick eyebrows, winks.

"Argus keeps showing up—everywhere one turns. Dicky had been led to think I wanted to lunch with him in order to talk over something about Arabesque, which I'd never heard of at the time. And, according to whatever documents Julia had and gave to you, I am alleged to have benefited from their shorting of Ergo's stock."

"That *is* what they show," Rupert admits, "but documents do not provide the last word on anything. They can be forged, or even contain innocent mistakes."

"Where are they now? I'd like to see them."

"I burned them, I'm afraid. For your protection. And Julia's. Everyone's—the firm's. Ashes can't very well be subpoenaed was my thought. At the end of the day, the funds are either there or they're not. It's the money itself that will or won't incriminate you."

"I wish that were true," I say, suppressing shock, "but unless I attempt to claim it, those banks, as I understand them, will never speak up, never say yeah or nay to anyone's questions."

"Fair point." Rupert ponders.

"Have you ever run across Jason Argus?"

"Never met him."

Our starter plates of whitebait are served. Rupert asks the waitress for a shot glass of Bushmills and, when it arrives, pours this as a floater into his pint.

"I did. But in Turkey, *not* Zurich. On Tuesday. I flew there. Incognito. On *his* air force."

"Incognito?"

"They took charge of all travel arrangements. Obviously, he wanted to evaluate me with his own eyes, without my ever being able to prove a connection. Unless, of course, you assume they were just playing games."

The whitebait is salty.

"You're not kidding me?" Rupert asks.

"I only wish I were."

"So do I. Because, if you really and truly aren't, then they're not playing games, John, and, frankly, I don't like the conclusion to which that leads. I mean, if a man like Argus is taking such a personal interest in all this, it implies that whoever's behind your problems is going to be much harder to deal with. Someone whom Argus would get into bed with would have to be, in his own right, on a certain level already."

When the steaks arrive and after the vegetables have been ladled and the Colman's mustard dolloped onto our plates, I say, "You feel let down by Wiley Ryan, don't you?"

Rupert hesitates reflectively. "He was my mistake."

"You thought he could go the distance and, in the end, he couldn't?"

"*Wouldn't*, is the way I'd put it. I wanted it to work out so much that I could taste it, so I allowed myself to look past his weaknesses. There's no one else I can blame. It was a chance to do something that hadn't been done before and I trusted his instincts, when I should have seen that we were going way too slowly and concentrating on all the wrong things."

The strong mustard immediately clears my sinuses. I breathe in, squint a little. "I'm sure you're right," I admit. "But I have a more imminent problem."

"We all do."

"You haven't been accused of anything."

"Not yet," Rupert replies. "But if they succeed in doing you, Philip and I will be next, no doubt about that. They'll string us end to end, turn over everything we've ever done, looking for whatever they can find or make look like something."

Momentarily, perversely, the notion of company—colleagues, friends, anyone—with whom to share my ordeal salves my nerves, yet I recognize that, as deeply as Rupert may wish to console me, he is being disingenuous. "Surely not," I say. "I've spoken to only one D.T.I. type so far—a very low-level fellow trying to work up a basic profile of the situation. But he didn't ask about any of you, didn't seem interested in anyone I'd had contact with—other than Dicky, of course. Also, he didn't give two hoots about anything that happened after the fact. My guess is they're looking for betrayal on a relatively intimate, relatively junior scale. Oh, I'm their man all right—at least the one who's left alive—not some tycoon who spends the majority of his time sailing the jet stream."

Rupert looks off obliquely into the smoky distance beyond and above me. "I wish I could help you," he replies. "But I honestly don't know how."

23

AFTER LUNCH A wind rises suddenly; it slaps our backs as we come into the open street. At the corner we separate, Rupert off to God knows which client's board meeting to dispel suspicion, infuse confidence. We shake hands. He waves, lowers his famous trilby on his brow.

Only one person has called during my absence, but, the instant I see the name, I shudder—by reflex, yet also out of a surprisingly avid curiosity. Chas Ledbetter is passing through London on business. He cannot be reached until after seven-thirty when he will be in the bar of the Connaught Hotel, where he is staying. Would I like to come by for a drink, he wonders in his message. My first thought is that I do not have time for such nonsense. I have not seen him since . . . our fifth . . . or perhaps it was our tenth reunion from high school. I have no idea what has become of his life—and yet one is inevitably keen to see for oneself how middle age has refined youth, especially youth of the golden variety. I decide to postpone my decision until the working day is farther along and I have paid a visit to the one remaining person who may be able to help me solve the riddle which is distorting my life out of its recognizable shape.

I spend the afternoon taking and placing calls to those who had hoped to be part of the Ergo syndication—especially to investment bankers and fund managers in America, which is, or was, my bailiwick. The purpose of these conversations is to protect our relationship in the aftermath of events which have stretched it dangerously—to accept a measure of blame yet, as subtly as is feasible, to spread that blame among the management clique that instructed us, to imply that the circumstances of our debacle were more complex, even more sinister than it would be discreet to elaborate over the transatlantic wire. The deal having come to a bad end, it is Battleman—my partners, our future— whose protection and survival must now be our first concern. Monotonously, I emphasize the venerable age of our partnership, our long reputation for probity, the improbability that we would compromise it. I stress the cutthroat a-ethical nature of modern competition, leaving it to our clients to infer whether we or Ryan—or mysterious forces in opposition to us both—are most likely to be culpable. Not too defensively, I draw attention to his avarice in wishing to vest his cadre's pensions ahead of others'—our astonishment as well as powerlessness when this was sprung on us. I acknowledge our mis-evaluation of his character and focal discipline. These days, it is a kind of catechism we are all pronouncing, acknowledging but also deflecting guilt. It is beneath us—beneath our historic and even recent self-conceptions—but, in the circumstances, we have no other choice. "Nothing to fret over, I promise," I hear myself repeat near the close of each such chat. "I'll fill you in when I see you. We'll have lunch. One side of the pond or the other. *You bet! You're on!*"

Later, in afternoon gusts so violent and fitful they rock my car as I motor along the Embankment then across the Albert Bridge, I set off for Wandsworth. The Thames is indigo, nearly opaque; waked by barges, it conjures a forbidding cold. In Battersea then in the Common, the branches of trees remain budless, but a soft birdsong carries everywhere in the distance, white noise of the approaching spring.

Hugh Basildon lives in the small terraced house he bought a decade before, in the last property boom, with the inheritance his mother bequeathed him. He opens the bright blue front door, with its polished central knob, to reveal case after case, box after box of still-packed china, bric-a-brac and books. "Forgive the state of things," he implores courteously. "I've been away for the last fortnight in Madeira. Do you know it?"

"No."

"We were somewhat ahead of season there, but not too badly so. Lovely seawater pool, balmy evenings and, of course, the price was right. I stayed with an old friend who's an artist there. He went years ago—for that exquisite sub-tropical light. Foolish, for a painter, to live in this climate really." He is a tall, soft man, just heavy-set, in whom the well-formed features and affected mannerisms of a young dandy have metamorphosed into something more petulant. As I look at him, I recall Julia's description when his name came up in conversation many years ago. "I'm afraid Hugh's a dreamer," she declared apodictically. "And dreamers never really seem to cut it."

"I've barely seen you since your wedding," Hugh Basildon continues, fussing among his crated store. "Would you like something to drink? I'm sure there's a bottle of bubbly still in the fridge. Must be. May have gone flat. Let's see."

"I see your father now and again. So we keep up with you that way. But we really should get something on the books."

"It would be nice," Hugh says, his voice full of unmistakable doubt. "Do you know, I thought I'd be married once—when I moved in here, in actual fact. I thought this might be a way station or, maybe, I'd end up living here, but not alone—you know, improving things along the way. Funny, still and all, how suddenly one's life stops evolving. Everything stops but the clock. . . . We're in luck, it's not gone off yet," he announces, as he pours and tastes the leftover champagne.

"Do you work here as well as live here?" I ask, wishing to avoid an excursion into his current philosophy.

"Yes. My studio and darkroom are downstairs."

"That's handy."

"It is—sort of."

"You free-lance?"

"Where and when I can. I've had staff assignments on and off over the years. In actual fact, there's a new mag starting up I was hoping might see its way to taking me aboard. Vaguely alternative sort of sheet, although its majority-owned by one of the big publishing companies. Sad to say, they've seen fit to hire elsewhere. Apparently the lucky candidate's a woman, or in some other way disadvantaged."

"I see. Well, if it's not that, it'll be something else. Everyone says you're very talented."

"Do they? I suppose I was when *they* knew me. Sorry, if that sounds glum, it's just that I'm a bit fed up at the moment."

"Don't get me going," I tell him. "You've been away. You probably haven't heard what's been happening here."

"Oh, I have. The London papers arrive every day in Funchal by late afternoon. I've felt so sorry for the two of you."

"Naturally, it's more complicated than has been reported."

"Naturally. They're not interested in the truth, you know. They're not even interested in making you look good or bad. They are solely concerned with making *the story* look good because it's all entertainment now, the whole modern fucking world. One has only to take photography, for example. Thought's dead. I mean, soon everything will be stimulus. It couldn't be more obvious which way it's all headed. And one either has what one should have—namely a body—and lacks what one should lack—namely a brain—or the picture isn't very pretty. I'm prattling. I know. Forgive me, I'm wound up."

"The friend in Madeira?"

"Boy I went with, actually—paid his airplane fare. Has found another friend. Not to worry. I'm the world's expert in handling this sort of thing. . . . So tell me, how are all my friends, the ones I never see anymore."

"Carrying on, those I know anyway."

Hugh affects a broadly disdainful grimace. "Not an artist among them."

"I couldn't argue with you there, although I'm sure I'm as guilty as the next fellow."

"I suspect not."

"Why is that?"

"Julia married you. Everyone she's ever cared for *or collected* has been artistic—except Piers, of course, but she was young then and mistook his sophistication for insight. It's a strain in that family. Rupert possessed the same thing once upon a time."

"I think I know what you mean," I say, then suddenly sneeze. "Sorry."

"*Gesundheit,*" Hugh offers.

"Thank you."

"Personally, I'd prefer a life of style and debt to one which involved neither. Clearly, others wouldn't. Oh, well. . . . Anyway, you wanted to see my photographs, didn't you? Isn't that what you said on the telephone?"

"Please."

He leads me a half-flight downstairs to a shuttered conservatory in the center of whose cold terrazzo floor a massive stack of albums rests on a throw rug of synthetic tiger-skin. I flip through the topmost, then several pages of the second large cowhide-spined volume, letting out an intermittent solo of admiring sighs. "Actually," I confess at last, "what I am most interested in is a video."

Hugh Basildon smiles ironically. "Ah, well, I've won a bet with myself in that case."

"Which was?"

"That 'what goes around comes around.' "

"Obviously, you know which video?"

"Of course, *I know*. What do I do now is the question: show it to you or not?"

"That's not necessary. I've already seen it."

"Perhaps. But without the outtakes."

"You shot it?"

"Who else? In Super Eight—all those summers ago. Of course, the editing and the transfer to tape were done more recently—no more than six months ago. Before that, it just lay in store with the rest of the past."

"Why, suddenly, then?"

"Why? Money—bills, all that. What did you think? I knew it would be an easy trick to trace it. Didn't seem to bother him, however."

"Bother whom?"

"I was just fooling around with some high-speed rolls of film. Practicing. Fulfilling my role, I suppose. It was my house, my garden so I didn't really require any other ticket." He confronts me directly. "It had nothing to do with your wife. That was not at all the intention."

"I understand."

"But everything to do with David. I didn't mean to invade anyone's privacy. Anyone *else's*. The image was just *irresistible*. No more to it than that. That luminous night—it was like some weird allegorical painting. The seduction of a class by this god who had sprung self-formed into their world." In his eyes, as he speaks, there is the glint of tragedy.

"You knew David very well, didn't you?" I ask, finally looking away.

"That's not a secret," he replies at once.

I sip some of the mediocre champagne, then draw a breath. "It was Matthew Paxton who asked you to edit the film and make that video, wasn't it?"

"Matthew's destructive. There's no question about it. He flaunts himself. Ultimately, however, he's not even interesting, except as David's brother." Hugh, too, now quaffs the last of his drink.

"It's difficult, looking at him," he soon resumes, "to remember that David's life was not easy. With so much in his favor you would have thought it would be, but the human brain is a peculiar place. I mean, who's kidding whom, we all receive and are denied."

I gaze at him and around the chilly conservatory, with its rickety table and chairs, its ragged curtains and upholstery creased by the perpetual weight of heavy boxes and dusty piles of books. It is as if he has decided that the story he is revealing must develop slowly, like a negative in fluid, before being pinned up on a wire and illuminated.

"What do you think Matthew meant to do with it, if not turn it over to the police?" I ask, ignoring his last remark.

"No idea. Did I say it was Matthew Paxton, by the way?"

"You didn't seem to object to my drawing that conclusion."

"This is very difficult for me," Hugh admits.

"I'm sure."

"No. For more reasons than even someone as clever as you can guess—beyond the fact that I loved David with a love as disabling as it was unrequited, all but once." His voice breaks.

I do not interrupt.

"I've been threatened, you see," he tells me. "Frankly, from the vividness of that threat, its sheer virulence, which I'll not go into, I'm surprised I wasn't dispatched then and there, as soon as the tape was in his hands. I can only guess he knows a coward when he sees one. You're shaking your head; your jaw's dropped open, John; you look surprised."

"Nothing surprises me anymore," I say.

"The person who threatened me is more than capable of carrying out that threat, mind you. I've known him long enough to recognize that in his make-up. Truth be told, I've hated him long enough, too." Hugh stares at me expectantly, then abruptly stretches himself across a corduroy divan, propping his head on its worn sidearm.

"Go on," I insist. "Please, Hugh, go on. Why do you hate this person so much?"

He hesitates. "Why else? Rejection—going back. He led me on— for sport. He was older. It ought to have been the other way round. He knew my inclination before I did practically, even if he didn't share it. Good for a laugh—with the other blokes, among the in-crowd."

"And since then?"

"Old injuries lodge in the heart, don't they? Or haven't you ever suffered any? In those days, which were long before your time, long before anyone in this country had ever heard of you, Piers dispensed the odd pill or powder and he dispensed humiliation. I don't know which is worse."

"Do I know this person?" I ask.

"Do you really want to know the answer to that is the question you should be asking."

"Tell me."

"Rupert . . . Rupert Midleton-Lygham, *now Cheviot,* paid me for the tape. *And* to put a certain sequence in rewind, then tape it over and insert it. Oldest special effect there is—astonishing it's still so reliable."

"I don't believe that for a minute."

"Why would I lie?"

"I don't know."

Hugh sits up. His blue eyes lock onto mine. "The whys and wherefores I can't tell you. But when you think about it carefully, you'll see it makes all the sense in the world: once you realize that Rupert is *and has always been* an actor and that his performance quite simply fooled you, as it did most other people. I don't even know what he's up to, I'm not party to any of it, but I can only imagine the scale."

"It's very important," I tell him deliberately, "that you not mention this conversation to anyone else—particularly to Rupert, or to anyone who could conceivably pass it on to him."

Hugh shrugs. "Whom would I talk to?" he murmurs.

"No idea," I say gently. "I'm just begging you not to speak to *anyone.*"

"Here," he says, pressing several Kodak boxes, a Maxell slipcase and video tape into my hand. "You and Julia should have the originals. Burn them, give them to the police, I don't mind. Whatever *His* Lordship is holding back will be the only copies left."

"Wouldn't it be nice to think so?" I say.

I AM SHAKEN by Hugh Basildon's accusation. At first, I do not, cannot make myself believe him. For, to accept Rupert's complicity in the nightmare we have been enduring would be to flavor enmity with betrayal, to call into question my own shrewd perspicacity, the future of my employment and employer, as well as that of the family into which my children were born. It is easier, more comfortable to discredit Hugh, whom I hardly know and whose very adulthood seems somehow unmoored from the safe harbor of his youth. Yet I cannot completely discount his logic. Certainly, Rupert possesses the requisite skill and access and resources to engineer a conspiracy as intricate and ominous as the one enveloping us. Clearly, in each arena of our lives—at Castlemorland as well as in the City—he has the most intimate information possible. Inevitably, at each pivot of events, he has been close by, hugging the tangent of our existence. And yet three balancing questions remain: what would he have to gain? Has not the injury to him—through the Ergo deal, to his reputation and finances—been second only to that we have suffered? Could he, would he so wholly deceive us?

Quickly, I have to separate myself into two people: one who thinks, questions; another who drives, turns right or left according to memory, slows for then starts up at lights, impelled by reflex. In the Latchmere Road, acting on instinct, I telephone Philip, but there is only voice mail at the office and his mobile is off. The traffic is heavy in both directions. I head for home. In front of a Paki take-away, a young black man with broad shoulders, a white leather Eisenhower jacket and Rastafarian dreadlocks steps unhesitantly from the curb. I swerve to avoid him, nearly swiping the left fender of a taxi in the passing lane. My adrenaline rushes. I accelerate. I *must* concentrate on the road, I tell myself—defer all other thought, calm down, come to rest. Very soon, I know, whatever happens, I will have no choice but to come to rest.

According to the clock in my dash, it is seven twenty-three as I approach Lower Sloane Street. I have been driving in silence, but I now flick on the radio and scan until I am sure there is nothing I would like to hear. Silence again; the wind against the car; the music of engine and gear box. If I do go home, I decide, I will fret, probably drink and forego dinner, thus get no closer to the answers I am seeking. I will feel Julia's absence, turn melancholy in the childless quiet. I swing a right, then left, into Bourne Street and again into Ormonde Place. Our house is shuttered, dark. I slow, stop the car in the front of our garage for a moment, keep it running. Then, as if injected with resolve, I make a U-turn around Hercules and speed away in the direction of Mayfair.

I find a space in front of the tobacconist's across Mount Street and enter the Connaught behind a party of Texans arriving for dinner. The women carry Chanel handbags. This hotel is a kind of home to me, a landmark in my life. It is where I stayed when I first travelled to England as one of Battleman's men in the Orient and each time I returned thereafter. In the Grill Room and Restaurant, I have entertained and been entertained by endless clients and customers of our firm, mostly foreign. And it was to a suite and bed here that I brought Julia on our wedding night.

In the oak-panelled American Bar, an electric log burns in the fireplace, whilst above it a stag head, slightly cocked, presides as usual over those who gather on the tapestry sofas and leather chairs, around the small tables he surveys. In the inside room, in an alcove of windows opposite the bar itself, a solitary man in a charcoal suit sits studying the martini before him. He is lean, bald for his age, with a fringe of prematurely silver hair; an artery rises from his left temple as veins do from the backs of his hands, remnants of ferociously athletic younger days. His glance rises and turns suddenly and I recollect the severe profile, that cruel, confident, adolescent jaw. "Chas," I say, going toward him, reminding myself that we last parted as friends.

"Oh, good! You made it."

"Just broke free. Would have left you a message otherwise. But I wouldn't have known what to say much before now."

"Sure, sure," Chas laughs. "Drink?"

"I think I'll join you," I tell him.

"Bombay martini—white bottle, not the sapphire—really dry, up, with a twist," he says aloud, simultaneously to the waiter and to me, as if to confirm my assent to each particular.

"Perfect," I say.

"Well?" Chas smiles.

"Well?" I laugh.

"It's nice to see you."

"You, too."

"You're doing well?"

"Yeah—by and large." I nod. "I've known better moments. You?"

"Same. It's normal enough at our age."

"Married?"

"Was once. Briefly. Not for a long time now."

"Oops. Sorry."

"Amazingly, I don't even think about it. We didn't have any children—spent a king's ransom trying—but it was probably for the best
that all that technology just missed the mark."

"Never too late to try again," I tell him, wondering, a moment afterward, if it might have been a careless thing to say.

Never mind; Chas lets it pass. "I saw your name in the paper," he explains.

"Sadly," I confess.

"As long as they spell the name correctly, right?"

"Wrong. I won't bore you with the details, but it's been one hell of
a cock-up. You wouldn't believe it: a chain reaction of things going
wrong. How much play has it gotten in the States?"

"Only in the financial pages. The *Journal*. The *FT*'s printed there
now; you know that. Guys in the business know, most of them.
Whether they remember's another question."

Our martinis arrive. Chas returns his finished glass, raises its re-
placement.

"To your very good health," I propose. The gin changes the atmosphere all at once, establishing a distance between us and the others in
the room. The day, up until now, recedes into the distant past; the
evening looms. "You in the business?" I inquire at last.

"In a manner of speaking. Not M and A, of course, and nothing to
do with Battleman Peale or Ergo, Incorporated. I'm an institutional
salesman."

"On Wall Street?"

"We moved to midtown ten years ago. But, yes, 'on Wall Street' is
the way I think most people would still put it."

"And doing well?"

"Holding my own. I couldn't ask for too much better. I've been
lucky."

"Great. Do you get over here often?"

"This is the first time in twenty years. Until recently, my customers
have all been domestic. I've just begun to handle some European accounts in the last year; nothing in Asia as yet."

"But you haven't called on our Asset Management Group?"

"No. They're on another broker's books."

"Good."

Balding, silver-haired or not, Chas has not lost the twinkle which drew Caroline Carswell and every other girl toward him in the days when his looks seemed unravagable. "I'll take that as I know it's meant," he replies. "I'm not looking for inside information."

"If I possessed any, I'd be the last person you'd ever want to get it from." I laugh. "I swear to God."

"The fact is there's some information *I'd* like to give *you.*"

I put down my glass and study him. "What kind of information?"

"Nothing improper. By accident," he continues, "I happened to see something, from which I've drawn a conclusion. That's all. Perhaps I'm onto something, perhaps not. You'll know, you'll have an instinct."

"I'll try."

"I told you I'd begun handling a few European accounts, to get my feet wet?"

"Um huh."

"One of them's in Liechtenstein."

I bolt back to hyper-consciousness. "And?"

"You've heard of Jason Argus?"

"Of course. Who hasn't?"

"His account is the one I'm talking about. . . . I know what you're thinking, that it's a strange and exalted place to start, but his American operations are customers of mine. We've done business together for a long time now. I've made them a lot of money."

I rest my elbow on the small table, my chin on my fist and peer at Chas Ledbetter. "Do you know anyone called Koestler," I ask, "in Vaduz?"

"Koestler? No. Why?"

"Sorry. Go on."

Charles stretches his legs before him, folds his hands behind his head. "Here's the point," he elaborates, drawing his elongated form together all of a sudden and leaning toward me. "I've been reading the papers, naturally, and, as I told you, following your story. So I may not know all the ins and outs, but I do have an elemental grasp of the situation. *And* I know two things that most people don't. First, I know that Arabesque *did* short Ergo before—almost up until—the buy-out blew up. I know with such certainty because many of their sell orders, on the U.S. markets, were executed through me."

"Very interesting," I admit.

"Second, I know that the Swiss guys who manage the Arabesque accounts for Argus were at Annabel's last night. With your cousin, or whatever—Rupert Cheviot."

"How do you know my cousin Rupert, Chas, if you don't handle Battleman and—"

"I don't know him. Profiles in the press, that's all. He cuts a figure. How do I know the Prince of Wales? I don't but I do—same answer. In point of fact, there are not many leading merchant bankers with titles. Or perhaps, there are? . . . I thought marquesses were French anyway."

"Those are *mar-keys* not *mar-kwisses*. So did I. It's tricky. I'll explain one day. Did you meet Rupert?"

"Only in a manner of speaking. He had his hand up some Italian girl's skirt. His mind was elsewhere."

"Steady, Chas," I say. "Steady. Why are you telling me all this? Now? Breaking your customer's confidentiality, not to mention whatever other risks may be involved. You're—"

"I don't know myself. Because your wife's cousin a prick? Because I see myself in him—what I once was and wanted to be? Because I've often felt I did you dirt when we were kids and never really apologized—and, strange as it may sound, like to think I've become a nicer person, more decent and Christian as I've grown older and, well, lived more. Or because Ash Wednesday's coming and I want to get it off my chest? I mean you have a wife and two children—isn't that right—who are more important; and how can I sit back and watch you destroyed and their lives with you when I know that whatever was done, whatever's happened, he had and has to be behind it?" Chas seems to hold his breath.

"Those are all good reasons," I assure him, my voice trailing into quiet.

"Okay, there is one more," he confesses.

"Having to do with your Swiss friends?"

"I suppose there is a certain consistency to all of us, isn't there?" Chas smiles wickedly. "They bet against me, through another broker, in an arbitrage deal of theirs. They moved the entire market. I came *this* close to going under. But what could I do? You can't fight City Hall. Assholes! They never even knew I knew. Naturally, when fate delivers me such a delicious chance to fuck them this royally—all because we happened to be a little thirsty and my customer thought we might just as well have one last drink and take in the female scenery—well, who am I to reject Providence? Save a friend and screw an enemy at the same time's nice work if you can get it."

"Sweet!" I agree.

He winks. "Can I buy you dinner—here or elsewhere?"

"Oh, you bet your life," I promise. "But not tonight. I've got to run. But, yes, absolutely—as soon as there's time, if there ever is."

24

MY FIRST INCLINATION is to tear off in the direction of
Castlemorland, to find Julia and relate to her everything I have
learned—first from Philip, then from Hugh, then Chas. But, before I
reach my car, my eye catches an unopened gate at the center of an interruption in the line of tall Victorian houses that have long ago been
converted to stylish shops and upstairs flats. The gate is heavy iron and
recessed. I venture through it tentatively, then, by habit, along the neat
path, bordered by slat-backed wooden benches plaqued in memory of
the dead, that curves down behind the Farm Street Church to the lower
steps of Mayfair. The Jesuits' church is still, lightless, locked at its altar
door. I gaze up at its cold stone facade, filling my lungs with the damp
London air. I exhale slowly. On my tongue I can taste delicious crystals
of moisture, not quite rain, in the thick, exuberant, metropolitan atmosphere.

I return to my car, but no sooner do I reach South Audley Street
than I can feel the martini dulling certain of my senses and heighten-
ing others. I am afraid to drive very far, so I turn abruptly and head instead to Islington. It is a much shorter distance, especially at this hour,
and, the longer I think about it, a more sensible starting point, too.

A few minutes from Philip's hotel, I ring him on my car phone. The
hotel takes a while to answer and, by the time my call is put through
from the switchboard, I can spot the white, double-fronted stucco
building along the side of the street in the distance. After seven rings,
there is no answer, which suits me. I pull into a vacant parking space just
opposite, leave the engine running and the heater on. It is eight forty-
three. Either Philip will return in the next few minutes, from a drink

with someone or other, or else, wherever he is, he will have stayed on through dinner and not be home until much later. I decide to wait until nine o'clock.

But, at nine the street is quiet. One or two innocuous couples and a few solitary others have entered or exited the little hotel, but neither Philip nor anyone I recognize has been among them. A police car, slowly and sirenless, drives by; later, a blue Volvo sedan, which hesitates long enough to discharge a tired-looking man, in the depths of middle-age, bearing a heavy sample case. The sight of him induces in my mood a certain atavistic melancholy, as if someone, in the distance, has begun to belt out the blues. I decide to wait another quarter hour in the un-eventful street. For Philip is not simply the best, but now, perhaps, the only person with whom I may be able to work out a strategy and tac-tics to put things right—to save my family from Rupert's machinations before they destroy us.

Ten minutes later, a taxi swerves round the corner, changes gears boisterously as it passes the local pub, then eventually stops by the curb. Philip alights.

I step out of my car cautiously, locking it with the remote, and fol-low Philip into the tiny townhouse lobby, with its muted marble floors and brass railings. With me, for plausible cover, I have brought my briefcase and, already in my right grip, a Battleman memo regarding a minor deal on which we are—and for some time have been—supposed to be working. Should anyone observing us make inquiries, this will serve as my excuse for having tracked Philip here.

"Philip," I call quietly, from a few steps behind.

Surprised, he turns. "I don't believe it," he replies.

For appearance, I thrust the memo immediately into his near view. He lowers his eyes to read it. "You know that hole to China we were talking about digging?" I whisper.

He looks up again, momentarily confused. "I think so."

"Well, my end's apparently about to come through."

"Oh," he says, "I see," immediately restoring his mock-attention to the memo. "In that case—"

"We should probably head off somewhere, what do you think? In-tending no disrespect to your hotel, of course, which is a very nice place."

"Isn't it? It's simple," Philip says, "but there are those of us who love it."

In the unlit car, driving aimlessly, I raise my finger to my lips and draw a zipper across them, just in case. "Have you decided yet what day you are going back?" I inquire.

"Day after tomorrow, more than likely." He studies me for permission to continue this course of conversation.

I nod.

I park west of Tottenham Court Road, just north of St. Giles Circus, and we wander down Greek Street then turn at a corner, deliberately losing ourselves in the crowds of diners, playgoers, tourists and night-blooming perverts.

"Really, day after tomorrow?" I ask.

"Really. So, what is this about?" Philip asks.

"In broadest outline: Rupert paid a friend of Julia's called Hugh Basildon to trick up a video showing Julia and David Paxton together on the night he died—of a drug overdose. Debatable how incriminating it really is, but it's scandal sheet stuff. He gave this to Matthew Paxton, who, whatever he says, I still believe used it to intimidate Julia even before Adrian died. Rupert also shorted Ergo shares, through a bank in Liechtenstein, among other places, long before the news of Dicky's trades broke."

"Christ!" exclaims Philip. "How do you know?"

"Basildon told me about the video himself. Matthew Paxton confessed to sending it to Julia. He claims he received it anonymously, which may be true, although I doubt it. More likely, he's afraid of Rupert."

We walk briskly, our collars up. "You have to *think*," I continue. "I know you said that Rupert was not really involved when you did that shipping deal with Argus, but did he ever *meet* him?"

"Not that I recall. Why is it so important? You'll forgive me if I say the whole business seems rather jumbled."

"It does. *If* you think about it as a single plan, with a single motive, straight from the beginning. That's where I've been getting lost myself. What I now think, however, is that there were a couple of different plans that ended up running into each other. Suppose, first of all, that Rupert *did* send a video to Matthew Paxton. He knows Matthew's a shit and would be bound to terrorize Julia with it. Anyway, if he didn't, Rupert could always plop it in the post himself later on. The idea was to frighten Julia into encouraging her brother to sell off a small but prime parcel of land to Paxton. Argus, more than likely, would have backed that development. And Rupert would naturally have had a silent piece—probably in another name, probably held abroad. Still, small change in the present context. Now, let's further suppose that, by the weekend Wiley and Tag Ryan came to shoot, the weekend Adrian was killed, Rupert had already begun to conclude that Ryan wasn't up to the task he had set himself. Subverting Castlemorland, whatever the ambitions or complexes behind it, had to be a minor ambition at best— small potatoes compared to his desire to see the Ergo deal through to where he was sure it would leave him: at the top of the City, essentially. It could be that he heard about Ryan's plans to vest his pensions prematurely, or something else entirely. Remember, there was plenty. Once he understood that the deal was unlikely to fly, he had to look for another way to profit."

"Short it and frame you."

"Short it *with* Argus's money, for a bundle, the price of which was merely to slip Arabesque advance notice of the scandal that would inevitably cause the deal to unravel on a date certain."

"So, if he were already involved with Argus, the two plots were thus joined."

"Julia was terrified. She called him. That must have been irresistible."

Philip bites his lip. "All Rupert had to do was produce that bottle of Armagnac," he speculates, "after everything else that was consumed that night, then lure Adrian onto the road—"

I stop midway across the beginning of a cobblestone mews. "I hadn't got that far," I tell him.

"It's only a hypothesis."

"That call: when it came, we were on our way upstairs, remember? I asked Adrian if everything was all right and he put his hand over the mouthpiece of the receiver and said 'Isabel's mother'. Naturally, I just assumed. But what if the call weren't *from* Isabel's mother, but *about* her?"

Philip pauses. "He could have made it, using his mobile, or had it made. He could also have tied the string across Adrian's door, making it look, to all of us, like he had retired for the night. Normally."

"They were going to elope. I promised to cover for him. That's something I've never told anyone but Julia. I don't know why. No reason not to. Anyway, with Adrian dead, Rupert had the title that had eluded his father. The house was in Julia's hands, but, soon enough, one way or another, he could be pretty sure of finding a way to scare her out of it. Or that might have been Matthew's job, so that Matthew could develop it."

"Do you think Rupert really wants to develop it?" Philip asks.

"Well, I don't think he cares about it, if that's what you mean—certainly not in the way that Adrian did or that Julia does. I think it would all depend on what he had in the bank, to tell you the truth. When that was very little, I can see that he might have shared Matthew's dream. Now that he must have socked away what he has, maybe not. Maybe he'll develop on the periphery and otherwise leave well enough alone, or double-deal Matthew completely."

Philip smiles. "I've just had a devious thought," he admits. "There may, in fact, be a way to redress things. I'm not sure yet. Give me a bit of time, will you? One thing I do remember, though, now that I think about it, is that Rupert definitely *did* come to a party at my sponsor's house after that shipping deal. In which case, I suppose, he would have had to have met Argus. Argus was there and Rupert's not one to have passed up the chance, although I never actually saw them together. The reason I suddenly remember it is that he brought the daughter of one of the taipans—to show her off, I think. He told me later that she went at it like a bunny, but I always suspected he was giving himself more credit, in that instance, than he deserved. She just didn't seem like that kind of girl. She was very nice, sweet really, when I talked with her. I told her about my father's wood-carving, in fact, and, sure enough, she went to his shop a few days later and bought a large chest for her parents for Christmas. That was a long time ago."

"I have to convince Julia," I say. "I have to talk to her and lay it all out so that there's absolutely no doubt in her mind."

"I could talk to her," Philip offers, "but how much that might mean . . . No, it will come down to *you*, to your word against Rupert's—her future against her past."

"I'm afraid she's so fair, by nature, she'll want to give Rupert a chance to defend himself."

"You can't let her do that."

"I know. Because if he knows that we know, then—"

"Do you want me to come with you?"

"No," I tell him. "I want you to follow through on that devious thought."

I SLEEP AT home in Ormonde Place then set off for Castlemorland after dawn, avoiding rush hour, even though I will be travelling counter to it. The morning is mild, offering too much hope for this time of year. When I arrive, Julia is in the garden beside Andrew and Louisa. They are dressed in matching green huskies. Julia holds papers in her hands, architectural drawings of some type. These have been folded, apparently for many years. She drops the hand in which she clasps them to her side as soon as she notices me.

"We're going to plant a garden," Louisa explains enthusiastically.

"We're going to build a ruin," Andrew says.

Now, Julia cannot help but smile.

"*Can* you build a ruin?" Julia inquires. "Really?"

"No, silly, it has to be very, very old, doesn't it, to be a ruin?" Louisa says.

"Yes," Andrew agrees. "But this is just a make-believe one. Don't forget that."

Julia kisses me without hint of the distance or tension between us, plainly fastidious in her desire to secret these from our children, at least for now. "I found these in the bottom drawer of my mother's desk, tucked in the back. They're plans my mother had for the garden. Her ideas. She had a young Dutch landscape architect she admired and he drew them up, I remember."

"May I see them?"

"Of course," she answers, opening them rather than handing them over. The center fold rests on the cement balcony which divides the garden's levels. The old paper crackles slightly in the breeze. "The idea was to have a long, shallow pool, with water lilies and vines right here," she says, pointing to the diagram then raising her gaze to the distant cedars, weeping cherry and willows. "You wouldn't see it from the house—not until you'd reached just about where we are standing. Beyond it, there would be two rows of three doric columns each, an arch and statues, heroic figures, among the spruce and heliotrope. Suddenly, amidst all this beauty, a garden so ripe for love in spring, past the wall of rambler roses to our left, the iris and the tall delphinium and pink astilbe, after froths of pastels and all the laurel at the door to the children's tea house, after jillions of blue and white bells, and so many herbaceous and higgledy-piggledy borders—out of nowhere, unexpectedly, an intimation of an entirely detrited world, a world to which there is no longer any viable bridge, whose very forms would seem to have been as much a gift from heaven as the nature which surrounds them."

I look carefully at this woman I love. "Why didn't she ever build it?" I ask, as the children pedal miniature John Deere combines across the hard ground.

"I haven't any idea. Perhaps it was too fanciful for Daddy, but maybe not. Something's on your mind, I can tell. Are they going to arrest you?"

I start at this notion, at the fact that it should surface first in her mind. "No . . . not as yet, anyway."

"Good."

"But I do have to talk to you."

"As you can see, you've picked an opportune moment. What about, John?"

"Everything. . . . Rupert."

"Rupert? Why Rupert? He's coming to dinner and to stay the night. You can talk to him yourself, if you want to. But, of course, you can do that most any day you like."

"When is he coming? Tonight?"

"Yes. He's in the area on business."

"Seeing Matthew Paxton?"

Julia studies me, a familiar anger brewing in her eyes and her demeanor. "Matthew? Why on earth would he have any reason to see Matthew?"

"I think it's time for the children to have their milk and bickies," I tell her. "We have to sit down somewhere by ourselves. You have to let me take you through everything that's happened from the very start—let me tell you what I've found out. You'll find it as hard to believe as I did—maybe harder—but I think you'll see that we have to plan our next moves more carefully than we've ever done anything."

"I'm prepared to listen," Julia says. "I can't promise what conclusion I'll come to."

It takes me over half an hour, scrupulously sifting what can be proved from what cannot, to limn the story as I have come to know it. As I speak, even when I pause, Julia does not react, but stares, entranced, at the chair and the mahogany side cabinet that are already directly in her view, across the library. I tell her that I believe Rupert may well have begun with one objective in mind, but that he appears to have craftily expanded his plan as circumstances changed. I convey Philip's intuition, Hugh's confession, Chas's stumbled-upon indictment of Rupert, by association. But these facts, like the story of my summons to Zurich then Vaduz then Antalya, and the supposed coincidence of my alleged accounts there, seem hardly to register in her appraising eyes. "No one else had so much to gain," I press. "Who else knew enough to reek such havoc in our lives?"

When I finish, she stands. "Done?" she asks, walking into the center of a shaft of silver light that pours through the long windows.

"Done," I assure her.

"The difficulty I have with that story," she informs me, "is that it casts Rupert utterly out of character. I've known him all my life. I can't believe he would conspire against me like that—or against you. He likes you; you're his partner. I certainly don't believe he killed my brother Adrian. If I did—"

"Start with the small things. Hugh Basildon's video. Why would Rupert pay to have it made up from film? And faked in reverse, at that?"

"To get it out of Hugh's possession? I don't know. Hugh's no good. Daddy used to say that anyone who asked to see the pictures or the furniture, as he always did, was either a thief or a poof. Well, he was right. Hugh's both. Not that I mind about the latter, but he stole my privacy. *He* did. Not Rupert. *Him.* So why take *his* word?"

"He has no reason to lie, Julia. Quite the opposite."

"Rupert rescued me from that scene—that horrible party of Hugh's. You have to remember that," my wife insists. "It couldn't be Rupert's fault. That would fly in the face of common sense. If he'd wanted to hurt me, he could have left me there then. Or called in the police, after David died."

"You were younger," I say, enforcing a soft refusal to become emotional upon my tone. "You were his ally then. You were not, realistically, any kind of threat to him—not yet. You weren't even an heiress. You were a scholar, that's where it began and ended; an impoverished and amateur one at that."

"Don't tease me," she declares. "This is not the moment."

I study her. "Fine. But, do you think you would have noticed a chip on his shoulder if one had been there?"

"Yes."

"Even if he had wanted to keep it hidden?"

"I don't know why you concentrate so on people's weaknesses," Julia says, "when those are usually responsible for the best things about them."

"So, you do admit—"

"It would be only natural. Rupert is the gifted son of a *second* son. So what? All the more get up and go as a consequence."

"Perhaps," I say.

"What about your client Ryan? He'd have rather a lot to gain. I mean, if you are right and Rupert was right and Ryan wasn't actually up to the deal on which he'd staked his future, how much handier for him to blame you, to bring you down?"

Matched pairs of recumbent sphinxes seem suddenly to stare at me from the ebony base of a mantle clock. I am getting nowhere. "Except," I say, "that there is no evidence, *at all*, that Wiley Ryan ever heard of Hugh Basildon, much less that he ever dealt with or passed anything on to Matthew Paxton; or that he would profit in any way by Adrian's death; *or* that he sold his own future short because, out of the blue, he'd ceased believing in himself. Let's agree on this, shall we? If there is anything that is not open to debate in this business, it is that Wiley Ryan will never stop believing in himself. Never. Ever."

"I suppose that is true," she confesses after a minute, finally stepping out of the light.

"You were ready to believe that I'd—"

"Only because there was evidence. *So much* evidence. *Lots*, and almost all in big, bold print. Here there's none," she insists, but weakly, as if to explain, even excuse the asymmetry of her reactions to the charges levelled against Rupert and me. "Nothing like that at all. Is there? Just a theory."

"It's a powerful theory, though, darling: one it's pretty hard to argue with."

"Yes. It is." Julia shudders outwardly. Next to me, now, she sits again, still looking toward something unpresent in the distance; a gaze that is the equivalent of a whisper. "What do you want me to do?" she inquires, without commitment.

"What do you want to do?"

"That's hard to say, right now. I don't believe Rupert's done this."

"Think it through. Take your time."

"But there isn't much time. I know that."

"There's enough," I promise. "You won't need much. Just think, slowly, through the whole thing. Forget any pressure."

"Is that what you've done?"

"No."

Julia hesitates. She closes her eyes.

"Think of the children—first," I suggest.

"Exactly what I'm trying to do."

"And don't be afraid."

"Of course, I'm afraid."

"I meant don't be afraid of where your thoughts lead you."

"Oh? No. I'm trying not to be." After a considerable pause, Julia looks up. She says, "I certainly owe Rupert the opportunity to defend himself."

"Do you?"

"I would have thought that you, of all people, would agree with that."

"In principle, I do—of course, I do. One would have to. But not in this case."

"Because—"

"Because a man who killed Adrian—directly or indirectly, it doesn't matter—a man who did that, who would do what I'm sure Rupert's done, wouldn't . . . No, let me put it another way, he would be dangerous, fatally so, to anyone who happened to be in his way unless . . . unless he thought his plan was working without his having to expose himself to that risk."

"So what you're saying is that you're afraid I'd give it away. You don't give me much credit for subtlety."

"On the contrary, but Rupert's clever. It's dangerous business trying to fool him."

"Then I'll try not to be caught out at it."

"There is a way to test him, to suss out the situation."

"I know. I could suggest I might be willing to give up Castlemorland after all—then see if he takes the bait." She turns, smiles faintly.

My breath all but vanishes. I ask, "You've had that in mind all along?"

"*All along. Because I'm positive he's innocent.* He'll clear himself without ever knowing he was accused."

"But if he *can* afford it, if he does take the bait—"

"If he can afford it, it means you're right, I suppose. He wouldn't have sufficient funds unless he'd made them shorting your precious Ergo, would he?"

"Not sufficient to take all this off your hands. There's no way in the world."

"Then we'll see, won't we?" Her tone is full of irony. Her hands clutch her jumper. I take them in my own.

THE CHILDREN ARE nearly through their jam roll when Rupert arrives. He strikes me as altogether too calm, as if he has shaven, bathed, splashed himself with some of his beloved Eau de Verveine before departing wherever he was. He has brought kites, blue for Andrew, yellow for Louisa. My son and daughter hold these up to the copper chandelier, whose light plays in the folds of their cellophane wrappers.

"Can we fly them tomorrow?"

"If there's wind," Julia promises.

"That's the forecast," Rupert says.

"Oh, *please*, then . . . I want to fly my kite above the temple," Andrew says, "all the way to the moon."

"Because the sun would burn it up," Louisa declares.

"But not the moon. May we fly our kites tonight?"

"No," Julia tells them.

When the children have fallen asleep, we drink Frascati in the sitting room. Julia has filled her glass with ice.

"I had no idea you were going to be in this part of the world," I tell Rupert. "We could have driven up together."

"Last minute sort of thing," he replies enigmatically.

"Well, I'm glad. Do you have to go back wherever you were to-morrow?"

"All done, thank God. London—early."

"Same."

"Not the ideal time of year round here," Rupert says, "but, there you are—"

We have an up-to-the-moment dinner: gourmet cuisine bought from a hyper-mart and reheated in the Aga. We sit at the butcher block table in the kitchen. Julia has laid it with pretty cotton placemats and napkins. The first course consists of steamed prawns with walnut oil and melon.

"Andrew and Louisa certainly look well," Rupert says.

"All things considered," Julia agrees. "They rather miss their school, but I've had so much to take care of here and, anyway, they're going to be changing after they break."

"So, John and I will be having a fair number of boys' dinners in town when he's baching it, is that what you're telling me?"

"That would be nice," Julia says.

There is circumspection in Rupert's voice. *"You'll* be missed," he assures her.

"I doubt it. Not after the first drink anyway."

"Don't be silly. But, seriously, won't you find it a bit lonely being here by yourself so much?"

"At times, I imagine, I will. But the children are getting to the age and stage where they need to live in one place or another. And I can't see my way clear to living in London from Sunday evening to Friday afternoon. With all the demands of this place, something's got to give—better me than them is the way I look at it."

"That has to be right," Rupert says, between sips of wine.

He quickly withdraws a hot prawn which has scalded the wall of his mouth. Steam floats away from the puncture his tooth has made in its skin. He drops it onto his plate and shrugs. "Wow! Be careful . . ."

"If things come crashing down at work," I say, "I can always put Ormonde Place on the market and take a job in the village."

"Touch wood that won't happen," Rupert says.

"I'd be a good headwaiter. Or bank manager in some High Street."

"Any news?" Rupert asks.

"Finally," Julia interrupts. "Candor! I feel better. Let's not talk around the point anymore. After all, we're all family."

"And there are few enough of us as it is," Rupert adds.

"No news of any importance," I reply. "I may as well have been abducted by aliens as by whomever's behind this."

"No more from the D.T.I.?"

"They're like the dog who doesn't bark, then lunges for your throat when your guard's down. Or that's my impression. The press is quiet, too—but for how long?"

"Lay low," Rupert advises. "Bore them."

I smile. "I wouldn't have thought I had any choice in the matter."

"Let time go by."

"All very well, but bills have a nasty way of accumulating. What I need to do is to bring in some business."

"Apparently, the Argus referral is genuine."

"I'm sure. I wouldn't touch it with a barge pole, though. That would be tantamount to pleading guilty."

"Do you really think so?"

"I'm sure of it."

For our main course, Julia heats *stringazza* in *riscotta de Felsi*, flat, triangular noodles with fish, mussels and morsels in a creamy, saffroned curry. "How long can this go on—without any sort of resolution?" she asks once it is served.

"A very long time, I'm afraid," Rupert tells her.

"It's the modern torture: perpetual limbo," I explain, sitting back in the chair to digest the pasta and the rich sauce in which it is smothered.

Julia puts down her fork and spoon and looks up, fixing her eyes on Rupert's. Hers seem suddenly lit with amusement. "Too bad you're not married," she tells him.

"So I've been told."

"No, I mean it. You've had—the experiences you've had. I'd think you'd want to try on another identity before it's too late in the day."

"Anyone in mind?"

"Hardly. I suppose I was just being wistful because, if, God forbid, things should go against us, the only person I'd ever feel comfortable turning all this over to would be—well, never mind. That's putting the cart way before the horse."

Inwardly, I flinch.

"I think you are," Rupert says.

"Still and all, better you than Matthew Paxton and his Planning Council mates."

"Well, certainly. But much better the four of you than me rattling around here alone."

"I'm glad you said that," Julia tells him. "It's not that I've felt guilty since Adrian died—not that at all. But I have wondered how you might feel sometimes. The names Cheviot and Castlemorland always rolled off the tongue together. Now, it looks like they're destined not to. It's just sad."

"Don't misunderstand me. Of course, I love this place. If you had come to me saying that you'd thought it all out—what you want to do and accomplish in life—and decided you'd prefer a greater degree of freedom than an estate like this one permits; that you wanted to keep on with your scholarship, to follow that streak, then, naturally, I'd've been interested." He glances my way and winks. "With or without—or, shall we say, pending—a wife."

"You would?" Julia prompts.

"I won't lie: sure. But I couldn't bear it any other way. I couldn't bear anything that smacked of a distress sale. Forcing you out."

"No distress sale."

"If ever I did take it off your hands, it would have to be because that's what you and John wanted."

"Once upon a time," Julia assures him, "I would have said 'Please, take it', and jumped for joy. Now, with kids, I'm inclined oppositely. Castlemorland is either a burden one willingly takes on and makes one's life because of one's history, or else it's a very rich man's toy. None of us is very rich—at least in cash."

Rupert hesitates, then breaks the silence. "No. Of course, we're not—although, I must admit, I've done better than I ever expected to lately."

"You haven't done *that* well," Julia replies mirthfully.

"I don't know. In any case, there is such a thing as a mortgage—or there was, last time I looked."

"In this instance, I think you'd need something more like one of your buyouts," Julia teases. "Sorry, bad joke."

"Perhaps you're right," Rupert says.

The telephone disturbs this train of thought. As Julia gets up to answer it, she smiles her old smile at me. It is as much as to say "You were right. I believe you now. I'm with you."

"It's Philip, John," Julia announces. "He'd like a word."

"Philip, hello," I answer once she has handed me the receiver and returned to the table. "Where on earth are you? Very noisy."

"The airport. Listen, John, do you remember that *thought* we were talking about?"

"Yes." Reflexively, I turn away from Rupert and Julia.

"And the people you wished me to look up? At the far end of that hole? Who might be able to be of some help?"

"How could I forget?"

"Would you be willing to follow their lead—with me as your guide, naturally?"

"I think so," I tell him.

"It's a very hierarchical situation," Philip admonishes me. "I warn you. No untoward questions."

"Fully agreed."

"Could you follow me out to Hong Kong?"

"Why not? When?"

"As soon as possible."

"Let me just clear it with Julia."

"Absolutely."

"She is indeed. Rupert, too." "And, while I'm at it, make sure Rupert has nothing else planned at the office. Which won't take a minute, because he's right here. He's staying the night." I turn now and smile at my beautiful wife and her handsome, hollow cousin.

"Rupert?" Philip repeats, plainly surprised.

"Do you want Philip for anything?" I call to the table.

"I don't think so. Give him my best."

"My love, too," Julia adds.

"He sends his back to both of you," I say. "He's at Heathrow."

"Safe journey, then."

"This is going to be easier than I'd thought," Philip continues. "John, by all means let it be known where you are going. Not why—better you don't know that in too much detail. Just say that I've asked you to help me and that, in view of everything that's happened, I've asked you into a deal."

"Word for word."

"I sense good *joss*," Philip laughs.

"And about time, too," I reply. When I hang up, I draw a deep breath and return to my chair. Julia is peeling a pear. "It seems I've got to be off to Hong Kong for a few days, I'm afraid."

"Hong Kong?" Rupert repeats inquisitively.

"Philip is desperate. He needs some help with this A & O business. I can't turn him down. Actually, to be honest, he obviously knows our circumstances and he's been nice enough to ask me into something else he thinks might turn a buck—which, God knows, we could use. I don't know enough about it at this point to say much more."

"How long do you think you'll be gone?" Julia asks.

"Not very."

Covered neck to toe in dark and day-glo pajamas, Andrew abruptly steals into the kitchen. "I couldn't sleep," he tells his mother plaintively, his pink face contrite.

"Did you try?"

"Yes," he whispers. In his small fingers he carries a book. "I did. Very hard, but I couldn't, Mummy. I want you to read me a story."

Julia pauses.

"What book is that?" Rupert interrupts.

"*Charlotte's Web*," Andrew tells him, "which is my favorite, just about."

"Shall I read it to you?" Rupert asks, searching for our permission as my son settles onto his lap.

"Only a few pages," Julia insists.

"One chapter," Andrew bargains.

"You're on," Rupert says then. Almost musing, he adds, "Bug all, John, perhaps it might be useful if I flew out with you for a few days. Let me see if I can't clear my calendar. Would you mind?"

"It would be my pleasure," I tell him, thinking *Anything—anything in the world—to keep you away from here.*

25

THE SKY'S ABLAZE. Above the harbor, gigantic chrysanthe-mums of orange and amber burst in furious succession. Roman candles pop and flare. Hot, copper-blue peonies flower blindingly. From twin barges, away from other boats in the vacated Star Ferry channel between Central and Kowloon, fountains of white fire ascend then drip over: explosions of aluminum and magnesium chlorate com-pounds. Green shells and bright red comets, all manner of pyrotechnic, illuminate the amphitheater which is Hong Kong—and on the top-most ledge of which, drinking champagne cocktails, we stand en-tranced.

Chinese New Year. We have been asked, through Philip, to celebrate with Chuan Ch'u at his house just below the crest of Victoria Peak, on Pollock's Path. The beginning of the short drive to it is from a precipice, at so steep an angle that one must take the existence of far-ther road on faith, or else risk falling vertically toward the pitchfork towers and pyramidal roof of the Bank of China building. The archi-tecture of Chuan Ch'u's residence is Mediterranean in lineage. This is also true of the garden in which it is set—a long, plush plateau of thick sod, spreading to a borderless pool, clay tennis court and stone barbe-cue pit, all balustraded above the world's ultimate market city.

"Do you know," I tell Philip, "as long as I lived here, I almost always managed to miss this day. I must either have been travelling, or—"

"That's too bad. Because, remember, we invented fireworks," Philip explains, "in the ninth century."

"You invented gunpowder, except you had no idea what to do with it."

"Bullshit! We used it to scare wizards away. Can you think of a better application?"

"Probably not." I smile.

Twenty yards along the balustrade, Rupert is engrossed in conversation with a square-jawed young Chinese man of less than medium height and an even younger woman. They are a pretty couple.

"*That's* Jonty Woo," Philip goes on, resisting his instinct to point.

"No kidding? The movie star?"

"In person."

"And the girl?"

"Does it matter? . . . I'll tell you something about *him*, though. The last woman I saw on any kind of regular basis I made the mistake of spoiling before—well, you know, *before*. She *loved* me, so she said, but she had no interest at all in the thing I had the greatest interest in, which, of course, was sex. I kept telling myself that she'd come around to it, teasing myself, I suppose. Then one day we happened to be with some people who were talking about Jonty Mak. He'd been caught with a prostitute and in the news not long before. Anyway, this girl that I'd convinced myself was practically frigid all of a sudden blurted out that she'd have done it with him for free. I don't think she understood how much that hurt."

"She clearly wasn't the right one," I tell him empathetically. "That's all."

"Seldom are."

"There's Chuan Ch'u," I say, spotting the great man among a small circle of neighbors, off to a side of the party. "You know, I've met him with you over the years, but this is actually the first time I've been up here. Does that surprise you? . . . Anyway, watching him, I must say it's as hard as ever to reconcile the fabulous image and the simple manner."

"There is an old Chinese saying," Philip informs me. " 'Humility is the final accomplishment.' "

"That's a good one. I like it," I say. "I'm putting a lot of faith in him right now."

"I know you are. Don't worry," Philip replies.

"We've had practically no time alone since we landed this morning," I tell him. "I have to admit I wish I had a better idea of what you and he have in mind."

"He is going to loan you the money to make a certain—at the end of the day, rather riskless—investment. Be grateful. It's as a favor to you that you'll know little more than that."

"I just wish Rupert hadn't come along. Or could be occupied elsewhere. I was afraid to leave him behind, but there was no choice."

"On the contrary," Philip suggests intriguingly, "it is, no doubt, all to the good that he's here. The idea is to lay a trap for him—essentially. Chuan Ch'u will do you a kindness, make you a proposition, which he will phrase in the form of an invitation. The point being that Rupert will only rise to an offer out of greed or jealousy or some mixture of both. Do you object?"

"Hell, no."

"If all goes well, we'll not only make him return what he caused you to lose. We'll transfer his winnings to your side of the ledger."

"You'd do something like that?" I ask facetiously.

"In a Hong Kong minute," Philip says.

Sparks of strontium, calcium, barium and sodium flash fissiparously across the night sky and reflect from the mirror-calm harbor, illuminating hundreds of berthed junks. In the almost mysterious placidity of his garden, dressed in a black ceremonial Tangs suit, Chuan Ch'u makes his way among his guests, a waifish, balding, deferential figure of sixty or so, inconspicuous but for the reputation which flatters him as dependably as the creped lantern light.

Half an hour after the fireworks, the cult hero of the Hong Kong film industry and his bosomy date are the last, but us, to leave. Having been beckoned by Chuan Ch'u to do so, we wait by the door to wave goodbye. Then we follow our host into the house, through the airy frescoed entrance hall to a staircase which flows clockwise and is inevitably northfacing as it opens onto successively higher floors. When we arrive at the summit, we find ourselves in a kind of solarium, a sleek octagon with panoramic views. Below the vast plate windows, rosewood cabinets inlaid with bronze line the room. Atop one of these rests a lucite humidor, from which Chuan Ch'u offers Rupert, Philip and me cigars before selecting one for himself. For the first time since his perfunctory greeting to us at the start of the evening, quietly but intensely, as though he has purposely deferred the matter, he speaks. "This house has excellent *fêng shui* connotations," he explains, then sighs. "You understand *fêng shui?*"

"I think so. Basically," Rupert says.

"The ancient Chinese art of geomancy, by which structures are located and designed in harmony with their environments, particularly their natural environment. *Fêng shui* means, literally, 'wind and water.' But the objective is always one of serenity. Tranquility with respect to the sea, tranquility with respect to the great hills, whose symbols are dragons. The most knowledgeable and experienced *fêng shui* masters gave their assent to *this* house—from its conception, through the drawing of its plans, its construction and, finally, upon its completion."

"That's fascinating," I say, once he has paused. "When was it built?"

"Nineteen thirty-one. It's never a bad idea to ground the new in the ancient. If only as insurance." Chuan Ch'u smiles. ". . . So, the outcome of Mr. Wiley Ryan's adventure proved rather bitter for us all."

"Indeed," Rupert at once agrees.

"Why?"

"We may have overestimated him, I'm afraid," offers Rupert.

"No doubt you did. Yet, he fell of more than his own weight."

"He was pushed," Philip says.

"Yes. Certainly, he was. Although not by your . . . miscalculations."

"No," I state firmly. "That's true." I am relieved and glad that he seems implicitly to understand this.

"That's what you and Philip have both told me and I accept your word of honor on the matter. I don't, for a moment, think you would have been foolish enough, much less so dishonorable, as to have traded on your information. The risk would outweigh the gain—over any term. You would suffer the complete loss of your integrity and reputation. What I do believe is that, for some reason we may never know, indeed probably never will, Wiley Ryan must have disappointed Jason Argus—wherever, however—so that Argus, in turn, first bet against him then manipulated a scandal he had every reason to think would be beyond Ryan's capacity to cope with. Correctly, as it turned out. That you, John, were the instrument of that scandal seems, unquestionably, an accident," he says, staring at me intently. "No, the conspiracy originated in other precincts, out of other motives and had nothing at all to do with you."

"Nor with Battleman," I tell him, stealing the moment to search Philip's face for some cue, Rupert's for any revelation of guilt.

"Of that I'm equally sure. Had anyone else been in your position, he would very likely have found himself with an identical problem. Conversely, had you *not* been there, your life, right now, would be going on as usual. You would have no cause for alarm."

I shudder at this thought. "I hope that's right," I tell him.

"It is my supposition," Chuan Ch'u says, inspecting the Cohiba torpedo he has chosen from the humidor, twirling it slowly, just away from his ear, listening for the tight, even pack of tobacco leaves.

Rupert produces a small appliance on a gold key chain and is about to offer our host the miniature guillotine when Chuan Ch'u waves a dismissive hand.

At this, the Marquess of Cheviot returns the cutter to his pocket.

"I learned this from a Cuban, so it's authentic," Chuan Ch'u relates. We have brought our champagne cocktails with us from the garden and he now dips the untorn mouth-end of his cigar into his glass, withdrawing it at once. Flicking the last liquid from it, he points the torpedo away, toward the ceiling, and blows a steady jet of air into the end he will light. It requires several puffs, but soon a perfect current of smoke, thin and white as string, trails from the cigar Chuan Ch'u pulls from his lips. "*Proof,* if you need it," he smiles. ". . . Now, what we are obliged to do, from here on, is to find our way forward."

Almost simultaneously, we attempt to start our cigars in mimetic fashion. Philip's and Rupert's take at once, but I find that I must draw harder on my own in order to draw back its fire. "If you are right," I inquire, a little winded, "how do we deal with Argus?"

"Argus is, if not a friend, a colleague of sorts, someone whose interests follow paths that now and then intersect with ours. We do not attempt to even the score in any way, if that is your question. We shall do so, of course," he elaborates, turning to Philip, "when fate provides us a chance. But fate must deliver that. We cannot reach for it ourselves."

"You just accept the loss?" Rupert asks incredulously.

"For now, for the time being. The important thing is the sustenance of our relationship, our relationships generally. I am sure that, in due course, you will find ways to help us recover ourselves. Just as we shall continue to do the same, whenever we can, for you. My first concern is for John, who has suffered most directly and substantially. And— doesn't it go without comment—an older man of any fortune owes certain things to a younger man of talent. So, of course, I'll be keeping an eye on and out for Philip, as I've long done. The point is that I am willing to loan you both the necessary funds to purchase the debt of a complex—hotel, resort and retail, basically—which has had a bad time of it lately, but whose situation, *I feel confident*, can soon be reversed."

"You're talking about the Highland project," Philip asks.

"Yes. Of course."

"It's near Shanghai," Philip tells me. "Just outside."

"In the best direction," Chuan Ch'u adds. "The most promising area. There *is* some urgency. You could travel there, if you like, but numbers on paper often give a more lucid picture than bulldozed land and half-completed structures. The only other harm in your going there, apart from the delay it would impose, relates to the possibility that your presence might tip our hand to other interested parties. But you would only be out this particular *opportunity*—not any *investment*—in that event."

Philip hesitates. He makes a show of studying me. "I think we are inclined to accept your judgment," he defers.

"Rupert, I'm sorry," Chuan Ch'u says, "this must be most boring for you. But I do want to get the personal out of the way before we talk a little further about A & O and Battleman Peale."

"By all means," Rupert says. "Please."

"Morgans have always done that. And Jardines and Swires, too: seen to their people's personal well-being. Kept up, kept alive their relationships—even after their associates have gone off on ventures of their own. Kept them in the family, so to speak."

"That has always been our approach," Rupert concurs.

Chuan Ch'u sits upright on the straight ebony wood chair over whose back a small blue afghan blanket has been folded. "Yes, I would have to say I think it has been. You, personally, haven't lost money, I gather, but as your reputation *has been a bit scuffed* by all this, perhaps you can find something less daunting—more secure and private—in which we can pool our talents and resources in future."

"We shall put on our thinking caps and keep them on until we do," Rupert assures him.

"I like Battleman Peale," Chuan Ch'u says. "Not everyone does, of course. There was a time—the same time when neither Philip nor I could have bought this house, nor lived in it. Nor come to it, for that matter, except as servants. And the effect of that lingers, understandably. But those days are past, really. There are different people now, altogether different. No one should be judged by the actions of his prede-cessors. Who would want to be? I'm not one of those who has viewed Britain's departure from this island and these territories with unmiti-gated joy—any more than I view it with unmitigated sorrow."

"Could we, I wonder," asks Rupert, puffing calmly on his cigar, "possibly be of any help with the venture in Shanghai you mentioned?"

Chuan Ch'u reflects in silence. "I don't think so," he answers fi-nally.

"I only ask because, as you describe it, it seems the kind of thing in which we are ordinarily interested. In principle. We have the necessary connections around the world to help something like this work once it is financed—assuming, of course, that it *is* first class in all its aspects."

"Oh, absolutely first class," Chuan Ch'u persists. "The debt fell through because of a sad addiction of its original backers to over-extending themselves elsewhere. Thus, as so often seems to be the case, was the good flushed with the not so good."

"Shanghai?" Rupert asks. A bead of sweat has appeared on his upper lip.

"Shanghai."

"I won't be coy. We'd like to do more business in China, with China."

"Market of a billion people and so on and so forth," Chuan Ch'u says. "I'm sure you would."

"So, then, it's fully subscribed?"

Chuan Ch'u smiles. "Too fully to bring a bank of Battleman's stature in at this stage. I'm sorry."

"Just a thought."

"No, I can see how you might have been very helpful, in exactly the ways to which you allude. Yet, we are past that moment and I hope you'll forgive me. I would suggest, however, that the shoe would seem to be on the other foot right now: that Battleman ought to be about the business of making us—at A & O—whole, not the reverse."

"That, I completely understand and agree with," Rupert assures him. "But the things on my plate right now do not represent the kind of deals for which I believe you are looking. As soon as one appears that does—"

"Thank you."

"Just that soon—don't worry."

"No, I won't."

"We want to keep our families together. We want that very much," Rupert promises. "I do, especially."

"Naturally, I must act in ours, but I must say I believe that to be in everyone's interest."

"Good," declares Rupert, his voice determined, quiet, full of camaraderie. Yet, I remark something uncharacteristic: a loss of balance and control in him. For an instant, it is as though he has had to reach for his own fallen mask and I am sure his mind is elsewhere, travelling as fast as his plan seems to be unravelling; his stomach queasy at the sudden, unimagined prospect of my actually being able to rescue Castlemorland and my marriage, at the inadvertent foiling of his plans.

"I think we all do," Philip agrees.

I nod.

Rupert says, "Speaking not as a partner of Battleman Peale, but for myself, if there were a small position still available in the Shanghai venture, I'd be interested in—learning more."

"I only wish there were."

"Do I hear a 'but' coming."

"You don't, *at all*. I was merely going to say that these particular units are rather pricey."

Rupert frowns. "For the right opportunity, perhaps one could find the money." His eagerness is beginning to alarm me. It is not a natural trait in his personality and I worry that he may have already deciphered our plan and now be ferreting for information rather than succumbing to it.

"Ten million sterling? Or a bit more?"

"For the right opportunity. But, if the deal is closed, well, never mind," Rupert says, backing away from the subject. "There are always others."

"Always," Chuan Ch'u echoes.

Rupert evaluates me.

"I don't," I say, parcelling my attention, "have to be greedy. If there is some way we can divide my share, I'm willing—"

"The same, of course, goes for me. All the more so," Philip says. "It's fairer to take any points out of my share than yours, John."

"Not necessary," Rupert says.

I feel shock.

"Let me top up your drink?" Chuan Ch'u asks, tilting a new bottle.

"Please," says Rupert.

"You don't mind," Chuan Ch'u asks Rupert, almost cavalierly, "if we wait until another day?" He smiles. "You won't feel *discriminated against?* . . . Englishmen, strangely, never do. It's not in the vocabulary—all to your credit."

The four of us sip the champagne, pink this time.

Rupert examines the slateboard sky, upon which fireworks were so recently written. "Not at all," he replies.

"Very decent of you," Chuan Ch'u avers.

With each minute, I am more sure that Rupert is lost to us, that he has understood our conversation for the skit it is and that some alternative plan, presuming any is ever possible, will have to be made if my life is not once again to spiral toward disaster. Clearly, one of Philip's and Chuan Ch'u's motives in wishing to keep me in the dark bout the Highland venture has been to insure the spontaneity of my reaction to their offer. Now, with equal clarity, I recognize that this has not sufficed. Judging Rupert's reaction, I see that I have no choice but to extend the bluff, to riff. "In actual fact," I tell Chuan Ch'u, "I wouldn't mind having a look, going to Shanghai if that's what's required. Instinctively, it feels like a big leap otherwise, I'm afraid, whatever the dangers."

This astonishes Philip and even Chuan Ch'u, whose more limited range of expression is less easily subjected to interpretation.

"Not to be difficult," I add. "A certain amount of managed risk is one thing, but I'm not a high roller by nature and, even as bad as things are, I'd hate to wind up owing you more than I could *ever* repay."

"What exactly do you hope to find out there that you can't here?" Rupert asks.

"Who knows?"

"Shall we each see what we can do then?" Chuan Ch'u proposes.

Smoke rises about the solarium, vapors cohering into clouds. Life is smoke, I think, assuming shapes that momentarily possess magical powers over us, that inspire or threaten, satisfy or punish us. And then dissolve.

THE WEEKEND IS brisk; it's less than a month now until the equinox. There are intimations of spring: myrobalan skies before and after sunsets; the enlargement of early-blooming buds. Still, the essential barrenness of winter persists, the night chill.

We spend our time, with quiet ostentation, entertaining senior executives of Asian and Omnibus in the Captain's Bar and on the Mezzanine of the Mandarin, as well as on the splendid Battleman junk. The wind is always strong. It is vital to layer jerseys and jackets against it.

Although I have no intention of travelling to Shanghai, I sense it is crucial to maintain that pretense steadfastly in front of Rupert. And so I talk of it more than once, as elliptically and in as brief snippets as possible. My reservations, I tell myself, must be firmly expressed and firmly acted upon if they are finally to persuade him that the deal is genuine, that any idea of its being a trap is merely a manifestation of his own paranoia, not indicated by fact. My reluctance must flow naturally from my predicament and personality, even as it confirms his own resilient sense of superiority. The pragmatist in him must be tempted to squeeze me from the venture, thereby eliminating my hopes of rebounding; the gambler, to replace my chips with his own.

Philip and I, as committed, undertake the valuation of a minor mainland project for A & O. Like the cases I was assigned in Business School and most such arrangements I have worked on since, the task is time–consuming, but not challenging intellectually. Columns of numbers—ratios of ratios—are marshalled in support of a thesis that, if one could only admit it, was subjective to begin with. This deal has nothing whatsoever to do with the venture near Shanghai with which we have, so unpredictably, become involved. But, when we are alone in the Battleman office, I cannot help asking Philip, "What does Chuan Ch'u expect of us in return?"

"Loyalty?" Philip replies.

"Fealty?"

"No."

"You're sure?"

"He'll have his own reward."

"I hope so," I say. "I mean even *I* wouldn't bet on *me* right now."

"Do you remember what I told you about *face*, a long time ago?" Philip asks.

"I do, as a matter of fact. It was one of those things that lodged in the mind. You said that it is something other people give you."

"That's it. You have shown Chuan Ch'u respect *and* deference—

not obsequiousness, which isn't called for anyway. What have Rupert and Jason Argus done—just the opposite! They've played him for a fool. First, Rupert uses me—and, admittedly, his own charm—to entice him into his first big Western deal. As a principal, with a high degree of visibility. And a deal that's very much on the cutting edge, at that. That done, for his own motives, he turns sides and works against his own deal—*and* A & O and Chuan Ch'u—with a cunning that is not only expensive but embarrassing. Humiliating. All of which suggests that he gives no respect to Chuan Ch'u's position or intelligence, because he has obviously assumed he will not be found out. The old arrogance of empire again. What is Chuan Ch'u to do, but reverse the process step by step? He cannot, for the time being, recover A & O's losses in the market from the Ergo transactions, but he can make a profound point through helping us. And, surely, we could never work our way out of present circumstances without him and his loan—of credibility as much as funding."

"It's all so intricate at this stage," I say. "I mean it's a real Chinese puzzle, if you'll excuse the expression. The prospect of solving it is gorgeous, but how? I can hardly wait."

I do not have to wait long. Just past midday on Monday, Chuan Ch'u's personal assistant leaves a message with the Battleman receptionist, saying that it has become urgent we decide on our participation in the Highland venture by tomorrow. There is a hard-to-resist clamor from other would-be investors and, although he would very much like to give us more time—to travel, to think—he fears he will be powerless to do so. Thus, on Tuesday, we gather in Chuan Ch'u's offices in Pedder Street. Panelled in waxed pine, with low ceilings and Persian rugs, these have the atmosphere of a ship's cabin. There is English silver atop most occasional tables and on the shelves of a breakfront.

Philip and I read and review the documents in a small conference room then, after an hour or so, sign them. As Chuan Ch'u has requested, we have brought Rupert as a witness. When we have completed our work, Chuan Ch'u's P.A. gathers the papers into a folio and thanks us. "Mr. Ch'u would like a moment with you," he says.

We are served tea by a young secretary. When Chuan Ch'u slips into the room, he makes it immediately apparent he is rushed. He smiles. He leans against a sideboard. "We will keep in touch" he declares graciously. Among the contracts we have signed is one giving him power of attorney in the matter of this investment. "I will let you know—as soon as we've finally and formally closed the deal."

Rupert looks up.

"And, naturally, whenever there are further developments."

"Thank you very much," I tell him.

"Indeed," Philip agrees, a jocular intimacy in his voice.

"How much *further* do you have to go?" Rupert inquires after a moment.

"Not too far, actually. One investor would seem to have come up a bit short at the last moment—for entirely extraneous reasons."

"I see."

Another pause.

"I am not a salesman," Chuan Ch'u explains.

"All right," Rupert says, "I *would*, in fact, be interested."

"As you suggested the other evening."

"Exactly so."

Chuan Ch'u hesitates. "Okay," he declares.

"How in hell are you going to finance that?" Philip asks Rupert later in the evening.

"You'll make double at least, perhaps five times on your money," Rupert says, "when the thing turns around. Which it will. Because—it couldn't possibly be more obvious—Chuan Ch'u knows something none of us does. He's giving you *entrée* and yet another present. And he's restoring John because they were both damaged by the same person. Not that I have any doubt he'll come back to you someday for something. Fine. Why shouldn't he? In the meantime, I can scrounge and borrow as well as the next man—for that sort of return."

"By tomorrow?" I ask.

"Certainly not without effort. But, yes, I think so."

THE NEXT DAY, after his own acquiescent signing and the confirmation of the wire transfer of Rupert's funds into the Highland venture, the three of us elect to celebrate our second partnership at the Man Wah where, in a way, our first was formed. It is still afternoon and not yet dark as we depart the last session with A & O and make our way along the Connaught Road, but there are already lights on in the windows of hotel rooms and offices, figures and shadows visible. We make a plan to meet in three hours, then separate. It is tangy, on the cusp of seasons.

In the lobby of the Mandarin, I pass a sweet-looking adolescent girl with a mark on her forehead, then, several steps on, a man of my own age, similarly cindered. With a bolt, it occurs to me what day this is. Immediately, I stride past the concierge and the bank of lifts, up the wide stairs and through the arcade, above the Chater Road until I am as near as I can get to St. John's Cathedral. It is five o'clock; the gong of a distant clock still strikes, a patterned sound against the randomness of traffic.

The garden of St. John's is filling now, not only with church-goers, while in the great Anglican cathedral itself, so imperial and semi-tropical, with its wood pews and rafters and ceiling fans, people shift to make room for one another, silent in their memories of all those things for which they have come to seek forgiveness. Everywhere, crosses are covered and tied with a gauzy lavender cloth.

At the Imposition of Ashes, I close my eyes. " 'Remember, O man, that thou art dust,' " the young priest repeats, " 'and unto dust shalt thou return.' "

In the Litany of Penitence, kneeling, we beg to be absolved, among other sins, for " 'Our laziness, intemperate love of worldly goods and comforts, and our dishonesty in daily life and work.' " Then, at the Communion, after the *Angus Dei*, the choir sings the *Lamentation of Jeremiah*: " 'Jerusalem, Jerusalem, return unto the Lord thy God.' "

Beyond the church's portal, in the clear twilight, I walk back to the hotel alone—slowly, feeling, if not salvation, at least that I am borne toward the shimmering evening on a new tide of hope.

26

T HE NEWS BREAKS with the storm front. As the drizzle lets up,
I tug an iron chaise from beneath the eaves of the house and,
avoiding puddles, onto the flagstone terrace above the garden. I plop its
long, worn canvas cushion, which I have removed from the storage
shed, atop it, then lie down quickly, stretching my legs forward, my
back at an angle to the earth. In the right distance, the temple still
hides, but soon reveals itself half-moment by half-moment. The fields
are tawny where the sunlight has forced itself through cloud; now and
then a blaze of the sunlight settles upon the empty limbs of trees, waiting there until the fast-moving weather obliterates it, then re-appearing
elsewhere, flaming pond or waterfall.

"RALPH AND LUCINDA are engaged," Julia says, drawing up a chaise
beside mine.

"So I've heard," I tell her.

"Their announcement was in the *Telegraph*. I don't know about the
Times," she continues.

"The *Telegraph* is where I saw it."

"Lucky Ralph."

"Lucky Lucinda?" I ask playfully.

"I think so, I do," my wife answers, after a brief hesitation. "I mean
I wouldn't ever have wanted to have married Ralph—too set in his
ways. But he's not so bad. He's good-hearted and, really, what more can
you ask for?"

"I agree."

"What else doesn't deteriorate?"

"A pure heart can be hard to glimpse, even so."

"I suppose that's one of the things that makes life interesting."

"I wish life weren't so interesting."

"Do you?"

"Right now, I do. I'm tired, Julia."

"I know," she whispers.

"I'm more than tired."

"I know, but you'll be fine. You need a rest."

"Yes, I'll be fine. I'm sure of that. But will I be the same again? I'm afraid the answer to that is no. I won't ever feel young again, in that wonderful way one did. Facing so many choices, oblivious of their risks."

"Neither will I. I won't ever feel—" Julia stumbles, then recovers her thought. "I won't ever feel *so good about myself.* Because I doubted you when I ought to have known better."

I press my lips together. A shudder of emotion has disrupted my ability to speak. "On paper," I say finally, "I looked pretty damned guilty. I have to admit that. For a while there, the evidence seemed pretty overwhelming."

"Screw the evidence," Julia tells me. "I should have trusted myself, had more faith in my own instincts. I should—" Her voice trembles and she stops. When she speaks again, that voice is lower, softer, her diction acute. "I should have remembered the vow I took when I married you."

"I don't blame you, Julia, for anything," I promise her.

" 'Wilt thou love him, comfort him, honor and keep him . . . ?' "

I can feel myself beginning to cry. "You've never done anything else," I say.

"Oh, yes I have. *I have.* And that's why I'm asking you to forgive me. Because I have to ask you and I have to know that you do. Damn it, John, there's just been so much piling up: my father's death, then Adrian's. Then, all of these calamities—what other word can one use? I didn't betray you, but I didn't uphold you either. And that is more than a lapse, darling, it's a sin. It's a sin I have to come to terms with, as God will, and I can only do that if I am sure that you have."

Her words, her quick glance away from then toward me once more still my breath. I reach across the meter or so between our chaises and take her hand, my fingers touching the engagement ring and wedding band she wears. Finally, I force words up from memory, through the emotion of the moment. " 'To love and to cherish, till death do us part, according to God's holy ordinance; and thereto I plight thee my troth.' "

Julia's eyes and lips break simultaneously into a smile. "What *is* a troth?" she asks.

"A pledge," I answer, "but more than a pledge. A confession, really—an outright confession of faith *and loyalty*. Didn't you know that?"

"I knew it. I just wanted to see if you did."

I laugh. "That's not fair," I tell her. "I love you, Julia. I've loved you since the moment I saw you, inauspicious as that was. I've doubted many things since, but never that love."

"And never our future together?"

I hesitate. "In retrospect?"

"Anything else would be too much to ask."

"Then absolutely *and utterly no.*"

"The awful thing is we keep racing, at the same speed even after the events which carried us have stopped. We can crash, can't we?"

"Too easily," I say and stand and move toward her. She makes room on her long divan. Her eyes close, then mine. We kiss passionately for the first time since my summons to Zurich.

NEW CLOUDS ARRIVE without warning: a brief encore of turbulence.

"What time is Rupert meant to be here?" I ask, although, of course, I know the answer. My question is a reflex, a way of focusing on what remains essential.

"Any minute?"

"Are you ready?"

"Do I look forward to this? No. But I'm ready. We have to get it over with. There's no other choice."

"Yes, it stinks, it's rotten," I say. "There's no question about that. Somehow I don't mind, however."

"He brought it on himself," Julia says. "Treason's always been the worst of crimes. And treason against your own family, the next generation! . . . Have you talked to Philip?"

"Yes."

"What time is it there?"

"Seven hours ahead. So it's late, very late."

"Poor Philip," Julia says.

When Rupert arrives, the storm outside is once again fierce. Beyond the door only fog stirs—until he seems to come forth from a pillar of rain, as a sculpted figure is said to release itself from marble, stepping into Castlemorland limply, without pungency.

"I'd thought you might not make it," I say.

"Truthfully, I almost didn't. Road's flooded out a few miles from here. My car left a helluva wake. Huge arcs of water. I could see them in my mirror, in the headlamps of the car behind me."

"Well, come in," I tell him. "Dry off."

"Good idea."

"Cup of tea?" Julia asks.

"Cup of whiskey," Rupert tells her "if I may?"

"Of course, you may."

"I don't know if Julia's told you," Rupert says as we sit across from one another in the library. "I've come to collect my guns."

"Yes. She did. But why on earth—"

"For cleaning, first of all. I want to take them down to London this year. Have it all seen to properly. Also, the feeling is I know these drives so well. Every covert and its inhabitants." He attempts a laugh. "You get to a certain point in life, it's time to try out new things. Or not. Now or never, you know."

"Where will you shoot?" I ask.

"Plenty of places. This is yours, John. You'll be able to keep it—and keep it up as it should be kept—if all goes as well as I expect it to. I'd be the odd man out. No offense."

Rather than reply, I look away, into the dusty almost-springtime light that has once more, abruptly, begun to flood the room. Outside, heard through the window frame, a hawk cry sounds loudly, again and again.

"I shan't be long," Rupert promises.

"You're not staying for dinner?" Julia asks.

"I can't, darling. I'm sorry," her cousin tells her, something unmistakably broken and tragic in his voice.

Between his whiskies, I lead Rupert to the gun room, unlocking its heavy door and venerable cupboards. When we return to the library, he angles his father's Purdeys, in their ancient leather case, against the enormous table behind the sofa.

"Don't expect me to understand," Julia says. "I don't."

Rupert grins wryly, opening the case and, all but absent-mindedly, studying his guns. "No, you wouldn't. I wouldn't have expected you to."

Three double rings of the telephone break the silence. Julia, nearest to it, answers and, as she listens, slides casually into the chair behind the Baumbauer *bureau plat.*

"Who is it?" I inquire, once her breathless gossip sounds on the point of winding down.

"Philip."

"From Hong Kong? It's awfully late there."

"He does that," Rupert reminds me.

"I know. It's a bad habit." I take the receiver, even the chair from Julia and listen, in silence, to the message Philip and I have rehearsed. I look toward Rupert, then, determinedly, away. "Oh, God," I exclaim. "That's *wonderful!*"

From the corner of my eye I read Rupert's eagerness. "Rupert's here," I tell Philip, rather volubly. "Yes. *Again.* I think he likes it here." Once more glancing toward Rupert, I pause. ". . . What? Bloody hell! I don't believe it. That's terrible," I say. "Are you absolutely sure, *absolutely* positive? . . . No, no, you tell him yourself." I press the speaker button, re-cradle the receiver."

"Rupert, hello, it's Philip," comes his voice, remarkably without static.

"Hello. What's the matter out there? *What's* 'terrible'?"

Philip is slow to answer. "Well, as I told John, there's good news and there's bad news. The good news is that John's okay. He got out before the bankruptcy."

"Bankruptcy? What bankruptcy?" Rupert interrogates anxiously.

"I'm sorry. The Highland venture's gone under. I thought you'd have heard by now."

"Not a word," I say.

"Oh, well—"

"Keep going," Rupert insists.

"Apparently, technically, we each bought into a different series of bonds," Philip explains. "I don't know about you, but it's something *I* didn't notice at the time. Your debt, Rupert, was, in actual fact, subordinated to mine—as, it turns out, mine was to John's."

"Meaning?" demands Rupert, his glare intensifying, his eyes large and obsidian.

"That's difficult to say. Maybe that we were blinded—by the scale and apparent effortlessness of it all. Wouldn't be the first time."

"Meaning?"

"John's in profit—well in. Your loss, I'm afraid, is . . . in point of fact, it's total."

Rupert pauses. "What about you?"

"Unclear as yet. I won't make anything. Probably get my money back, I suppose, in due course. The whole thing's pretty impenetrable. All offshore. Holding companies holding other companies—you can imagine. Sooner or later, with any luck, I suppose I should come out about even."

Rupert draws a deep breath. He rises and walks toward one of the long windows between bookshelves, waiting. "Philip," he says at last. "Yes?"

"Well done," Rupert tells him, by now holding a Purdey up to the light, then suddenly loading it with a cartridge he has extracted from his pocket. He points the barrel to the much-disturbed sky, to a line of slow-moving birds.

"Turnabout is fair play," comes Philip's voice, then its echo. "That's what I was taught. By the English, actually . . . I'll ring you back tomorrow, John, if that's all right. Bye, for now."

"No, hold on a minute," I say, but Philip is already gone.

Still at the window, Rupert seems disoriented, lost in thought. "When did you figure it out?" he asks. "Don't bluff me."

"Gradually. There wasn't one moment. Talking to Hugh Basildon, I suppose, is when it all began to fit together persuasively."

"If I were what you think I am, I'd have popped him. Has that occurred to you?"

"Have I wondered why you didn't?"

"It's a reasonable question."

"No. Because you're not that sort. You don't conceive of yourself that way. With you, there has to be a certain level of ambiguity. It's always a matter of surfaces—style, flair, whatever one chooses to call it. If only so that you can escape accusations from yourself."

"Perhaps that's right," Rupert agrees, but too readily.

"It will all become public," Julia declares, "no matter what now. What you did, what's happened to you."

Rupert shifts his stance and stares at us for a long moment. "Too complicated for the papers, all of it, much less television. No one will understand. They won't take time to. They'll assume we're both thieves."

"The hell they will," Julia shouts. "I'll see that they don't. I will."

"Why?" I ask finally.

"Why?" Rupert immediately throws my question back at me, as though its answer lies in every direction I might look.

"That's not an answer," Julia cries.

"I'll be damned if it isn't. One thing led to another—is that what you want me to say?"

"I don't want you to say anything—particularly," she replies.

"It was never a matter of hate. I never hated you, either one of you— quite the reverse. We had good times. It was always, much more, a question of instinct, if that makes any sense. It was always so easy for you, so much harder for me. Everything I didn't want came so easily I eventually came to want it even less. Everything I yearned for always stayed . . . just out of reach."

"So you killed Adrian?" Julia says, working herself into a choler.

"Only if it's a crime to give a thirsty man a drink. There's no deny-ing I might have found some other way—if what happened hadn't. But, to my surprise and delight, it did. Anyway, he bequeathed you Castle-morland and all its glories. That can't be so bad."

"Go to hell," Julia says.

Once more the telephone rings. I study Rupert, the gun in his hand, as if for permission to answer it. He makes no signal, his eye on the ir-resolute sky.

"It's Wilson Blaine," I say.

"Who?" Julia asks. "Oh, I remember. For a second, I'd blocked his name."

"Fucking terrier journalist," Rupert says. "Don't bother with the speaker phone this time."

"He seems to have got it pretty well pieced together," I explain, after pretending to listen to Blaine for a few minutes.

"I'm sure he has."

"Philip was right," I say, keeping the line open. "There weren't any funds in those supposed accounts. There never were—not in Liechtenstein, or anywhere else."

"Not altogether true," Rupert interrupts.

"Well, if there were, you parked them there—but only for as long as necessary. Then you moved them on."

"How insightful of you!"

"Once I claimed them—"

"—found the nerve to claim them."

"Once they were claimed, they vanished."

"So, now, after your Highland scam, I've effectively repaid you. Isn't that how it's all worked out?"

"Everything you stole," Julia answers.

"And completely legally, which is the nicest part," I add. "Not a 'scam'—in any way."

"Do you really want to avenge your little brother?" Rupert inquires. "If so, *here*," he shouts, abruptly handing off the locked Purdey to my wife. "*Presto con fugato*, quickly with fire!"

Julia's spirit seems cauterized. Her finger settles quickly, firmly on the trigger, the shotgun now pointing slightly to the side of Rupert's hip. "Killing you," she says finally, "is quite out of the question."

"Your decision."

"No, it's not. Tempted as I am."

"Whose is it then?"

"You don't have children," Julia says, loosening her grip just a little. "If you *did*, you'd have to take . . . have to have taken a different view of things. You would, you just would. Trust me. . . . Why did you come here, Rupert, after all?"

"For my guns, I told you. Surely not to give you a chance to kill me."

"I don't fully believe you," Julia tells him. "But, I suppose, in certain ways, guns *can* be very useful."

"I'd rather run."

"Run then," Julia says.

"I'm sure there's time. By the very nature of the—"

"*Crimes.*"

"*Events* is the word I think I prefer. It will take the authorities weeks, maybe months to get up off their asses." Rupert straightens his tall body, his thin lips smile as Julia breaks the gun and casts the cartridge to the floor. "I guess it's goodbye," he says, hurriedly collecting his weapons and coat. "Forgive me?"

"Forgive you?" Julia's voice implodes with the question mark.

When he has gone, Julia breaks down into sobs. I gather her tightly against me on the double-depth sofa.

"What will we tell the children?" she asks eventually, in a brutalized voice. "They loved him."

"We'll tell them he's lost," I say quietly.

"Yes. We can make a fairy tale of it. We'll tell them a great long story, but we won't make him its hero. . . . I love you so much."

"I love you, too," I say, steadying her. "We'll just tell them Rupert's tired. Very, *very tired*—and lost."

At MIDNIGHT, ESPIED only by the old plaster knight riding the column of fire, I track the familiar waist, the neck, the piquant lips and nipples of my wife. I have no sense of drawing or expelling breath, am without awareness of mortality. I close my eyes, then, at last, in calculation of the children's early waking, attempt to fall asleep.

Palm Sunday tomorrow—and the four of us alone; Easter in the air. On the eve of vindication—albeit accidentally, in the very pages and over the same airwaves that would have as nimbly seen to our demise— I suddenly experience a weightless, transient freedom. Andrew and Louisa, Julia and I will soon fly to New York for our holiday. There— as here, as elsewhere—my wife and I will confront, repel and absorb the cultures our children so naturally bind. It pleases me, sends a happy shudder through my soul, to imagine them negotiating, without second thought, the multiple allegiances to which their lives can and will and should reply.

The entire tenantry of Castlemorland sleeps in the last of winter's slumbers. Yet I cannot. For there is one thing I know: time is the object of the game, not money. Money obsesses people, impels strangers, tantalizes friends. But time—good days, more days—is, perhaps only after love, the one commodity of real value in the world. Capital is memory, after all. And you cannot win time by skill. Only fate can give it to you in the end. Only fate.